ALSO BY PAT CUNNINGHAM DEVOTO

Out of the Night That Covers Me
My Last Days as Roy Rogers

Pat Cunningham Devoto

The

Summer We
Got Saved

WARNER BOOKS

NEW YORK   BOSTON

For my parents
Sara Thackston Cunningham and
Wells Rutland Cunningham

Copyright © 2005 by Patricia Cunningham Devoto
Epilogue and Author's Comments copyright © 2006 by Patricia Cunningham Devoto
Discussion Questions copyright © 2006 by Warner Books
All rights reserved.

Warner Books

Time Warner Book Group
1271 Avenue of the Americas, New York, NY 10020
Visit our Web site at www.twbookmark.com.

Printed in the United States of America
Originally published in hardcover by Warner Books
First Trade Edition: April 2006
10 9 8 7 6 5 4 3 2 1

The Library of Congress has cataloged the hardcover edition as follows:

Devoto, Pat Cunningham.
    The summer we got saved / Pat Cunningham Devoto.
      p. cm.
    ISBN 0-446-57696-4
    1. Highlander Folk School (Monteagle, Tenn.)—Fiction. 2. Civil
rights movements—Fiction. 3. Political campaigns—Fiction. 4. Voter
registration—Fiction. 5. Race relations—Fiction. 6. Segregation—Fiction.
7. Friendship—Fiction. 8. Alabama—Fiction. 9. Racism—Fiction. I. Title.

PS3554.E92835S86 2005
813'.54—dc22

                                                                    2004010408

Book design, endpaper map, and text composition by L&G McRee

ISBN 0-446-69715-X (pbk.)
ISBN-13:978-0-446-69715-6 (pbk.)

I have no way and therefore want no eyes. I stumbled when I saw.

—*King Lear*

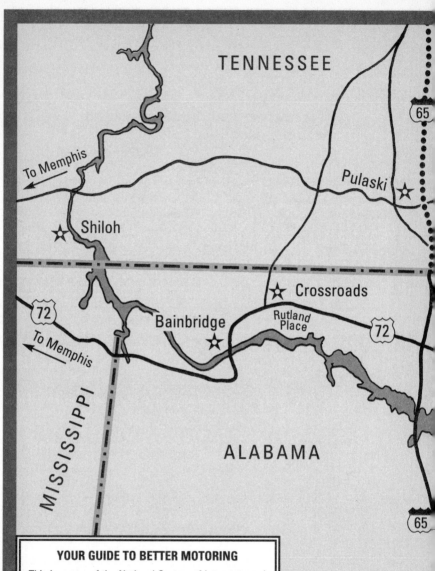

TENNESSEE

To Memphis

Shiloh

Pulaski

65

72

To Memphis

Crossroads

Bainbridge

Rutland Place

72

MISSISSIPPI

ALABAMA

65

YOUR GUIDE TO BETTER MOTORING

This is a map of the National System of Interstate and Defense Highways. Scheduled for completion in 1972, this vast network is designed for traffic needs 20 years in the future and will cost 41 billion dollars. Use these roads whenever possible and reap the benefits of American technology and the free enterprise system!

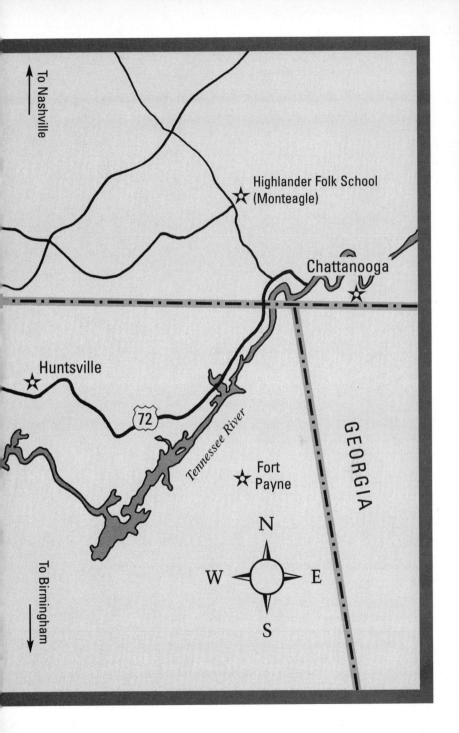

*T*here is a road: It runs east west out of Chattanooga, bound for Memphis, following the path of the Tennessee River as it dips down into the northern edge of Alabama. Turn off Highway 72 just out of Chattanooga and the road leads to Highlander Folk School, campground for the revolutionary leaders of the civil rights movement. Stay on 72, turning north some miles later, and that road winds into Pulaski, Tennessee, birthplace of the Ku Klux Klan.

PROLOGUE

*I*T WAS YEARS LATER, after their father died, that they came across it. Both of them were sitting on the front porch, taking a breather, halfway through cleaning out the old house on Walnut Street, the one their parents had moved to when the grandparents passed. The leavings of a lifetime were stacked in boxes on the porch and in the front hall. Tab had plugged in one of Miss Hattie's old GE floor fans and it was blowing around memories. Tina finished her Chick-Fil-A, pitched the sack and half the fries in the trash, and flipped the top off an old shoe box, beginning again to sort.

It fell out on the floor between them, and Tab put down her Coke to pick it up. "How in the world did this survive?"

"How do you think? Mother saved everything, and then some."

"Kids stopped using pencil boxes like this years ago." Inside was the stub of a pencil, bits of eraser, and a crinkled piece of paper. When Tab tried to unfold it, blue remnants fell in her lap. "I am holding, or trying to hold, here in my hand, the thing dreams were made of—back then."

"Well, I don't remember that we had reefer paper back then, so what is it?"

"It's a Blue Horse loose-leaf-paper filler band," Tab said, reading from the faded label. "Says you can get a free camera or a bicycle headlight by saving a mere two hundred bands. Maudie and I were saving for a camera. She gave me this pencil box for safekeeping when she got polio and had to leave to go down to Tuskegee."

"That black girl you were friends with when you were a kid. I remember." Tina took a sip of Coke. "Of course, you realize that back then, in order to save two hundred bands, you and Maudie would have had to use up maybe ten tons of paper."

"Back then"—Tab smiled at the long ago—"that kind of reasoning seemed perfectly logical." She folded what was left of the paper, placed it carefully back in the pencil box, and pitched it in the trash.

CHAPTER 1

Their Father

SO INEVITABLE were its comings and goings that the Ford Ranchero seemed to steer itself off Highway 72 and onto the red clay roads of the Rutland place. As soon as it stopped, Charles Junior jumped out to play on the split-rail fencing that edged the pasture. Charles propped the morning paper against the steering wheel and read the article on the upcoming governor's race, not because he was interested, but because he was loath to go inside to what his foreman had said he would find. The paper predicted Wallace the winner. He glanced up at Charles Junior, then lazed over to an article about Ike playing golf at Augusta. He had a notion that right here and now he might be able to take himself out of time— let the sun, beating down against the top of the cab, pressure-cook his little cubicle and ease him into a gentle, lasting sleep. Instead, he skimmed the movie section, folded the paper and placed it on the seat beside him, got out of the truck, and went inside.

Clyde, his foreman, stood off in a corner, watching. Charles raised the lid on the stainless-steel vat that was the receptacle for milk taken from the dairy cows. The heavy aroma of wild onions wafted up out of the vat. He let the metal top bang back down into place. "Four damn days' worth of milking gone to waste—the second time this month." A few of the dairy cows had broken through a fence and grazed on a field with wild onions.

"Ain't nothing to do but pitch it," Clyde said. "This rate, you ain't never gonna get Will that new house." Rather than sympathy, Charles thought he detected a note of satisfaction in Clyde's voice.

He left the barn and walked down the road to Will's. Mary had said something about new clothes for the girls. The boys didn't matter—blue jeans and a T-shirt—but the older girls, Tab and Tina, were coming to an age when that sort of thing did matter. Will's new house would have to wait.

Out on the sagging front porch, which was a good part of his living space, the old man was sitting in a straight-back cane-bottomed chair. Charles could hear the sounds of a hymn drifting through the old screen door, which had long ago lost its usefulness—poked with holes and bowed out at its bottom from the banging of grandchildren, the scratching of dogs. Will's daughter, inside fixing the noon meal, was stuck on the same verse: "Oooh—sometimes it causes me to wonder . . . to wonderrrr." It began to blend with the other sounds of the day: a tractor motor in the distance, chickens out in the yard fighting over the last bits of corn, the house dog chased by the yard rooster. Charles took a seat on the wooden swing that hung at the end of the porch. He got out a cigarette and struck a match on the back of the oak ribs.

"You got plenty of firewood? I'll have Tot come up here and cut you some if you need it."

"Nawsir, got plenty of wood."

They had known each other since Charles was a boy.

Will had worked for his father, had gone to fetch the doctor the day Charles was born. "Did he get by here with your check yesterday?"

"Yessir, sho did."

Charles looked out to the rectangle of concrete, way past curing, that was to be the foundation for the new house.

Will whittled. His knife disappeared into a calloused hand, churning away at a piece of white oak that would eventually reappear as a whistle for the grandchildren.

"Some bad news with the milk just now. The cows . . ." His voice trailed off because it didn't matter why. "We'll have to hold up on starting the walls." He threw what was left of his cigarette out in the yard, watching the chickens come up to inspect the smoldering butt before they backed off in search of real sustenance.

He left and went back to the farm store to check on Charles Junior and to tell Clyde, "Be back. I'm going to check the springhouse," and he was—in a way.

The natural spring sat in a draw, down in deep woods near the river. Tall birch trees and oaks towered over the old springhouse. Nurtured for over a hundred years by the spring, the trees were giants now. They must have already been big when his great-grandfather first came here and carved his name—Jonathan McDavid Rutland, 1820.

"The Cherokees weren't good and gone before he was here, claiming the land for us," his father had told him. There were all manner of things cut into the trees: initials of young lovers, Indian symbols, or what he thought were Indian symbols. Maybe the slaves had carved messages in the trees when they had come down to fetch water up to the main house, which was over a mile away. The main house had always had its own water, but this spring was supposed to have the best-tasting water in the county.

Carved into the tree nearest the spring was what appeared to be a Confederate battle flag and, carved beside it, "Franklin Blues." Perhaps young boys had come for a drink in the sweltering midsummer heat, shedding their wool uniforms, squatting down, ducking their heads into the cool water, filling canteens for the long march. He liked to think of them sitting there, momentarily refreshed before they took to the hot, dusty roads again—great numbers of them to be killed.

When he was a boy, he had carved "Charles Lane Westmoreland Rutland." He had been named in the English fashion—bestowing multiple middle names—partly because his father wanted to show ties to his British heritage, and as a practical matter because there were so many relatives to be placated and there would be only one firstborn son.

There had been a sister, Eugenia, born before him and received pleasantly enough. She was healthy, would be a wonderful companion to her mother and perhaps marry well, but she had not been afforded extra names. It would have been pretentious. When she was young, she had been immediately precocious, talking early, reading by the time she was five. Her father had been very proud, but she was not a boy, would not be there to ensure his step off into eternity.

Charles stooped down by the springhouse and listened for the hum of the motor that pumped water back over the hill to the south field's watering troughs. He splashed his face and took a drink. It might be the best-drinking water in the county, but nobody seemed to care about that anymore. Too many other choices now—tea and Coca-Cola and Kool-Aid. People didn't appreciate good water anymore.

From here, he always walked up the hill to the family graveyard, sat down on one of the raised markers, and pulled out a cigarette. It was pleasant, always a breeze and a good view of the river. This routine—going to the spring, looking at the river from the graves—always made him feel better; or if not better, then more secure in what he was doing—in what he was meant to do.

CHAPTER 2

The Seduction

CHARLES HAD BEGUN WORK on the farm as a young boy, on weekends and during the summers. By the time he was ten, he had been made responsible for one of the most important, if menial, jobs on the Rutland place—weighing the cotton during picking season. His sister, Eugenia, would watch from under the shade of the big oaks in the front yard of the main house, begging to be allowed to go to the fields and work, too. Mr. Ben would pat her on the head. "Too much sun isn't good for a lady's skin, Eugenia."

Charles would stand by the cotton wagons situated in the middle of the field in the heat of the late summer, responsible for weighing the cotton sacks that were brought back to the wagon by the pickers. It was a job of huge importance. Some farms were known to adjust the scales to give the owner advantage. Some pickers were known to add rocks to their sacks. He had been proud that he checked the adjusting screw periodically, that he felt each sack and watched as it was dumped in the wagon, to make sure no rocks rolled out in among the bolls. He never gave a short weight to anyone who had been hours in the sun. The pickers, black and white, had timed their picking to end at Charles's wagon so he could do the weighing. From the time he was a child, he had felt his place—and liked it. Eugenia had never felt her place and never liked it.

Later, there would be another sister, Helen, and a younger brother, Arland. They had never questioned the way of things. Eugenia had always questioned everything.

Charles had been given his own horse, with a roll-top saddle like his father's, and would ride behind him out into the fields to inspect the crops. One afternoon, he was sitting on the steps of the log cabin that served as the farm office. His father had been called away to another part of the property. Charles was eating his sack lunch and waiting for Mr. Ben's return when he noticed one of the tenants running up the road toward him. She had been quite a distance away and had come close before Charles had seen the distress in her eyes. Sue Ann was breathless by the time she reached him.

"Waylon done turned the wagon over on hisself, Little Boss. You gotta come." He was up and running with her back along the dirt road, wondering why she thought that he, at twelve years old, could do anything about it. As it happened, he saw that he could do something. He immediately began unloading the sacks of corn off the heavy wagon, Waylon moaning underneath.

"Go ring the bell, Sue Ann. Go, run," he had shouted. He could hear the big plantation bell echoing all over the fields as he dragged sack after sack off the fallen wagon. By the time he had lightened the load enough, other workers had come in response to the bell and could help right the wagon. The man under, suffering a broken leg, had stopped the men who were carrying him off long enough to call him "Mr. Charles" when he thanked him. His father, upon hearing the story, had reached in his pocket and given him his penknife. He couldn't imagine ever being any happier. He had gone to the springhouse that very afternoon and carved his name.

Later that same summer, on one of their rides, his father had looked out over the fields and said to Charles that someday he would be responsible for all of this, and Charles, at that moment, had felt there could be no better job, that there could be no finer place to live than in a world in which he was the hero.

He had not noticed the large gullies that had formed as a result of years of planting the same thing over and over, had not known that the end result of fields of healthy green bushes sprouting white puffs was brought about by large loans that had to be paid off at the end of each growing season, or—if not paid off—they would sink the farm into deeper and deeper debt. By then, he was twelve and king of the hill. He had not observed that the hill seemed to be shrinking as small parts of what had once been a huge tract of land were sold off each season to satisfy unpaid debt. It had not entered his mind, at that young age, that even then his debt to the system which was breeding him had become insurmountable.

—•—

Early on, the family had moved to town so that Charles and his siblings could attend public school. After graduation, his best friend, Reuben, had gone up east to college. Charles had gone to a state university, nearby and inexpensive, the University of Tennessee. He worked part-time to make room and board, and he met Mary, the daughter of the president of the university.

It was not until he came home to settle in with his new

bride that the enormity of what he had committed to began to sink in. It was not until his father let him take a look at the farm ledgers, let him take them home and study them, that he began to comprehend.

Thoughts of the Great Depression still lingered somewhere out there, pushed back out of sight by each turn of the sixteen-disk harrow in red clay, by backbreaking summers on the hay baler, hot, sweaty bodies coated like flypaper with the swirling chaff. From a distance, the word *plantation* sounded dim, diffused, even romantic; up close, it was hot, grueling, worn-out.

—•—

He and Mary had spent the first five years of their marriage scrimping and saving, living in the run-down old plantation house out in the country. At the end of those five years, when they were four—two girls, Tina and Tab, had arrived—Mary had insisted they be allowed to attend a town school. They moved into Bainbridge and Charles began driving out to the farm every day.

Now he had been farming for over nineteen years and, in that time, three more children had arrived. His first two, Tab and Tina, were on the verge of becoming young women. He was beginning to notice specks of gray. It was a life he had settled into, much like chocolate poured into a mold fills up every nook and cranny to gain the perfect likeness.

This was the way of men of his generation. The job of nurturing had been left up to the women. For men, the assigned measure of love took the form of provider and protector. A man's love was not weighed in any outward expression, but in a lifetime of being there, and that was not fully indemnified until the whole lifetime had played out. Though a man might feel the pressure of such responsibility and take to the bottle, and though he might squander what money he was able to earn on gambling or enjoy extra time with worldly women, all was forgiven, or overlooked, if he could be counted on to be there. If he did not stay the course, he became like so many tinkling ice cubes melting away in an afternoon's glass of tea.

CHAPTER 3

The Girls

Out of Memphis, headed east, Highway 72 crosses the Tennessee River near the Natchez Trace and pulls the hill into the village of Bainbridge. Blowing over the solid black tarmac—a chilled wind from the west.

Tina loved her coming. Tab loathed it. Stir things up was what she did, get people agitated, and Tab was not of an age to need agitation, having enough put upon her already—it being the first afternoon of her life that she had gotten up the nerve, along with Mary Leigh and Harriett, to come in and take a booth at Trowbridge's. High school people were welcome. Adults were endured. Junior high persons were not tolerated. Whereas derogatory looks, or no looks at all, could have shamed them into leaving had they gone in and waited at the cashier's stand, they stood outside, the three of them, anxiously glancing in the front window, hoping for a booth to clear and then pouncing on it when it did, settling in and disregarding the odd looks.

It was a predictable place for Tina, a rising senior. She was sitting in a window booth, talking to three boys, pretending not to notice any other comings and goings.

The senior booth could be looked upon by others and admired, but not sat in.

A sack of new nail polish from Woolworth's was something for Tab to do with her hands while they waited for their drinks. After she had ordered a Cherry Coke float—Mary Leigh and Harriett had done the same— she rummaged in the bag, got out a bottle of Orange Blush, and began painting her nails, from time to time showing the color to Mary Leigh. Harriett was pretending to look through the jukebox selections, absent any money to waste on "Smoke Gets in Your Eyes"—their favorite—as sung by the Platters. "Teen Angel" was playing at the time.

"It would look a lot better if you didn't bite your fingernails down to the nub."

"I can't help it if I'm high-strung, Mary Leigh."

They all made a point of not noticing as Tina got up and walked to their table, Jack Carter's letter jacket so big on her that she had to roll the sleeves three times to find her fingers. A large gold *B* on the front was adorned with small silver charms—a winged shoe for track, three basketballs, two footballs. Prizes for every year he had lettered and then bestowed upon her, his personal chastity belt.

"Come on. We have to go home, remember?'

"Are you talking to me?"

"You know I'm talking to you. They spent the night in Memphis and they're driving in from there. Mother said we all have to be home to greet Aunt Eugenia. It would be impolite if we weren't."

Tab tried to prolong it, taking a sip of Cherry Coke float and changing the subject. "Lately, I've been thinking of calling myself Tabitha," she said, then, turning to the others, "it's my God-given name, you know." The others nodded in appreciation. Mary Leigh had been thinking of shortening hers to Leigh. Harriett was considering Lana. Anything to indicate a more mature self was in the offing.

"Tabitha, Smabitha, get up and let's go."

"I don't need to be there. She doesn't even like me. Besides, as you can see, we are enjoying our Coke floats."

"You're too young to be here anyway." Tina turned toward the door.

"I have just as much right to be here as you." Tab gathered up her sack, took one last suck, and followed after.

"And that nail polish is gross." Tina let the door come close to slamming in Tab's face. Tab reopened it and turned to give the V for victory sign to Mary Leigh and Harriett, which meant, Stay in that booth as long as you can.

—•—

They walked three blocks down River Street before turning right. Tina smiled at Mr. Clovis, who was standing outside Woolworth's, taking a break. "Hope Tab is gonna share some of that nail paint with you, Tina. She got enough for Cox's army."

"I hope so, too, Mr. Clovis." Then, out of hearing, "Fat chance I would be caught dead."

Tab waved to two of the men sitting on benches out in front of the courthouse. "I coulda used Tangerine Twist, but it seemed too bright."

"What you have on"—Tina tried to look bored when a carful of boys slowed to whistle—"has to be the grossest thing yet. Tangerine, whatever, couldn't possibly be any grosser." She ran bright red nails through long blond hair, then took off the heavy letter jacket, draping it over her shoulders—the better to see a matching pink sweater set.

Tab inspected her nails as they turned right on Dogwood, past Fuzzie's Fine Feeds and Farm Supply, and on to the next block, which was lined with houses set back in among the dogwoods. A breeze scattered the shriveled remains of white blossoms across the sidewalk. Tab skip-stepped to come along beside. "I am not just too thrilled about this visit from Aunt Eugenia, you know. I have other things I have to do this summer. It could be a gross time."

"That is not how you use the word *gross*." Tina stopped short and looked both ways before crossing the street. "Besides, that's what you always say, every time she comes, and then you end up tagging along with us."

"She always asks me, and you're just jealous."

"She always asks you because she's so polite and she doesn't want to hurt your feelings."

"I don't see what you see in her. All the time I'm with her, I feel nervous, like something terrible might happen."

"It's because she's so worldly."

"It's because she's so weird. Why are we walking past our house?"

"Because, dim brain, we're all supposed to meet up at Grandmother's to welcome her. And another thing—I could modernize your hairstyle if you'd let me cut it."

"Ponytails? Ponytails are very popular."

Eyes at half-mast, the head flipping back a mane of blond hair. "On ponies."

—•—

From a block away, they could see the cars pulled up in the drive. The twins, their youngest brother and sister, were in the front yard, playing with cousins.

Charles Junior, slightly older, was taking turns riding the Radio Flyer down the front walk, careening around cracks in the concrete, dodging scattering cousins. Sunlight filtered down through the big oak trees that lined the street, dappling the front yard grass in painterly shades of green. The red Radio Flyer shot through the picture again. Delighted screams from those on the brink of annihilation. Brightly colored polo shirts and pinafores ran laughing to the four corners of the yard. Soft voices called warnings from the front porch. It was a picture so beautiful and so familiar as to be completely ignored.

The house, a two-story Georgian set squarely in the center of its two acres, was one of many that lined the easy, long-settled block. Four white columns anchored the porch, which had been added years after the building. Tiny piles of sawdust at the bottom of the columns evidenced the carpenter ants that were slowly coring out the insides.

Gliders and a swing, rocking chairs, and heavy iron rock-back rockers spread out under two large overhead fans. They—Uncle Tom and Aunt Helen, their father and mother and grandparents—were gathered there talking, reminding themselves anew of what it would be like when Eugenia arrived.

Tina and Tab were the oldest of the children, somewhere in understanding between those in the front yard and those on the front porch. They sat down near the top of the six wide steps that were the entrance. Their father, Charles, pointed to them as a welcome, never slowing in his story, but including them. "Your grandfather, seeing she was so smart, decided to send her up north to a school that would challenge her. That's how come she ended up going to college in Virginia." He took out a cigarette and picked up a *Life* magazine off the wicker side table. Conversation alone was not enough to warrant the men just sitting there. "That's about as far north as he was willing to go with it." He winked at his wife, Mary, before he began to read.

Then Aunt Helen: "Eugenia would be fine if she just wouldn't arrive in a whirlwind every year and upset everybody so. That's what drives me to distraction. Doesn't she know I have to live here after she goes? I spend a month getting the pieces back together every summer after she visits."

Tab's grandmother, Miss Hattie, was sitting in her wicker rocker, reading the paper. They could hear a warning rattle of pages. Tina, clasping her hands to her elbows and looking out into the yard, said it loudly enough for Tab's ears. "Here comes the one about her giving away Aunt Eugenia when she was a baby."

One of the twins had run up and shoved an untied shoe into Tab's lap. She was tying it too tight. "Grandmother couldn't help it if she got sick. Gad, Tina, what do you expect?"

"I couldn't help that I had to let her go stay with my sister for a while when the next baby came." Miss Hattie held the paper wide out and gave the pages an extra pop, folding them back. "It was right after Helen, and I got sick. Couldn't handle two toddlers and a baby. She always said that had a traumatic effect on the rest of her life. She felt abandoned. That was more than forty years ago." She looked up over her glasses to anyone who was listening. Nobody much was. "She still brings it up. To this very day, she still brings it up, for heaven sakes. Now you tell me if you can remember what happened back when you were all of three years old. I can't even remember what I had for breakfast yesterday." She picked up the paper, but wasn't finished. "The thing about it is, Mr. Ben spoiled her, that's all, sending her to that progressive women's school in Virginia. She was bound to come away with strange ideas. That's where it all started—not when she was staying with my sister till she was four and crying her eyes out because she had to use somebody else's teddy bear." Something on the front page caught her eye. "Says here Wallace is running again, as if we didn't know it." She settled down into reading. "Besides, everybody loves Eugenia. We all love Eugenia."

"Driving all the way from California in a jeep—if you can believe that's perfectly normal—at her age," Aunt Helen said.

Tina sighed, looking straight down at the steps, cheeks resting in palms. "You wish you had the nerve," she whispered.

"She's gonna hear you."

"She is not, and so what if she does?"

Aunt Helen was swinging a crossed leg to the rhythm of the rocking chair she was sitting in. "Can you see Tom if I decided to go out and help organize a labor union—in Alabama—a labor union? And then she has to go and marry a professor that teaches at Berkeley. In California? Lord. The only thing worse would have been if he was a Communist, only we didn't know Communists were so evil back then." Helen rose halfway up out of the chaise and blew smoke in the air. "Has it ever occurred to y'all he might have been a Com—" She stopped herself in midsentence and glanced around to see if anybody was looking. Everybody was. "Well, it was only a logical progression in my brain. I couldn't help it."

"You must admit Val is not half-bad-looking," Mary said.

"Which is amazing. She obviously doesn't have the same ammunition as the rest of us. Let's face it, the girl is flat-chested as they come."

Tina, face still resting in her palms, muttered, "Gravy, that is definitely not supposed to make a difference. Aunt Helen is so, so behind the times."

"You're just saying that 'cause you don't have to worry about it," Tab whispered.

"If I was speaking to you, I would explain that it is not something we worry about. We have all talked it over in Miss Graham's home ec class."

"Mary Leigh says it's of the utmost importance."

"Mary Leigh is gross."

"Well, the proof is in the pudding, or whatever it is they say," Tab's mother was saying. "Look what she got. I mean, look at Val, six four, broad shoulders, square jaw. He looks like Superman. I swear I think of Superman every time I see him."

Aunt Helen took the last Camel out of the pack and lifted the coupon before she dropped the empty package in the big ashtray on the table beside her. "Remember that summer she came in fresh out of New York, had just spent a year up there getting analyzed? She acted like it was perfectly normal, getting analyzed. Nobody does that down here—not unless they're crazy as a betsy bug."

Tina almost shouted when she stood up to face them. "Well, I *like it* when she comes, you know."

Everyone looked up, startled, then rushed to agreement. "Of course you do, honey. We do, too. We all love Eugenia coming—and Val, too."

Charles put down his magazine. "We all adore Eugenia, Tina. What gave you the idea we didn't?"

Helen looked to Mary. "Where did your daughter ever get the idea we didn't like Eugenia coming?"

Tina's shoulders sagged. "Oh, gravy." She turned back around and sat down. Her mother smiled at the others and mouthed *teenager,* and everyone felt fine again.

A minute later Tina hopped off the steps and ran halfway down the front walk before she turned and ran back to them. "It's her. The white jeep."

CHAPTER 4

Maudie

THE SUN WAS ARCING WESTWARD when Reverend Earl turned his old Chevy onto Highway 72. The trip had taken longer than he'd planned. Not wanting to be noticed, Reverend Earl had decided to detour around Birmingham. They had taken the back road up to Huntsville and were now on a straight line into the sun.

Since he had picked up Maudie in Tuskegee that morning, Reverend Earl had tried intermittently to start a conversation, but they had driven mostly in silence.

Some three hours before, they had stopped for gas at a Negro-owned general store outside of Oneonta. The boy who filled their tank had begun flirting with her while he washed the windshield; at least as she looked back, she thought that's what it must have been, flirting. She had seen the nurses and orderlies in the halls at Tuskegee.

"Now lookie here. If you ain't something in that green dress. Where's the party at, girl?" Maudie had smiled but said nothing, bringing her arm inside the car and fiddling with the ashtray on the door, trying not to grin like a child. The boy had leaned down to catch another glimpse as he wiped off the outside mirror on the driver's side. "Reverend Earl, think she might be old enough to go on down to the Royal Blue and do some dancing next time y'all down this way?"

Reverend Earl had laughed as he opened the door to get out and go inside to use the rest room and pay for the gas. "Hush up there, Jimmy. This here one's seventeen going on forty-five. She run circles round you."

"That's the kind I like, Reverend, smart and sassy." He said it loudly, to be sure she heard. She had smiled at him and then quickly looked away.

When Reverend Earl got back in the car, he had brought both of them a Coke and crackers. "Sure you don't wanta go on in and use the facilities? We been riding for a long time and we got a long time to go 'fore we can stop again."

"I'm just fine, thank you, Reverend Earl," she said, and waved to Jimmy, who was watching her while he checked the hood of the car next to them.

"Suit yourself."

Now, hours later, she was furious with herself for having been so vain and for having drunk the Coca-Cola. She had wanted to go to the rest room when they stopped in Oneonta. Now she was dying to go.

Finally, Reverend Earl pulled the car onto a dirt road that led down to a little stream with large limestone rocks along one side. It was owned, he said, by a colored man, who wouldn't mind if they used it. "This was gonna be a picnic lunch, but since we so late, it'll have to be a early picnic supper." He turned off the car. "Well now, miss, time to get out and stretch our legs, and I could use me a trip to the gentlemen's room also." He got out of the car and closed his door. "Be back in a minute to get out that picnic the folks down in Tuskegee made up for us," and he disappeared into the bushes beside the stream.

He had left without thinking to get her crutch out of the backseat. She unlocked the door of the old Chevrolet and pushed against it. The car was so ancient and the door so off center, it had to be shoved hard for it to move at all. She pushed several times before it gave way. Then she stood and her leg brace locked into place. The rear door was as stubborn and creaky as the front. After several tries, she gave one last yank. The door swung open so hard, it knocked her backward on the ground. Her leg brace clanked against small stones and hard red clay. She lay there, her eyes closed to the sky. It was always like this—every molehill a mountain.

When Reverend Earl reappeared, walking out of the woods, leisurely fanning himself with his hat, she was standing, holding her crutch under one arm and brushing dust off of her dress with the other. "Well now, Maudie," he said, chuckling, "you wasn't trying to get in some of that fried chicken before I was, were you?"

She was tempted to swing at him with the crutch. "No, sir, just stretching my legs." While he laid out the picnic, she hurried back up the dirt road to find a level place to enter the woods and get some relief.

They sat on the limestone outcroppings near the creek and ate their fried chicken and biscuits. There were fried peach pies for dessert. The cicadas were cranking up in the trees. A late-afternoon breeze was carrying cooler air. She could feel she was coming into familiar territory. The land rolled more. Spanish moss had disappeared from the trees.

"You know," Reverend Earl said, handing her a fried pie, "I been thinking one reason you might be being so quiet is you done changed your mind 'bout doing this

here job, and if you have, that's all right. I can just as
soon drive us back on down to Tuskegee, let somebody
else do it."

"I can do it, Reverend Earl."

"This here is gonna be a hard job, and it ain't gonna
get done overnight."

"Yes, sir, I know that."

"Lots of folks, white and colored, don't want no
change. Fact is, I was one of 'em, thinking like that,
afraid you was gonna upset the applecart, but the ladies
of the church kept at me, wouldn't let it drop, 'til finally
I give in."

She nodded her head. He droned on and on.

She was not really paying much attention to him now.
He was like all the others, hemming and hawing around
what they really wanted to say, so she did what she always
did—changed the subject. "This is a mighty good-tasting
fried pie, Reverend." She mustered a smile for him.
"How in the world did you ever get the ladies of the
church to make such a feast for us?" She knew this would
do it. Reverend Earl had been a widower for several
years, and all the maiden ladies of the churches he visited were quick to do his bidding. "I noticed Miss Rosabell giving you a big hug when we left this morning."

Reverend Earl grinned and ran fingers through
graying hair. "Been knowing Rosabell since we was children together. Raised down at Tuskegee—till I was
called to preach up at Crossroads."

Maudie had heard the whole story from Miss Rosabell
when she first came to the polio clinic as a nurse's aide.
She would stand by Maudie's bed, rubbing her aching
legs with peanut oil and talking about her church's work
with the voter-registration drives. Although Maudie pretended interest, she had not cared about the church or

voter registration. It was the part about those who were involved in the program getting to go new places that intrigued her. She had imagined herself in Atlanta or Birmingham.

Now Reverend Earl was going on and on about his childhood in Tuskegee. She smiled at him, and she knew that she looked for all the world like she was listening to him. Her eyes stared, as if she was hanging on every word, and she wasn't hearing a thing. Down in Tuskegee, she had developed this into an art form, pretending to be in the here and now while she was really miles away—in this instance, years away—lying on the sweat-soaked stretcher in the railroad station in Birmingham, her legs aching, refusing to respond to any commands she might give them, her hands gripping the side poles of the stretcher, making certain she was still right side up in the world, her eyes closed to what she might find in the thick smell of tobacco smoke and diesel fuel that was in every breath. Now as she looked at Reverend Earl, she could feel the breeze on her face each time her mother waved the paper fan in front of her.

—•—

She and her mother and two little brothers had arrived in the Birmingham station in the early afternoon. Then they had waited for hours before they could get a train going south to Tuskegee, the only place Negroes with polio could go for rehabilitation. An hour would pass, with Maudie counting each tick of the station clock. It was well past midnight when their train finally pulled in. She hadn't remembered being loaded.

When they had come into the Tuskegee station, there had been another train arriving right behind them with polio children from an epidemic over in Mississippi. The second train arrived with clanging and hissing, but no passenger cars, only cattle cars. Her mother had told her not to look when the big doors of the cattle cars had been rolled back and iron lungs—each with a person inside—were eased off the ramps by their attendants and onto the waiting wagons and old pickups, their portable generators hissing and groaning.

By the time she had been carried into the clinic, it was deep dark. The orderlies stood holding her stretcher at the front desk, waiting for assigned space. All she could see was the ceiling and, when she turned her head, a lamp at the reception desk that was shedding dim light on hands studying the papers her mother had given up. Outside the triangle of lamplight, she was uncertain of anything. The hands, brown, with short, sensible nails and no rings, began to flip through the papers. "I think you need to put this one on the first floor." The woman paused and turned to Maudie. "How old are you, child?"

"Old enough to know I ain't studying staying here no long period of time." She turned back to look at her mother, who grimaced but said nothing. The lamplit hands were still for a moment before they placed the papers down on the desk.

"I've changed my mind. Put her on the second floor, in that empty bed next to the windows."

Her mother kissed her good-bye and told her she would be back to visit when she had rented a house and gotten settled. From the doorway, the brothers lifted their hands. The orderlies carried her to the second floor and then to a bed in the corner of the room. On one side was a bank of windows, ratcheted out to let in a breeze. On the other side, the thing next to her wasn't another bed at all, but a round metal tube like the ones she had seen being unloaded at the train station. She glanced at it, at the head sticking out of the end, and then looked away, feeling she might have looked at something she wasn't supposed to. She hadn't really seen the head—rather, a reflection of it in the mirror attached to the iron lung just above the head. She decided to pretend sleep, but the head didn't care to see that.

"Where'd you—come from?"

Maudie kept her eyes closed.

The head persisted. "Where 'bouts?" She appeared to be six or seven years old, although it was hard to tell, having to judge from a head alone. Maudie thought she had seen buckteeth and curly black hair.

The orderlies were tucking in sheets and fluffing up her pillow. Maudie opened one eye and looked directly at the face in the mirror. "From here, up round the river."

"Been here—two years."

"That right," keeping it short to discourage conversation.

"Name Yolanda—from Indianola. — That's in Mississippi. — You can—know me—by the ribbons—in my hair—always wear—ribbons."

I know you from that big fat barrel you got round you, no mind them ribbons, she was thinking, but she said, "What you look like underneath there? You fat, you skinny, what?"

"I used to be—fat—but now—I think—I'm skinny," Yolanda said in the faltering way the in-and-out rhythm of the iron lung allowed her to speak.

She said she had come from the Delta, from a family of eleven children. "But I don't know—maybe—I'm still fat—good—food here."

"That right?"

A nurse had come along after the orderlies left, and

she told them to stop talking and go to sleep. The head said nothing else, but the iron lungs—there seemed to be others in the room—made constant hissing sounds and wouldn't let Maudie drift off. That first night, she felt it would drive her crazy, the incessant noise.

The next morning when she woke up, the face was lying there looking at her through the reflection in the mirror.

"Thought you—gonna sleep—all day. — Miss Betty—be here soon."

"She up yet?"

"Yeah, she up—just barely."

Maudie raised her head to find the new voice conversing with Yolanda.

It came from the bed in the other corner, directly across from hers. The girl, dark black, probably eight or nine, was up on her elbows, looking at Maudie. "How old are you, girl? Don't you know no better?"

"Thirteen. Older than you I 'spect." Maudie dropped back down on to her pillow and closed her eyes. "And I ain't finished sleeping yet."

There was a sound like giggling from the iron lung and from the girl across the way. Yolanda turned her head. "Macy, she say—she believe she gonna—sleep more." Macy, who was in the iron lung next to Yolanda, was passing it along to whoever was next to her.

Doreen was up on her elbows, looking at Maudie. "You better get awake, girl. When Miss Betty say eat, you gotta eat."

Maudie kept her eyes closed. "We see who gotta do what."

"You hear that? — Say she gonna—" Yolanda passed it on again.

A thin woman in a starched white uniform, a white

nurse's hat pinned to her graying hair, arrived with breakfast trays and two assistants. Maudie could hear plates rattling and silverware clanging. Those who could eat on their own were propped up and given trays. Assistants fed the others.

Nurse Betty held the tray of food over her bed. Maudie recognized the hands that had shuffled papers under the lamplight in the lobby. Wire-rimmed glasses gazed down at her. "Breakfast is served from seven to seven-thirty. You may eat or you may sleep, but you can't do both."

Maudie kept her eyes closed and breathed deeply, pretending to snore. She could hear someone giggling.

Nurse Betty sighed. "We have to be a little sassy at first, don't we?" She set the tray down on Maudie's stomach and turned to feed Yolanda.

The smell of bacon and eggs drifted to her. She hadn't realized she was starving, had had nothing to eat since the Coke in the train station the day before.

The bacon and eggs went cold perched on her stomach. Nurse Betty took the food away at precisely seven-thirty.

An hour later, a nurse walked in, pushing something heavy. It looked like an old washing machine with a ringer on the outside. She rolled it to the other end of the room. Maudie could hear the wheels creaking under the weight of it. There was steam rising off the thing. With its coming, the whole room went silent.

"What you suppose is that?"

"It's for—hot packs. — Ain't you never—had—no hot packs—help—the healing?"

Maudie put her hands behind her head. "Ain't never had no hot packs and I ain't gonna have none now."

Yolanda laughed out loud at this new entertainment. It was not a laugh exactly, but a stuttered hoot. Maudie could see her little head with the red bows in the hair jerking from side to side, too tickled. "Say she ain't— gonna have—no hot packs. —She do—beat all."

The big machine rolled slowly from bed to bed. Steam twisted up out of the tub. The nurse fished down in the water with a stick to retrieve a towel and push it through the ringer before placing it on various body parts. The stench of scorching wet wool hung in the air. Maudie pretended to be looking out the window as she watched the steam rising off the scalding towels that were placed on Doreen's legs. She heard Doreen's muffled cry when they touched her skin.

The iron pot rolled up to her bedside. She tried to strike a casual pose; hands behind her head, wavering smile, eyes examining the view from the windows. "Don't believe I'll have me none of them hot towels today. Still tired out from my traveling." She could hear one of the other girls crying.

"Now honey, everybody has hot packs. It helps with the healing," the nurse said. She looked much younger than Nurse Betty.

"Well now, you see, ma'am, the truth is, my doctor, where I come from, he say I shouldn't have none of them hot packs. Be bad for me. It's right there in my report I brung with me last night. Right down there at the desk lobby. Yes'm, everybody but me had them hot packs where I come from."

"Really?" The young nurse looked like she might believe her. "I never heard of it before, but I'll go get Miss Betty and ask her."

"You don't have to do that. Just pass on by me today, that's all."

"Oh, I couldn't do that. I'll be right back." She walked out of the room.

"Now you—done it." Yolanda turned to pass it on. "Now she done it—done called—Miss Betty. — And she—don't like—no—calling."

The anguish of hot packs on legs and arms and thighs was forgotten while the room listened for the footfalls of Nurse Betty. A minute or two later, they could be heard clicking on the tiles in the hall and then turning into their ward. Miss Betty stood over her, expressionless. "I see we are awake now."

"Yes, ma'am. Now what I been thinking is . . ." She was saying it loudly, for the others.

"Never mind what you were thinking. You will have hot packs every day, for as long as we deem it necessary. If you are able to get better, this is the only thing that will help. Do you understand?"

"Well, I do, but . . ."

"Everyone gets hot packs twice a day."

"*Twice a day?*" She looked at Yolanda. "You didn't tell me nothing 'bout no twice a day."

"And don't go giving my nurses any more trouble about it. Do you understand?" Nurse Betty dipped down into the hot water with a wooden ruler and put a towel through the wringer. She turned Maudie on her stomach and draped the steaming wool cloth across her calf muscles. When the cloth touched her leg, "Hey! Hell. What's you doing? Take it off." She couldn't move away from the searing pain.

"And another thing—we do not use profanity." Betty slapped another blistering, water-soaked wool towel on her other leg.

Maudie bit down on her lip until she felt the salty taste of blood.

"Miss Charlotte will continue," she said, and left.

The younger nurse placed towels up and down her legs and then proceeded to the far end of the room to start the process over again.

Maudie looked up and saw the head staring at her, waiting for some explanation. She sighed. "Look here, Yolanda, I wasn't yelling 'cause it hurt. I was pure and simple yelling at old Nurse Betty."

Yolanda grinned. "Hear that? — She yelling—at Nurse Betty. — She do—beat all."

Maudie buried her face in the pillow, waiting for the pain to ease. That afternoon, the hot packs came again—as they did every morning and afternoon for weeks after she arrived.

—•—

Reverend Earl was gathering up picnic paraphernalia and eating the last fried pie. "Better be getting a move on, Miss Maudie. Wanta get there in time for prayer meeting tonight."

Maudie nodded and reached for her crutch.

CHAPTER 5

Eugenia

She wore sandals and she was driving the white jeep. Eugenia was thinner than her sister, Helen, and taller, almost as tall as the men. She had a long, angular face—the nose was rather large and the teeth did tend to stand out a bit—not beautiful within the exacting confines of classic American beauty. There was the hint of her travels to India in the dangling brass earrings, the look of California in her long, flowing skirt and tie-dyed blouse. The short, wavy hair had never felt hair spray. The beauty in Eugenia was born of experience.

"Will you look at you." They were all trying to crowd around her, but she hadn't finished hugging Tina, who had been the first one there and who had opened the door for her.

Helen said, "I would never have thought to travel without a hat and gloves. Genia, you look wonderful, so, so carefree."

Eugenia laughed and reached out to pull in Tab. "A hat and gloves, in a jeep? I would have burned up. Going through Mississippi earlier today, it was scorching." Everyone lined up for the obligatory hug. The men walked around to the other side and shook hands with

Val, pulled suitcases out of the white jeep, and marveled to one another with raised eyebrows that anyone could drive all the way from California in a jeep—would want to in the first place. The women followed, found Val, and gave him cheek kisses. Admittedly, he was a strange duck, but they would try to make him feel at home. The group of them walked arm in arm, carrying the suitcases up to the front steps. Miss Hattie rushed inside for more ice and fresh mint for the tea.

Eugenia and Val sat themselves down on the wicker porch swing with the blue-and-green-flowered cushions. Eugenia gestured for Tina to come sit between them. Tab stayed on the porch steps. The others scattered out in rocking chairs and gliders. Overhead fans trudged around in slow circles, giving the notion of a breeze, rippling the fronds of the hanging ferns, and stirring up the leaves of the green-and-white caladiums Miss Hattie had planted in the wicker stand next to the porch railing. The GE floor fan that was attached to an extension cord running back through the front window did the real work.

As she looked around, there were tears in Aunt Eugenia's eyes. There were always tears in her eyes when she first came back. They all thought it was the emotion of the moment, of seeing them again, of wondering if she had done the wrong thing by leaving them. That's what they thought.

Everyone was staying for dinner, of course. They would all come for meals the first few days of a visit from Eugenia. Miss Hattie insisted. There was strength in numbers. Besides, they could find out what Eugenia had in mind for this stay.

—•—

There was an easy quiet as they took their places at the old mahogany dining table half of them had known since childhood. The lace tablecloth had been spread out along the length of the long rectangular top. The floor fan ruffled its hanging edges and spread the smell of fresh roses that composed the centerpiece. So many containers had been set in preparation, there was hardly room for the food: tea glasses and water goblets, dinner plates and bread plates, salad plates, coffee cups, saltcellars. Polished pieces of silverware had been laid out along the sides of the dinner plates. A large linen napkin rested in the center of each plate. Tina had set the table. She had learned the art in home economics, had been tested on it and had gotten an *A*. It carried the same credit as algebra and chemistry and was more important. She had opened the heavy damask drapes slightly. She had lit the candles, which were set in cut-glass holders on each side of the American Beauty roses gathered out of Miss Hattie's garden. All of that had been covered in the chapter entitled: "A Restful, Wholesome Place for Family Dining." She had helped Ora Lee bring in the roast and potatoes, the green beans and crowder peas. At each place, they had set down salad plates with molded rings of fruit-filled Jell-O topped with dabs of mayonnaise.

Miss Hattie had rung the handbell next to her place at the table before deciding to go into the kitchen to take the rolls directly out of the oven and check to see that the younger children were seated at the kitchen table, watched over by Ora Lee.

The women, who were up in the bedroom eyeing the unpacking of California dresses, followed Eugenia down the stairs into the dining room. The men, entertaining Val with football stories—the better to stay away from politics or religion—came in from the living room. Tab had already seated herself in the chair she knew would be next to Tina, because Tina would sit next to Aunt Eugenia, and Aunt Eugenia would sit where a visitor always sat on the first night—to the left of the grandfather.

"Who asked you?" as Tina sat down beside her.

"I was here first, as you can plainly see. Where you sit, I couldn't care less."

The prayer was long and blessed everyone, especially giving thanks for the visitors having arrived safely. It was given by the grandmother, as appointed by the grandfather. Mr. Ben carved the roast and passed plates first to Eugenia, then to the other ladies, and last to the men. Other dishes began a clockwise trip around the table.

Eugenia took up her napkin, dabbing her cheeks and forehead. "My, but it's nice to be back home and so much going on down here."

The others shifted in their seats. They had been too long at too many dinners with Eugenia not to know this was the opening salvo. Presently, Uncle Tom caught on. "Uh-oh, y'all hold on to your hats, 'cause Eugenia's fixing to let us in on what's the latest thing in California. Hey, maybe she's gonna talk us into some of that communal-style living they're doing out there now. I read in *Time* magazine—"

"Don't you pay a bit of attention to Tom, Genia," Helen said, patting his arm to shut him up, which everyone knew was impossible. "You say what you want to say."

Mr. Ben put down his fork, waiting. Miss Hattie excused herself to go get more rolls from the kitchen. This was the part Tab liked, where they would all jump on Aunt Eugenia and set her straight. It was like watching a play, being right in the middle of it and not having to say a word if she didn't want to. She put her elbows on the table and grinned at Tina, who was not looking at her on purpose. When the grandmother frowned, she took her elbows off the table.

"I know you know all the terrible inequities we suffer down here," Eugenia began. She would include herself when she was getting ready to tell them how they were falling short. They had heard it enough to know it was a warning of things to come. "Groups of people from all over the United States are beginning to organize. They're getting ready to come on down here and help out."

"Help out with what?" Tab asked.

"Why are people always wanting to come down here and help us out?" Tom said. "The last time they helped us out, half the place ended up being burned down."

"Tom! You are such a scream. My husband is funny as Red Skelton."

Eugenia ignored it and plowed ahead. "After all these years of hideous injustice, it's high time we did something."

"They can't stay home and tend to their own injustices?" Tom asked.

Tab glanced at Tina and mouthed I told you so.

"Well, maybe we *should* do something," Tina said, and then, head down, talking into her lap, "whatever it is you want us to do." Aunt Eugenia reached around to give her a hug. "You would be willing to stand by me, wouldn't you, Tina?"

"Oh sure, yes, ma'am. I sure would."

"And you, Tab?"

Tab, trying to imitate Uncle Tom, and going for the laughs, "Oh sure, Aunt Eugenia, anything you wanted me to do. Why, if you wanted me to, I'd probably go on up to Pulaski and take a hammer to the plaque." She had thought it a great joke, everyone at the table knowing about the plaque, knowing it was sacred to Mr. Ben and so completely out of the range of possibility. She looked around, expecting to see the others at the point of laughter at a thought so ridiculous. She imagined she might even elicit a smile from Mr. Ben. Instead, he looked gray-faced.

"Are you forgetting about your cousin John Lester?" It had been the last thing she meant to do—offend her grandfather—one more reason to hate Aunt Eugenia. "If Cousin John Lester hadn't come along when he did, southern women might not be able to hold their heads up in public. In Cousin John Lester's time, there was no rule of law."

Itching to counter, Aunt Eugenia tapped her knife on the china plate, full of food she hadn't touched. "It seems to me, southern men are threatened more than southern women. The problem has always been that southern men are scared to death to relinquish any power, sexual or otherwise, and"—she took a breath—"and Cousin John Lester was no exception."

There was dead silence. This had to be the final straw. Tab almost laughed out loud, so thankful was she that in one fell swoop the onus had been taken off her and put where it belonged, where she knew it had belonged from the very beginning.

On the one hand, Aunt Eugenia had insulted Cousin John Lester, and on the other, she had said "sexual" at the dinner table—like throwing up all over the Jell-O salad.

Mr. Ben had been born a few years after Reconstruction ended. Before he was old enough to sit a horse, he had been dipped headfirst into the well of family tales and had come up drenched, ready to shake off any excess onto the next generations. He had grown up with stories of the Klan, hooded and ghostlike, sweeping down in the night, saving his aunts and cousins from marauding colored people just freed from slavery and not knowing what to do with themselves but to go out and kill white people. It was not their fault, he had explained to Tab; it was just the nature of things.

At an age when the greater meaning of controversy is lost in the thrill of the fight, Tab wiggled in her chair and brought the napkin in her lap up to her face, pretending to cough, not being able to control the smile that was showing itself.

"Genia, what has got into you?" Miss Hattie whispered across the table.

"She's developed some kinda familial death wish is all I can figure," Helen said, not whispering at all.

Now Charles cleared his throat to speak for the first time, measuring every word. "Well now, Dad . . ." He pushed back slightly from the table, studying his half-eaten dinner. Tab still held the napkin over her mouth, watching him, disappointed that her father would stop the argument, like he always did. "You know, a lot of people, and certainly all of us here at this table, consider the Ku Klux Klan a group of—well, the Ku Klux Klan today"—he paused to select his words carefully—"a group of redneck rabble-rousers." He qualified immediately. "Now I'm talking about the Klan today, certainly not the Klan of Cousin John Lester's day."

"Rabble-rousers are they? I don't give a tinker's damn about the Klan today, but Cousin John Lester—" He slammed down his napkin. "Miss Hattie, I'll have my dessert in the library."

And then, as if tuning in for the first time, Val got in on the act by seeming to think he was owed some explanation. Since he was sitting next to Tab, he turned to her. "You know, Tab, I'm having trouble following the family tree in this particular instance. Just who is, or was, your venerable cousin John Lester?"

Tab, hoping to make it up to her grandfather, "Oh, Cousin John Lester, nobody better than him. He was our first cousin and one of the five original founding fathers of the Ku Klux Klan."

Val turned as white as a sheet—it was true—his sparkling Superman eyes popping. He coughed to regain his voice and, in what he must have hoped would sound like unflappable academia, "You never mentioned that, Eugenia."

"Well, he wasn't exactly my first cousin," Tab was rambling on. "Course he couldn't be. He was probably my second or third cousin, but we are *very* kin in some way." She grinned at her grandmother.

Eugenia, in turn, bore up as well as could be expected under this heretofore-unopened closet skeleton that had just jumped out at poor Uncle Val like some dangling bloody body to fly in the face of his scholarly self.

"I really never thought . . . thought about it, Val. It's just one of those things one lives with."

Helen hooted. "You never thought to tell Val, of all people, about John Lester?"

Aunt Eugenia snapped back, "I never saw *you* broadcasting it around the neighborhood, Helen."

Helen had settled back into eating and had a bite of roast in her mouth, but couldn't let it pass. "What's to tell? Everybody around here already knows. Besides, around here we already know we aren't perfect"—a grin to Tom.

Val cleared his throat again, trying to remain calm. "You never thought to tell me that you were kin to one of the founding fathers of the Klan?"

And Tab, "Heck, that's no secret. It started right up there in Pulaski, not two hours from our doorstep. I been up there to see it."

"I think I've lost my appetite." Val got his hurt self up out of his chair and retired to their upstairs bedroom.

Aunt Eugenia trailed behind, iced tea glass in hand. "Now darling, I told you when we married that my past was . . . well, marred."

"I thought you meant ordinary things, being southern, having unresolved family issues."

"Is that California talk, 'unresolved family issues'? Is he talking about us?" Uncle Tom wanted to know as he helped himself to more crowder peas.

It was customary to have dinners like this when Aunt Eugenia came to town.

CHAPTER 6

Shiloh

By the time they moved out to the porch for ice cream, the mood had taken a 180-degree turn. "Discussions," as Miss Hattie called them, just happened with Eugenia. "You have to get on with it, or your whole life will end up being one big discussion, round and round all the time, because the minute you say *black,* Eugenia is bound to say *white.*"

Miss Hattie took the top off the freezer and pulled out the dasher. "You let Eugenia worry you, and you'll end up frazzle-minded." She motioned for Tina to come hold the dasher while she used a spoon to scrape ice cream off into the canister. "Mind you hold it still. I don't want any rock salt in my cream. Hand me those bowls over there, Tab." She took the dasher from Tina and laid it aside, then began filling bowls, which she gave, one by one, to Tina and Tab to pass out to the yard children, if they would come and sit quietly on the front steps to eat.

Eugenia came out on the porch without Val. He was in the middle of a much-needed rest, she said. Mr. Ben was in his study. Miss Hattie spooned out an extra-large portion and sent Tab in with it.

Tab closed the screened door, the porch voices fading as she walked the long hall to the back of the house. She felt, as she always felt when she visited with him, as if she were walking back in time to meet him. The grandfather clock was striking the quarter hour as she passed. A cool, almost cold, breeze from some other place in the house drifted by. Opening the door to his study made her feel she was entering another house, or maybe another place altogether—old light that had faded everything to quiet colors, old air that had been used and reused. Legal bookcases were stacked on two walls. There were the requisite volumes of Lee, of Stonewall, of Johnston, the Joel Chandler Harris–edited set of *The Library of Southern Literature,* and the complete *Photographic History of the Civil War,* but most of the books were about leaders and battles in the Tennessee Valley, where he lived, where he and his family had spent generations.

Above one bookcase was a large portrait of Lee on Traveler. Mr. Ben sat in an old swivel chair, one he had brought from the farm office when he retired. His legs were crossed and stretched out in front of him. His head was bent down to his book, his chin cutting into the stiff white collar of his dress shirt. On rare occasions, she had seen him take off his suit coat, but she had never seen him without his tie and vest and dress shirt. In lean times, the whole assemblage might be a little threadbare, but it was always clean and pressed, and a formidable layer of protection against those who might imagine familiarity.

He had felt that passing everything on to his elder son and giving up control would be distressing. He had heard that was sometimes the case. In reality, it had been just the opposite. He was free to do as he pleased and let his son worry about the future. Now he was rereading his copy of *Cleburne and His Command.*

Tab closed the door quietly. She brought the ice cream in and set it on the desk, being careful not to speak unless he spoke. He had opened the windows over the desk, and a fan sat on top of it, turning slowly back and forth, pulling in scents from the backyard garden. Tab turned to go and was almost out the door before he said, "My father's company was positioned to the right of Cleburne's Brigade, you know."

She turned around and came back to him, waiting for one of his stories. She loved this one. "Yes, sir," she said. "Company A, Sixteenth Alabama Infantry." She had heard it many times, but it didn't matter. She was partial to the ones he told and retold.

"Up at Shiloh."

"Yes, sir, just down the river apiece," she said. She walked over and pulled the old leather ottoman away from the other end of the room to take a seat opposite him.

He looked up from the book and stared out the window at the backyard garden Miss Hattie kept each summer. Irises were growing along the border of flagstones that led to the center walk-around. Purple thrift surrounded the birdbath. Cosmos was beginning to stick up behind a border of candytuft. Pollen and dust drifted down through shafts of sunlight and he saw artillery smoke rising off the hills to the east, along the Tennessee River. "It was a beautiful day, weather like this," he said. "I have always wondered why the Lord visited such death and destruction upon us on a day like this. He told me he stepped in a clump of wildflowers growing near the creekbed when his company was given the order to form up. Said he could hear the howitzers firing down the line as they moved east up near Owl Creek."

Mr. Ben had grown up and grown old with the stories of his father's war, and on his deathbed, when he was delirious, his father had gone back there one last time to live out that day—the high point or the low point of his life—there in the dirt and sweat and death that was the Battle of Shiloh. Mr. Ben had been a young man when he sat by his father's bedside and listened for the last time. "It was surprise we had on our side," he said now. "The Yanks never knew we were coming."

"We had to attack before the Yanks could bring up reinforcements," Tab said. "They were coming upriver with reinforcements. When was it his brother Arthur got there?"

Mr. Ben was still watching the garden. "His brother Arthur, your great-great-uncle, he was just seventeen. He had been home on sick leave—had dysentery. People did that back then, left their company and came home on leave." She nodded her head. She knew all about it. "A few days before, he had heard troops were massing up for a big battle. His brother Charles was still up there. Arthur got out of his sick bed and put on his uniform and left to rejoin them. He walked the eighteen miles into Bainbridge, had one of the old fishermen row him down river to a place he could cross to the south and rejoin his company—had to skirt around the Union gunboats."

Tab had leaned forward and put her elbows on her knees, her head in her hands. She could smell the smoke and hear a saber rattling as a courier dashed by on his horse, carrying orders to the other end of the line. His mount's neck arched back as the courier momentarily reined in to appraise the situation, then

dashed off, hoofs spitting out dirt. "Course, his mama
didn't want him to go," she said. She could see Arthur—
sallow-cheeked, turning his back on his mother, walking
down the long drive, and disappearing into the country-
side. "She stood in the door and cried when he left,
knowing he might not come back." She watched Mr.
Ben. "And he was very handsome. At seventeen, he was
very handsome."

"I showed you that picture of him, didn't I?" Mr. Ben
said. She nodded. She had studied the picture, had
imagined having a boyfriend like Arthur, curly blond
hair, his gray private's hat sitting at a jaunty angle,
smiling out at her. She had never seen another picture
of a soldier smiling. Soldiers didn't usually smile in pictures. He seemed bursting with confidence, with pride at
being permitted to take part in what was about to
happen. She waited for the charge to commence.

"It was early morning when he got there. It's not that
far, you know. He had brought back, in his haversack,
some tea cakes his mother had made with the last of the
sugar she had. Eventually, he found his brother. They sat
down under a giant poplar and ate every last one of
them—the tea cakes." Mr. Ben watched blue jays light on
Miss Hattie's birdbath. Tiny sprays of water caught the
sunlight as the birds fluttered their wings, cooling themselves. "My father told me he should have saved some,
but he was always glad they ate all of them right then and
there.

"Arthur had been feverish, but he had kept saying he
was all right. They had filled their canteens out of the
creek right before they heard the command to form up
and start moving." Mr. Ben looked away from the
window and down at Tab. "The infantry line alone was
almost three miles long. The Yankees were so surprised,

they had left water boiling on their campfires and beans cooking in their pots. Our boys swarmed like mosquitoes—shooting and yelling. They ran past overturned pots of beans, grabbing up blankets and canteens left in their wake, running forward, almost laughing at the ease of it. Bullets were whizzing by but never made a mark. Once, a cannonball came so close to my father, he could feel the wind of it."

"But when they came to the Sunken Road," she said, "to the Hornet's Nest?"

"Then they came to the Sunken Road. Suddenly, there rose up out of the road a line of Yanks, right in their path, firing at close range and then ducking back down for cover. Whole lines of men fell, and those who were left retreated to reload and charge again."

"Arthur was too quick with his reloading," she said.

"Arthur had reloaded the new Springfield his father had given him. Charles took longer because his was an old smoothbore. He ran to catch up. He wanted to kneel and fire alongside his brother. Just as he got there, Arthur fell, a hole blown in his neck, his head lying in a small patch of violets and the violets turning red. He remembered seeing the violets as he knelt down beside Arthur."

"Arthur's eyes were open, but he couldn't say anything, just looked up at his brother," she said, her voice cracking. She was seeing the beautiful blue eyes, searching and desperate, the blood running down his neck, soaking the blond curls.

"In the next moment, my father saw a line of boots and blue pants running toward him and he felt someone grab him and pull him backward toward the cover of the trees.

"When they charged again, he ran to the spot where

he thought he had last seen Arthur. By this time, there were bodies all around." Mr. Ben looked out at the garden again. "Couldn't even find the violets. He was searching, turning over bodies, when he heard the order to fall back.

"After that, their company waited hours for the artillery—sixty-two pieces, so they say—to clear a path, throwing shells into the breech, obliterating everything.

"By then, it was late afternoon and dark was coming on. By then, there was no way of telling. Buell had come up to reinforce Grant." Mr. Ben looked down at his book, seeming to have finished with the story.

But she wanted him to go on. "We know the place he was buried with all the others," she said.

"I showed you the grave my father said he *thought* he was buried in with all the others." He picked up his book and opened it to his marked place, thumbing a few pages back to reenter the narrative. "My grandmother always liked to pretend that somehow he got out alive and went to live in Texas."

"But we know most likely he didn't," she said.

"Yes," he said, and picked up his ice cream as he began reading.

She got up off the ottoman and turned to leave. "Now, your Aunt Eugenia, she just forgets. Nothing against her for forgetting, but you won't, will you?"

"No, sir. I *never* would!"

—•—

Back out on the front porch, Eugenia had them all to herself, absent the objections of Mr. Ben and the worry over what Val might think.

"Negroes have lived too long riding in the back of life's bus. It's time we did something about it."

"What do you want, Genia, for us to set the whole place on fire? Burn it down and start over? We're going as fast as we can, and still maintain some kind of sanity," Charles said.

And Tom, completely serious, "There aren't even any buses here in Bainbridge for them to sit in the front of."

Charles glanced at Mary and looked to the ceiling.

Eugenia persisted. "Now, about the Southern Christian Leadership Conference."

There was silence as each one waited for someone else to do the defending. Finally Miss Hattie spoke up. "That's a group for colored people, isn't it?"

"I'm sending them money. I think we should all send them money."

Tom rose halfway up off the glider. "Wait a minute. Are you kidding?"

"Oh my Lord." Miss Hattie's face paled.

Tab's mother snickered, then pursed her lips. "Sorry, Genia. I'm not laughing at you, just the thought. Wait till Bainbridge hears this: 'Hometown girl leads SCLC.'"

"Eugenia, are you trying to get us all run out of town?" Charles said. "Look, sweetheart, there are limits. We're doing the best we can, given the circumstances."

"Run out of town?" Miss Hattie almost shouted. "Is it that bad? I knew it was a colored group, but is it that bad? What is it full of anarchists, or Communists or something?"

"It's not that bad, Mother," Charles said.

"What would the summer be like without some cockamamy idea from Eugenia?" Uncle Tom said, and lowered the sports section over his head, preparing for a short snooze.

"What's cockamamy?" Tab let the screen door swing

shut and walked over to pick up her bowl of melted ice cream.

From under the sports section, "Your aunt—wants us to take the pledge to disown all our friends and family, burn down the place our fathers and grandfathers sweat blood over. Seems they're all Simon-pure out in California."

"I'll never disown my family that died for me," Tab said. "Why would I ever do that?"

"Tab, nobody that I personally know died for you," her mother said then, with a quick nod to Miss Hattie, "except for your uncle Arland—in the last war. I know she didn't mean to be impolite, Eugenia."

"Yes they did. Yes they did." Tab pointed her spoon in Aunt Eugenia's direction, seeing the swirling smoke, hearing the rounds of howitzers thunder across the fields of Shiloh. "They died. It was a day like today. There was smoke so thick, you couldn't see in front of you." She turned to Tina for help. "You know it's right, Tina."

"Egads, Tab. Will you sit down?"

"No! There was blood everywhere. He was hit in the throat and couldn't even talk. I won't forget, even if Yankee Aunt Eugenia does."

"*Tab.*" Her father jerked up out of his chair. "Apologize this instant to your aunt and then go to the kitchen until we're ready to go home."

"Yes, sir." Tab ran over to the front screen door and pulled it open hard. "I'm sorry, Aunt Eugenia. Please accept my apology." She swirled and was gone.

Charles sat back down. "Sorry, Genia. Obviously, Dad has been at his stories again."

"Well, they're true," Tom said from beneath the newspaper. "Train up a child in the way he should go, or in this case, she should go." They could all feel him smiling under the pages of the *Bainbridge Times*.

This, of course, made it quite obvious to Eugenia that she had arrived for her summer visit just in time.

CHAPTER 7

Tuskegee

REVEREND EARL HAD TURNED on the car radio to get the latest news. "See if anything's going on we need to know about," he said. Maudie leaned her head back against the front seat and began to doze.

Upon entering Tuskegee's polio clinic, she had been given over to another world. Before this, Maudie had lived most of her life in the outdoors, was used to earth smells and season changes and being surrounded by children and dogs and dirt. At the polio clinic, everything was a pale green and sterile and green again: the walls, the upstairs wards, the downstairs offices, the therapy pool in the basement. Her eyes couldn't seem to find any variables.

She had always lived with great swings in color. Huge gray-black thunderclouds rolling up the blue-green of the Tennessee River and, in the fall, shuffling through the woods, ankle-deep in red and yellow and more floating down as she walked. She had always lived in a world that let fly with emotion—yelling at her brothers for some wrongdoing, being hugged by her mother for some right.

When she entered Tuskegee, she had been on the

plump side, a residue of years of corn bread and fried chicken, pigs feet and grits, all seasoned with large portions of lard. She had made most of the meals for her little brothers and had free reign over their woodstove and icebox. Mealtime had been when she had decided that she, and therefore they, felt hungry. On summer mornings, she and her brothers would see their mother off to work and then sit on the front porch of their cabin—situated on one of the dirt roads leading out of Bainbridge—eating cold biscuits and last night's fried chicken, throwing the leftovers to the dogs, who were coming out from under the porch and stretching for a day's run with them.

She had had a friend, a white girl who lived on a paved road near her house. Tab was a few years younger. The summer before she got polio, she and Tab and the brothers had roamed the woods and river together. Once, they had fished the big river and almost been run down by a huge barge. Even as a child she had been, for the most part, free to live as she pleased. Everyone in Bainbridge had known her, chubby and boisterous, bossing the brothers down the street, daring anyone to take advantage of her—of them.

And then suddenly, her role as caretaker was gone. She couldn't even care for herself.

—•—

She had been at Tuskegee for several months when she graduated to a wheelchair. One day, she had rolled into the ward and seen all the nurses singing "Happy Birthday" to little Yolanda and holding a cake. Yolanda had seemed pleased and surprised by the sight of the cake, but its presence must have reminded her, and all of them, that she had been in Tuskegee a long, long time.

"A—whole year?" she said when they had finished singing. "Didn't—know that. What—that make—Miss Betty?" Nurse Betty ignored the question. She had brought presents: a new toothbrush and a picture post-card of Mississippi. She took tape out of her nurse's pocket and began taping the postcard to the side of Yolanda's mirror. "This is the picture of a town square over in Mississippi. See the magnolias in bloom? I know it must remind you of your home."

"Didn't live in no town—lived in—the country. — How many years?"

Nurse Betty looked over to Nurse Charlotte. "We have been amazed to have you with us—what is it now, Charlotte, over two years?"

"Around that," Charlotte said. "I'm not sure how many. Now look at this toothbrush we got for you. It has Donald Duck on the handle."

Yolanda gazed at the picture postcard. "Don't re-member—besides—me and Maudie—when we leave—we gonna have—a house—in California—where the stars stay."

"You've been telling her that, have you? That someday she'll leave here?"

"Yes, ma'am. Got it all planned." Maudie put her hands behind her head and stared back at Nurse Betty. "Going out to where Doris Day and all them people stay."

Yolanda said the first piece of cake after hers should go to Maudie. Nurse Charlotte fed Yolanda a small piece of her cake, but she had trouble swallowing after the first bite. She said she would rather have a drink of Coke in-stead. After she had a few sips, Nurse Charlotte left to help the other children. Yolanda turned to watch Maudie eating. "You knowed—?"

"Course I knowed it was your birthday." Maudie scraped icing off the plate and called to a nurse for another piece. "Course I knowed. What's you think, Yolanda? Miss Charlotte done told me. Everybody been talking 'bout it." Maudie finished her second piece and set the plate on her bedside table. "Got me a surprise for you, too."

It was late in the evening when Maudie wheeled back into their room, coming to a stop between Macy and Yolanda. There was a noticeable lump in her lap, covered over by her pajama top. "Have to wait 'til all them other peoples gone to give you mine." Her hands patted her lap. "It's that good-looking."

"Told you—Macy—she'd get—me—a present."

Slowly, she lifted up her pajama top. It lay there in her lap, two gold-braided ropes the thickness of her fingers. She raised them slowly, giving high drama to the viewing. Equally gaudy gold tassels were attached to the ends of the braids. "Something I done picked up for you last week at the store, since I knowed your birthday was coming up."

Yolanda was at first breathless, letting the iron lung take up the slack. Then she was teary at the sight of such stunning beauty. "Got it at the five-and-dime. Done wheeled all the way into Tuskegee to get it," she said with only the slightest hesitation.

"Say she done—wheeled all the way—"

"I—hear her," Macy said.

"Never mind that, y'all. Wait till Macy see how you look with 'em on." Maudie came closer and pulled up out of her chair, using Yolanda's lung for support. She began tying the gold braids in her hair, draping the abundant excess artfully over her pillow, letting the tassels come to rest to give the impression of dangling earrings.

"Course now there's one thing." She sat back down to view her handiwork, wheeling around to get a good look through the mirror, noticing that Yolanda seemed thinner in the face. "Can't wear these 'cept when nobody but us is around. They is a rule Nurse Betty done told me 'bout. No fancy hair ribbons on the iron lung people. Other peoples might get jealous. In the day, I'll keep 'em under my mattress, outta the way."

Yolanda hadn't heard a word, so enchanted was she with the gorgeous gold braid–laden person in the mirror.

—•—

And after that night, Yolanda would not be denied. "We best pals—like sisters—ain't we—Maudie?"

Maudie had glanced at the little bucktoothed smile and turned to look out the window. "What's you 'spect, Yolanda? I ain't hardly broke out with friends, lying in this here corner of the room. Can't even hardly see nobody else. Guess you'll have to do." Maudie flattened out her pillow and turned so she could get a better look at the smile. "Well now, listen here, Yolanda. If we sisters, why don't you get on out of here and go get me a Coca-Cola?"

Yolanda got so tickled, she couldn't even pass it on to Macy. And Macy kept saying, "What—so funny. — What—she say?"

Maudie watched Yolanda laughing when the barrel allowed it, remembering the night she had first seen her, too embarrassed to look at a detached head. Now the barrel, the head, the swishing sounds were all Yolanda.

—•—

Maudie turned to watch Reverend Earl's profile forward of the darkening scenery rushing past behind him. When she had imagined herself involved in voter registration, she had hoped for Atlanta or Birmingham, leading a new life in the big city. The drawback was that before you were eligible to take part in a voter project, you had to attend a voter workshop up in the mountains of Tennessee.

It was an obstacle she was determined to overcome, because by this time she had been in and out of the polio clinic for most of four years, enduring weeks of searing hot packs and then months of grueling physical therapy, all in a futile attempt to bring both of her legs back to life. One had responded; the other could not hold its own.

After a time, she had been allowed to go home and visit her mother and brothers on weekends. The first visit to the little house her mother had rented in Tuskegee had been a disaster. It was full of unknowns; steep steps, and thresholds she tripped over. She didn't know the town, didn't know the neighbors. Her mother was working all day as a maid, and her little brothers had gone on with their lives without her. She was seventeen, almost grown. If she didn't get away soon, she might never leave, might be stuck there for the rest of her life, trapped in some sit-down job at a mill or, worse, sitting on the porch of her mother's house.

—•—

At first, the church had been lukewarm about letting her go up to the Highlander Folk School, but she had pestered and pestered. Finally, the day had come and six of them from Tuskegee had boarded an old church bus, rumbling along the flatlands and then gradually rising up into the ranges of larger hills that were the beginnings of the Appalachian Mountains.

She really hadn't cared about the experience of living with coloreds and whites all mixed together, but it was prerequisite to running a voter-registration citizenship school, so she had pretended great enthusiasm. After two days at Highlander, she had learned her way around and had begun to make friends with her three bunk mates. She had been surprised that she didn't like the other colored girl, who was always whining about something, but that she had liked the two white girls. She had met Reverend Earl at Highlander. He had been there at the same time. He had spied her on her first day and kept an eye out for her the rest of the time, especially after he had found out that she was born up in his part of Alabama, in Bainbridge, and that she had spent a summer with her aunt up near Crossroads, his community. He hadn't talked to any others, probably because nobody else had wanted to come to this backwater county. It wasn't even in the town of Bainbridge, but more like fifteen miles outside of Bainbridge. Nobody cared what happened out here. She knew she was being thrown to the dregs of the movement. Reverend Earl's voice faded back in to her consciousness.

"And I know you got more education than most—all them classes you took down at Tuskegee."

"Yes, sir. I did," she said. They were coming up on Crossroads—not a town, just a place for country people to get gas and food.

"We'll be there directly," he said, "if you're a mind to do any combing and primping."

She recognized some few changes: a new advertisement for Camels stuck in the window of the grocery store, a new pump at the gas station, a billboard built on creosote poles carrying a paint-splattered picture of Martin Luther King sitting together with some white people.

When she was eleven, Maudie and her younger brothers had spent the summer in the country with their aunt Carrie. Then, Crossroads had consisted of a general store, a gas station, and the drive-in movie. The drive-in had been the only form of entertainment anywhere around, and it was only open on weekends. That summer, she had talked the manager into letting her go out among the white folks' cars and wash windshields for ten cents each before the movie started. At first, it had worked beautifully. She had made good money, and after she finished and the movie started, she and her brothers were allowed to watch the feature film from back behind the last row of white cars, sitting on the split-rail fence that separated the white cars from the colored ones. She could vaguely remember the round-faced fat girl who went from car to car, cajoling people into having their windshields washed. "You ain't gonna wanta make out the whole time. You gonna wanta watch the movie for a minute or two. Well, ain't ya?" The white boy sitting on the driver's side would begin to protest, but she would interrupt. "Don't have that windshield clear, that girl gonna think you up to no good." It worked every time. The boys would begin to dig in their pockets. They all knew ten cents was a cheap price to pay for the veneer of good intentions.

Remembering now, she could feel the light on her face flickering off the big screen as she sat on the fence eating popcorn and drinking Coca-Cola with her little brothers.

Now in the fading light of the sunset, she looked out at the image in the car's side mirror. A thin-faced girl with dark watching eyes stared back at her. There was no trace of that other person, the fat, happy one, twisting and shaping life to her satisfaction. She thought not one remnant of that person remained.

CHAPTER 8

The Rutland Place

$\mathcal{E}$IGHTEEN TWENTY, isn't that how long it's been in the family? Didn't we steal it from the Cherokees about that time, or was it the Creeks?"

"The original government land sale, Eugenia, is up on the wall in the office, as you well know." Eugenia always felt obliged to go out to the plantation at least once every visit. She had decided to do it early this time and get it over with. They were all in the car, their father driving, Eugenia beside him in the front seat, Tab and Tina in the back. Uncle Val had flown back to California the day before. He had to teach the summer session. Eugenia had decided to stay on for a while. No one knew for how long. It would have been impolite to ask. And on this visit, she had seemed to make sure that both the girls were invited along on her every outing.

"She's trying to convert us to being strange, like she is."

"She's trying to be polite, else she wouldn't invite you along."

"Oh sure."

They drove the eighteen or so miles out of Bainbridge along Highway 72, just past the small community of Crossroads, and turned right. Red clay fields rolled out on either side of them as they came onto the property. This coming was instant guilt for Eugenia. She looked out, her eyes filling with tears as she saw the ghosts of slaves laboring to clear the land. "It must be very hard for you to stand in those fields day after day," she said.

And Charles, unaware of her meaning, "Are you kidding? I'm delighted that after years of sweating it out, I've finally got the land—some of it—back where it belongs. Maybe this year I'll be able to make a good profit on the Williams place for you girls." The Williams place was a part of the farm that Mr. Ben had given over to his daughters. Of course they, being women, were not expected to run the place. That was up to the elder son. They did, however, expect to reap the profits, if there were any.

He pulled the car up to the one thing on the farm that he knew would impress her, the thing that he wanted to show off to her—the house for Will. "What do you think?" He had parked in front of the beginnings of the cinder-block house. Framing boards held plumb lines that marked the edges of what would one day be the walls.

"What is it?"

"It's the house for Will. You know, I always told you if I ever got the money, I wanted to start redoing all the tenant houses on the place. Well, this is the first one. It's Will's house. He's been with us longest, so his comes first."

"He's the only Negro—the only black man left on the place," she said.

"Some of the other tenants weren't too happy about

it, but I thought, Will has been with us forever, and with Dad. He deserves it."

She said nothing as she got out of the car to go next door and speak to the old man who would be the recipient of the cinder-block house. He sat rocking on the front porch and stood for her coming. She insisted that he take a seat after she had given him a hug. Charles got out and walked straight to the building site. The girls watched from the car. Tina folded her arms on the top of the front seat. "She told me she thinks Will is no better than a slave."

"Why would she say that?" Tab leaned forward, rested her arms next to Tina's, and peered out the window. "He doesn't even work anymore. Pop says he's too old."

"Because he's tied to the land and he doesn't have freedom of choice."

"He's lived here always. Where would he go if he did leave? How would he get any money?"

"I don't know. Aunt Eugenia says that's not the point. It's the philosophical question of the individual's merit that warrants our concern."

"What a crock. You got it from Aunt Eugenia. I bet you don't even know what it means."

"You are obviously not old enough to comprehend the problems we are having with the coloreds right now."

"More crock. What do you think me and Maudie May were? We were best friends. Before she got polio. Before she had to leave town."

"That was years ago. You and your little colored friend did nothing but run around town getting into mischief." Tina began quoting Aunt Eugenia again, babbling on and on, making no sense to Tab's ears. She looked out the car window, thinking of Maudie and the summer they were together, smiling as she remembered. Once, she and Maudie had gone to the river fishing—a place completely off-limits to Tab. She must have been around ten at the time. "We gonna get enough fish to sell so we can buy the brothers some school supplies," she had said. Before Tab knew it, they had ended up in the middle of the river in a leaky boat. The two of them had come too close to a barge on the river. It had been the scare and the thrill of her life—and a miracle that they had escaped drowning.

It was early evening when they left the farm and headed back home. Their car stopped momentarily, waiting for an old Chevy sedan to pass by before they pulled out onto Highway 72. As their car picked up speed, Eugenia turned to the backseat. She reached over and patted Tab on the knee. "I have a wonderful surprise for you girls later on."

CHAPTER 9

The Surprise

EVERYONE HAD CONGREGATED at Miss Hattie's for supper. As soon as napkins were down, Eugenia was the first to speak, "You know I told you girls I would have a surprise for you. Well, I had a letter from Bebe before I left California. He—*she* wants me to come visit while I'm here." Eugenia looked down at the untouched squash casserole on her plate and picked at the slivered almonds on top. "So close to Chattanooga and all."

"Bebe who?" Uncle Tom asked.

"You know, Bebe Palmer. I went to college with her."

Various family members shifted in their seats. They didn't like to be reminded of Bebe Palmer. "Oh yeah." Tom took a Parker House roll out of the bread basket and remembered what everyone else already had. "The nutty one—helped you get that job as youth director at the Methodist church over there. Is she still speaking to you after all that commotion you caused, insulting her church and all?"

"I don't think—" Miss Hattie began.

"Insult her? I did *not* insult her." The fork came down and scooped up an almond sliver. She chewed slowly, remembering, and then swallowed. "Besides, she forgave me, after awhile."

"You don't call asking those colored children to the youth fellowship—and it was her church—insulting?"

"For what was"—Eugenia pointed her fork at him and tried to lower her voice—"for what was a positive experience and a great awakening for her church—what should have been a great awakening." She reached for her iced tea, not bothering to finish explaining to him, to them.

After she had taken a small sip, "My thought was that I might take Tab along with me for the visit." She smiled at Tab. "Bebe's youngest is about your age."

"Me? You wanta take me?"

"Yes, you. Won't we all have fun?"

Tab looked to her mother for help that wasn't forthcoming. "Well, uh, I guess."

"We'll love riding the Incline up Lookout Mountain and"—she glanced at the head of the table—"and I'll make sure she gets to look at all the monuments up on Missionary Ridge."

Everyone else at the table was, for the moment, silent. The women tried not to smile at one another. Eugenia had been with them only a few days, and already nerves were on edge. This way, she would still be visiting, they would still be extending their hospitality, they would still be loving her, and yet she wouldn't be visiting, wouldn't be making everybody nervous for two whole weeks—or maybe longer, if Bebe asked them to extend their stay. A ripple of calm passed down the table. "Why, that's so thoughtful of you, Eugenia," Mary said, and picked up the basket of rolls and handed it across the table to her daughter. "We're almost out of rolls. Tab, will you bring us more, please?"

"Me?"

"Yes, you."

"But Tina likes to do all that housekeeping stuff. I don't take home ec 'til next year."

"Now."

"Yes, ma'am."

And as she walked out of the room with the basket still half-full of rolls, she could hear her mother trying to cover for her. "Eugenia, that's so thoughtful. What a treat for the girls."

Tab flung the bread basket on the kitchen table so hard that rolls scattered over the table and off on the floor. She was in the process of picking up the rolls when her mother walked in, calling back to the others. "I'll just see what's keeping her."

"Tab. That was the most impolite, halfhearted response I ever heard. What is the matter with you? You know better. Where are your manners? When someone invites you someplace, you must say how grateful you are, even if it's the Devil himself. You know that."

"I don't wanta go. I'm not going. Aunt Eugenia, she makes me nervous."

"Why would you say that? Y'all will have a marvelous time going to parties, riding the Incline. You may even meet some of the boys who go to Baylor Military School up there. They always look so handsome in those uniforms."

"They do?" She reconsidered, but only for a moment. "I don't care." She tapped fingers on the top of the kitchen table. "Not going."

Her mother sighed. "Well, that's a shame. Tina just told Aunt Eugenia she would love to go, even if you can't come along."

"Tina?" Tab's eyes shifted off the table and to her mother's face.

"Yes. Didn't Tina tell you Eugenia invited her this afternoon?" Suddenly, her mother seemed to see something very amusing out the kitchen window. "I guess it slipped her mind."

"Nothing ever slips her mind," fingers still tapping the table.

Her mother turned to go. "Well, I guess I'll just tell her you can't—"

"Okay, I'm going."

"I'll tell her you're delighted."

Tab picked up the last roll off the floor, blew on it, and dumped it in the basket before she walked back out to join everybody else.

Miss Hattie even offered her car up for the trip. "It's much nicer to ride in than that jeep, more comfortable for the girls."

Mr. Ben said nothing, but he did shake his head slowly in the affirmative, thinking perhaps of all the statues and cannons Tab would want to see.

—•—

She had on a hat they all thought must be a California-style. Nobody in Alabama would wear a thing like that. Red felt, with the brim pulled down on one side, and a long scarf wrapped around her neck and trailing behind her, as Tina was trailing behind her now.

Mary had taken the other children to swimming lessons, so Charles drove the girls over to Miss Hattie's in the farm pickup, taking the morning off to unload suitcases from their car into the Buick and tell the girls good-bye.

"Now you take good care of my beauties," he said to

Eugenia as he stood on the porch with his girls, giving them alternate hugs.

"Oh, I will. They'll love this trip, an awakening—oh, and fun, full of fun."

Charles motioned for Tab to come and sit in the porch swing with him for a minute while the others were loading. "You know the other night, when you got upset with Eugenia about how different her ideas are from . . . well, say, your grandfather's?"

She nodded, half-listening. "Yes, sir," watching the car to make sure Tina remembered she, Tab, had dibs on the backseat.

"I know you haven't traveled much."

"Two times to Birmingham and once to Memphis."

"Right, but that was with me and your mother. Now when you go on this trip, you may meet people who don't feel like we do about things."

"Yes, sir," she said again, not hearing.

"Well, just try to keep your eyes open to new things. When I went off to college for the first time, it was—"

She turned abruptly and gave him a big hug. "I sure will, Pops. I gotta go. They're waiting."

CHAPTER 10

On the Road

$\mathcal{T}$HE DAY WAS BRIGHT AND SUNNY, a forerunner to glaring and baking.

Tina had taken off the football letter jacket as soon as they were out of town and had flung it to Tab to store on the backseat. She rolled her window all the way down as they passed over Twelve Mile Creek Bridge. The muggy morning air ran at their faces like high-powered hoses, tearing at the ponytail Tab had earlier curled and sprayed. For a whole two weeks, they were to be pampered and treated to the high life in Chattanooga. Aunt Eugenia's friend Bebe Palmer, it was rumored, had inherited bargeloads of money when her father, a maritime lawyer, had sued the heck out of one of the big barge companies whose boats would, from time to time, run into each other in the river. Miss Bebe probably had money to burn and would think nothing of spending trifling amounts on the likes of them: holding barbecues and afternoon teas, sending them to ride up and down the Chattanooga Incline till their fannies were sore, going to dances where the boys would come over and ask to be put on their dance cards. Tab found herself biting off bits of Purple Passion.

Tina had run down to the drugstore just before they left and bought yet another orange lipstick. Tab had taken the time to pack her two starchiest crinolines. They were not that far out of style. Now Tina was sitting in the front seat with Eugenia, keeping time to the radio on the dashboard. They would make a great impression with their grandmother's new car. People would think they were rich also. Tina had turned the radio to the highest brow station around—"Charlie Mac and His Classic Swing Hour"—to show Aunt Eugenia that they were not altogether backward in this part of Alabama. Jo Stafford was singing an oldie but goodie, "Shrimp Boats." Tina and Aunt Eugenia joined in: "Shrimp boats are a-comin' / Their sails are in sight / Shrimp boats are a-comin' / There's dancin' tonight."

Eugenia slowed the car to make a left turn off Highway 72 and head north. Tina hardly noticed. The wind in her face would not allow eyes that open, but Tab did, and—thinking Eugenia had taken a wrong turn—"Aunt Eugenia, you know the way we always go is straight on out Seventy-two to Huntsville."

Eugenia took off the red felt hat with one hand, placed it on the seat beside her, and ran fingers through her hair. There followed one of those conversations everyone in the family seemed to have with Aunt Eugenia from time to time—Tab every time.

"When I was your age," Aunt Eugenia said, glancing at Tab in the rearview mirror, "I would have given anything to get out from under, even for a few weeks."

"Get out from under what?"

"Sometimes I felt as if I would suffocate."

"The heat? Guess they don't have it so bad in California."

"I knew they loved me, in their own way. I knew that."

"Oh yeah, the family, oh yeah," trying to accommo-date. "They said it about a million times, on the porch the other day, before you came, said they just all loved you." After all, Aunt Eugenia was the one taking them to Miss Bebe's to have the barbecues and meet the boys from Baylor.

"I've been thinking about you two so much lately. What could I do for you to assuage that feeling you must have every morning when you get up—at your age and here in this state—knowing there must be some-thing else out there and not being able to make con-tact. You probably say, If only I could touch it, see it, be a part of it."

She looked at them expectantly.

They looked back, eyes squinting.

Then Tina smiled knowingly. "Aunt Eugenia, how did you know I always wanted to meet some Baylor boys?"

Tab was beginning to connect the direction of the road with the direction of the conversation. "I don't know what she means, but she doesn't mean that."

"Of course she means that. Don't you ever get any-thing?" Tina said.

"Me? You should talk. Will you look around? I don't even think we're going to Chattanooga."

"Now girls, enough of that. I know how you feel, how suffocated you must feel, even if you don't understand your own feelings at this point."

"I understand my feelings."

"Be quiet, Tab. Aunt Eugenia is trying to talk." Tina was taking a good look at the outside scenery, trying to gauge where they might be.

"Yes, well, we—that is, I—got a call this morning from Bebe. She had to go out of town unexpectedly, and so I decided to alter our plans slightly."

"Oh no, is there something wrong in her family?" Tina rolled up her window so she could listen better.

"Uh, no—just business, as I understand it. She sends her regrets, but she won't be able to be there." The car had slowed considerably. Aunt Eugenia couldn't drive at her usual breakneck speed and make up stories at the same time.

"But what about the visits to Missionary Ridge, the barbecue parties, the boys in the uniforms?" Tina's lower lip might be quivering.

"She said she's so sorry. We'll have to do it next time we visit."

"We could go and stay in her house and let the servants wait on us." Tab's voice trailed off, "You know, so they would have something to do while she's gone."

The car began to speed up again as Aunt Eugenia was over the flat-out lying part of her story. "I knew you would be too disappointed for words if I told you right before we left." She shifted into third gear. "And soooo." She had put her sunglasses on, the ones shaped like pointy cat's eyes. Her scarf caught the breeze and flipped out in the wind. "I have made alternate plans. It's a little unusual, but in the end . . . a fabulous experience, and one you both sorely need."

"Uh-oh."

"What do you mean, 'Uh-oh,' Tab? Aunt Eugenia has gone to the trouble of making other plans just so we won't be disappointed. Sometimes you can be so disagreeable." She turned to Aunt Eugenia and put a hand on her shoulder. "That's so thoughtful of you, Aunt Eugenia. What might be our alternate plans? I hear they have some fun things to do up in Gatlinburg. That's not far. Mama said someday we might visit there."

Tab didn't hear her. She had flopped against the

backseat, wind from the two open back windows slapping hair across her face like some flogging she didn't
deserve. Now she would never get to meet up with the
boys from Baylor. Her head crashed against the roof of
the car. Aunt Eugenia had hit a pothole going fifty miles
an hour while she was in the throws of the explanation
of their alternate plans.

"We're going where?" She heard Tina almost shout
and then she heard her mumble, "Oh my God," and
Tina never said 'my God'—out loud—in Grandmother's
car.

"What—what is it?" Tab was rubbing the top of her
head.

"The Highlander Folk School."

"What?" She was trying to remember where she had
heard the name before, and then she remembered.
"That place? The one you see on the billboards?"

"Yes, Highlander Folk School." Aunt Eugenia seemed
to say the name without any problem. It floated off her
tongue without the least bit of effort. They had never
heard it said like that. Before, when it had been mentioned, it had been spit out like sour milk, or included
along with a string of cusswords, as in "that damn Highlander Folk School," or "the no-good, Commie-breeding
Highlander Folk School," or "those sorry-ass, nigger-
loving Highlander Folk School people." A camp hidden
away in the hills of Tennessee that trained outsiders and
coloreds and turncoat southerners in ways to integrate
the schools, the buses, the rest rooms at the filling sta-
tions—everything of importance known to mankind.
After training, people who went there were sent out to
do destruction all over the South. Martin Luther King
had been to Highlander Folk School. Eleanor Roosevelt
had been there. Even the colored bus lady from Mont-

gomery, she got her training at Highlander Folk School before she decided to go sit at the front of the bus and not get up.

Awhile back, on their way out of Bainbridge, they had passed the billboard about Highlander. "COMMUNIST TRAINING SCHOOL" was the caption underneath a huge picture of Martin Luther King sitting with some white people at Highlander Folk School.

Aunt Eugenia was pulling the car over to the side of the road. She parked beside a store that sold used clothing, Joyce Ann's Fashions. A few cars and pickups were parked in the dirt drive. "There's just one thing," she said. "You probably won't understand this, but there are some people who think Highlander Folk School is not . . . well, is not, would not be, the best influence on impressionable young girls." She drummed her fingers on the steering wheel. "That, of course, is ridiculous. I know from personal experience that is *not* the case." She adjusted the rearview mirror. "This will be a much-needed broadening experience for you both, a breath of fresh air. What I would have given when I was a child to have had an experience like this." Now she paused, choosing her words carefully. "But I don't think it is an experience that your parents, or any of the family, need to know about—not just yet."

The girls stared at her openmouthed, waiting for more. Surely there was more, some caveat that would absolve them of the responsibility of actually entering the enemy camp. There had to be some convoluted reasoning they could use that would, if tied in knots, make what she was asking them to do seem right. Was she expecting them to lie to their parents, to their grandparents? To keep quiet about where they had gone and never reveal that they had been into the very heart and

soul of the one place that was dead set against everything they did in life and every way they did it?

A big truck passed by, kicking puffs of dusty wind into
their windows. Cicadas whined in the pine trees. Tina
cleared her throat. "Are you saying that we should not
tell, that we should never tell where we've been? That we
should pretend when we get back that we really did go
to see Miss Bebe?"

"No, I don't want you to lie. When we get back, I'll explain everything to them: how the whole thing was im-
perative for both of you, to your understanding and
growth. How I felt it was vital for you to begin to take
your place in a new order of things down here. I'll take
full responsibility."

There was silence as a Ford pickup passed, loaded
with hay bales, swirling straw wisps out in the breeze.
Aunt Eugenia took her cat's-eye sunglasses off and
looked just beyond Tina, out into the tops of the pine
trees. "I am saying that it would not be appropriate at
this time—at this time."

"Wait a minute." Tab was still rubbing her head.
Maybe the bump was harder than she had thought. "Are
you serious about this?"

"Yes. When we return, I'll explain the whole thing.
I'm just saying that right now I think it's very important
for both of you—especially you, Tab—to develop some
kind of perspective about things."

"I got perspective. Tell her, Tina. I got perspective."

Tina was not interested in perspective. Other
thoughts were occurring to her. "What kind of people
will we meet up there? Will they be our age—any of
them?"

"Why, yes, yes, there very well might be," Aunt Eugenia said. "Young college boys, men, from up north
often come down for the summer to help out."

"What does that have to do with my perspective, me, my perspective?" Tab was also beginning to see possibilities—of a different kind.

Tina flipped up the door handle. "Just a minute, Aunt Eugenia. Tab and I need to talk about this. I'm sure it would be a lovely pleasure to go visit your place in the mountains, almost like we were going to Gatlinburg to see the sights, but instead we are going to"—she paused—"to that place. Listen, Aunt Eugenia, I need to have a word with Tab." She got out, opened Tab's door, then walked around to the back bumper.

Tab, taking her time, got out and followed, a slow smirk building. "I'm telling."

"You are not. That would be so gross."

"Yeah, I'm telling." She was so glad she had come. Opportunities like this didn't come along every day.

"She thinks she's doing something nice for us. You know people in California think strange. It would be impolite to argue. Besides, who knows who we'll meet up there. Maybe some Yankee college boys down for the summer to save us from segregation. Did you think of that?"

"Did you think about that billboard out on the highway? It says it's a Communist place. Did you think about Cousin John Lester?"

"I don't know what billboard you're talking about and I don't give a hoot for Cousin John Lester. Look, how bad could it be? I don't know what the place is. I've just heard them mention it at the supper table. It couldn't be all that bad."

Tab didn't say anything, waiting.

"Aunt Eugenia wouldn't take us any place all that bad." Tab looked out at the highway in front of them, following it with her eyes until it disappeared over the hill. She waited until she glimpsed Tina drumming her fingers, hands on both hips.

"I get three of your lipsticks and two of your nail polishes and all that eye shadow you got in that purse."

"All the eye shadow? Forget it. Two lipsticks and one nail polish and no eye shadow. You're too young for eye shadow anyway. Besides, it's the only one I have."

Tab turned to look at Aunt Eugenia through the back window and smile at her. "The eye shadow. Hand it over."

—•—

Back in the car, Tab was charm come to call. "Aunt Eugenia, we've talked it over and we think it's a lovely invitation and so sweet of you to think up alternate plans when Miss Bebe flaked—I mean, through no fault of her own, had to withdraw her invitation."

"Oh gravy," Tina mumbled, sitting there with her elbow on the armrest, her chin in her palm, her purse devoid of eye shadow.

Aunt Eugenia nodded her head, knowing they were bound to see the light—not as quickly as she would have had she been in their place, had the same opportunity presented itself to her way back when. She adjusted her cat's-eye sunglasses and flipped the chiffon scarf back over her shoulder. "These little details have to be attended to." She shifted into first gear. They burned rubber back onto the highway.

In just that time, that few minutes off the highway, the whole drift of the day had changed. In just that moment, what it would be like to ride the Incline and be served afternoon tea had changed to imagining what lay ahead in the wilds of the woods of Tennessee. The very air had turned sinister. The wind, whipping in through the windows, made the hair on Tab's arms stand on end. She rested her hands on the back of the front seat and looked out at the road, which had turned into a winding black thing, laying a slithering path out before them. Dresses were out. Dark green shorts and a baseball cap, dirty tennis shoes. She did have one pair she would have to scuff up. That would have to do. She had left her dirty shoes at home, for fear of offending Miss Bebe.

There would be guards at the entrance, spiraling razor wire on the top of the high fences that encircled the place, maybe machine guns. The car sped north.

Aunt Eugenia was chattering on. "You will have a chance to interact with people of all racial and ethnic backgrounds. You lead such provincial lives. It's time you were exposed to other things."

"Maudie May. I had a friend, Maudie May, and she was colored. We used to go down by the river and fish, and one time we almost drowned. She was this girl I used to play with before she got polio and had to leave town."

"That's just my point." Aunt Eugenia had interrupted her train of thought just long enough to hear Tab's last few words. "You see, Tab? Why should she have had to leave town? She had polio, like so many other people, but she had to leave town to get treatment."

"She had to go down there to get cured. They were gonna cure her down at Tuskegee. They told me that, only they never told me what happened to her."

"*They, they, they.* My point exactly. 'They' seem to dictate the course of our lives, of your life—down here—and it is patently unfair."

"My parents?"

"No, society at large—down here—don't you see?"

Tab didn't see. She was thinking about Maudie May, wondering if she still had polio, if she was cured. Probably she was married by now and maybe had children. "They get married early, you know."

"What did you say? I couldn't hear you back there."

"Oh, nothing."

"I've been active in raising money for Highlander for some time now," Aunt Eugenia was saying. "I think because of that they asked me to come and help out with several sessions. I knew when I got the letter that it was a godsend for me, for you girls."

No one bothered to ask how long ago she had gotten the letter.

CHAPTER 11

The Word of Truth Missionary Baptist Church

*M*AUDIE HAD AWAKENED ALONE, in a tiny unfamiliar room. It had taken a minute or so of staring at the blank walls to get her bearings.

The Word of Truth Missionary Baptist Church had not been what she had expected, what she had thought she remembered. The church itself had turned out to be nothing more than a plain rectangle of a building made of rough-hewn wooden planks topped by a shingled roof and situated below road level. It sat in a small clearing, surrounded by woods on two sides and fields out back. She had hoped she remembered stained glass or a steeple. She had not.

Singing had drifted out to them when they pulled in among the other cars and trucks parked around the front stoop. "Wednesday-night prayer meeting. Good crowd. Knowed we was coming," Reverend Earl said.

Maudie had said nothing. She had gotten out of the car and was concentrating on what she could see of the dark uneven ground, trying to gauge how high the front steps of the church might be. Reverend Earl had gone ahead of her to hold open the front door.

The congregation was singing in the dim glow of three lightbulbs on long wires hanging from the middle of the ceiling and spaced out down the aisle. The light was not enough to read by, but enough to find the way to a seat. Forward of the ten or so pews on either side of the aisle, there was a raised platform and a single podium of white pine. Behind that and nailed to the back wall was a homemade pine cross that touched the ceiling.

Reverend Earl walked down the aisle and shooed children out of the first pew. The congregation was on the last verse: "Ain't but one train runs this track . . ." Reverend Earl's friendly large hands motioned her to the empty seat. She began to walk, listening to the singing slow as members touched one another, signaling to look.

An older woman at the piano ruffled up and down the keys one last time as the final verse died out. Maudie had unlocked her leg brace and taken a seat. Reverend Earl walked to the podium and nodded a thank-you to the piano player.

He looked different to her now, more commanding as he stood there before his people. His black suit coat, already wet-ringed under the arms, had been a long time too tight across the belly. Pull creases from the front buttons were permanent.

Reverend Earl had begun with the business of Wednesday-night prayer meeting: a new baby at the Brown house; "Miss Randa sick again and everybody need to bring some little food by to help her get along." And finally, the roof-repair collection was still hurting.

Paper fans were out and pushing around the scents of the congregation. She hadn't needed to turn and look to know them. There were men who had spent the day in hot fields, red clay still caked to their shoes, women who had scrubbed someone else's house with Old Dutch cleanser and come home to coat their hands in Vaseline, babies still being breast-fed, and little children who had earlier played outside the church door in the fresh-cut grass around the front steps.

Ushers passed collection plates and some few coins could be heard dropping.

Reverend Earl mopped sweat off his face with a handkerchief retrieved from his suit pocket and began. "Got somebody new among us tonight. Girl had a choice to come here or not, and you got a choice to welcome her or not." He took off his glasses and looked at his congregation, one eye closed and the other one staring directly at them, as if he were watching through a microscope. He began telling them where he had met Maudie—"at the Highlander Folk School up there in Tennessee, and everybody good, from Mrs. Rosa Parks to Dr. King hisself, been up there. Somebody famous as Mrs. Eleanor Roosevelt visit up there. It's that good a place. A place where coloreds and whites live together without no fuss." So although they might make her out to be just a child, she had already taken two years' worth of college courses down at Tuskegee. "All that time at the polio hospital wasn't for no reason, 'cause she spent that time getting educated." He pointed a finger at his audience. "The Lord works in mysterious ways, His wonders to perform," he had said. "So don't you go thinking we ain't been sent the best, 'cause we have." Reverend Earl droned on, praising her long enough to wipe out any good that might have come from it. When he appeared to be nearing the end of his sermon, the woman at the old upright piano next to the wall had begun softly playing chords that wound into the melody of the final hymn just as Reverend Earl announced its singing. Some few members had already started humming and swaying before the whole joined in.

When it was over, Reverend Earl had rushed down to her and waved others over to greet her. They seemed to stay back, hesitant to come forward.

An older woman brought her son up to speak to Reverend Earl. "Edward want to have a word with you, Reverend." He looked like he was in his late teens, a body grown into an adult, but a face absent any lines of experience. His mother elbowed Edward.

"I just wanta say, Reverend . . ." He glanced at Maudie and hesitated until his mother took his arm. "Much obliged for the shoes. Couldn'ta got the job without no work boots."

"It was bounty from the Lord, Edward, bounty from the Lord." He slapped Edward on the shoulder. "Now you're a working man, I'm gonna 'spect to see some of that bounty in the collection plate."

"Yes, sir." He had backed away, his mother satisfied.

Reverend Earl turned Maudie around to meet an older lady in a dark dress, her hat and gloves kept on for the introduction. "This Miss Laura, our music master, head of the church welcoming committee. Ladies been working night and day getting ready for you coming. She be a friend of your aunt Carrie 'fore she pass."

The piano player, perhaps in her seventies, came forward. "Mighty happy to have you, child. Seems like I remember Carrie having some little ones stay with her one summer, but I never woulda knowed you grown." She looked Maudie straight in the face, eyes never straying.

"You gonna like it here. Lots a good peoples here. Been telling Earl we need somebody like you."

"I enjoyed your piano playing," Maudie said.

"I try my best what with half them keys sticking." She took off her glasses to clean them with a small lace handkerchief retrieved from her pocket. "Don't need these 'cept to read what songs we gonna sing; otherwise, they a nuisance."

"They a nuisance less she wanta see where it is she's going." Another woman, about the same age had walked up behind Miss Laura.

"Hush up there, Viola." Miss Laura didn't even turn to look at a voice all too familiar. "Who was it couldn't thread that needle at Sewing Club the other day?"

"Wasn't 'cause I couldn't see it," Viola said. "Needle head too small. Ain't that right, Dottie Sue?" She nodded her head to a third woman standing beside her. "She seen how small it was, didn't you?" Dottie Sue was the same age but slight, not as overgrown as Misses Laura and Viola.

She smiled and shook her head. "Needles too small nowdays."

"Dottie Sue, you'd take Viola's side if she say the moon's purple."

"Now ladies, you gonna have Miss Maudie here thinking you mean all that bad-mouthing. Viola and Dottie Sue and Laura been knowing each other since— how long is it now, ladies?"

"Lord, longer than I wanna think about." Miss Laura was readjusting her glasses. "Since cotton-picking season and I was three years old and riding on my mama's picking sack, her pulling me through the fields."

"Wasn't neither. It was the first day of school when we

was all eight. Ain't that right, Dottie Sue? Down at Cross-
road school."

"I wasn't eight; I was ten."

"Now ladies, why don't we tell Maudie here what you
done for her, since you the ones been wanting her here
for so long?" Reverend Earl put his arm around two of
the women, steering them to the back of the church.

"I appreciate y'all putting me up," Maudie said.
"Hope I won't be trouble to you."

"Oh now honey." Miss Laura stopped. "You ain't
gonna be no trouble to me. I, we—my committee—been
thinking you rather have a place of your own." She
glanced at the floor. They walked on into a room that
Maudie guessed must serve as Reverend Earl's office.
There was a metal desk and chair, dusty from disuse. A
picture of Jesus praying hung lopsided on the wall. "This
here is what I call my office, but I don't spend no time
here. You know, I got two more churches to tend to," he
said.

"Right this way." Miss Laura was holding out her hand
and pointing to what looked like a closet door. "Better
than staying with old ladies like us. We done fixed you
up a place right here at the church." When the others
hesitated, Miss Laura walked over and opened the door.

Before being converted, the room must have been a
place to store supplies. There was an old desk to one
side and an American flag leaning against the wall in the
corner. The ladies of the church had made curtains for
the two windows that looked out on the backyard. A
brightly colored quilt was on the single bed that had
been brought in and placed in the far corner. At one
end of the old oak desk there was a washbowl and
pitcher. At the other end was a two-burner hot plate,

which was plugged into the one outlet in the room. A small black floor fan took up the other socket. The ladies had placed a rag rug by the bed and a rocking chair on the edge of that. Someone had contributed an icebox. "Not cold enough to keep ice cream," Miss Laura said, "but it do keep things cool, and the ice last four, sometimes five days when the weather ain't too hot."

"And lookie here"—Reverend Earl pointed—"got you your own battery radio to keep up with what going on, and your own private entrance." He walked over and opened a door that led out to the back of the church. They were all too happy, too effusive, making it too obvious that none of the welcoming committee had been willing to take her in.

Maudie had imagined herself living with one of them, taking dinner with them every night, talking about the events of the day. She fixed a smile, tried to look as if she was pleased with what they had done. She could feel her eyes watering, betraying her, and then, just as quickly, what she was seeing and what she was feeling separated and saved her.

She lay there now in her new room, remembering how she had gone along with them, telling them they had done a wonderful job with the quilt and the curtains, chitchatting about the other things they had made. She remembered Reverend Earl bringing in her suitcases. The next thing she knew, she was sitting by herself on the bed and wondering where the bathroom was. She had gotten up and gone to the window to search for what she had suspected was there, off in the woods, a small clapboard building probably just big enough for one seat. That had not been part of the show-and-tell. After she had negotiated the two back steps and the path to and from the outhouse, she sat on the bed and took off her brace, too tired to move, until she realized she needed to walk back over to the back door and bolt the brand-new sliding lock they had installed.

CHAPTER 12

The Water Boy

*S*UN STREAMED IN through the back window and across her bed. There was food in the icebox: a cake, collards, and black-eyed peas cooked with a large piece of fatback. The ladies welcoming committee might not have wanted her to live with them, but they weren't going to let her starve. She took out a piece of corn bread and went back to sit on her bed and click open one of her suitcases. It was full of books she had taken from the Tuskegee library. She meant to return them sometime, of course.

It was early yet. The sun was just up. She picked a book the librarian had recommended. "I wouldn't have given this one to you earlier, but now you're seventeen, that's old enough." Maudie flipped to the first chapter and began to read: "'Brrrrrriiiiinng An alarm clock clanged in the dark and silent room . . .'" She nestled in among her books. When it turned her way, the floor fan ruffled the pages. The breeze cooled her face. This was not half-bad. If they wanted to leave her down here, they could. She lay with her head at the foot of the bed, her weak leg propped up on some books. Maudie continued to read and was back in Chicago in the 1930s.

—•—

Before Tuskegee, the only schooling she'd ever had was what her mother taught her, and the only subject they had studied was Hollywood. She and her mother would pore over old movie magazines her mother brought from other people's houses. First, her mother would read them to her, with Maudie looking on. Very soon, Maudie began to see the words her mother was saying. Before long, she was reading to her mother every day when she got home from work. Her mother would take off her shoes, lie down on the couch, and hand Maudie the magazines she had collected. Maudie began reading all the articles and keeping track of all the stars. Her mother would fall asleep on the couch, listening. After a time, the brothers would come in off the front porch to sit and listen.

—•—

At Tuskegee, she had watched out the window as students at the Institute carried books to and from classes. By that time, she was fairly skilled with two crutches. She began to pester the nurses to let her out. The library was not that far from the hospital. Nurse Betty had finally arranged for her to go.

She drove the librarian to distraction, roaming the stacks, pulling books down for no rhyme or reason. The librarian decided it would be a good idea for Maudie to audit an American history course. The librarian told the dean of students. The dean of students felt sorry for Maudie, but more for the librarian. "Professor Tuffel wouldn't mind having her. Old Tuffs can handle anything. We'll stick her in there."

In that manner, she had been passed about the campus, bouncing from one professor to the other, learning first this thing and then that, listening closely to the way the professors talked, learning to adjust her speech patterns to sound more and more like someone else. When she wanted to, her grammar could be almost flawless.

—•—

A shaft of sunlight eased its way onto the page, and Maudie realized she had dozed off. She wouldn't want someone coming on her first day—surely someone would come—and finding her still in bed. She got up, using her crutch to get over to the washbasin and wash her face while she looked out the window situated over the desk. She realized the well she saw in the distance must be her source of water. She cut herself a piece of cake, poured a glass of water, and, without putting on her brace, used her crutch to take the few steps to the outside back stoop. She sat down, leaned back, and closed her eyes, enjoying the sun on her face. This might not be what she had imagined, but she was back out in the world. When she opened her eyes, Maudie noticed a boy of eight or ten walking in her direction from the field back of the church. In an effortless movement he must have mastered about the time he learned to walk, he lifted one of the barbed wires and slithered through, untouched by the waiting barbs. He walked over to the well to lower its bucket. When it was filled, he brought it up and began walking toward her, bucket in hand, indifferent to what he was bringing. Water sloshed out on his jeans and down into the worn black canvas of his high-top Keds. He came to stand in front of her, shifting the bucket from one hand to the other and looking over to the back door, which she had left ajar. "She told me, 'Find the one with leg irons on and get her fresh water.' You ain't the one. Somebody else inside?"

She glared at the boy, deciding that she was happy not to be teaching children. "What do you want?"

"I'm the one gonna bring you water every morning—for as long as you here."

"What do you mean, for as long as I'm here? Is this only temporary?"

"If you don't get run off. That's what I mean."

He stepped past her and opened the back door. She could hear him setting the heavy bucket on the floor. He came out to the door again, holding the washbasin full of soapy water.

"I can do that."

He splashed water out on the ground and went back inside. She heard him filling the basin with clean water and then filling the pitcher.

As he passed her on his way back out the door with his empty bucket, "You the one. I seen the leg iron on the floor." He walked on off toward the well.

—•—

Along about noon—she had been inside dressing—Reverend Earl drove up in his ancient car, red dust coating the back fenders, whitewalls obscured by caked clay. "I knowed you was gonna need some teaching supplies, and this the day I can find time to take you to town." He sat down on the porch and talked to her through the back door while she finished dressing. "You know I done told you I got three churches in all. Pleasant Valley, over near Twelve Mile Creek, and Harvest Moon, out past Crossroads."

"I remember," she said, wondering why he hadn't chosen to put her in one of those churches.

"Gonna have to let you do for yourself a lot of the time."

"It's all right," she said. "I can do it." She had forgotten that she might need teaching supplies.

They rode quietly for the first few miles into town. She could tell Reverend Earl had something on his mind, as he was glancing at her and back at the road. He slowed to a stop at the Twelve Mile Creek Bridge to get in line behind two other cars.

"Trouble on the bridge?"

"A cotton-picking machine using up both lanes coming across. Probably headed to the Rutland place." He peered through the dirty windshield. "Now like I was saying, after figuring on it, I was just as glad you was coming, but"—he stuck his head out the window to watch the big farm machine inching its way across the bridge, with little room to spare—"but now some of the others wasn't that glad." He pulled his head back inside. "Fact is, we took a vote and they was several didn't care 'bout you coming a'tall."

She had suspected it. "What others? You mean like some one of the men?"

"Well, don't matter who. Wouldn't be right of me to say, but I just don't know how many you gonna have coming to your voting classes. What I'm saying is, when we get to the Woolworth's, don't go spending all you got on paper and things, 'cause ain't no telling who might show up"—he hesitated—"if any."

"What do you mean, 'if any'? I thought you said, when we were up at Highlander, that y'all needed—wanted— somebody to start trying to get people registered."

"Well now, the county folks do—Miss Laura and her ladies all for it—but now the folks got jobs in town ain't so sure. They saying as how they got the jobs in town and they getting along and you gonna come in here and mess with things." He reached over and patted her shoulder. Maudie glanced at him, beginning to wonder what he really thought. "But you didn't feel that way?" she said.

"Course I don't feel that way. Wouldn't had you come all this way if I did. Just feel like you got a right to know, you buying supplies and all."

The big cotton picker finally made it across the bridge and the cars in front of them began to move forward. She sat there pretending what he had said had not fazed her. "They'll listen to me," she said, not thinking for one minute that was true.

CHAPTER 13

Mon Amie

$\mathcal{E}$UGENIA HAD STOPPED THE CAR at a roadside park built by CCC workers during the Depression. Tab and Tina got out and carried their lunch over to one of the concrete picnic tables. Aunt Eugenia sat opposite, unfolding the map. She wasn't sure exactly where she was going. She had raised money for Highlander Folk School but had never been there. As they all searched, pickle juice from the girls' bologna sandwiches dripped down on parts of Kentucky.

"There it is"—Tab pointed—"just an inch or two away from Cousin John Lester's place." Eugenia pulled the map to her, fingers tracing along the roads. "Why didn't you tell him about it, Aunt Eugenia?" Tab took a drink of Coke and a bite of potato chip to mix in with the bologna and pickle. "Uncle Val—about Cousin John Lester being kin. You coulda, you know."

Aunt Eugenia didn't answer.

"We could take him to see the plaque next time he comes to visit, it being so close to home and all."

Eugenia looked up from the map. "Your uncle Val will *never* see that plaque, if I have anything to say about it."

She looked down again and began measuring the distance between Highlander and Pulaski with her fingers. "At times," she muttered as she measured, "I have thought seriously about going up there and lodging some kind of nonviolent protest in front of that plaque."

Even Tina was put off by that notion, elbowing Tab. "Ha-ha, Aunt Eugenia, you're such a joker. Granddaddy wouldn't let us back in the house if we did something like that."

"He may not let us back in the house anyway, once he finds out where we're going," Tab said.

"Remember, Aunt Eugenia"—Tina had grabbed the back of Tab's neck to shut her up—"we need to have our horizons broadened at this other place, at this Highlander place."

Eugenia began slowly folding the map, smiling at them. She seemed so pleased to do this for them. She was taking a chance, risking family censure to have them see whatever it was she wanted them to see. Tab knew she would never have risked the same. There was beginning to build a grudging respect for old Aunt Eugenia.

"You're absolutely right, Tina," Aunt Eugenia said. "First things first." She stuffed the map back in the picnic basket and they were off.

The hills got higher, the roads more winding. When they were at the top of a rise, they could see tiers of jagged blue lines off in the distance. They finally reached the mountain crest and turned onto an ordinary-looking country road. Farmhouses were set off in the trees and in weedy fields scattered with scrub pines. Quite suddenly, they came upon Highlander Folk School. A turn in the road and it spread out before them, this place everyone talked about in the newspapers and on the billboards but which nobody had seen.

There were no guards or even a fence. Several buildings were scattered haphazardly around a small lake. It all looked so familiar, like a thousand little communities the girls had seen beside a thousand county roads. "This is it?"

"See, I told you. Isn't it lovely?" Eugenia flung her arms out. "This is where it's all happening, girls, the makings of a new day in the South, across the nation really. It's all right here. Look at that lovely old house." She pulled the car up to what looked like the main building—a large two-story clapboard. Split-oak rocking chairs filled the length of the porch running across the front. It reminded Tab of Girl Scout camp. The air smelled of pine. Shouts came from the lake. This was nothing like she had imagined from the pictures on the billboard, from hearing Uncle Tom talk, from reading about it in the paper.

Two people came out to meet Eugenia, as if they knew she was coming all along. They greeted one another like old friends, a white man and a colored woman. The girls stayed put in the car, unnoticed. Off to the left, there was a building with a sign that read LI-BRARY. In the shadow of the front entrance, a colored girl stood holding a book and watching them. Other buildings around the lake looked like they might be bunkhouses.

"Oh gad." Tina squinted her eyes to get a closer look, but it was not close enough to really see, so she reached down in her purse and got out the prescription glasses she wore in dire circumstances. "Oh gad, do you see, over there, that colored man and the white woman getting ready to jump off the float in the middle of the lake? What is this place—them swimming together like that?"

Tab couldn't help the grin. In her wildest dreams, she

could not have imagined getting herself in a situation of such advantage. "Did you bring those fake eyelashes with you, the ones you hide in the top of your dresser?"

Glasses were jerked off and thrown back in her purse. "No, I did not, and forget it."

"Granddaddy would like to hear about this place." It sounded like the first line of a song, and she was ready to sing endless verses.

Eugenia broke away from those greeting her and came back to the car to get them. "Isn't this unique? Don't you love the setting, the trees all around, and the little lake? You know, we're on the very top of the mountain." She took a deep breath. "Sort of symbolic, don't you think?" She swung the car door open. "What's the matter with you two? Come on out and see for yourself."

"It's pleasant to me as all get-out," Tab said, and hopped out, stretching her arms to mimic Eugenia. "You know how to pick 'em, Aunt Eugenia," she added, and opened the door wide for Tina.

Eugenia introduced them to the two people she had been talking with. The leader was Myles—Tab didn't catch the last name—a white man, and the colored woman Aunt Eugenia called Septima. Both looked pleasant enough and were a vague disappointment to Tab, as she'd been expecting to glimpse a gun or some other evidence of serious intent.

All of them walked toward the main house, carrying suitcases. "We'll take a bus over to pick up the children tomorrow and bring them back here for the weekend," the leader was telling Eugenia. "It's been a hard time for those kids. I'm afraid they'll all back out of trying to integrate the high school over there if we don't give them more support."

They took the girls and the luggage to their assigned

bunk room and left, still discussing their plans, Eugenia engrossed in every word. "I'll be delighted to help." They could hear Aunt Eugenia's voice trail off as she walked down the hall, away from them.

—•—

On the first floor, the house accommodated several bunk rooms and the dining room. Tab sat down on the bottom bunk she had been assigned. Tina had the top. Eugenia was rooming upstairs with older people. This room had two bunk beds, small orange crates stacked at the end of each bed to store clothes, and one small closet. "Course it's not so pleasant that I wouldn't go on right now and send a letter home if anybody happened to think about not giving me what they promised."

"Don't give me that. You're in this just like I am. If I get in trouble, you get in trouble."

"You're the older one." Tab was sing-songing again. "The older one is responsible for the younger one."

"Oh shut up." Tina flipped open her suitcase on the bottom bunk and began pitching clothes to Tab. "That's my crate over there. Put this in and then we'll do yours." Tab caught shorts and shirts, socks and shoes, then placed them in the upturned orange crate, which had one shelf and served as a wardrobe. Tina left the other— the dresses, hats, and gloves—in the suitcase, snapped it closed, and stuck it under the bed before she got to Tab's. She was beginning to pitch stuff to Tab when they heard, or half-saw, movement on the top of the other bunk in the room. Someone was lying in the top bunk, with a sheet pulled up to the neck and a comic book over the face, like she, or he, had been sleeping when they arrived.

And that's what she said, from under the comic, that

she had been sleeping when they came in, and they immediately said they were sorry they had awakened her. It was a girl's voice, and she said, in what was a distinct Yankee accent, that she was from Connecticut and—apropos of nothing—liked Elvis, and that it was all right, because she needed to wake up anyway. Tab and Tina shrugged shoulders at each other. They still couldn't see her, only the comic book and the body form under the sheet.

"So, do you like Elvis? My father doesn't like Elvis, but I do."

"Well, yeah, we like Elvis, don't we, Tina?" Tab took some socks from Tina, still watching the bunk.

"Sure, we like Elvis."

"My father is a minister, Clarence Calder. You've probably heard of him. He's famous in the movement. We may go to Memphis when we finish here, so I can see where Elvis lives."

Tab moved around the room to see if she could get a better view. "Guess you're in junior high like me?"

"Uh, yeah, but tall for my age." The sheets were shaking, as if she might be trying to keep from laughing. "Have you ever seen Elvis?"

"No, but that's a good idea, going to see where he lives. Don't you think so, Tina?"

"I said I did." Tina was not interested in the lump under the sheets.

Tab was resisting the urge to go up and jerk the comic off. "So, did your father come down to help out with training coloreds on how to get to vote?"

The voice snickered. "Yes. Yes he did, to train coloreds, as you say. And your aunt?"

"Yeah, she's crazy about coloreds, too. Hey, I got a idea. If you go to Memphis from here, you're bound to go through Pulaski. It's on the way. You could stop to see the plaque of—"

"Don't start that again, Tab. She's not interested. They have a lot more interesting things up north, like the Liberty Bell, things like that." Tina pitched a pair of tennis shoes to Tab, who put them away as a bell clanged out on the front porch.

Dominique Calder tossed the comic book to the far end of the bed and sat up. Long brown legs swung around to dangle over the side of the bunk. Bushy black hair that framed her face stood out perhaps four inches on all sides of her head, and there was a sly grin. "It's the hairdo you're staring at, isn't it?" They shook their heads yes. "It's called an Afro." One hand reached up, fingers plumping it into shape. "Most people down here don't wear this style yet. It's new. I realize you people down here don't get fashions until much later. In a few years, you'll see it all over the place."

She slipped off the bunk, not using the ladder, which was no problem, given the length of the legs. She was tall for her age, if she was, as she had said, the same age as Tab. She looked years older, and, Tab thought, slightly weird with the bushed-out hair and a gap between her two front teeth. The face was hard and narrow, the lips thick and large—not pretty. Tab was trying to remember if she had ever seen a beautiful black person. No, but striking. That was it—she was striking.

"That's the dinner bell." She stood facing them, her feet planted apart, her hands jammed in her jeans pockets—daring them. "Better hurry and unpack. I can tell we're having fried chicken. I know you people are used to fried chicken down here, but ah, *c'est un bizarre plaisir pour moi.*" She strode toward the door. "*Et, je m'appelle Dominique.*" And then she caught the door frame and turned back to them. "Oh, sorry, I was telling you that my name is Dominique. My father cautioned me about speaking French down here, with you people."

Tina waited until Dominique was well down the hall before she burst out. *"Is your father down here to help the colored people learn how to vote?"* She fell over on the bunk, laughing. "How gross can you get?"

"Well, how did I know . . . this weird body, lying up there covered up like that? Have you ever heard of a colored person with a Yankee accent? Well, have you?" Tab hit her sister with a pair of socks, trying to make her stop laughing and confess. "I'm serious. Have you ever heard of such a thing?" Certainly they had not seen or heard anything like it in Bainbridge, and although they had visited Birmingham and Memphis on two occasions, nothing of that sort had made itself known to them in those cities—or on television. The set they had had for two years now showed *I Love Lucy,* and *The Andy Griffith Show* or *My Three Sons,* and only after homework was done.

"And you were gonna tell her about the plaque. I loved that part!"

"Well, she mighta wanted to see the plaque."

"Oh sure, colored people just love to see anything associated with the Ku Klux Klan." Tina pitched more socks on her bunk. "You're too much," she said, and pretended an exaggerated check of her own hair. "Well, I must take leave of you now, since it's dinnertime. Adios." She started toward the door and walked out before turning around and sticking her head back through the frame. "Oh, sorry, that's Spanish for 'I think our colored roommate is gonna be a jerk.'"

—•—

They met the other roommate that night at supper, sat across from her at one of the tables in a dining room that accommodated forty or so people. Eloise was from South Carolina and, Tab thought, had a regular-looking colored person's hair—slicked down with what was probably Vaseline and tied in the back with a yellow ribbon. Her way of talking was not grating to Tab's ear, more like her own. She was younger, eleven, and she reminded Tab in a way of Maudie May, the girl she had played with before she got polio and had to leave Bainbridge. She felt immediately comfortable with Eloise. She had come up to Highlander with her mother. When they finished here, they were going on back to South Carolina and start a citizenship school to teach people to read and get them registered to vote. "Leastways that's what Mama say we was gonna do. It ain't none of me. I be here 'cause Mama here."

Dominique was sitting at a table at the far end of the room with a tall, thin colored man. Eugenia was with them, listening with rapt attention every time the man spoke.

"They talking about going on over to Troy Town tomorrow, if you're wondering what they talking about." Eloise had seen Tab watching Dominique's table. "Gonna see if they can't bring back some of them colored children scared to go to school with the whites. Let 'em be here for the weekend so they can play." Eloise sneered. "Looka here. I ain't scared of no whites. Sitting right here at the table with 'em, ain't I?" Tab looked around to see whom she might be talking about. There were only Tina and herself and one of the lifeguards.

"Are you scared of him?" she whispered. No one had ever explained to Tab that she was supposed to be afraid—of anyone. For someone to mention the possibility of a predator—of any kind—to a girl would have been impolite, even common. She had heard the words, batted around at slumber parties, like balloons floating in the air, things they would say for the fun of it, to show they knew the words: *whore, bitch, rape*—and they knew the definitions, because they had looked them up.

"I ain't scared of no women," Eloise said. "You gotta be careful 'bout the men, though." Tab eyed the lifeguard suspiciously, trying to imagine him as a villain in a movie—the closest she could come to disquieting social interchange. There was that story she had heard her grandmother tell one night on the porch, when Grandmother had had three glasses of peach wine. She didn't like to remember the details of that story, and anyway, Grandmother had told her never to repeat it. Girls didn't hear stories like that.

"So, Eloise, do you like Elvis? He's white, and Dominique likes him."

"Don't like Elvis. My mama say the Devil in them hips. I like Fats, Fats Domino. Try to get him on the radio up here, but all I can get up here in these mountains is 'Grand Ole Opry.' That ain't my type of music."

"Me neither."

"Tina doesn't like it, either, do you, Tina?"

Tina nodded. She hadn't said much to them. There were two boys sitting across from her, lifeguards for the lake, among other things, down for the summer to help out, they said—the one black and the other white. Tina had been talking to the white one and watching everything the black one did. Tab looked up from her fried chicken to give the black one a passing glance. He didn't look colored except for his skin.

Supper was fried chicken, crowder peas, sliced tomatoes, string beans, corn bread, and all the iced tea they wanted. It didn't taste any different from the iced tea they had at home, although the fried chicken was not the same—cornmeal in the batter.

After supper, the three of them—Tina, Eloise, and Tab—helped stack chairs in the dining room. It had been decided that there should be a square dance. "I think," Tina whispered, "we're gonna dance—with everybody participating."

"So? I am very good at square dancing."

"So what if someone asks me to dance?" And sure enough, someone did, and Tina went out on the floor and wasn't half as good as the colored man who had asked her, and she came off red-faced.

Tab was sitting on a pushed-back table, legs swinging. "You see, your problem there was, you were do-si-doing the wrong way and bumping into the people behind you that first time, and then when you were supposed to alle-mande right, you allemanded left and messed up the whole thing."

"Thank you, *Miss Swan Lake,* but that had nothing to do with it."

"If you don't mind me saying so, it's because you can't dance worth a hoot, Tina."

"It most certainly is not. It's because it's against the law; otherwise, I would have been just as good or better than everybody else."

Tab took a drink of punch. She held the cup up in Tina's face. "I have heard that swimming is against the law, but nowhere is it written that square dancing is against the law—or drinking punch."

"I can't believe you. We're up here not more than one day and you're acting more like Aunt Eugenia than Aunt Eugenia. Here we are, in the midst of Tennessee, breaking the law. Where is all that hate you had for Aunt Eugenia and all that stuff you're always spouting about

Cousin John Lester and our poor ancestors at the Battle of Shiloh?"

Tab sighed heavily, feeling put-upon that she must clarify the simple but irrefutable logic of it all. "If you do not remember, I will tell you. It was not colored people who killed Great-Great-Uncle Arthur. It was—do I need to explain this to you, Tina?—Yankee white people."

—•—

Eugenia, out of breath, walked over to them at the end of the Virginia reel. Another dance was starting. "Isn't this fun?"

They nodded their heads.

"And so many interesting people here. Do you like your roommates?"

They nodded again, forcing smiles.

"Good, good. I told you you would. Do you see that man over there?" She was pointing to the man who had been sitting next to Dominique at dinner. "I know you haven't heard of him, but that's Clarence Calder. He's—"

"A famous preacher in the movement?" Tab said.

"Why, yes. How did you know?"

Tab shrugged and looked around, but she didn't see Dominique.

The dance ended and Eugenia was back out on the floor again, acting like the social director, grabbing poor colored people who didn't want to dance and making them join in the fun—out of the kindness of her heart, of course—because Aunt Eugenia was so anxious to do good, she was going to do it no matter who suffered.

CHAPTER 14

Divorce

THE BUS HAD COME BACK from Troy Town late the next afternoon. Eugenia, the leader, and Reverend Calder were the only ones on board. Eugenia, looking crestfallen, was sitting on the porch, waiting for dinner. "They couldn't see, or maybe they didn't want to see," she said.

"Eugenia, you can't expect it to be like you want it to be. It's like it is. That's the reality we work with," the leader said.

"Did I ruin the whole thing?"

The leader looked tired. "No, it was probably bound to happen anyway. When the parents saw you arguing—discussing—with the protestors, they got scared for their children." He could see that Eugenia was near tears, and so could Tab. She had been sitting on the edge of the porch, listening. She got up and took Aunt Eugenia's arm. "Whatever you did, Aunt Eugenia, I know it was good." And after she had said it, she realized she felt sorry for Aunt Eugenia and never had before.

"We need to forget it and move on," the leader was saying. "Envelope stuffing tonight after dinner."

"I'll be there," Eugenia said, brightening. "I'll bring the girls. We'll be there."

That night, Tab, Dominique, Eloise, Tina, and the two lifeguards were all sitting around one of the dining room tables, stuffing envelopes, when Dominique had to say it: "You people just don't have the temperament it takes. Your aunt botched up the whole thing over in Troy Town today."

Tab felt duty-bound to take it as an insult, even if Dominique was right about Aunt Eugenia. She had been taught to defend family, always, no matter that you personally didn't like what they said or who they were. She had never really thought about it before, but she wasn't so fond of Uncle Tom. That night, in a halfhearted effort at reprisal, she short-sheeted Dominique's bunk. The next day, she was amazed that Dominique didn't accuse her, didn't seem to know who had done it. She figured Dominique must not have heard about the family loyalty thing.

—•—

The younger ones—about eight children who had come to Highlander with their parents—would do other things during the day, work on crafts or take hikes or go swimming. Eloise had never learned to swim, and so one of the lifeguards was giving her lessons. Tina had volunteered to help out with the lifeguards because, she said, she had her senior lifesaving certificate. Dominique and Tab were left together by default. And when the two of them went swimming in the afternoon and Dominique said she didn't have any aunts or uncles and that she was an only child, it was something unusual, but not unheard of. But when they reached the float in the middle of the lake and were sitting there catching their breath and Dominique said her parents were divorced, now that was news—Tab having never been acquainted with a child of divorce. It was not an occasion for sorrow as much as it presented itself as an oddity, like a two-headed cow at the fair or something out of a *Ripley's Believe It or Not!* This announcement brought on a dull thud of silence, Dominique gazing out at the water. Tab tried not to stare, because any minute Dominique was going to make a fool of her by laughing at her gullibility. Tab thought it must be another attempt at cleverness, much like throwing around the French phrases.

Tab had friends whose fathers drank to excess. She had one acquaintance whose mother always seemed to have bruises on her arms. She could come to Tab's house, but Tab couldn't go visit. It was never discussed. Discussion might require imagining the details.

With it all, divorce was not an option. It would have been shrinking from one's duty. It would have garnered the whole community's contempt. And her father, Dominique's father, was a minister. Tab stared long enough at Dominique to realize she was not joking. "Are you sure?"

"Am I sure?" Dominique looked to the heavens, rolling her eyes. "You are so pathetic."

"Why am I pathetic? You're the one with the divorced parents, and you just come right out and say it in public. And you don't even know me that much."

There was silence again, except for shouts and splashes off in the swimming area. "I just don't know anybody with divorced parents, that's all. So shoot me." Tab looked out at the water. "Besides, if you do get a divorce, it is not something you go around telling people." Other people did things like that—movie stars, Elizabeth Taylor, people like that—but nobody in the real world. She sat there trying to think of anyone her parents might have mentioned. She lay back on the float and closed her eyes, completely absorbed in this new thought. There was a cousin. Did she remember her parents, maybe her grandmother, mentioning that he got a divorce and moved to Texas? People were constantly moving to Texas when they did something strange. And then she realized Dominique was still sitting there. "You know what, Dominique? You are the most unusual person I've ever met: a colored with a Yankee accent, whose father got a divorce, and he's a minister on top of that." She lay there, amazed by it all, and then heard a splash.

Dominique had jumped back in the water and was swimming ashore.

"Hey, wait up."

—•—

"You should hear them people when they get going on a argument. Everybody saying things every which-a-way." Eloise was talking. She and Tab and Dominique had gone down the hall to the showers, hurrying because they were already late for breakfast. Tina had told them so before she left.

"Tab, you go on—go to one of them meetings they have. You can sit outside the windows and listen. They don't mind that. You gonna hear a bunch of arguing fools."

They were in and out of the showers in a hurry, flipping sheets, tucking in blankets—beds had to be made if you wanted breakfast—and walking fast back down the hall. Meals didn't last long.

All three paused at the door to the dining room.

"Follow me. I know where to sit," Dominique instructed them as they entered. She seemed to feel it was her job to tell them what to do and how to do it, going to great lengths to make sure everyone knew she was leading. It had been like that since their arrival. She had, at first, been mistaken enough to try to enlist Tina. "That's not the way you fold clothes properly," she had said, coming down off her bunk to demonstrate. Tina stood up from stacking clothes in her orange crate and gave her a look of such contempt that Dominique had physically backed off. From the beginning, their fences were up and firmly in place. Tab, on the other hand, was fascinated by the way Dominique talked, by her hair, by the barefaced arrogance.

Tab and Eloise followed along, Dominique leading the way into the dining room, speaking to everyone she met, making sure they saw her leading. The two would stand behind and wait as she conversed with one and then another. She moved toward her father's table; and they were halfway across the room when Eloise pulled on Tab's shirt and motioned for her to follow. "Come on," she whispered. "Don't wanna get caught at that table."

"Why?" Tab watched Dominique go on, unaware that they were not behind her.

"'Cause her pa don't never stop talking. Can't get a word in edgewise, and if he ain't talking, he's having her do the talking. Showing off what she know, having her say foreign things. She talk strange enough already." Eloise pointed to two empty chairs. "Let's us sit over there." They sat down at a table brimming with eggs and bacon, grits and hot biscuits. "That's Dora," Eloise said, gesturing to the girl seated next to Tab. "She go over to Fisk in Nashville, a colored school."

"Hi." Tab sat down and glanced across the room. Dominique was turning to introduce them to her father, only to discover they weren't behind her.

—•—

Tab was buttering her third biscuit when there was a tap on her shoulder. "I told Father you were too shy to come sit with us, but he wants to meet you anyway."

Dominique's father had stopped halfway across the room to talk to another man. She turned. "Father, I want you to meet—" She stopped and walked over to him. "You said you would come."

"I will, Dominique, one minute." She stood there waiting on him. They were the same, both tall and lean. He was the darker, even had the gap in his front teeth that she did, but a mustache overrode it. His eyes weren't particularly large, but they seemed to shine, as if he might be on the verge of tears, which, of course, he was not, but the impression was that of a man poised to tell you interesting, even great things. When he walked over and turned his attention to Tab, for that instant, Tab felt she was in the center of his focus. "So this is Dominique's new friend." He took her hand and placed his other one on top of hers, smiling at her, his eyes gleaming. "You mustn't be shy. I know Dominique can be imposing on occasion, and sometimes that—" He turned his head and the light turned off. "James, let me have a word with you before you go." And then back to Dominique. "I need to have a meeting with James there. I'm afraid we won't be able to swim. Why not get Tab here to swim with you?" He patted Tab's hand. "You girls have a good time," and followed James out of the dining room.

Tab sat back down and found some strawberry jam for

her biscuit. The dining room was emptying out. The Fisk student had gone and Dominique sat down in her chair. "Shy? You told him I was shy and didn't want to meet him? Why did you say that?"

"Well, I turned around and you weren't there. What else was I supposed to think—that you people just don't have any manners?"

CHAPTER 15

Miss Laura

No one showed up for Maudie's first Thursday night of voter-registration school. Others from her Highlander class were at sit-ins in Raleigh or marching down near Mobile or in Mississippi. On some nights, the little radio in her room would pick up news of what was happening in those places.

No one came on the second Thursday night.

—•—

The next Sunday, she asked Reverend Earl if she might say a few words to the congregation to remind them of the voting-registration classes. Reverend Earl said he was the only one who made announcements when he was in the pulpit. He would remind the congregation. It was a hot day and the paper fans were out in full force, trying to keep babies from crying and children from squirming. Maudie sat next to Miss Laura in the front row. "I want to thank you for sending the little boy to bring fresh water every day. Does he stay with you?"

"Lord no, child. I'm too old to keep a handle on JD. He worse than a swarm of bees. He stay at my house when his mama ain't home. He belong full-time to my nephew Jessie, stay up the road from me." She turned in her seat. "He back there in the last row now. Have to stay back there to keep a eye on JD. He always up to some no-good."

"He does seem to have a mind of his own."

Miss Laura looked over her glasses to Maudie. "He ain't been giving you no sass, has he? If he do, you just tell me and I'll tell his daddy."

"Oh no, he's just fine. Comes every day without fail. I was just wondering."

Maudie turned around in her seat, to see JD intently watching her conversation with his great-aunt. She smiled at him. He glared back at her. She talked on to Miss Laura just so JD would know they were discussing him. "Is that his daddy sitting next to him?"

"That's Jessie."

Maudie glanced back at a tall man who looked like a grown version of JD, dark brown skin, darker eyes set wide apart, the forearms and shoulders of a laboring man. Next to JD was a mousy-looking woman. "And is that his mother on the other side?"

Miss Laura didn't bother to turn around. "Whoever it is, she ain't his mother. She ain't been in this church since she married Jessie, and that's more years than I care to count."

At the end of the preaching, Maudie noticed, out of the corner of her eye, that Miss Laura was having a disagreement with JD's father and Reverend Earl. Miss Laura turned abruptly and left them to walk toward her. She interrupted the others gathered around Maudie. "I come to see if you might take dinner with me and Jessie and JD. Ain't got nothing fancy—ham, biscuits, peach cobbler—but we'd be happy to have you."

There were knowing looks from the others in the

group. Viola touched her arm. Miss Laura pulled away. "Ain't gonna have nobody in my church don't feel welcome. This child come all the way up here—" She looked around at the others. "Come all the way up here, least we can do is—" She looked at Maudie. "Would you like to come?"

"Yes, ma'am. I do love peach cobbler."

"Then let's go. Don't nobody want to drive us, we can walk. Just over the hill beyond them trees." But they didn't have to walk. Jessie was waiting for them in his car when they came out of the church.

—•—

Maudie was surprised to see that the house was only a few hundred feet away from the church, around a curve in the road and hidden by dense woods. It was situated just off the road on a slight rise, having been built by some early settler who saw the promise of the rise in the land combined with the shelter of good hardwoods. A chicken coop, a garden, and an old hay barn lay sprinkled out around the house. Jessie pulled the car up beside the neat brown clapboard homestead. A porch ran the length of the front. Each window was decked out with shutters that were painted a bright blue. To the right of the blue front door was a wood swing on chains. On the other side of the door were four old bent-metal rocking chairs with flowered cotton cushions faded from use. Running up the front steps and along the rim of the porch were containers bought originally for the coffee they contained and now home to flowering plants, mostly petunias, which cascaded over the red-and-black Eight O'clock coffee cans. In the front yard, in the space between the road and the porch, was a huge oak—probably growing there long before the house was built, probably the reason for the house being situated there in the first place.

Miss Laura laughed when she saw Maudie staring. "I know what you looking at, them shutters and that door, brightest blue I could find. People say go on down the road and look out after that blue house. That's where Laura stay." She was taking her hat pin out, removing her Sunday hat, and smoothing down her hair. Don't nobody have trouble finding my house."

"It's nice, Miss Laura. I was thinking how friendly."

Miss Laura glanced at Jessie. "That's what it is, friendly, and that's the way it's gonna be, even if some folks don't see it that way."

Jessie got out of the car, taking no notice of Miss Laura. He was looking at one of the blue shutters, which sat askew. He walked over and used his fist to knock it back in place. His hard hands and oversized shoulders and arms were from his work at the foundry in Bainbridge. Miss Laura had told her that several of the men of the church had been lucky enough to get work at the foundry in Bainbridge. Jessie had been the first, and he had recommended others for jobs.

What was a round, slightly chubby face on JD had turned into a hard angular one on the father, but the resemblances were unmistakable. After thirty-five, maybe forty years, this is what JD would look like. She imagined their baby pictures must be identical. How must it feel, she wondered, to produce an exact replica?

"Sit for hours on this here porch," Miss Laura said. "Say howdy to everybody come down the road." By this time, she had reached the front steps and now she held her hand out for Maudie. "Come on, ain't but three of 'em to climb." Maudie took Miss Laura's hand.

The porch gave a view of rolling cultivated fields that began on the other side of the road and lasted out to a tree line. Miss Laura settled herself into one of the rockers. Maudie remained standing, taking in the view. "My daddy come by that land, before Worlds War Two. Saved up and bought it off the Rutland place." Miss Laura swept her hand out in front of her. "Now I rent out." She pointed off to her right. "Starts over there by that blackberry draw. Jessie used to farm it, but wasn't enough of it to do no good. Had to go to town to get a job at the foundry."

Jessie had settled himself in one of the other chairs beside them.

"You and JD stay here with Miss Laura, Mr. Jessie?"

He nodded toward the road running away from the church. "Me and my wife live on down aways."

"Speaking of Carlie," Miss Laura said. "She gonna be gracing us with her presence today?"

"You know she say she coming, just like usual."

Miss Laura laid her hat on a side table and began to get out of her chair. "Just like usual," she mumbled, and stood to go inside. "Come on here, JD. Your job to set the table."

Maudie and Jessie stayed on the front porch, an awkward silence between them.

When Miss Laura called them in to dinner, there were five places set at a long table in the dining room, which was just off the kitchen. Straight-back chairs of various origins were gathered around a table spilling over with so much food, it barely left room for dinner plates: a large bowl of green beans with new potatoes in among pieces of ham hock, pickled beets in a glass bowl, squash and onions cooked together, and a large platter of country ham, another of cold fried chicken, fried apples swimming in butter and brown sugar, and large glasses of iced tea dripping circles of moisture onto the white tablecloth. Maudie walked over to one of the empty places, ready for her best meal since arriving. Jessie sat down opposite. "You wasn't expecting the Queen of Sheba, was you, Auntie?"

Aunt Laura took her place at the head of the table and began to take down her napkin. "Had me a few leftovers needed to get shed of." She gave a long prayer and then passed the green beans. "Eat on up, child. We need to get some meat on them bones."

"Let's us take our peach cobbler out on the porch," Aunt Laura said when she and JD had cleared the table. Jessie began to get up out of his chair and then thought better of it. "I'd just as soon have mine inside." He glanced at his aunt. "Cooler in here."

Without a word, Aunt Laura put the dishes of cobbler down on the table and they ate there in the dining room.

Later, Maudie stood by the kitchen sink, helping to dry.

"You doing all right down at the church? Got you plenty to eat, enough covers at night?"

"Yes, ma'am. I'm doing fine."

"Sorry we ain't got no indoor plumbing down there yet. We gonna have some one of these days."

"It's fine."

"Sure it ain't too much bother for you?"

"No, ma'am, it's fine."

"You can take home some peach cobbler. We got plenty."

"I'm fine," Maudie said, "but one thing I'd like to ask you."

"What's that, child? Anything you want. You want some fried chicken to take with you?"

"No, ma'am. I was noticing when I went to wash my hands—you got a big tub back there. Would you mind if I took a bath?"

Aunt Laura's hands went slack in the dishwater and she started shaking her head. "Of course you can. Course you can," she almost shouted. "Everybody deserve to take a bath. Lord Almighty, everybody deserve to take a bath." She shook the suds off her hands and grabbed Maudie's arm. "Come on here right now." She pulled Maudie back to the hall that led to the bathroom and got three fresh towels and a bar of soap out of the linen closet. "Here, child. You go on in there right now and stay as long as you like."

—•—

Maudie sat in the tub, which was filled with hot soapy water, and listened to them arguing in the living room.

"To save my soul, I don't know why I ever listen to no men. That girl down there, ain't even got no way to take a bath, and we acting like nothing wrong and we acting like we Christians. I'm standing here letting you and Brother Earl talk me into doing something I knowed was wrong. All the time I knowed it was wrong."

"You want this house burned down round your ears? This house been give to you by your daddy. You gonna pass it on to JD." Jessie's voice was loud enough that Maudie knew he didn't care if she heard.

"What's wrong is wrong. What good is a house if I'm living in sin? Ain't I taught you nothing, boy?"

"Everybody, black and white, pass by on that road out there. You think they ain't gonna know it if you keeping some outside troublemaker in here? Don't you think the first thing they gonna do is take it out on whoever keeping her? We done decided this long time ago, Auntie. If you and the ladies wanted to talk Brother Earl into bringing her up here, church best place to keep her."

"I ain't decided it. You men decided it. Done gone on and decided it and now I'm gonna have my say. I'm undeciding it."

Maudie could hear the door slam and his car engine start as Jessie left from the side yard. She soaked a few more minutes and then re-dressed in her Sunday clothes and fastened her leg brace back on before walking out to sit at the dining table.

Miss Laura was bringing dishes from the kitchen to put in the corner cupboard.

"I'm just fine down at the church, Miss Laura, but I'd count it a favor if you let me come up and take a bath now and again. Sponge bath just isn't the same."

Miss Laura slung the dishes in on top of one another. "Course you can, child." She turned and went back in the kitchen and brought out more dishes. She set them down on the dining table, and when she looked up, there were tears in her eyes. "Shamed of myself, I ain't done more than I done, but that's gonna change. That's gonna change." She turned and started noisily stacking dishes in the cupboard again. "Them men scared of they own shadow. Well, I ain't." She pointed toward the hall without looking at Maudie. "I got three bedrooms. I stay in one. JD in the other one when he stay here, which is most of the time, and I got another one that you welcome to move into, anytime."

"I don't want to put you out, Miss Laura. I'm fine

where I am," she said, knowing that if she accepted, no one in the church might speak to her.

"Ain't nothing gonna happen to me, nothing." Miss Laura closed the door of the corner cupboard and walked back into the kitchen.

CHAPTER 16

The Card Game

*I*T WAS A RAIN SO SLIMY AND THICK, the drops seemed connected, long, slippery strands coming out of the sky. Maudie was using her hands, trying to push them aside. She was only a few feet away from the safety of the clinic. She could see Nurse Betty motioning to her to come in, but she couldn't move forward. She looked down and saw that her legs below the knees were sending out roots, like snakes popping out of the skin, writhing and slithering, boring down into the ground, holding her fast in place, even as she twisted and screamed to escape.

The reflection of car lights bouncing against the wall opposite her window woke her. She was lying on her bed in the back room of the church. She could hear women laughing and talking as the car drove away. Miss Viola's son had brought the three of them to the church. Miss Laura was carrying a cake and talking as she came in the back door of the preacher's office. Viola and Dottie Sue followed behind her, looking around nervously, having never been there when it was so dark in the corners; very seldom had they entered the church at night when they weren't called to enter. Miss Laura walked into Maudie's room and held up the cake.

"Thought if we was gonna have us a school, we need us some refreshments."

Miss Laura kept up a steady stream of talk, putting down the cake and beginning to take off her hat. "Had us a time getting here. Jessie had to work late at the foundry. Course I coulda walked, but not Viola. She too far away." Maudie stared at them, still waking from her dream, trying to get her bearings. "And Dottie Sue, she too lazy."

"Don't you go starting on me, Laura Jean Osborn."

Dottie Sue put down the bag she was carrying and began taking out paper napkins and forks. "Who was it baked three cakes for the last church cakewalk?"

"Yeah, and then go out there and win one of 'em back. Walking round in that circle till she get the right number," Miss Laura said.

Dottie Sue was grinning big now. "Can't help it if I'm lucky and you girls ain't."

The other two looked at each other. "Luck? Your cousin Daniel the one doing the number calling."

Finally, Miss Laura took notice of Maudie. "Well, here we are. Now what you want us to do?"

She realized they had come because it was Thursday night. She was supposed to be waiting for somebody to show up for her class. She hadn't even bothered to put out her materials. She had spent the day reading and dozing.

"Guess the first thing we can do is eat us some of that cake," Miss Viola said and took a seat on the only chair in the room. "I done told Laura if she gonna get me hung, I'd just as soon have some of her caramel cake 'fore they string me up." The three women laughed until they had to wipe away tears, their boldness bringing on the high spirits.

"Yessir," Miss Laura winked at the other women. "Didn't know how much being a troublemaker could work up a appetite." She began to cut pieces of cake. "Now what is it you want us to do at this here voting school?"

"Are y'all really coming for the voting school, or are you just out for a night on the town?" She slid the book she had been reading under her pillow, pulled her legs off the bed, and sat up.

"We ain't coming for no cooking lessons," Miss Viola said. "Course we coming for the voting school. Thursday night, ain't it? Here we are, your first customers."

"You think your coming is going to shame the men into coming, is that it?"

"Honey, you can't shame mens into doing nothing. If they take a notion to come, they gonna come. If they don't, well . . ." She took up a paper napkin and wiped her hands. "We coming 'cause the children need to know somebody coming."

Finding nothing else to say, the other women inspected the walls and floor of Maudie's room.

"Well . . ." Maudie cleared her throat. "I'm supposed to teach y'all how to read and write enough so you can go register to vote." She got up and walked over to the shelf where she kept her materials.

"I thought as much." Miss Laura had cut four pieces of cake and laid them out on napkins. "I'm already registered to vote. Viola and Dottie here, they ain't registered, but they already know how to read, and I told 'em if they come on out here with me, I wouldn't make 'em go down to register 'less they wanted to." She gave a big slice of cake to each of the ladies. "So here's what I been thinking." She walked over and snapped open her black cloth handbag. "While we waiting for more people to join our class, we could have us a game of cards."

Dottie Sue put hands to her cheeks. "Playing cards in the church?"

"I know," Laura said. "Ain't this gonna be fun." She pulled out a pack of Rook cards and the ladies began rubbing hands together and twittering about how naughty she was.

"Well now, ladies, seeing as how they ain't face cards, I don't think Brother Earl would have no problem with it—and besides, he ain't here, is he?"

Viola and Dottie Sue were immediately reminded of other occasions when Laura had led them astray. While they walked their cake into the sanctuary, they carried on about how Laura had always been the wild one, even when they were children, leading them into all sorts of mischief, reminding each other of the times they had been punished for some of Laura's misdoings.

"Y'all sure you need me?" Maudie was coming along behind, her crutch in one hand, her slice of cake and some writing materials she had grabbed off the shelf in the other.

"Sure we need you, honey," Miss Viola said, drawing chairs up to the teaching table. "You gonna make up the fourth player."

"I don't know how to play Rook. Don't know anything about it."

Miss Laura sat down and began to shuffle the cards like she was born to it. "Look like we gonna have to teach the teacher." The cards flashed out in a blur, distributing themselves into four neat piles. "Go get the rest of that cake and bring it back in here, Dottie. I'm gonna need plenty of brain food tonight."

They played for the rest of the evening, gathered

around the table they had pulled directly under one of the lights in the sanctuary. Their shadows moved back and forth whenever a breeze took a notion to come in one of the open windows and sway the lightbulb hanging from its wire.

There, in their little pool of light, surrounded by darkness, Miss Laura told the story of how she became a registered voter. "Tried ten times 'fore I could find the registration office open. Every time they seen me coming, they close up the place. Finally one day, I snuck in the back and come in 'fore they could see me. That day, they say the registration done been changed to another place. I say where is it at and they say it's out Seventy-two to the Houston place. And I say, 'What you mean in the farmhouse?' And they smile and say no, it on the farm, but ain't *in* the house, and for me to go on out there if I want to register. So I says all right, I'll just do that. Wasn't gonna call my bluff." She shuffled the cards and dealt another hand. "Well, let me tell you, honey, when I got out there, sure enough a sign was pointing off in the dark woods, saying, 'Voting This Way,' and I says to myself, This ain't gonna stop me. And so I walk on down this road, and it got smaller and smaller and darker and darker, and finally I end up down in the swamp, by a creek, and sure enough there was a table and some white men sitting round talking. I know everyone of 'em and they know me. They commence laughing. 'Laura, you the only one in the county got the nerve to come all the way back here to vote, and if you got that nerve, then you gonna get to vote,' they say like they was making a game out of it. 'You the first colored come back here, and it would be you and not a man.' I didn't say nothing 'cept where was I supposed to sign, and they showed me and asked me to read some sentences, and I walked out of there my legs weak as water."

Miss Viola picked up her cards. "And you think you gonna get me out to vote in amongst them crazy white folks?" She slapped a card on the table. "Laura Jean Osborn, you ain't friends with no fool."

Just then, car lights flashed through the windows. Miss Laura looked down at her watch. "Jessie a little early."

But the lights weren't Jessie's. After a minute, the car backed up, pulled out of the churchyard, and was gone.

CHAPTER 17

Highlander

JAB WAS SITTING ON HER BUNK, telling Tina about going to discussion group with the adults. "Well, not actually being in the group, but sitting on the windowsill and listening. They don't mind that." Tina, half-listening, was painting her nails.

"You woulda thought I had given her a birthday present, the way Aunt Eugenia beamed when I ask her if I could sit in the window and listen to what was going on. Oh sure I could—'It'll let you see the real dynamic of the way things work up here.' That's what she said, 'the real dynamic.' Oh, and guess what else she said. She said, 'How is your sister getting along? I haven't seen her lately.' And so then I said, 'I think she has a crush on that lifeguard from Wisconsin, Jeremy what's his name. She hangs around with him all day.'"

"You are so pathetic."

"Pathetic? You sound like her. That's what Dominique says to me all the time. Anyway, then Aunt Eugenia says, 'Which one do you mean, the white one or the black one?' Do you believe that? And I said, 'Gad, Aunt Eugenia, what do you think?'"

"And what did she say?" Tina held her brush in mid-stroke.

"She didn't say a thing. It would have been too silly to say a thing. So anyway, at first it wasn't anything like Eloise had described—the meeting, you know. People talked, yeah—they're planning ways to integrate their towns when they go back home—but they didn't argue, not like Eloise said they might. I almost went to sleep. Anyway, they were going along, talking about their ideas, first one and then the other speaking up, and the leader, Mr. Horton you know, is standing over in the corner listening and saying, 'You have the power to do whatever it is you want to do,' when this black man—it is the new thing to say, 'black man' instead of 'colored man'—he says in a very agitated way that it is the pitiful white heritage that has caused the whole thing and that the Ku Klux Klan is not worth killing. And Aunt Eugenia is violently shaking her head yes, when I say—'cause I couldn't help it, it just came out, and this is a subject I know something about—I say that of course Cousin John Lester wasn't like that at all. And when they ask me who is Cousin John Lester and I tell them, Aunt Eugenia is turning a very deep gray color, especially when everybody turns to stare at her."

"Tab, will you never learn?" Tina was shaking the bottle, readying it to polish her toes. "How could you embarrass Aunt Eugenia like that?"

"It serves her right, disowning Cousin John Lester, and in *public*. I think it was the ultimate in bad manners. Grandmother would think that, too. Anyway, the leader is smiling and talking about the irony of it all—that's what he said, 'the irony of it all'—and Aunt Eugenia is looking sick, and the colored—the black man—he is looking mighty disgusted at Aunt Eugenia. This, of course, takes Aunt Eugenia's breath away, and I think she is gonna get on her knees and beg him to forget that she is kin to Cousin John Lester, which I would never do in a million years. Even the leader said Aunt Eugenia sometimes has unrealistic enthusiasm. That's what he said, 'unrealistic enthusiasm.' Grandmother would agree with that, but I would never tell Dominique."

"Will you stop talking long enough to answer a question? Did she ask anything else about what I was doing?"

"Nah, she wasn't interested in anything after that."

Tab went over and sat down next to Tina. "But *I* am. And what have you been doing? I saw you walking with both the lifeguards the other day, the black one and the white one, and the white one is very handsome." She elbowed Tina.

"So is the black one," Tina said.

"Are you crazy?"

"Well, he is. Admit it."

"Okay, he is, but it's not something you say, even if he does look almost white."

"At least I am not going around insulting my aunt in front of every last person up here."

"It wasn't my fault, Tina. If you are kin to Cousin John Lester, you are kin to Cousin John Lester and that's that."

"Peachy." She didn't look up from doing her toes.

"Well, I got to go. I need to go talk to Dominique. I haven't seen her around. Maybe she's mad at me."

"Probably she's mad at you, although why you would want to hang around with that snob, I don't know."

"She is not a snob. A black person cannot be a snob."

"Ask Eloise if she's a snob. She says Dominique is always calling her 'Little Eloiseee from the boonieeees.' That's tacky."

"So how about giving me that other thing of nail polish you owe me?"

Tina finished with her toes, screwed the top on the bottle, and pitched it. Tab was down the hall before she remembered and turned back. "And guess what else? Dominique's parents are divorced, and she gets all mad at me 'cause I don't know anybody with divorced parents. Do you remember if that cousin from south Georgia—what's his name? Didn't he get a divorce before he moved to Texas?"

Tina was blowing on her toenails but shook her head. "I don't remember."

"Well, can't you think of anybody who got a divorce, so I'll know somebody?"

"Elizabeth Taylor, people like that. Oh, yeah, there was that one grass widow Mama used to be friends with. She had a daughter older than me, but that lady died a long time ago."

Tab stood in the doorway smiling. "Can you think of what might happen if they knew—I mean anybody in Bainbridge—sitting down there watching *Father Knows Best* every Wednesday night and we are up here with all these crazy as a betsy bug people?" She hit the wall with the palm of her hand and skipped back down the hall.

—•—

"I used to favor Purple Passion. Now I like"—Tab looked at the label—"Coral Crush. I thought you might like it." Dominique was sitting out by the Ping-Pong table. She had been at lunch and had chosen to sit with them rather than with her father, but she hadn't said much, had not bored them with diatribes in French and even longer translations. She had left the table before Tab and Eloise had finished. Now Eloise was visiting with her mother.

Tab held out the bottle of polish too long before Dominique took it. "Go ahead, try it. If you don't like it, I got remover in our room. You could try it on your feet. It looks good on feet."

Dominique unbuckled her sandals and brushed dust off her toes. "I've worn nail polish before, of course, French colors." She took the bottle and held it, looking down at the label before she began to unscrew the top and pull out the brush. "This is a tad garish. French colors are more subtle." She looked up at Tab. "It's okay, though."

"Now listen, Dominique, I didn't mean anything about what I said the other day on the float, about your being, you know, unusual—in *several* ways." Tab sat down beside her. "I been thinking about it, and I do remember now that I have a cousin who got divorced— least my daddy said he did and that's why he went on off to Texas."

She watched Dominique finish one foot. Tab felt it was not such a good job. The polish was outside the lines in places. "So see, you're not the only one I ever met— you know, divorced."

Dominique closed the bottle and shook it before she got started on the other foot.

Tab had expected a lecture—"you people are so backward, not knowing anyone who is divorced"—but she didn't get one. Dominique finished up her toes and closed the bottle, waiting for them to dry before starting a second coat.

"I don't see her much."

It took a second for Tab to realize what she might be talking about.

"Not since she left and Daddy got all caught up in this

stuff." She nodded toward the meeting room. "Now this is all he thinks about."

She shook the bottle of nail polish harder and longer than she needed to. "And since we are talking about it, don't you think I get tired of meeting you people all the time?" She opened the bottle and looked at Tab. "I'm popular; I have lots of friends up there where I live." She began a second coat, brushing more evenly now. "He's planning to go down to Mississippi after this. He can't get enough. I would rather go on back and forget about this stuff."

Tab pulled her knees up and put her arms around them. "See, that's the way it is with us—we're supposed to be over in Chattanooga, but Aunt Eugenia had to come bring us up here instead. I think it's because she can't get enough, either."

"They're going to close this place down pretty soon anyway. Did you know that? Did you see the paper today?"

"You're kidding. I just got here. Are you making that up, Dominique?"

"C'est la vie, n'est-ce pas?

"Did you say you weren't making that up?"

"Oui."

"I know that one."

Dominique looked skyward. "Sound the trumpets."

Tab didn't hear the sarcasm, and edged closer, whispering. "Are they gonna have a sit-in in Nashville? I heard Dora at dinner the other day. She was talking to some of the other Fisk students. Somebody said they were gonna have a sit-in at Woolworth's in Nashville, but I didn't believe it. I never even heard of a sit-in 'til I came up here. Course I wouldn't mind doing one, since I love their hot dogs."

Dominique looked up at Tab and did this little thing with her eyes, blinking them and narrowing them at the same time. She went back to her polishing, finishing one foot before she said, "You like hot dogs, do you?"

"We *people* eat other things besides corn bread, you know."

Dominique wiped excess polish from her toes and smiled down at them. Then in a low voice, "I did hear there was a group from here going to the Nashville sit-in. You understand it's very hush-hush, though. Not everyone should be included."

Tab edged closer. "I wouldn't say anything, honest. What do they say?"

"Well . . ." Dominique pretended to search behind bushes and trees. "They say there's a group going out of here to the sit-in in Nashville. Of course it's just gossip, probably not true, but if it is, would you like to go?"

"Sure," Tab whispered. "We won't be gone long, will we?"

"Oh, maybe a few hours."

"Aunt Eugenia would probably love me to do that."

"Oh, you can't tell her. You wouldn't even be able to tell your sister."

"I wouldn't tell *her* even if I could. She might try to horn in. What about the police? Won't the police come up here and close the place down if that happens, especially since this place is against the law anyway?"

"Why is it against the law? Just tell me. Why?"

"It's against the law because . . . because it is. I didn't make the laws. They were here before I was born."

"You people are unbelievable." Dominique grabbed her sandals and walked away, pitching the polish on the ground.

"If we're so unbelievable, you didn't have to come

down here, you know. Who asked you anyway? Go to France and stay with your mother and speak nothing but French all the time." Tab was up off the ground, brushing the dust off her shorts. "And," she yelled after her, "if you're so smart, how come you're walking in the dust with wet polish on?"

CHAPTER 18

Scrimmage

*L*ATE AFTERNOONS would find everyone gathered on the front porch and steps of the main house at Highlander, talking and relaxing before dinner—that is, those who were not assigned to help with kitchen duties. Tab had never really gotten a long look at Dominique's father, and so she made a point of going over to sit next to him as he rocked in the sunlight that crept in under the eaves of the west-facing house.

She had heard him in the morning meetings—by now, she had attended several, sitting outside and listening through the window, always with Dominique. Dominique would soon become bored probably, Tab thought, because she had heard it so many times. She would usually take a scrap of paper and draw up a game of battleship, out of her father's sight. They would play that or tic-tac-toe to pass the time. Tab didn't pay much attention to what was going on while she was trying to beat Dominique. When she did listen, Dominique's father seemed to be the one who would always interrupt and say that compromise was not possible and that the ultimate goal should be to integrate everything, not tomorrow or in gradual steps, but today, right this very minute. When he spoke, he used big words; she could tell that the others didn't understand them, either. There were some college students in the group, but mostly they were people off of farms, workers in the cotton mills, people from rural communities who had perhaps seen, although seldom touched, the outside world. In a meeting one morning, one of the mill workers had said that he could only get news of what was going on when he went to a neighbor's house to listen to the radio. Dominique had touched Tab's shoulder. "Do you believe he never even saw a television set?"

"That's amazing," Tab had said, when in fact her family had only come around to getting a black-and-white set two years ago, and then they had not been allowed to watch it that much.

She wanted to find out about Dominique's mother. Dominique would never talk about her, would never answer Tab's questions, so she had stopped asking.

Having taken the rocker next to Reverend Calder, Tab sat pushing off the floor, propelling herself into an exaggerated rocking motion. She thought she would pretend to be there for the rocking alone. This would not arouse his suspicion. She would go unnoticed as she took full measure of him.

"I understand this is the little lady that is rooming with my Dominique," he said, laying his hand on the arm of her chair to slow her. "Tell me, how are you two getting along?" Did he not remember that they had met before, in the dining room? "I have great plans for Dominique"—he patted Tab's hand, which was resting on the rocker arm—"as I'm sure your parents have for you."

Tab had noticed Dominique strolling across the yard and then stopping when she saw them talking. Now she was walking toward them, so there wasn't much time. "I was just wondering, does she take more after her mother or you? Since I never met her mother, I can't tell. Not that she doesn't take after you. I'm sure she does."

He leaned back in his chair and let go of her arm. "Dominique is a rare combination, a living symbol of what we are about here at Highlander. For that matter, what we are about—should be about—in the whole country."

Dominique was getting closer.

"'A living symbol'?"

"When I married Dominique's mother, that was one of our goals, to be an example to the rest of the world." Dominique was on the steps and listening now.

"We were going to have several children, but unfortunately, things didn't work out. Her mother is back in France now—I'm sure Dominique told you. It didn't have anything to do with that philosophy, as I'm sure Dominique told you." Dominique was at his side now. "We are very open about things with each other." He reached up and patted Dominique's hand, which had come to rest on the back of his rocker. "Since it's just the two of us now." He brought her hand around, like he did with most people, and clasped it in his two hands. "Dominique hasn't seen her mother since she was five. She doesn't influence our life now. Her mother is—"

"Daddy, you don't need to tell Tab things I've already told her."

He smiled. "Don't want the old dad interfering, do you? I know you girls like to have your secrets." He turned to Tab. "What's your family like, Tab? I'm sure large. Most of you people have large families down here."

Immediately, Dominique's expression changed. She was almost smirking now. "Do tell us about your family,

Tab. I'm sure we'll be enthralled." She put an elbow on the back of the rocker and rested her chin on her hand, pretending to be spellbound.

"Your aunt told me you're an agricultural family. I know you need a number of children to help out in the fields," Reverend Calder said.

"Have you picked much cotton?" Dominique asked, all innocence.

"I have two brothers and two sisters. We live in Bainbridge, not on the farm. I've lived there all my life, and I have a grandmother and lots of aunts and uncles and a grandfather, very good at telling stories and—" She was determined to counter with as much as she could, but Dominique was just as determined.

"I'm sure we don't want to hear your whole all-American family saga."

"Now Dominique, Tab must have an interesting, if somewhat provincial, story. You should be open to the various regional folkways."

The bell rang for dinner. "Father Calder"—some people called him "Father" even though he wasn't Catholic—"could I have a word with you?" A young man came up the steps, and Reverend Calder got up to follow him into the dining room, Dominique behind them.

Tab didn't break stride following Dominique. "And we go to the river and have picnics and we eat ice cream on the front porch every Sunday in the summer and—"

"And you probably have a tattoo of an American flag on your fanny."

"And my *mother* makes the best fried chicken."

"And your brothers probably hunt up a possum every Saturday *niiiight* for Sunday *eatin'.*"

"And every Christmas we have . . . have the biggest tree in the whole town."

Dominique watched her father walk off to another table with some other adults. She turned on Tab. "And don't even think about me being your best friend—if that's what he told you I said. I just told him that as a joke."

Tab had taken the seat at the head of the table, two seats away from Dominique, still seething at Dominique's insults to her family. Mr. Spivey—from the Delta country in Mississippi—was in between them.

Tab picked up the big bowl of mashed potatoes in front of her. "Could you pass these mashed potatoes to Dominique, Mr. Spivey? Of course, they may not eat mashed potatoes where she comes from."

"I have mashed potatoes," she said, her head turned away. Mr. Spivey, who was in his eighties and had come to Highlander because he was "too long being stepped on," was also very hard of hearing.

"SHE SAY SHE GOT MASHED POTATOES, TAB." The whole table looked up whenever Mr. Spivey said anything. It was impossible not to.

"I don't see any on her plate." The bowl of mashed potatoes was cradled in Tab's palm ready for Mr. Spivey to pass on.

Mr. Spivey turned to Dominique. "SAY SHE DON'T SEE NONE ON YOUR PLATE." Everyone at the table turned to look at Dominique's plate and, seeing no mashed potatoes, waited for Dominique to acquiesce.

"I don't care for mashed potatoes, thank you. I prefer boiled new potatoes with fresh parsley, but they never seem to have that down here." Dominique grabbed her iced tea glass. "Like a lot of other things they don't have around here."

"SAY SHE DON'T LIKE THEM MASHED POTATOES, WANTS SOME PARSLEY INSTEAD."

The bowl was swaying precariously in Tab's hand. "Well, you might tell her we have lots of parsley down here. We usually feed it to the hogs."

Mr. Spivey looked rather perplexed before he passed it on. "SHE SAY SHE KNOW 'BOUT PARSLEY AND HOGS AND FOR YOU TO HAVE SOME MASHED POTATOES SO'S I CAN GET ON WITH EATING MY SUPPER." Mr. Spivey took the mashed potato bowl out of Tab's hand and passed it on to Dominique, who could not refuse, especially since other members of the table were also perturbed by now—"Take the mashed potatoes, for God sakes."

Dominique took the bowl of mashed potatoes from Mr. Spivey. Tab was smiling now—and she should not have. Dominique stood up, still holding the bowl, took a heaping tablespoon of potatoes off the top, and reached over Mr. Spivey to slam a glob on Tab's plate. Then she did it again. The table had gone quiet while watching this unfolding drama, all except for Mr. Spivey, who had resumed his eating. Tab pushed her chair back and stood up. "I was *just* trying to help you out, but I can see you don't understand people with decent manners."

"*Manners?* You call saying that I'm a freak just because my parents are divorced good manners? You call telling me all about your low-life family good manners? Here's some more good manners for you." Dominique dug the spoon once again into what was left of the mashed potatoes and sailed a spoonful across Mr. Spivey and onto Tab's T-shirt.

"*What're you doing?* Look at my shirt." For a moment, she and everyone else at the table stared down at her shirt, but for only a moment. Tab grabbed a handful of potato from her plate and started after Dominique.

"Let's just see how this is gonna look in your bushy colored person's hair."

"You ignorant redneck backwoods cracker." Dominique backed away to fend Tab off, but she was too late. They both ended up on the floor, shouting and kicking, arms flailing, rolling into chairs and tables.

Dominique was much stronger and she knew what she was about in a fight. By the time the two lifeguards pulled them apart, Tab was much the worse for wear.

—•—

An hour later, Eugenia was still incredulous. "Did you actually call her a bushy-haired colored person? How could you? How *could* you? I am responsible for bringing you up here, and what do you do but make a mockery of everything this, we, I, stand for? Didn't your mother teach you any manners?"

"But we don't have manners up here." She spoke to the floor. "You said yourself that we do what we want to up here. We're free."

They were sitting in Tab's bunk room. That is to say, Tab was sitting. Tina was lying prostrate on her bed, an arm flung over her eyes. Eugenia was standing in the doorway. She had not come in to dinner, had been sitting on the front porch when the commotion started.

Tina jerked up to a sitting position. "And I had to go screaming like some idiot out to the porch to get Aunt Eugenia." She flopped back down on her mattress.

Tab moved the cold washcloth from the cut on her leg to the black eye that was developing. She had bumped into a chair on one roll and then into a table leg when Dominique had grabbed her hair and yanked it. That had been right after Tab had twisted Dominique's arm behind her back.

Tina suddenly rose up again, feeling the gravity of the

situation warranted a better description. "You know what you are. You're common. I've told you you're gross, but have I told you you're common? I have *never* been so embarrassed in my life. Fighting, and with a colored person."

"That'll be enough, Tina." Aunt Eugenia had one hand on the bunk to steady herself.

"Rolling on the floor like some common criminal. Egads, if our father ever finds out."

"That's quite enough, Tina."

"Well, aren't you going to say anything else to her, Aunt Eugenia? You need to tell her what an embarrassment she is to the whole family."

"I *will* if you will let me get a word in," she almost shouted, then caught and calmed herself. "Tab, do you understand that you have violated every principle that this place and these people stand for? For nonviolence, for racial harmony?"

"Tell her how common it was. There I had to go and try to pull her away kicking and screaming." She slumped back down. "I broke a nail, you know."

"You told us."

"If it hadn't been for Greg and Jeremy, I never would have gotten them apart. And they were laughing like it was some big joke, pulling those two hellions apart." She leaned over the side of their bunk to get in Tab's face. "That's what Greg called y'all, 'hellions.'"

"It takes one to know one" was all Tab could think to say, and she knew it was vastly inadequate, but her eye was beginning to hurt and she had to save her good stuff for Aunt Eugenia.

"Oh, you are so, so—"

Eugenia looked to the heavens. "Let me guess—

gross." and instantly reneged. "Oh, I'm sorry, sweet-heart. I didn't mean that."

"*Aunt Eugenia!*" Tina rose up again, devastated.

"I'm so sorry. I didn't mean it." Eugenia rushed to pat Tina's arm. "It's just been a long day, sweetheart. *Gross* is a very nice word." She tried to hug Tina, who was already tearing up. "Listen, I know you had a huge responsibility being in there when I wasn't, and you did yeoman's duty. You know what I think you should do?"—still patting— "I think you should go find Greg and Jeremy and thank them for helping out this afternoon."

"Do you think so?" wiping away tears and trying not to smear her eyeliner.

"Oh yes. That would be the correct thing to do, pre-serving the family name and all. Why don't you do that? As a matter of fact, when I was coming in just now, one of them asked if you were all right."

"They did? Which one?"

"I'm not sure, but one of them. Why don't you go find them and tell them how much you appreciate their help?"

"That probably would be the right thing to do." Tina was already looking in the mirror she had nailed to the wall next to her bunk. "I'll just," she was already unzip-ping the makeup bag she kept up there with her, "just freshen up my lipstick. Does my hair look okay?" She popped back the lipstick and slipped down off the top bunk. "At least I," a disdainful nod back over her shoulder to the lower bunk as she left the room, tucking in her blouse, "know the honorable thing to do."

Tab and Eugenia were left alone in the quiet. Sounds could be heard from the dining room down the hall— clinking glasses, moving chairs—as the tables were being cleared and floors were being swept.

"I don't know what to say to you. Have you been so influenced by others that you don't see what you've done? Is that it? Or is it all my fault?"

No answer from the lower bunk.

"What did I do wrong?" Aunt Eugenia asked again.

"They said in the meeting the other day to express your feelings. That's what I was doing, expressing my feelings." Tab moved the washcloth to her knee and dabbed at the scrape. "Besides, I hate her." The sound of dishes being stacked echoed in to them. "I was trying to be nice. I was offering her the mashed potatoes, wasn't I?" It sounded so innocent when she said it, she decided to take that tack, because she knew there was no reason, other than she must hate her—must hate colored people—but that was not what Aunt Eugenia would hear. "That's right. All I was doing was offering her the mashed potatoes, and she threw them back at me for no good reason whatsoever. Granddaddy said . . ."

"What did Granddaddy say?"

"He said that they have terrible tempers. If you don't watch them, they can flare out on you." Okay, that was not reasonable, but she was grasping at straws.

"That is absolute nonsense. Don't you know that? What ever happened to 'turn the other cheek'?"

"I don't care about that. I just care about her—I mean, I hate her."

"No you don't."

"Yes I do."

"You couldn't possibly. I don't want to hear that. You couldn't possibly."

"What do you mean, she couldn't possibly?" The leader was standing in the doorway. "She says she does and she obviously means what she says." Eugenia went red. "Myles, I'm so sorry. I . . . I don't know what to say.

Here we—I—bring these children into a place they are obviously not ready to come to and they upset the whole group. I can't tell you how sorry I am."

"Eugenia. You told her she was free to express her feelings, and she was doing just that. Isn't that what we've been talking about?"

"I know, but Myles—"

"Don't be so quick to embrace the philosophy if you aren't ready to accept the reality that goes along with it."

Tab disappeared back in her bunk, draping the wet cloth over as much of her face as possible. He bent down to look at her. "Gave you a shiner, did she?"

Tab jerked away the cloth. "No, sir. She sure did not. I gave it to myself." She closed her eyes so he could see the purple swelling on the lid and around the lashes. "Well, I knocked into one of the table legs, that's all."

"You should see what Dominique gave to herself." He laughed.

"She's okay?"

"Says she's got that busted lip because she hit the floor too hard. Says you're too weak to really hurt her."

Tab studied the dotted specks of blood against the white washcloth. "I didn't hit her in the mouth. I wouldn't do that. But I coulda. Maybe I shoulda."

"Well, it looks to me like you'll both live through it."

Eloise stuck her head in the door. "You mind if I come in and get my swimsuit? Ain't no other way for me to get it 'cept to come in here, even if y'all are having a big argument." She looked to the leader.

"Come on in here and get your bathing suit, Eloise." The leader turned to go. "I'll get out of your way. Think I'll get mine and take a swim, too."

"Look, Myles." Eugenia followed him out the door. "I know she violated every rule, probably offended every black person here. We'll understand if you ask us to leave."

"On the contrary, Eugenia. I think you should stay longer, at least a couple more weeks. See what those two can work out." He walked off down the hall, with Eugenia following along, asking for pardon again and again when a pardon was not in order. "Eugenia, there wouldn't be any need for us, for Highlander, if everybody sprang from the womb in harmony with the rest of the world—especially teenage girls."

Eloise came in, glancing at Tab before she began digging through the stack of clothes in her orange crate. "You done busted up Dominique pretty good."

"She deserved it."

"That's what she say 'bout you."

"Well, she deserves it more than me."

"'Cause she's colored and got bushy hair? I heard you at the dinner table yelling at her." She pulled out the top half of her suit and kept looking for the other half. "Guess that means you don't like me, neither."

Tab looked up at Eloise, astonished she would think such a thing. "Of course not, Eloise. I like you. You're . . . you're black. She's light brown. I don't like light brown people with bushy hair."

"I got nappy hair."

"No you don't. Yours is slicked down nice and you don't have a Yankee accent." Tab put down the washcloth so that she might clarify for Eloise—using her fingers to enumerate—the more sophisticated parts of her newfound code. "Here is what I don't like, Eloise. I don't like light brown"—index finger—"bushy-haired people"—middle finger—"with Yankee accents"—ring finger—"who think they're smarter than everybody else just because they speak French"—little finger. She smiled at Eloise and held her hands out, palms up. "See, you're not any of those things. I like you."

"You sure must have a hard time keeping all them categories straight." Eloise found the bottom of her suit and began taking off her shorts to change. "You wanna go swimming?"

"Oh, sure." Tab eased over to the door to see if Aunt Eugenia might be coming back. "Yeah, I think I can come. I'll find my suit."

"She do think she's the smartest thing walking round, but somehow I feel sorry for her. You shoulda heard what her daddy say to her. Say she a disgrace, acting that way. Say she gonna have to spend hours doing stuff to make up for it. Say she gotta learn herself how to be more high-minded. Say she acting like her mother. Even when Mr. Myles come in and say he didn't think she need to do all that, it just make her daddy madder. Her pa say he can take care of the situation. Course I wasn't listening outside the reverend's door. I was just passing by." She slipped on her swimsuit bottoms and took off her T-shirt to slip on her top.

—•—

That night, Aunt Eugenia called the girls out for a walk around the lake. She told them what the leader had said—that they should stay another two weeks, if that was possible. "So what do you think? Perhaps a little longer would be helpful." She looked at Tab. "It certainly couldn't make matters any worse. I can write to Charles and Mary and say Bebe wants us to stay longer. I'm sure they won't mind. I hear the governor's race is beginning to heat up, and you know how you father likes to dabble in politics, no matter that it's a hopeless cause. They're probably so busy, they won't miss us. In fact, I'll call them tonight, if that's what we want to do."

Tab was not interested in being helped, but knowing that it would take at least a week for her eye to get back to normal, "Okay with me if you can pretend like that. I couldn't do it."

Eugenia looked to Tina. "Fine with me as long as she"—pointed but did not look—"doesn't make a fool of us again. And I do feel I have an obligation to the water safety around here."

CHAPTER 19

Reuben

*W*HEN CHARLES WALKED IN from the farm, Mary was waiting in the kitchen. "A.W. called earlier, said he might drop by tonight. You better hurry and take a bath so we can eat early."

"Tonight?"

"I thought you would rather do it tonight and get it over with. Here, this'll cheer you up. A letter from the travelers."

"Bebe must be showing them a good time, since they're staying on."

"I guess. It's from Tab, and you know Tab."

Charles pitched his hat onto the hall hat rack, smiling even before he took the letter out of the envelope. "I'll bet this is a doozy—oil and water, Tab and her aunt Eugenia." He stood silently, reading the letter, his grin widening. "Ha, I love this part about them having an 'enrichment experience beyond belief.' Does that sound like Eugenia? It's amazing how children pick up on what adults say."

He put the letter back in its envelope. "Probably is a good experience for them, though a little out of the ordinary. Says she's met a girl who speaks French. She's never had a friend who speaks a foreign language."

Mary stood in the doorway. "I know if Eugenia and Bebe are sending them to a day camp, it's out-the-door progressive, Unitarian or something. We won't mention that to your mother, but what did she mean, they're sleeping in bunk beds? She said it was a day camp."

"Oh, probably they take naps after lunch, or they're all on the sleeping porch at Bebe's. She has scores of cousins." He dropped the letter on the side table and picked up the rest of the mail.

—•—

A. W. Ladd had been coming to ask for Charles's support every election year since he started running for governor. How many times was this, seven or eight? He couldn't remember. Of course, no sensible person could beat the rabble-rouser types that seemed to be winning nowadays. The only alternative was to find someone who was halfway decent and throw your support behind him. A.W. was a nice-enough old gentleman. Charles's family had known his family for generations back. One year, he had even agreed to be A.W.'s campaign manager for the northern part of the state. Charles's efforts never had much impact, but he was expected—he wanted—to take part in the political process. His grandfather had been a county judge. His great-grandfather had been a state senator.

A.W. seemed to know when they would finish supper and so timed his visit accordingly. He settled himself in a chair and said "Much obliged" when Mary offered drinks. "Milk, thank you, ma'am." He winked at Charles. "The farmers like that, milk prices being what they are." Milk was one of A.W.'s trademarks. Everybody knew A.W. would ask for milk—and he drank it. Rather than think it was hackneyed, Charles liked it. Showed the old fellow was trying to have the courage of his convictions. Not like the others, who would ask for something benign but want to have it laced with whiskey, as in their politics. Of course, that was probably why he never polled more than 2 percent of the vote. People expected a certain amount of duplicity from their candidates. Too much purity was not to be trusted.

A.W. had put together this wonderful pie-in-the-sky education reform bill, which wouldn't have a tinker's damn worth of a chance of passing the state legislature even if he were, by some God-sent miracle, elected. Had money in it for the colored schools as well as the whites—of course, a lot more for the whites. You couldn't go too far. Candidates couldn't be expected to offer themselves up to be shot in the back in some dark alley. After thirty minutes of pleasantries, A.W. got to the point.

"Charles, I hope I can count on you for your support this year." No one ever came to Charles for money. They knew better, but people knew he was willing to give his time, and pledging his support to A.W. wouldn't take much effort, because Charles knew there wasn't much that could be done anyway.

"I suspect you can have my support and gladly, A.W., but I don't even know who's running yet—besides the usual.

"Except for Wallace, not many, as I know of. Heard tell Randolph Comer, state senator from down in the Black Belt, and Jennings Hardman, the road commissioner. That's all I know about at this early date." He smiled. "But ain't nobody gonna beat me this time out. Been planning my strategy since the last time."

Charles tried not to wince at the grammar politicians

used, no matter how well educated. He remembered the
first time A.W. ran. The man had put together a decent
sentence then—one of the weaknesses he had corrected
on running a second time.

"Well, I got to be getting on. Want to go over and
speak to Big Abe Rosenstein while I'm in the neighborhood. Much obliged for the milk.

"Oh, I thought of another one." A.W. had paused on
the front threshold. "La Forte from down around
Tuscaloosa, Brad La Forte. Too young, ain't paid his
dues, but they say he's gonna run anyway. Waste of
money, if you ask me."

"Brad? Really?" Charles stood holding the door. "I
know him. Good family. I can't believe he'd want to run,
subject himself to all that. . . ." He caught A.W.'s ques-
tioning look. "Well, A.W., like you say, he's too young to
know . . . to know the pitfalls like you do."

A.W. laughed. "I sure as hell know them pitfalls,
wouldn't you say?"

Charles said he sure must by now, then shook hands
and stood in the door, watching A.W. walk to his car.

Brad La Forte—if that was true, he'd be a halfway decent candidate. In fact, more than halfway decent—
respectable. Probably wasn't true, probably just another
one of those rumors that got started every election year.
He would have to ask Reuben if he knew anything about
that. Reuben always seemed to know what was going on
in political circles. It was because of Reuben's father—
Big Abe Rosenstein.

—•—

Maybe once a month, Charles and Reuben would
play chess together. Reuben had suggested they meet
more often, but Charles could barely squeeze in this
time.

They always played at Reuben's. He couldn't imagine Reuben coming to his house, with his children and their friends in and out all the time. Reuben would have been completely out of his element, and Reuben hardly ever got out of his element. He had children also, two girls, but they were away at school all winter, and in the summer Charles never seemed to see them, although he knew they must be somewhere around. Maybe off visiting, as Tab and Tina were now.

That evening, he walked to Reuben's. Charles didn't live on Hawthorne, but a few blocks away, in an area of smaller homes. Hawthorne was lined with stately old Victorians and gas streetlights. Most Bainbridge houses that were older than these had been burned down during the war, when Federal troops rode through looking for Forrest and his band.

Set off from the others, Reuben's house was enclosed by a stucco wall and wrought-iron gates. Big Abe had wanted Reuben to live in the best part of town, and this had necessitated tearing down a perfectly good house on Hawthorne and replacing it. Reuben's only other sibling, his younger brother, Stanley, had been killed in a car accident when he had gone up east to live. Everyone assumed that this house was Big Abe's bid to keep Reuben on home ground.

The older ladies of Bainbridge were seen to purse their lips and shake their heads when they passed the house on Hawthorne. It was perfectly understandable for Big Abe to indulge his son in this way, keeping him home where he belonged, but really—the color, the size.

Cypress trees lined the driveway and led up to a front sidewalk that was paved with hand-painted Spanish tiles. Charles stood before the massive wooden double doors, hesitating to ring the bell; gas lanterns silently flickered on either side. It was cave-quiet even out here on the front porch. The house overwhelmed its small plot of ground, reminding him of something out of *Sunset Boulevard.* Cream stucco walls were topped with turrets on each corner of the red tile roof. Every time the front door opened, Charles half-expected to see Gloria Swanson or Zorro come dashing out.

He could hear the door chime echoing down the inside hall. Eventually, Reuben appeared, looking completely out of scale to his surroundings. A scrawny gnome with big ears was the first impression. The large dark brown eyes were what there was to see of the outside of Reuben. Apart from that, he was skin stretched over lanky bones, wearing clothes that always seemed too large. He didn't say anything, just smiled and held the door for Charles to enter, closed it and walked down the hall, a routine they had developed over the years. Inside, there was an ancient knight's sword hanging in the foyer. Smaller replicas of the outside gaslights wavered as they passed, their footsteps echoing on the floor tiles. Charles could see Big Abe in his mind's eye, sitting in one of his many theaters, sketching drawings of this house from scenes he had seen in the movies. What Big Abe had hoped would be the talk of the town was, but not in the way he might have imagined.

Charles smiled when he first settled himself in and looked around the den. It was such a man's room: high-back leather chairs, exposed beams, hunting prints on the wall. There was a deer head mounted over the fireplace. And there was Reuben.

It was general knowledge that Big Abe had built the house and that Reuben hadn't had much say in what it looked like, or hadn't cared. Big Abe had also picked out a bride, gone up north to find a good Jewish girl, since there were few to none to choose from in Bainbridge. The house had been a wedding present.

Owning movie houses was a good business, especially if you owned them all over the state of Alabama and a few up in Tennessee, as well. It was understood, although never mentioned in public, that the Rosensteins stood atop the cash-money pyramid in Bainbridge. They were, in fact, the whole pyramid, which must have been disconcerting for Abe, as this gave him no competition. In a town—in a state—almost completely devoid of monetary largesse, other criteria for social acceptance held sway: being long-lived in the town, residing in the right neighborhood. Of course, Big Abe had no way of competing in the first category. Had he lived here even longer than his present forty-year residency, he would still be fresh out of New York. The big house, built for his only surviving son, was his winning entry in the second category. Big Abe himself had chosen to remain completely out of the fray and had acquired large acreage out of town, on the banks of the river. He had built something that would not possibly fit on the lot or lots on Hawthorne Street.

On the other hand, Charles's family had an ample supply of longevity and right-sided residence, but after the war, from one generation to the next, there had been constant worry about where the next dollar might come from, and in Bainbridge society this had somehow been perverted, to the point of making it downright honorable to be constantly stretching to make ends meet.

Charles got out the chessmen as Reuben lit his pipe. Reuben had never warmed to the task of running movie houses. Charles, Reuben's mother, his wife, and probably his children all knew that, but not Big Abe. Reuben flipped the match out and puffed several times. "May I ask what you are smiling about?" he said in the high-pitched voice that belonged to his physique.

"Oh, I was just remembering that time we were standing in here having drinks with the fellow visiting you from New York and he asked you if you had shot the deer over the fireplace and had it mounted."

"Oh yes, and I said, 'Why would I want to do a thing like that?'"

"You know, that kind of deer isn't even native to the southeast."

Reuben turned to look at the glass eyes staring down at him. "Abe ordered it from Montana." He never said "Dad" or "Father," always "Abe." Big, fat, cigar-chomping, loudmouthed Abe had spawned . . . Charles wondered where the genes had come from.

"The thought of killing an animal is revolting."

"Your go." Charles studied the board and waited for Reuben to make the next move. "That's why I never invite you to the fall dove hunts on the farm." The truth was that Charles never invited Reuben to the fall dove hunts with the rest of his friends because he thought Reuben might accidentally blow an arm off if he ever tried to pick up a shotgun. Not the most coordinated fellow on the planet.

Reuben chewed on his pipe stem and moved his pawn. "I am right in the middle of *Lanterns on the Levee*. Do you know it?"

"Of course, but why would you bother? You're not interested in the South."

This was always the way the evening went, although they never acknowledged it. Usually, the chess game got as far as two moves at the most before they launched into conversation about other things; books or politics, or sometimes Reuben would tell about a trip he had taken with his wife. Charles and his family seldom had the extra money to travel, except to see relatives in neighboring states. They would drift from one subject to the next, never forced or awkward. For the one who didn't travel, it was a languid trip into other realms; for the one who could, it was a grounding in a sense of place. At least that's how Charles thought of their friendship. He wasn't sure what Reuben thought.

After awhile, Bernice would appear with coffee and say hello. Charles would stand, asking after their two girls. Then she would disappear back into the house. Time with Reuben would pass so quickly, Charles was always surprised when he looked down at his watch. "I'm already an hour past the time I told Mary I'd be back," he said now. He got up and headed toward the door. "By the way, did A.W. come by here to line up your support for the governor's race?"

"No, he goes straight to Abe for that." Reuben picked up a book to carry to the door with him. He would turn from the door and begin reading as soon as Charles left. "Did you know Brad La Forte was running?"

"Did you hear that, too?" Charles opened the door to leave.

"I know he is. He called Abe the other day. Of course, Abe says he's voting for A.W., like everybody else we know. All you old-timers would rather save face than put it on the line, wouldn't you?" He gave that inquiring smile, raising his eyebrows, pretending it was a valid question.

"Reuben"—Charles paused at the door—"don't be a smart-ass."

CHAPTER 20

Reuben: The Early Years

THEY HAD KNOWN EACH OTHER since grade school. Charles remembered first seeing him on the playground at recess. Reuben was lying on the seesaw, pretending to be asleep, while everyone else dashed around, frantic to take full advantage of outdoor playtime. One of the bigger boys had come over and pushed the other end of the seesaw down to the ground with his foot and Reuben had tumbled off on his head. On that occasion and many others, Charles had gone over to help Reuben up. Even back then, his ears had been too big for his head: his head too large for his body. They were seated next to each other most of their school years: Rosenstein, Rutland.

They had gone to each other's birthday parties when they were small—at least Charles had gone to Reuben's. Reuben had been at only one of Charles's parties. Dressed in a dark suit, he had spent the whole time sitting on the porch steps, holding his present and watching as the other children played in the front yard. He had insisted on holding his gift until he could present it.

It had been a beautiful, very delicate porcelain

replica of a sailing ship done up in pastel blues and pinks and grays, imported from England, tiny porcelain flags flying from its masts. Reuben had fidgeted as Charles opened it, twisting his little fingers, pulling his shoulders up almost to the point of blocking his hearing, instructing Charles as to how the present should be unwrapped, explaining that he had picked it out all by himself. His mother had given him permission to go to Roland's Department Store and use her account.

Charles's mother gasped when it came out of the box. She had moved immediately to spirit it away from clumsy little fingers, but in the process, one of the children—"Look, Reuben gave a old-lady present"—had touched one of the little porcelain flags and it had broken off.

Reuben had turned ashen. "I . . . I was afraid, afraid of that, afraid of that," he had said over and over, pulling at his shirt. "Now it's all ruined." Later, when cake and ice cream were served, he had said he was not hungry.

Reuben never seemed to be able to mold into acceptable behavior his most heartfelt desires to communicate. The other children immediately sensed this and took advantage. Each time he did something totally inappropriate—the china sailing ship—he became the laughingstock. All of the naturally kind but always awkward gestures were ridiculed by his peers. Others had already learned to erect social fences. He couldn't seem to. He was brilliant in other ways. He read early and often. He stayed ahead of everyone else in math and science. Most of the time, his teachers would leave him to his own devices: reading during class time. To try to engage him in class discussions would only end in confusion—for the class or for Reuben.

Big Abe had sent Reuben off to boarding school in

his early teens. He and Charles saw each other only in the summer. Every summer, Charles had expected him to be changed when he came home, but he was always the same, his hair disheveled, his glasses a little thicker, shirt and pants hanging off a frame that only grew taller and thinner.

Something had happened his junior year at boarding school—Reuben never said what—that caused Big Abe to bring him home for his final two years in high school.

Everyone had assumed that Reuben coming home for those last two years would have Charles fuming because it would ruin his chances to be valedictorian—something Charles had had a lock on in their graduating class of fifty-two girls and forty-eight boys. With Reuben home, his chances went begging. Everyone was wrong. Secretly, Charles had been pleased. It had taken the pressure off. Now he didn't have to stay up past midnight before a big game to study for a test the next day. It was enough to be president of the class and tight end on the football team.

That junior year when his son came home, it happened that Big Abe wanted Reuben to be on the football team—laughable to everyone but Big Abe. His subsequent contribution of new uniforms to the whole team had resulted in Reuben's being appointed second-string goal kicker—never kicking a point—and team manager—sitting on the bench, pretending to keep statistics but all the while reading a book.

On the long bus trips to and from away games, they had ended up sitting next to each other and talking about anything that came to mind: girls, books, movies they had seen. There was something about Reuben that drew Charles—his kindness maybe, or perhaps Reuben's complete inability to develop any kind of veneer, the way one would develop an immunity to ward off disease.

"Look," he had said to Reuben one night when they were coming out of the gym after a late football practice, "will you stop letting Joiner take advantage of you? He does the same damn thing every day—asks you to repeat all those plays in the playbook. He's just doing it to make you look like a fool—you repeating it day after day, and all the others laughing at you because you do it every time. Don't you care that he's making you look like a dunce?"

Reuben had walked along in silence. "But what if he really can't understand it and he needs my help?"

"Even if he does need your help, he's just trying to show off, calling you 'Repeatin' Reuben.' Don't you see that?" They got in Reuben's car for the drive home and didn't say another word until Charles got out at his stop.

"Well, he might not know all the plays by now," Reuben said. Charles slammed the door and shouted at him as he drove off. "He's the damn quarterback, Reuben."

And then came the night of the big game against Huntsville. Billy Joiner had been on the sidelines and the coach had said, "I want you to run something different—XYZ play." Billy was pumping his legs up and down and shaking his head as if he understood and was about to go back in the game, but he sidestepped to where Reuben was sitting on the bench, ostensibly to get a drink of water. Charles saw the panic in his eyes. Reuben quietly explained the play to him, which resulted in their team winning the game. Then the following Monday, for fear some of Billy's friends might have heard their exchange, Billy pushed Reuben, clothes and all, in the shower stall and held him there for a good five minutes before Charles came in and saw him still yelling at Reuben, saying that he had some nerve trying to tell him the goddamn plays.

He should have learned his lesson right then, but no, he stood there in front of Charles, wringing wet, vindicated. "I told you he needed my help," Reuben had said. Charles had almost hit him.

CHAPTER 21

The Candidate

O<small>F COURSE WE'RE SUPPORTING</small> A.W. again this year. Who do you like for lieutenant governor?" Mr. Ben took a biscuit. It was Sunday dinner. Ora Lee walked on around the table from person to person until she reached Charles. He took a biscuit but not the bait.

His brother-in-law Tom was saying, "Hell yes—excuse me, ladies—A.W. is the only reasonable choice, given the circumstances. I wish to hell—excuse me, ladies—somebody decent would run. Some of the boys down at the office say they are gonna vote for Wallace this time. Course I told them not to do it, but they wouldn't listen."

Charles stirred his iced tea and tested the waters. "I hear Brad La Forte may be running."

"Who's he?"

"He's a state senator from down in the middle of the state, supposed to be levelheaded. Supposed to have some sensible ideas about the integration thing."

"Well if he's levelheaded, why is he running for governor?" Tom said, looking to the ladies at the table and waiting for them to laugh—and they did.

"Too young, wasted vote," Mr. Ben said.

"Well, so is A.W., wasting a vote I mean."

"No, a vote for A.W. shows there is a certain percentage of the population in this state that has some sense."

"What difference does it make? He lost," Charles said. "Sometimes we act like voting for the loser is going to put us in the category of the high and holy, but really it's nothing but voting for a loser."

Mr. Ben didn't look up from his plate. "It's voting for the right loser. You know, we can lose with honor. There are worse things."

"Maybe we ought to stop losing with honor, stop shrinking back and go out on a limb. Like maybe I'm thinking of supporting Brad La Forte this time."

Tom gulped down a mouthful of food and burst out laughing. "And maybe I'm thinking of supporting Elmer Fudd. Charlie boy, you want to make us look like a bunch of fools, supporting a nobody."

"There's nothing wrong with Brad. In fact, I think I like what I've heard. He doesn't go wild-eyed crazy about the segregation thing and he seems to have a good education plan."

Mr. Ben turned to address his comment to Tom. "Looks like Charles has been talking to his friend Reuben again. I guess the rest of us men are gonna have to hold the line during this election."

Mary looked over to Helen. "I forgot. Did we women get the vote yet?"

"Course we got the vote, honey. They just tell us what to do with it, don't you, Mr. Ben?" Helen smiled and put a hand on Mr. Ben's sleeve.

—•—

"You *what?*"

Reuben cleared his throat and repeated, "I said I invited Brad La Forte to the house. He was calling to talk to Abe. The secretary put him through to me by mistake."

"Reuben!" Charles laughed. "As my field hands would say, 'What's got into you, son?' You haven't invited anybody to this house in—well, let's see, five years? What did Big Abe say?"

"He doesn't know I'm having him. It will be a small meeting of a few businessmen. . . ." Reuben trailed off, waiting for the next question.

"What businessmen?"

"Well, so far, you." Reuben's fingers fumbled with the pawn he held, turning it over and over in his hand. "He's very persuasive, Charles, and seems to have good sense—and he's levelheaded about the integration thing. He told me what he thought about it up front, and he doesn't even know me."

"Yeah, but he knew you were Jewish and in the movie business. He probably had a good idea going into the conversation what you thought about the subject."

"Just because I'm a Jew? Charles, you obviously don't know a lot of Jews. In fact, I know you don't know a lot of Jews."

"I know the families here in town—what, five, six? But get back to your conversation with Brad La Forte. When's he coming up and who else are you going to invite to meet him? I don't think he has any supporters here."

"That's where you come in."

Charles's shoulders sagged. "Damn, I knew you were going say that. I don't know anybody. I don't want to do this."

"You know everybody. You're the one everybody looks up to, the handsome one. What are you, six three, six four? They can see you. They'll listen to you."

"They can see me? What the hell is that supposed to mean, Reuben? Why do you want to do this? This isn't like you."

"That's what you always say whenever I mention anything out of the ordinary."

"Well, it isn't." Charles picked up a pawn and twirled it on the board.

Reuben's gaze wandered to the deer head. "Sometimes I get tired of being so removed."

"It's what you like," Charles said, watching the pawn spin. He had heard this so many times, he wasn't listening. "You've always been that way. Hell, look at you." He thumped Reuben's book, which was lying on the table next to the chessboard. "What I wouldn't give to be able to sit down and read uninterrupted for thirty minutes, much less three hours. Reuben, you have a great life."

"Did I tell you I'm thinking about integrating one of our theaters?"

Charles shook his head and couldn't help smiling. He sat back in his chair, easy with an old subject. "Yeah, about fifty times. How many times have you mentioned it to Big Abe?"

"He doesn't know what I do with the drive-ins. He's left those completely up to me."

"He will know if you go integrating them. Listen, Reuben: You know I'm against segregation. We need change, but you can get somebody killed if you go too fast on a thing like that."

Reuben half-smiled at him. "You have no way and therefore want no eyes. Is that it?"

Charles sighed. "Very dramatic—if you're sitting in freshman English at Yale, but not very practical if you have to get in the car and go to work every day. You act like it's a homework assignment you can do overnight."

One of Reuben's arms was at his waist, holding the elbow of his other arm, fingers drumming his chin, a body posture Charles was very familiar with. He had made up his mind. "About the La Forte matter: How many do you think you can get to come? I don't want a lot, just enough to fill this room."

"Is that all?" Charles searched the ceiling.

—•—

The candidate stood beneath the deer head.

Charles had thought of several men who would come as a courtesy to him and also who would be delighted to go home and tell their wives about being in Reuben Rosenstein's den with the fabled mule deer that wasn't even found around these parts.

Reuben had had his man Horace build a fire, which now flickered shadows out into the room, changing and rechanging the perceived direction of the antlers. Even though the house was cool as a tomb, it was way too warm for a fire. Typical Reuben. The other men pretended not to notice. Charles watched the deer as Brad La Forte made his bid for their support. The antlers seemed at once menacing and then, as the light changed, blunted and innocuous. The guests were mildly listening as the candidate droned on about education and tax reform. They were waiting for the segregation thing, and Charles wanted to watch closely to see how most of this group would react. He had chosen people he knew were not Wallace men—an amalgam of backing for other candidates was sprinkled around the room. He knew when Brad got to the segregation thing, that would make or break it.

Reuben had made himself almost invisible. He had, at first, greeted everyone as they entered, intermittently taking his hands in and out of his pockets, buttoning and unbuttoning his sports coat, clearing his throat in a vain effort to lower his voice from its natural high pitch. He had worn an ill-fitting tweed jacket with leather elbow patches, an attempt to look casual. The others had worn dark suits. Very soon, he had stepped back into the shadows and let Charles take over.

Brad was getting to the important part now. The others stopped fingering their drinks and listened intently to see if they could find common ground in what he said.

—•—

The candidate and guests had left with thanks and without much comment. That was expected. No one wanted to commit, and Charles certainly didn't ask for donations. That they had come was enough for now. He had been aware that there were no noticeable winces when the candidate talked about integration, about what he would do. He had taken what Charles thought was a perfectly reasonable middle ground. He would abide by the federal law. It was the only responsible thing to do, while at the same time he'd take every measure to preserve their way of life, moving slowly forward toward the inevitable. Not bad, he had thought, especially since Brad wasn't one of them. He was a man's man, no doubt about that, but he did wear his hair slightly longer than theirs. His suit was in the style of south Alabama, lighter in color, almost the white linen of the Black Belt farmers. Not that any of these men would have been aware of the individual differences. They would have felt not quite as at home with Brad as they might have with some other candidate, displaying a vague uneasiness, somewhat akin to the way they felt about Reuben.

In another world, it would have been blatantly admitted that Reuben was a misfit, but so much of what Reuben's family had given the town was hard evidence, against which no reasoning, and practical, Bainbridgian could or would take exception. The Rosensteins had given money to set up the town library, had contributed to every worthwhile charitable cause in the county. Big Abe had even bailed out the Bainbridge Methodist Church when it fell on hard times and the bank wouldn't extend its loan. It was not that they overlooked Reuben being a strange duck; it was simply accepted and attributed to his Jewishness, there being so few Jews within the city limits of Bainbridge with which to strike a comparison.

He and Reuben had pulled up to the fire. Bernice had brought them coffee and then disappeared. "I think it went well. Don't you think it went well?" Reuben was packing his pipe and saying this as a matter of course, not because he could in any way judge the tenor of the evening. Reuben was not at home with these men, had no way of estimating their mood. He looked to Charles, holding his match in midair and waiting.

Charles drew on his cigarette. "I think . . . I think so. You know you never can tell about these things, but I saw several indicators. Morris Trapp didn't get that disgusted look on his face that he gets at Rotary when a vote doesn't go his way, and James Mitchell, he's always looking out for what's best for the bank. He was paying attention to every word Brad said."

Reuben let out a sigh and put match to pipe.

"And that was another thing," Charles said. "I liked the way Brad couched everything in economic terms, even the integration thing. I think all these men are worried about the economic impact if we start having trouble up here like in Montgomery. He was smart to do that."

"That was the part of his talk that I found slightly disgusting." Reuben took a sip of coffee. "I thought it an obvious ploy to gain their support. He shouldn't deign to hedge his moral commitment."

"Spoken like a man who never had to worry about where his next dollar was coming from. You know it was James's brother, the one down in Demopolis, who had to close up his Ford dealership when the Ford Foundation started contributing to the NAACP. Not one white down there would buy a car from the poor fellow. Went flat broke in six months. Had to close up shop and start all over again.

"I thought he was realistic without being condescending," Charles said. "And we need a realist to squash some of this stuff that's going on. Have you seen the billboard that's been put up out on the highway—that picture of Martin Luther King at Highlander Folk School—implies he's a Communist?"

"I saw it—outright nonsense." Reuben looked into the embers. "Then you will think about helping to support Brad?"

"He asked me to be his campaign manager for this part of the state when he was leaving, and I said I would." Reuben looked down at his shoes. Charles set his coffee cup on the side table and got up to put on his suit coat. "Of course he did preface that request by saying that you told him I would do it."

"You were always an honorable man, Charles." Reuben smiled through pipe smoke.

"Yeah, right." Charles walked toward the door.

Reuben picked up a book and followed. "By the way, what do you know about the Highlander Folk School, other than they're a bunch of rabble-rousing crazies up there?"

"They're not crazy; they simply advocate radical social reform."

"As if we didn't have enough of that going on already."

That night as Charles walked home along Hawthorne, a breeze blew the low-hanging branches of the dogwood trees planted between the lampposts. The intermittent light cast eerie shadows along his path.

CHAPTER 22

The Rally

*I*INTEGRATED A THEATER TODAY." It was the first thing he said when Charles sat down. "I've been meaning to do it, and I did it today." He opened the box that held the chess pieces and let them tumble out on the board.

"Oh really." Charles took out a cigarette. "Which one this time?"

"The Princess, over in Russellville. Sat in the balcony with all the blacks—that's what you're supposed to call them now, blacks. I sat there through the whole feature. That was the worst part. It was a Western." He picked up the two kings and placed them on opposite ends. "My God, it was boring. I would have gone to sleep, but everybody was looking at me."

"You always sit in the balcony to check the projection booth when you visit your theaters, and every time you call it integration."

He looked up at Charles and tapped his bishop on the board. "I have never sat in the balcony of the Princess in Russellville and watched the whole movie. They were all astounded."

"The colored children who were there to see the Saturday movie and cartoons?"

Reuben's eyes were half-closed to Charles's chiding. "Every little bit helps." He began placing the other chess pieces. "And I suppose you were roundly applauded when you got up at the dinner table and told Mr. Ben and that redneck brother-in-law of yours that you were supporting La Forte."

Charles grinned. "Actually, I didn't have to take much heat. They blamed it all on you. Tom said I might as well be listening to the women."

"Ah, Tom. He must run intellectual circles around you. How do you bear it?"

"Always, your deep affection for my family."

"And the father? No doubt the father had a few words."

"He didn't say anything, which means he was furious. Tom, of course, fell back on Genesis—Negroes are all descendants of Canaan. We shouldn't rush into anything that might go against the Bible." He took a deep drag. "What could I say that I haven't said a million times? They're scared to death any talk of integration is going to trigger Armageddon."

He sat watching Reuben realigning. They never proceeded until Reuben was satisfied that things were right. "Look, it doesn't mean that they don't like Negroes or care about them. There's Will, up there on the place. My father took care of him. I'll continue to take care of him until he dies. It just means they think they're following the Bible."

Reuben didn't look up. "Certainly it does."

"Okay, it doesn't, but what do you want me to do, boil them in oil? They're family. I don't see you throwing off any traces."

Reuben finished with his arrangement and completed it by straightening the board. "That's because we're both stuck in what we are."

Charles stubbed out his cigarette. "Hell, I'm not stuck. I'm free white and twenty-one"—he grinned—"with a wife and children and a fistful of mortgaged land to prove it."

"We can make choices—within limits." Reuben readjusted the piece Charles had just put down. "Take me, for instance. I know what choices I've made, given the circumstances, and I live within them very nicely, don't you think? I mean, given the type of person I am?" He paused to look at Charles. "Don't you think?"

Charles lit up again, studying the board, feeling the conversation moving to an uneasy place. Then he moved, as he always did, to another subject. "Speaking of choices, our candidate called today and said I needed to appoint a finance chairman for my area. We need to raise a considerable amount of money."

"How about James Mitchell, down at the bank? He seems competent. Not brilliant, but competent."

"I told him I would have you do it."

"Me?" Reuben immediately stiffened. "No one will listen to me. You need somebody with—"

"With what—more money, more time? You have an abundance of both, and you're always implying I should take a stand. Now you take a stand—publicly."

"Big Abe—"

"Never mind Big Abe.

—•—

The candidate had written Charles, saying that it was time for him to visit Bainbridge. It was high time they had a rally to measure their support in that part of the state. Charles had demurred as long as he could. He said he felt the time wasn't right yet. Actually, he felt the turnout would be miserable and do more harm than good, but Brad La Forte and his lieutenants had insisted.

Within a two-week period, Charles and Reuben had spent long hours and loads of Reuben's money in preparation—signs, posters, telephone calls. Mary had been drafted to work in a newly opened campaign office. Friends had been badgered to help out—all the while Charles feeling that it was a hopeless cause. But he had been wrong.

The night had been a success beyond anything they had imagined. With not much enthusiasm Charles had reserved the town park, had brought out the volunteers holding their obligatory signs, had asked the local Baptist minister to give the opening prayer. All along, he had imagined that there would be a small, uninterested crowd, people who either knew him and came out of friendship or just happened to be in the park anyway. The big event had been scheduled to start at 7:00 P.M. By 6:30, all the folding chairs that had been set up around the podium had been taken. By 7:00, people were standing in the grassy area behind the chairs. By 7:30, when Charles had introduced Brad La Forte as the next governor of the state of Alabama, there had been such clapping and cheering, he had stood there dazed as flashbulbs blinded him to the audience. He had momentarily forgotten to step aside and let Brad take the speaker's podium. And Brad had seemed to be what they had come looking for. The audience was not loud or boisterous. They were quiet and attentive, as if trying to learn what he was about. He touched on the regular—money, state budgeting, education. It was when he got to the integration part that they seemed to listen—not unlike the men at Reuben's. Several hecklers—probably from the Wallace camp—had made no headway with the audience and had quieted after a time.

They, Charles and Reuben and now Mary, had hoped a scattering of people would show up, and to their utter astonishment, hundreds had shown up. It had been the biggest political rally since '55, when Big Jim Folsom had come to town. Nobody—not Randolph Comer, Jennings Hardman, A. W. Ladd, least of all A. W. Ladd—had ever raised such a crowd.

Charles and Mary stood at the base of the speaker's platform, watching the children run around gathering up balloons and confetti. Reuben appeared out of the shadows just as the last of the volunteers were turning in their cardboard signs and heading to Trowbridge's down on River Street to celebrate. Charles had waved them on and said he would join them in awhile.

"Reuben. Where were you? I haven't seen you since this afternoon. Did you see it? Where did all those people come from—women and children, even some coloreds out around the edges of the crowd? Did you see that?"

Reuben walked up along one of the sidewalks that led to the center of the park and took a seat in one of the folding chairs. He was dressed in a way he must have felt would be appropriate to this kind of gathering: gray dress slacks and a short-sleeve white shirt with a bright blue tie that had red balls drifting down the center. He had probably been the only man there with a tie on in weather that was still ninety degrees two hours after the sun had gone down. He couldn't suppress a grin. His long arms were adrift, first hanging at his sides, then crossing at his waist, and finally resting themselves in his lap, fingers clasping fingers. "I must say that, all and all, it seems to have been quite a successful evening."

"Is that all you have to say, 'all and all, a successful evening'? Reuben, you started this." Charles put an arm around Mary's shoulder. "Will you look at that tie? I think Reuben thought he was going partying tonight."

Reuben's hand went involuntarily to the tie. "I thought . . . since this was a festive occasion . . ."

"Don't let Charles give you a hard time, Reuben. I like that party tie." She got up and began to call the children to her.

"Reuben," Charles harassed, "what if I had needed you to give a speech, my man? Where were you?"

Reuben rested against the chair, folding his hands in his lap, regaining his composure as quickly as he had lost it. "Quite possibly, I could have gotten up and told them what a godsend you think you are to the general population."

From across the way, Mary called out, "You tell him, Reuben." She had one of the twins by the hand and was chasing the other. "Can't have him getting the big head."

Reuben's knees came together and he perched his clasped hands on his legs. "In all seriousness, Charles, I do believe our efforts were well rewarded tonight."

"Are you kidding? Look at this. The place is a mess. What a crowd."

"I think it's his charisma," Mary said. She had gathered up a child in each hand. "They read about him in the paper after that Birmingham speech the other night and wanted to come see for themselves."

"And I saw people I know voted for A.W. last time, and some Comer supporters."

"It doesn't mean they'll vote for Brad, Charles." Reuben had taken a small notebook out of his breast pocket and was making notes.

"No, but they came out and listened, and several people told me later they felt like it was time for a man like Brad."

Mary said good night and began walking home with the children. The men sat watching the remaining volunteers pick up trash and stack the last of the banners. The moon rose up over the big oak trees that circled the park and a late breeze ruffled the red-white-and-blue bunting on the speaker's platform.

It was a feeling Charles had never had before in all his years of dabbling in state politics. The thought that maybe his side had a chance of making a strong showing was startling. He got up and moved another chair around as an ottoman. "I can't believe it. Do we have a chance?"

Paul Davis, editor of the *Bainbridge Daily*, walked across the lawn toward them. "I'm saying a crowd of around a thousand."

"Sounds good to me, unless you want to say two thousand." Charles pushed a chair in his direction. "Sit on down here, Paul, and tell us what a hell of a candidate you think we have."

"Can't. Got to make a deadline, but he did make a credible showing tonight." Paul strolled off across the grass to the newspaper office, which was a block off the park.

"Old Paul may have to rethink his endorsement— heard he was all set to go with A.W." Charles blew smoke in Paul's direction and eased back in his chair. "One thousand? We must have had people come in from across the river and over near Huntsville." He shook his head and tried not to grin. "A moderate on segregation, in Alabama, and he has a chance? I never thought I'd see the day."

Lightning bugs began rising out of the grass, landing on the backs of benches, settling in the trees. Willow flies were circling the lampposts. Charles lit up another cigarette. "Reuben, if we keep this up, you might be able to abandon your mythical integration of the drive-ins and do some good in the real world."

Reuben was carefully removing his party tie and folding it neatly. "Charles, don't be a smart-ass."

CHAPTER 23

The Drive-in

HAT'S A GOOD IDEA. I can go. I can go with ya to the drive-in movie."

"You can, can you? How 'bout you, Maudie? You like to go to the drive-in? We'll pop us some popcorn, get old Jessie here to do the driving. My birthday, and I get to say where it is we go." Miss Laura turned the chicken wing over in her fingers, making sure she hadn't missed a sliver. It was another Sunday dinner and they were all seated around the table, waiting for Miss Laura, always the last to finish. "Take me two hours to fix it. Ain't gonna take me no two minutes to eat it."

Maudie had been coming to dinner every Sunday now and on most Wednesdays. After weeks, no one, other than the card-playing ladies, had come for voting school. She had passed the time by reading and digging a little garden out back of the church. Reverend Earl had suggested a garden and had been happy to bring seeds and a hoe. Probably, she thought, he was embarrassed at the turnout and wanted to give her something to do. After some initial difficulty with managing a crutch and hoe, she had adjusted and come to enjoy her time alone in the garden. She had planted tomatoes and cucumbers, a row of lettuce and one of pole beans. There was not much else to do and no way to get out unless Reverend Earl took her. He said he was too busy this time of the summer.

JD was squirming in his seat and fiddling with his fork, anxious to get on with dessert. Jessie was looking out the window, half-listening. "Don't know. Say they was some trouble over at the drive-in couple months back."

"They always trouble someplace." Miss Laura took the last piece of fried chicken off the platter and held it up for the taking. The others at the table shook their heads and she began to eat.

"One summer," Maudie said, "when I was staying up here with my aunt Carrie, we went almost every weekend. Used to put me in the trunk so they wouldn't have to pay for me."

"That's what I do," JD said, "get on the back floor and cover up with a blanket."

Maudie picked up a piece of biscuit left on her plate. "Course I guess it's all changed now. Probably all integrated now. Black folks don't have to park out back in the field, where there aren't any speakers, so they can see but can't hear. That right, Mr. Jessie?"

"You ain't been since you was a child, remember? Yeah, it's changed." He sat back in his chair and crossed his long legs under the table. "Reverend seen to that."

"Reverend integrated the drive-in?"

"Better than integrating. Still over in the field, but now we got our own road in and out, got our own ticket taker. Don't have to have no business with them white boys. Old Bowie, fellow runs the place, mean as a snake. Don't have to be studying him no more. Don't have to stand out back at the white food stand no more. Got our own place now."

"You got speakers in your cars now?"

"*No, we ain't got speakers in cars,*" he mimicked, tapping his knife against the plate, "but Reverend working on that." Aunt Laura smiled and ate her fried chicken, her eyes shifting from one to the other.

"Now, you pay your money and park right up at the wood fence over there back of the white food stand."

Maudie reached for a cold biscuit. "Say you don't have any speakers and you have your own entrance now." She took her time buttering half of the biscuit. Jessie tapped his knife, setting up a rhythm, watching her. She took a bite and considered. "My goodness, things sure have changed, haven't they?"

"Yeah they have." He glared. "Course, we been waiting on a child like you to give us the blessing over it."

She took another bite of biscuit and dropped the remainder onto her plate, slowly turning to him. "Probably still gonna be like that when JD's a grown man." She put her napkin on the table. "Probably by then, we'll have our own separate drive-in altogether."

He dropped the knife on his plate. "Suit me if we had us one for the men and the women was set off in the corner somewhere."

"Weee Lord," Aunt Laura. "I ain't enjoyed a meal so much in a long time. What's you think about that, JD?"

JD was still contemplating his sneak into the drive-in. "That's when I pop out and commence to saying, 'Fooled you, fooled you.' We going, ain't we?" He looked to Aunt Laura. "Even with them bad-mouthing 'bout it?"

"Sure we going. My birthday, ain't it?"

—•—

On the surface, it was not much changed from her childhood days. The back of the towering screen faced the highway and displayed a gigantic neon cowboy mounted on a quarter horse, chasing a neon steer on the run. In better days, his lasso had twirled in neon light down over the steer's head. Forward of this, pocked with chipping paint and sitting in weeds just off Highway 72, was the marquee announcing the current movies. Letters were missing, but still enough for patrons to know that there were two features currently showing: *Revenge f The Creature* and *ld Yeller*. It was the current fad to commandeer *O*'s for bedroom decor.

The only change was off to the side of the main entrance. There, a path led past a break in the barbed wire fencing surrounding the drive-in. It served as a separate entrance for colored cars that paid their money at a makeshift box office just beyond the barbed wire and then drove to parking places directly behind the white concession stand and behind the split-rail fence that separated blacks from whites. Leading up to the ticket booth, in Burma Shave fashion, hand-printed signs gave direction to the patrons: WELCOME TO CROSSROADS DRIVE-IN. TURN OFF LIGHTS AFTER ENTERING. 50 CENTS PER PERSON. NO ALCOHOL ALLOWED.

Black or white, this was the gathering place for everyone within twenty miles of Crossroads. For farmhands tired after a long day in the fields, driving miles into town to the indoor movie was too much time and trouble. More than convenience, the ease of familiarity was the main pull. This seemed especially true for the black families, who had found a socially acceptable gathering place other than the church.

As they pulled into the ticket line, Aunt Laura waved to cars she recognized. Maudie sat up front with Jessie. Aunt Laura sat in the back, with her feet on the blanket that covered JD. Reverend Earl was standing on the platform by the ticket booth, laughing and joking with each car as it came in.

"Wasn't for Reverend Earl, wouldn't had none of this here," Aunt Laura said. "When he come, been having all sorts of mess going on, ticket takers messing with the colored. Reverend Earl talked to Old Bowie—only one to get along with the man. He say we want a separate place and no more dealings with them cracker ticket takers. Been working good ever since Reverend Earl talked to him."

"'Cept for once in awhile," Jessie said.

"What you talking, 'once in awhile'?" Aunt Laura said. "Look here at all them cars. The man ain't gonna mess with it long as he making a heap o' money."

"Long as he's getting it all," Maudie said, and she hadn't meant to. She had meant to leave it be, not to antagonize. She guessed it was being back at the drive-in, remembering the old days, the way she used to mouth off every time she felt like it.

Reverend Earl was standing by the ticket booth when their car pulled alongside. "I got this here one, Buddy." He stooped down to see inside. "I'm guessing we got some peoples celebrating Miss Laura's birthday."

"You guessing right, Reverend," Jessie said. "Didn't know we was gonna have the big boss taking tickets. What's you doing out here?"

"Just come by to check on Buddy, see how things was going." He winked at Jessie. "But I don't see JD. Musta took sick with a tummy ache, missing a night at the movies."

"Oh, worse tummy ache you ever saw, Brother Earl," Aunt Laura said. "He laying flat on his back and can't get up for nothing. Had to leave him at home."

"Ain't that a shame," Reverend Earl chuckled. "Hope

he got plenty of blankets covering him up, keep him from getting the chills."

"More like keeping him quiet for a while. How much you giving for the movie tonight, Reverend?"

"Be a dollar fifty, Jessie. Twelve and under free."

Jessie reached in his pocket for the money. "Y'all have a good time now, and don't shine them lights on the screen. Old Bowie have a fit."

They drove on into the field, following the cars in front of them. Aunt Laura nudged the blanket on the floor. "You can get on up here now, Jessie James. You done fooled 'em all." JD squirmed out of the blanket and jumped to the window, calling out to the evening air, "Fooled you, fooled you."

Aunt Laura took the blanket to fold it. "Oh, you a master of disguise, boy."

As they drove up to the front row, pulling in next to the split-rail fence, other cars had already begun to line up behind them. People were getting out to sit on front bumpers. Some had spread blankets on the space in front of their cars. Others had brought folding chairs. JD immediately jumped out of the car to join some friends.

"Least we got here in time to get a good place." Jessie had pulled into one of the last places in the first row.

"I remember when I was little," Maudie said. "I used to think this was the best place, too."

Jessie turned off the motor. "You being smart with me?"

"Me? I ain't being smart with you, Mr. Jessie." She tried to look wide-eyed, but her face had lost its child's countenance. Must be the smell of the popcorn in the air.

"All right, all right," Miss Laura said. "Don't wanta

have no arguments on my birthday. Now ain't this nice? Done forgot what this is like, like a party. Hey there, Cora." She waved to a little girl. "Viola's grandbaby."

Elvis could be heard singing "All Shook Up" over the concession stand's loudspeakers, which blared out across the split-rail fence. The last of the afternoon sun was a faint orange glow. The big screen, made of old housing planks, loomed up in the distance. JD came back to the car. "Johnnie's daddy gone to get him a hot dog. You get me one?"

"Don't need no hot dogs," Aunt Laura said. "Got plenty right here." She held up a large brown sack. "Fried chicken, left over from last night, popped some popcorn this afternoon, and got some homemade oatmeal cookies. Now if that ain't a feast." She opened up the popcorn sack and held it out to JD.

"We don't need no food stand charging us twice what it's worth," Jessie said.

"What about a Coke? I need something to drink," JD whined.

Jessie shook his head. "Naw, don't need none of that." He was watching the line of people approaching the stand. Suddenly, he flipped the handle on the car door and got out. "All right, I'll go." He held the door open and pushed JD in. "Get on in here and wait for me." JD reached over and helped himself to more popcorn. Miss Laura held out the sack to him, but she was watching Jessie.

"I mighta knowed Miss Self have something to do with that."

Jessie reached the line just in time to stand next to a group of women. One put her arm around Jessie and gave him a kiss on the cheek. The others laughed and patted him on the back.

"Who are they?"

JD looked up from the popcorn bag. "It's Mama and Lou Ann and Izzy."

Miss Laura took the popcorn bag and offered some to Maudie. "Nobody else get your daddy outta the car that fast."

They watched as the girls laughed and talked to Jessie and most everybody else coming up to the line. Jessie motioned in their direction. All three women waved at the car. Two of them began walking toward it, all the while calling back over their shoulders the orders of food Jessie was to bring. They were dressed as if they might have found their outfits in a child's box of dress-up clothes. The tight skirts and even tighter sequined tops were faded and stained, the pointed spike heels scuffed at the point. They sauntered over, waving to JD and Miss Laura, eyeing Maudie. "Hey, Miss Laura." They began talking two cars away, high heels unsteady on the rough, patchy ground, making more out of the uneven surface than there was to make, walking to the looks they were getting. "Hear you done gone and had your-self a birthday."

Miss Laura watched them approaching, fingering the popcorn kernels she still held, mumbling under her breath. Maudie straightened her skirt and resisted the urge to glance in the rearview mirror.

Izzy reached the car first, long black arms hanging over the edge of the open window. JD offered up the cookie box. She took two. "How y'all doing?" "Happy birthday to you, Miss Laura."

Miss Laura nodded her head. "Much obliged." Lou Ann's face joined Izzy's in the window, ample breasts, covered by a tattered lace camisole, resting on the window frame. "Happy birthday, Miss Laura. Hear you done got yourself a visitor staying with you." Lou Ann accepted a cookie and took a bite, all the while looking at Maudie. "You must be the one we been hearing 'bout." She nudged Izzy. "Hear you come all the way from fancy Tuskegee, up here to the back woods, teach all our mens how to go to voting."

Maudie was determined to be nice. "And the women, too," she said. They had come to make fun of her because Mr. Jessie had been making fun of her, but she would control herself. "The women should register to vote also."

"The women, too?" they both repeated, shouldering each other and grinning. "Well honey, I don't 'spect you can teach me much," the one named Izzy.

"I 'spect us backwoods girls could dance circles round you, honey," Lou Ann said. The reference to dancing, but still she was holding her temper. In the old days, she would have been out of the car by now, talking in their faces.

"Jessie say you gonna teach the mens how to"—Izzy shifted her shoulders and wiggled her hips—"*stand up and be counted.*"

Lou Ann banged her hand against the side of the car. "Izzy, you a devil."

And that was enough. Maudie looked out the front and then slowly turned toward them, resting her elbow on the window frame. "Looks to me like you already been teaching them how to lie down and be counted."

Miss Laura sucked in air. There was a moment of silence as the girls blinked in recognition, and then a burst of laughter and slapping of hands on the top of the car. "Lawd, Miss Laura, you done gone and got yourself a sister here. What's you talking, girl?" Izzy turned to

Miss Laura. "Sound like she been doing some counting herself."

Behind them, the third one had walked up—beautiful by comparison, a bright pink sheath and matching pink heels to broadcast the striking figure. "Sound like they teach them crippled girls more than walking down there at the cripple-girl school." The ladies-in-waiting shifted aside, moving to the back window, still laughing.

JD's mother leaned down to pat the top of his head and say no to his cookie box, all the while keeping an eye on Maudie, looking at her hair and dress, staring at her leg brace. "Is that right? Do them doctors down there love them cripple girls?"

"You hush your mouth." Miss Laura reached over and pushed at the hands of the girls at the back window. "Don't wanta hear no smart-mouthing from y'all. Get on outta here." Izzy and Lou Ann backed out of the window, still giggling.

JD's mother held fast, playing with the curls on the top of JD's head. "We just come over to wish you a happy birthday, Aunt Laura. We ain't the ones doing the bad-mouthing." She eased up out of the front window, bored by now. "Besides, we got to wait for Mr. Jessie to bring us our hot dogs, seeing as how he insisting on gettin' 'em for us." She bent down. "That right? You call him *Mr. Jessie*?"

Jessie walked up, carrying a large box filled with Cokes, hot dogs, and candy bars. They gathered around him, taking one of each and laughing as they teetered away, walking the length of the front row of cars, carrying their hot dogs and Cokes and slipping the candy bars in their cleavage.

He brought to the car what was left—three Cokes.

"I didn't get no hot dog? How come I didn't get no hot dog and Mama and them others got one?"

"Go on and crawl in the backseat. I brung you a Coke. You make yourself sick eating all that junk."

"But you said—"

"Mind me, boy." He gave JD a hard swat on the fanny.

The boy got to the backseat just as the lights went out and the cartoon came on.

Maudie stirred her Coke with its straw and watched the screen, trying to let the drumming in her head slow. She pumped the straw up and down through the ice, wishing she had said more, wishing she hadn't said a thing. Miss Laura held the popcorn bag up for her to take some. "Don't pay no mind to them foulmouth women." She patted Maudie on the shoulder.

"Which one was JD's mother?"

"The good-looking one," Jessie said. He reached over and got the sack of popcorn from Aunt Laura. "Told her I was bringing Aunt Laura to the movies tonight so she could go on out with them girls."

"Oh, and I'll bet the good-looking one does just as she's told." Maudie jammed her straw up and down.

"Sho do." He washed down the popcorn with Coke. "What you 'spect?"

"How long have you two been married . . . Jessie?"

"Best-looking woman in the whole damn county." He stuck his hand in the popcorn again and grabbed a fistful and crammed it in his mouth. "Fifteen years."

"Fifteen years? That's been going on for fifteen years?"

He turned on her. "You don't know nothing 'bout my life, and it ain't none of your business anyway." He reached his arm over the back of the seat to lean closer to her. "Look at you. And you got to go disrespecting folks. Who you think you are, coming in here telling us how to do?"

He grabbed her Coke, pulled it to him, and pitched it out the window. "You don't deserve nothing to drink. If it wasn't for Aunt Laura—"

"Hush up there," Aunt Laura barked. "Can't hear what they saying up on the screen. Can't see nothing, neither. Jessie, get back on over to your side." She pushed at his shoulder. "That girl ain't worth nobody arguing over."

Jessie jerked open his door, still staring at Maudie. "Why don't you look at your own self 'fore you go talking 'bout somebody else." He said it in a low voice the backseat wouldn't hear. Before he left, he picked up her crutch, which lay on the seat between them, and pushed it over to her. "You ain't nothing to be bragging 'bout." He got out and slammed the door.

On the screen, Roadrunner was suspended in midair at the top of a bottomless cliff.

—•—

By the time he came back, the newsreel and the coming attractions had finished. *Revenge of the Creature* was starting. He opened the door and sat down, easing it closed. The smell of beer mingled in with popcorn. He took a sip and rested the can on the steering wheel, keeping his eyes on the monster.

"What I smell, beer?" Aunt Laura said. "How you getting beer?"

Jessie didn't answer. He moved his arm, letting the can dangle out the window, pulling it back in to take drinks.

They sat silently, watching the movie, only those in the backseat commenting. "That girl be crazy if she don't know that creature down there in them woods waiting for her."

"The creature done got her under his spell," Aunt Laura said.

"Ain't no creature made could get me down in them woods. Get on outta there, girl! Hand me them cookies, JD."

"Aunt Laura, you taking four cookies at a time."

"Lord, I'm gonna have to close my eyes if that girl take one more step closer to that no-good creature."

"Aunt Laura, you ruining the movie."

"I ain't ruining the movie. It's that no-count girl up yonder in them woods."

"The creature gonna control her and keep her doing what he want."

Aunt Laura raised an eyebrow and glanced at JD. "And what you think that creature gonna want outta that girl, Mr. Smart Boy?"

JD helped himself to cookies. "Want her to cook and clean, probably got a house down there in the swamp."

"Yeah, uh-huh, that's probably it." Aunt Laura rolled her eyes.

—•—

When the lights came on, JD was gone, chasing friends in and out of the rows of cars. Aunt Laura got out to stretch her legs and go look at Reverend Earl's new food stand. There was a long line talking and laughing as they waited for a turn. Smoke rose from off the charcoal grill that sat to one side of the small wood building that held Cokes, candy bars, and anything else Reverend Earl thought might sell. The ticket taker had changed hats and was now the cook, being assisted by another boy. Aunt Laura could be seen inspecting the chicken and hot dogs on the grill.

Jessie drank the last of his beer and rested the can on the window frame. "You want another Coke? I get you one."

"No, thank you."

"You want a hot dog?"

"No."

He pitched the beer can on the ground, got out of the car, and slammed the door.

Maudie sat alone, watching the movement all around her. By this time, Miss Laura had taken over the grill and was serving everyone who had paid for a bun and brought it to her. Some others had bought paper plates at the food stand as a ticket for the barbecued chicken. Smoke rose and curled along car tops. The loudspeaker from the white concession stand was playing Nat King Cole. "You're so like the lady with the mystic smile . . ." His voice floated over the night air, drifting in and out of the smoke. "Many dreams have been brought to your doorstep . . ." Out of the corner of her eye, Maudie noticed Jessie with another beer, sitting on the split-rail fence and talking to a group that included other men and the three women. By now, Reverend Earl had joined Aunt Laura and they were serving up sauce on the barbecued chicken. Aunt Laura was taking hot dog buns from customers' hands and warming them on the grill. Reverend Earl had put a white paper hat on her head, matching those of his other workers. Maudie leaned out her window to catch the conversation, but couldn't, so she eased her door open and felt the gravelly ground with her crutch. It seemed stable. She got out and walked toward all the others gathered around Aunt Laura and the smoking grill that swirled its siren-song smell.

The screen had gone to still frames of cartoon characters eating various concession-stand treats. Intermittently, it was flashing a countdown to the next feature. *Ten minutes—and don't forget the candy at the concession stand.*

She had almost reached the grill. Miss Laura had just looked up and was smiling at her when a sound—the rush of people backing away from the split-rail fence—stopped everyone and had them turning to see what was going on.

From a distance, they watched the top rail, where Jessie had been sitting, roll off and rattle along the ground as all those in its path backed out of the way. Jessie had hit the ground hard. A white boy was standing over him. He looked much younger than Jessie, but just as big. Jessie scrambled to his feet and lunged for him.

Off to the side, the three women were smiling. The white boy was trying to pick up a rail to swing at Jessie. It was too clumsy, and this gave Jessie time to run at the boy, butting him in the stomach, sending both of them into the black crowd on their side of the fence. Shrill whistles could be heard in the distance. The crowd—black and white—knew what this meant and began to rush away. Maudie, caught standing in the path of the runners, was knocked down, her crutch thrown up under a car. She kept her hands over her head until it was safe to look again. Four white men were trying to separate Jessie and the white boy.

Maudie sat up and began brushing off her skirt. Reverend Earl rushed over to the fence.

Jessie yelled at the men with whistles. "I got a right, much as anybody." Two of the men, acting as security guards, pushed back the white onlookers, telling them to go to their cars. Reverend Earl did the same on his side of the fence.

The screen said *Two minutes left—be sure to buy popcorn.*

One of the security guards picked a beer can up off the ground and showed it to Reverend Earl. Jessie jerked away, said something to Reverend Earl, and they started to argue. Finally, Reverend Earl gestured for Jessie to get back on his side of the fence, and then he walked toward the white concession stand with the guards and disappeared behind a back door that said, EMPLOYEES ONLY.

Zero minutes till show time. The lights began to dim for the second feature.

"JD, will you get under that car over there and grab my crutch?" Maudie had seen him near the car, holding his Coke cup, worry on his face.

"They gonna get him and take him away?"

She held out her hand for him to help her up. "No, they aren't gonna take your daddy. Didn't you see Reverend Earl go in there to talk to them? He'll fix it. Must be talking to Old Bowie."

In a few minutes, Reverend Earl came out and walked over to Jessie. They both watched as he pointed a finger in Jessie's face and lectured.

"Under that one," she said.

JD handed her his Coke cup and scrambled under to get the crutch. "When I get big, Reverend Earl say I can have a job taking tickets. Gonna come out here every night, see every movie." He stood up and handed her the crutch. "Reverend say I can do it."

"I'm sure you can," she said, brushing dirt off her crutch. "When you get big, he'll probably still have that same job open for you."

CHAPTER 24

Jessie

THE NEXT SUNDAY, Reverend Earl asked Maudie to walk with him to his truck, as he was late for a dinner on the grounds over at Pleasant Valley. He needed to talk with her for a minute. He was trying to get a sluggish battery to cooperate when he told her that Jessie's atonement for fighting would be that he must come to her school for at least three sessions. "Is that what Old Mr. Bowie wanted, for you to make Jessie come to voting school?"

"Lord no, child. Bowie don't know nothing 'bout no voting school. If he did, he'd sure enough close me down."

The thought of having Jessie in a class for three sessions made her feel slightly panicked. She listened but said nothing. "You know Jessie a grown man. Can't say he'll come, but he usually don't go back on his word." He said he had told Jessie that it was either that or he wouldn't vouch for him, and the security guards might have taken him away for drinking on the grounds. "Don't know what come over Jessie sometimes. He's usually not bad to get in with the wrong crowd. Plain as day, you ain't supposed to be drinking on the grounds.

That's why I put that sign out there, to remind people."
The motor was whirring but not catching. He got out of
the truck and lifted the hood. "Had to deal with Old
Bowie 'cause of that. He the one run the place. Say next
time that happen, he gonna close down my food stand,
like it was all my fault." After jiggling some wires, he
slammed the hood down and got back in. "Can't have
that happen, no matter what." The truck started on the
next try. "Now you let me know if he don't show. I'll have
his hide, much of it as I can." He backed the truck
around so it could get a good running start up the steep
hill out to the road. He said that would give her one
person in her class. He could tell the Highlander folks
and the ones down at Tuskegee they did have some sort
of class, not just the ladies coming to socialize. Her
summer wouldn't be wasted altogether.

She knew what it meant, how important it was. If she
could just have one man, even if she did have to put up
with Jessie, then maybe others would come. Maybe
others would hear about it and want to come, wouldn't
be scared to come, if that was what it was, if it wasn't that
they just didn't like her to begin with.

She spent hours in preparation, half-thinking he
wouldn't come, half-hoping he might not. She had let
her gardening go, had temporarily given up her
reading.

—•—

She sat at her teaching table long after starting time,
listening for the sound of a car. She heard one on the
road along about seven o'clock. It seemed to slow but
then drove on by.

The first thing he said when he jerked open the front
door and walked in thirty minutes late, "You know I
gotta be here 'cause I give my word to Reverend." He

moved down the aisle toward her and her books. "But it ain't but for three times."

She gestured for him to sit on the front pew. He sat, legs sprawling, arms folded in front, eyes on the floor. She cleared her throat. He looked at his watch, then unfolded his arms and drummed fingers on his pant legs, fixing her with a steady gaze. She began straightening a stack of papers on the table, waiting for the tightness in her throat to ease. Suddenly, the papers seemed to have their own mind, becoming more and more uneven to her stacking and finally overflowing, several of them landing on the floor, others slipping out onto the table.

She didn't look at him when he leaned forward to pick the pieces up, but she could feel the smirk. He stacked them neatly and put them on the table beside her. Then he returned to his seat, casually resting his arms over the back of the pew. "I done passed the first part. Leastways I can keep them papers in hand."

She had known it was there all along, but once he spoke his contempt, it seemed to harden her. After a moment, she felt more even and picked up the cards she had made for their first lesson. They were large white cardboard signs made to replicate the Burma Shave–like signs at the drive-in movie.

His eyes narrowed as she stood them up on the table in a row, resting them against her books. WELCOME TO CROSSROADS DRIVE-IN. He sat up, his back stiffening. TURN OFF LIGHTS AFTER ENTERING. 50 CENTS PER PERSON. NO ALCOHOL ALLOWED. He glared at her with all the contempt he could muster, but it was not enough to hide in.

"Do you remember seeing signs like these?"

"Hell, course I do. What you think? I ain't no idiot." He stuck his hands in his pockets, then just as quickly drew them out and folded them in front of him. "I ain't coming to no drive-in school. I'm coming to a voting school. You supposed to tell me how to vote. None of this." He waved his hand.

His harshness had calmed her. "What do you think the words say?"

He uncrossed his legs, pulled them in, and glared at her, his arms still folded in front of him. "I don't care what them words say. Hell, they just drive-in words." The muscles in his jaw twitched, as if he might get up and hit her. "I'm a grown man. Got better things to do with my time than sitting here playing movies with you." He got up and turned to walk away.

"Reverend Earl said for me to let him know if you didn't stay."

He stopped, mumbling something that she knew must be insulting. Finally, he turned and came back to sit down in front of her.

She put her elbows on the table, clasped her hands together, and rested her chin on them to continue. "Do you know what the words say?" She folded her hands down in front of her. "Do you know that one of them says you can't drink beer at the drive-in and that one says you need to pay fifty cents per person for the movie?"

His hands reached for the top of his legs and he rubbed them against his jeans. "You think you such a . . . I know them signs. Seem 'em a million times."

"Well?" she said. "I thought we would start with these, since they're familiar."

He bit his lower lip, looking at the signs, studying the squiggly lines on the pieces of cardboard that stood in front of him. Slowly, he pointed to the third sign. "That word, right yonder on that one, say, 'fifty cents.' I know that there is 'fifty cents.'"

"Good. It says, 'fifty cents per person,'" she said. " It means—"

"Hell, I know what it means. What you think, I'm a fool?" He turned from her and studied the sign more intently now, seeming to forget she was there, almost talking to himself. "I knowed the 'fifty cents,' but not them others—'per person.'" He repeated it again, sinking it into his memory, "'per person,' 'per person.'"

He pointed to the sign that started with the word *No.* "'No—I know that one, so what you say the next thing say?"

"'No alcohol allowed.'" She pointed to each word as she pronounced it very slowly. "It means if they catch you drinking—"

"All right, all right," he said, dismissing her, concentrating on the signs. "Don't give me no sass, girl. What this here next one say?"

"'Turn off lights after entering.'" He studied it and laughed. "One time, I left my lights on all the way to parking and the movie already going. Was them white boys having a yelling fit, screaming at me from over the fence." He rubbed his chin. "It say that?" He looked at her for a moment. "Course I know you supposed to. I just done it to rile 'em. And this here one?"

"It says, 'Welcome to the—'"

"I know the rest. I seen them same words outside on the big sign." He looked at them, repeating them to himself in a whisper, his lips moving to form the sounds.

She almost smiled. She almost laughed out loud, she was so relieved, but he wouldn't have noticed if she had. After years of wondering and watching and never knowing that it colored every other part of his being, he had, on this night, when he thought only to fulfill his obligation, been forced to take the key he'd never dared ask for. He didn't take his eyes from the signs, pointing as he got up off the church pew and pulled a straight chair up to the table. "This one, what's this here one say again?"

Now she was watching him through swimming eyes. He and the signs and the room were blending into hazy shapes and colors, and she was so surprised. There hadn't been tears for a long time. She knew her voice would sound scratchy. "It says, 'Turn off lights after entering.'" She had to excuse herself, saying that she wanted to get a drink from the back room. He never noticed her voice or her tears. He was too busy reading the words.

CHAPTER 25

Mr. Calvin K. Jerome

AFTER THE SECOND LESSON, Jessie knew every written word that might ever have been seen at a drive-in. They had gone over all the words that appeared on the screen during, before, and after intermission. They had taken up what might be on the wall menu at the concession stand. He had brought old candy wrappers for them to read, matchbook covers that he wanted to know about, notices he had gotten at work, advertisements he had received in the mail.

He came every Thursday night, promptly at 7:00 P.M., and never mentioned his three-time limit.

Sometime after the third or fourth lesson, he had appeared in the church door, a sheepish grin. "You say you a regular citizenship school, don't you, or voting school, whatever. Well, I brung you more students."

She had been sitting at the table in front of the church, listing all the names of movies and movie stars she could think of. She watched him disappear and then appear again in a few minutes with two other men. "This here Mr. Calvin. Mr. Calvin K. Jerome and Roy Boy." Two men, one older than Jessie and one who looked about her age, stepped from the church stoop into the sanctuary. They were so far away and the light was so bad, she couldn't see them clearly.

"Evening," she said, and tried to get a better look by shading her hand to block the bulb that hung down halfway between the door and her place at the table. They lingered back in the shadows, but Jessie would have none of it.

"Y'all come on up here." He walked in front of them, assuming they would follow, and when they didn't. "Come on now. She ain't gonna mess with you."

They took off their hats and walked slowly forward, looking around the sanctuary. "Calvin and Roy Boy here work down at the foundry where I work at. Been there twenty years or more."

"Forty-two years." The one called Calvin stepped forward. "Got a job sweeping floors when I was a boy. Been there ever since." He sat down on the front pew and placed his hat beside him on the bench. He wore a coat and tie; gray hair curled around his ears. "Went straight from picking cotton to foundry work. Never had no time for nothing else."

"Nice to meet you, Mr. Jerome," she said, holding on to the table and half standing. She felt his age required it. "You live around these parts?"

"Live in Bainbridge." He looked over to Jessie. "But Jessie say the voting school free to everybody."

"Sure is, free to everybody," Jessie said.

"Oh yes," she said. "Just sorry you have to come so far."

"That's all right." He stretched his legs out and white socks showed from under trousers that were too short. He picked up his hat and began to finger the brim. "Come to find out 'bout banking. Course I could learn me some other things, too, but need to know 'bout banking more'n anything. Jessie here says you can learn me."

"Banking?" She looked at Jessie.

"Yeah, yeah, you know, banking." Jessie seemed perturbed at her hesitation. "Calvin here want to know all about it. Want to open up a banking account, and he ain't sure of how to read about it. He take it to his preacher, he gonna be getting all Mr. Calvin's savings for his church . . . or for hisself."

The other one, Roy Boy, had taken a seat in the row behind Mr. Calvin. "That's sure enough the truth. Brother Simmons knowed for that—get all your money 'fore you can turn round."

"Show her the papers, Calvin. She help you." Jessie said it as casually as if he were offering up his own secretary.

Mr. Calvin stood up and began taking papers out of every pocket in his suit coat and placing them on the table in front of Maudie.

"I don't know much about banking. I never—" She stopped short when she saw the expression on Jessie's face. "Course all there is to it is to read the papers and figure it out."

"That's all they is to it." Jessie rocked back on his heels. "All they is to it."

They spent the rest of the lesson learning words that had to do with banking—reading the various papers that came out of Mr. Calvin K. Jerome's pockets.

—•—

After that first session, Mr. Calvin didn't seem interested in discussing banking anymore; in fact, he would avoid the subject if she brought it up. All the same, he and Roy Boy began coming to the voting school on a regular basis.

From the very beginning, she had called him Mr. Jerome or, later on, Mr. Calvin. He had given her permission to call him Calvin, but she felt the name by itself, Calvin, seemed incongruous for a man of his age and dignity—and Mr. Calvin K. Jerome was a man she judged to be in his late sixties, maybe early seventies, a man of natural dignity. He always stood when she came into the room. He always wore a suit and hat and immediately removed the hat when he entered the church.

She gave them each a notebook and they began to copy things in it: their names and addresses, the name of the foundry where they worked, the names of their family members. Mr. Calvin and Jessie picked it up immediately. In fact, Mr. Calvin knew quite a few words and phrases. He would wait patiently as the others would learn things he already knew. She began to wonder why he kept coming. He was obviously familiar with all the vocabulary he would need to work in the foundry.

Roy Boy was not. He was younger and stronger than both of the others, but he couldn't seem to form the letters on the paper as well as they could and he didn't seem to remember from time to time what he had learned before. Maudie suggested that they all start coming on Tuesdays and Thursdays. They all said they thought they could do that.

As time went on, Jessie, and certainly Mr. Calvin, came to feel some familiarity with the pencils in their hands, with the problem of bending large calloused fingers around a small yellow piece of wood. This was not the case with Roy Boy. There was a constant bead of perspiration on his forehead. Each time, his fingers seemed to have to learn anew how to grip the pencil.

The first time she put her hand on his shoulder to look over his writing, she felt nothing but solid muscle on a frame that she thought must be six three or four. She was tempted to touch the hair that grew down his neck in soft brown curls. He would look up for her approval each time he completed a word that had taken him twice as long as the others and required three times the effort. She had been glad to take the time to compliment him and to have a chance to look at him without seeming obvious. He reminded her of the pictures she had seen of the new boxer, Cassius Clay.

—•—

This night, Jessie and Maudie were waiting for the others to show up. It was fifteen past the hour, and they were usually here by now. They were the ones who were always early, sometimes getting there before Maudie was ready. At twenty-five past, they heard Mr. Calvin's truck, an old Ford with a loose flatbed that rattled as he drove down the steep grade of dirt road that led to the church. He came in all smiles, dressed in his coat and tie, a large cardboard shoe box under one arm. He greeted each one individually, took off his hat, and laid it on the front pew, still smiling.

Jessie had been writing in his notebook, but looked up to watch the way Mr. Calvin couldn't seem to keep from grinning. "Look like the cat done swallowed the canary." Roy Boy couldn't keep a straight face, either. "What y'all been up to?"

Mr. Calvin sat down on one of the chairs, the box still in his hand. "Decided it's 'bout time for me to go on and take my money to the bank, like I was talking 'bout."

"That? Thought you done done that long time ago."

"No, I ain't done it long time ago. Take some figuring, knowing who I'm dealing with."

"Who to do what?" Jessie was watching them carefully now.

Maudie had settled herself in one of the other chairs at the teaching table. "You need some help filling out the forms, Mr. Calvin?"

He put the cardboard box on the table and flipped off the top. "Need some help counting," he said. Twenty-dollar bills that had been crammed in the box scattered out on the table.

"The Lord." Jessie dropped his pencil. "What you been—robbing a bank?"

"Ain't been robbing, been saving."

They all stared at the box overflowing with bills. Mr. Calvin put his big hand on top of the pile. "Got me some fifties down there in the bottom, too."

"How'd you come by all that money?"

"Same place you get money from. Working. Only I ain't no big spender like you young'uns. Always have some left over and all these years been saving. Me and Claudell used to take it out and count it 'bout every Friday, that being payday. Since she passed, ain't done that no more. Been thinking ever since Jeremiah Brown's house burned down, been thinking it's time to do something with this here, but I didn't have no notion what to do with it, so I started coming to the voting class." He looked over to Maudie. "Figured you could help me count it proper. Then I'll put it in the bank, the big one down by the courthouse."

"You mean you had all that at home, all this time? Weren't you afraid somebody would take it?"

"Didn't nobody know it was there. Thought I was poor, like everybody else round here. Figured I used up my money on drinking and foolishness, like everybody else." He grinned, showing teeth worn down from years of the pipe. "But I been saving it. Gonna put it in the bank, now I know how to sign for it. Figure Maudie here can go on down to the bank with me, make sure everything done right." His big hand ran over the money. "Figure I'll give her one or two of these here for her time."

"Oh now Mr. Calvin, I couldn't do that, but I'll gladly go with you."

"Wouldn't have it no other way—that you was to go with me," he said.

They counted and recounted for the next hour—Maudie counting and Jessie restacking. Mr. Calvin K. Jerome stood off to the side, his hands in his pockets, shaking his head each time Maudie completed a stack and wrote the total down on the inside of the shoe box's lid. Roy Boy grinned and rubbed his hands together, reaching over to touch each counted stack.

As they were counting the last few bills, lights flashed by the church window.

A car pulled around back and the motor cut off. Before any of them could move, they heard the car door slam.

"Who's coming? Didn't know nobody was coming—don't nobody come round here." Calvin looked to Jessie and began grabbing for the money on the table.

He was stuffing it back in the shoe box as fast as he could when the door to the back of the church opened. "Anybody in there learning how to vote?" he called from his back-room office.

"It's Reverend Earl." Maudie sighed, letting the money she had picked up drop to the table.

The others continued to stuff. There were a few twenty-dollar bills left on the table as Jessie slipped the box under the table and the preacher walked in the room.

"It's only Reverend Earl," she said.

"What you mean, 'only Reverend Earl'? Ain't I some-body?" He came into the room, a big grin on a sweaty face wiped down with his handkerchief.

"What's going on here? Y'all ready to go to voting?"

Roy Boy placed his notebook over the remaining money and sat perfectly still, his head down.

"Nothing much, Brother Earl." Jessie got up to walk toward him. "Nothing much. You come to join up?" For a moment, he placed his hand on Reverend Earl's shoulder, a gesture unfamiliar to Jessie and the preacher.

"Heard tell we got us some new members." Reverend Earl was looking over Jessie's shoulder. "Been so busy, ain't had time to come by and say welcome."

Mr. Calvin stood up.

"This here Calvin K. Jerome, Brother Earl. You know him. Work down at the foundry with me."

"Hear y'all from Brother Ben Simmons's church over on the bluff."

"Yes sir, Reverend. Me and Roy here come on out with Jessie." Mr. Calvin smoothed his coat and stuck out his hand, but didn't move from his place at the table.

"I said they was welcome to come out, Reverend."

"Course they are, course they welcome." Reverend Earl shook hands with Mr. Calvin and looked around the room, feeling the awkwardness. "Did I interrupt the lesson? Sure didn't want to stop the voting school."

Heads shook almost in unison. "Naw, naw, didn't do that."

Jessie picked up a pencil and tapped it on the table. "We was just learning a few things, not exactly 'bout voting."

"Like what?" Reverend Earl walked to the table and began to look down at the scattered papers.

"Well, Reverend, to tell you the truth of the matter, we were doing a few things that don't have much to do with voting," Maudie said.

The other men stared at her. "We were, uh, learning how to read the signs at the drive-in, stuff like that. Guess it wasn't exactly what we was supposed to be learning in a voting school."

Reverend Earl looked down at the notebooks on the table for a moment and then raised his head and laughed. "Y'all looking so guilty. Thought you was in here planning to build a still out back."

There was tentative laughter and then they all started talking at once. "Wasn't like that. No, just studying 'bout other things."

The reverend sat down at the table, leaned back in the chair, and looked at them with his one eye cocked on them and the other one closed. "Now listen here: Don't go worrying 'bout staying on voting things all the time. Plenty time for that. Ain't nothing wrong with learning other things, too—along the way." He let the chair slide forward and banged a hand on the table. "Long as you using my church for learning, that's good enough for me." He opened both eyes and stood up. "Well now, brought along some Coca-Colas for y'all to celebrate. You know this here is the start of a real voting school." He winked at Maudie. "Knowed it would take some time, but we coming along.

"Come on out to the car, Jessie, I'll give you them Cokes. I got to be going on over to Jackson's Gap to check on Miss Luella. She down in the back and I got to figure how to feed them children of hers while she out of work."

He started toward the door and then turned back to them. "Miss Luella got three grandchildrens she trying to raise up, could sure use some . . ." He paused and looked at them, then seemed to think better of it. "Never mind. I think I got Miss Luella took care of for the time being."

Jessie followed him out the door

"You give Brother Ben my regards," he said over his shoulder. Roy Boy and Mr. Calvin said they sure would.

For the rest of the evening, they drank Cokes—Reverend Earl had added a little something extra to the men's bottles before he left—and recounted the money. "I think Reverend Earl would have been happy for you, Mr. Calvin." Maudie was looking down at her column of numbers.

"No sense telling nobody your business. Don't need to know it," Jessie said.

Calvin had been saving for the forty-plus years he had been working at the foundry and not once had he ever put any extra money anyplace but the Buster Brown shoe box. There was $5,631.25 in the box—enough for a new house or two or three cars—a fortune.

Mr. Calvin said he would take off early for the first time in all his years of working at the foundry.

CHAPTER 26

Banking Business

*T*HAT DAY, he wore his blue suit, one of the two he owned. The seat was slick and the knees were noticeably worn, but she thought he looked the picture of a gentleman when he opened the front door of the bank for her, removed his hat, and walked up to the nearest teller, holding his box. He had told her on the way to town that he wanted to make sure the safe was fireproof and that it was locked up good and tight every night. She had said she thought that would be a good idea.

Of course everybody knew Calvin. He had been around Bainbridge all his life. Still, there was much consternation over the Buster Brown box. The teller told the vice president, a young boy not long out of the university, and the vice president came out to see the box. He then called the head of the foundry to see if Calvin had really been working there as long as he claimed. With each query, they stood patiently at the front teller's window, waiting. Maudie began to think that she should not have let Mr. Calvin bring his money here. They were looking at him as if he were some kind of a thief. Each time another question was asked, Calvin's head took on that crouched look she had seen on nights when he didn't know the answer to something she might ask him. His eyes scanned the floor and then the wall behind the person who was speaking. She stepped up and began explaining why he had the box of money. It had not helped, probably even made it worse. The teller and the vice president had asked who she was, and when she had mentioned the voting school, there was more silence and staring and shifting of feet. It was the first time she had felt pride at being connected with the voting school. Finally, the vice president said he guessed it was all right, that they would accept the money provisionally and wait to see if any had been reported missing.

There was silence as the teller and the vice president stood on one side of the teller cage and Maudie and Mr. Calvin on the other.

"Provisionally?" Maudie glared at the vice president. "*Provisionally?*" She began taking the stacks of money that were already on the counter and putting them back in the box. "Mr. Calvin Jerome has been in this town, has worked in this town, all his life. He doesn't need anything provisionally. He needs a good bank that will protect his money, and I think the one down the block will do just fine."

Calvin picked up the box top, waiting to cover his money once she had finished repacking.

There was a voice from behind them. "Donald, don't tell me you're letting all that good money get out of here and end up at the First National." Maudie kept packing. "Donald, everybody in town knows Cal. He's worked at the foundry for—what is it, Cal, forty years?"

The man came up and put a hand on Mr. Calvin's shoulder.

The vice president began to sputter. "Mr. Mitchell, course I know Cal, but all those old bills, mostly in tens and twenties . . . I just thought to be on the safe side—"

"Cal is probably the safest side you could be on, Donald. Do you think he robbed a bank? Use your eyes, man." He turned to Mr. Calvin. "Cal, we'd be proud to have your money."

But Calvin was not to be mollified. "I thank you, Mr. Mitchell, but"—he put the box top down hard on his money and picked the whole thing up—"don't believe I'll be doing no banking here."

He turned to Maudie. "Ain't even been offered a look at where they gonna keep it. Don't even know if it safe from fire and being stole."

The president of the bank thought this was wildly funny and laughed so loudly that it echoed up to the marble ceiling and bounced down off the marble floor.

"Donald." He still shook with laughter. "Miss Finley. Y'all give Cal here a tour of our walk-in safe and show him each and every fire extinguisher. And, for good measure, you might give him one of those toasters we're giving all our new accounts."

Before he walked off to greet another customer, he said to the vice president and the teller, "I hope you two will be able to convince him to keep his money here—as that was his plan in the first place, before y'all got hold of him."

They were another hour touring the bank, looking at the fire protection, walking inside the safe and seeing some real money. Finally, the new vice president, sweat soaking the underarms of his white dress shirt, had been able to convince Calvin that the Bank of Bainbridge was the place to keep his money.

The final total came to $5,611.00. Calvin had taken

out a twenty-dollar bill and change to celebrate and buy food for the next few weeks. And he left with a new toaster.

They backed out of the parking place in front of the bank and said nothing until they were almost out of town. He rolled down his window to catch some fresh air and signal a left turn. "Them folks act like they doing me a favor taking my money. Seem strange to me." They passed the foundry and Calvin waved to a coworker. "Leastways it's in there now, and if the place burn down, they have to make it up to me, just like"—he hesitated—"just like *Donald* say."

They were still laughing when they pulled into Lowry's Barbecue. "Make you wanna set a match to it, just on a general notion, don't it?"

"Just to see them all running out the front door, screaming and yelling and carrying the money," she said.

They had stopped at the best barbecue place in town—black-owned, but so renowned there was a carryout window for whites. They sat in one of the booths and ordered barbecue, Brunswick stew, french fries, coleslaw, loaf bread, sweet tea, and fried peach pies with ice cream for dessert.

She had never felt so satisfied—with a meal, with a day. "You have the power," she remembered they had told her at Highlander, "you just don't know it's there."

CHAPTER 27

The Con

$\mathcal{F}$OR DAYS AFTER their fight in the dining room, Tab saw only snatches of Dominique. She wouldn't ask, and Dominique didn't volunteer anything, but Eloise could. "So where you been keeping yourself?"

"*Laisse tomber, ma copine,*" and walked out of the room.

Eloise stood holding a shoe she was about to put on. "What she say?"

Tina was searching up under the bed for her life-guard's whistle on the gimp-plaited lariat. "Who knows? Probably 'Kiss my foot,' something like that."

It took two days of following to find out where she was going, what she was doing. The first morning after breakfast, Tab stayed back some distance and lost her when she went into the woods. The next day, she went to the woods early and watched undercover as Dominique came out and doubled back to go into the library. Tab waited several minutes before sneaking up to the door. The front door was open, but the screen was blocking a quiet entrance. She went around to the side of the building to get a look through the window.

Dominique was the only one in the room, sitting at a table, writing furiously. She would glance at the book that lay open next to her and then write. Glance again and write again, over and over, her pencil jammed into the paper. At one point, she broke the lead, pitched it across the room, and took up another.

Tab turned away and leaned against the side of the building. The sun was just above the tops of the big oaks on the other side of the lake. She could hear splashes. Eloise was at it again, spending every waking hour in the water. Tina was probably watching, whistle at the ready. Tab could smell the beginnings of the noon meal drifting by in the morning air. When she turned back, Dominique was slamming the book down on top of the stack of papers she had accumulated and throwing her pencil across the room. She sat there for a while, looking at the bookshelves opposite, before she got up and pulled out a book with a bright green cover. She went back to her seat, opened the book, and was immediately off in another place, her shoulders relaxed, her breathing easy.

Tab watched her, thinking that the strangeness she first thought she saw in Dominique was really a type of beauty she had never considered before. Beauty that didn't own up to anything she had ever been taught— the image of blue eyes and blond hair fogged over with hair spray. This look was cool and distant. It was the dark skin that conveyed it, smooth, without a blemish. She turned away, embarrassed at the thought. No one in her acquaintance would think of calling Dominique beautiful—but she was.

Tab decided to go swimming.

—•—

That afternoon, Tab was in the library, her feet propped up on a table reading a travel book on France, when Dominique came in from lunch. "What are you doing with my book?" Tab pushed the book across the table and watched as Dominique slowly opened it to a dog-eared page and began reading.

"He's making you write out a bunch of stuff for punishment, isn't he?"

Dominique didn't answer. Tab looked at the stack of paper anchored by a heavy book. "What are you having to do, translate it?"

"Yes."

"The whole thing?"

"Yes."

"Does he speak French?"

"Only a few phrases." There was a slight smile.

"And you?"

"And me what?"

"What is your aunt making you do?"

"Stay two more weeks."

There was a loud exhale. "Jeez." Dominique picked up a pencil and tapped it on the table, studying Tab. "I been meaning to talk to you about something," she said, looking around to make sure no one else was within earshot and then lowering her voice too much. "You know that time I talked to you about how there might be a sit-in in Nashville?"

"What?"

She sighed. "You know, the sit-in, in Nashville, some people might be going from here—early in the morning and come back that day."

"Oh yeah. I remember now. You were thinking about going."

"It's very secret. You can't tell anybody, not your sister or your aunt, but how would you like to go, if I can get you a seat on the bus?"

"Well, I don't know. Is it against the law?"

"It's civil disobedience. Your aunt would be proud."

"Maybe. I'll think about it."

"Sure." She touched Tab's arm, and she never touched Tab. "There's nothing to it. You might read things in the paper about sit-ins, but really most of them are routine. You won't have any problem. You go in and sit at Woolworth's counter and order a hot dog or whatever, and eat it—if they let you—and then come out again. It just officially integrates the lunch counter, and then we come back here."

"I guess it sounds okay to me. I remember them talking a little about it at the meetings, but we're always talking or playing battleship. I didn't pay much attention."

She was thrilled Dominique had asked her. She still felt the place on her arm Dominique had touched. "Like they said in the meeting the other day, 'Everybody should be allowed to eat where they want to.'" She knew Dominique would like hearing that. It meant nothing to her.

"All right, then, I can count you in." She got up to leave. "Now don't tell anybody else about this. It has to be our secret." She looked down at Tab and smiled, and that turned to a grin. Then she laughed out loud as she got up to leave, walking off, never looking back.

"What's so funny?"

Dominique didn't answer.

—•—

"They'll just think you got up early and took a hike or something." Dominique was whispering in her ear. It wasn't light yet.

"What?"

"It's time to go. Remember? The sit-in? Did you get out some good clothes like I told you?"

"Yeah, I hid 'em in the hall closet," Tab whispered.

Dominique stood watching her in the dim light of the bathroom. She was already dressed in a black dress with white patent-leather belt and black patent flats. She combed her hair and watched Tab through the mirror. "Are you people still wearing crinolines? That went out five years ago."

"You said, 'Put on your best stuff.' This is the best I got. And you talk about behind the times. Gravy. Who ever heard of dressing up to go to Woolworth's?" She slipped her black felt skirt with the pink poodle appliqué on over her crinoline slip. It stood out in waves around her, a hand-me-down from Tina. The poodle was faded and the fake gold chain that was his collar had tarnished, but it was Tab's favorite. On top, she wore a pink pullover sweater and an angora collar that tied in the front, leaving pom-poms dangling. "I only wear this on the most special occasions, so this better be a lot of fun—well, not fun exactly." She watched herself in the mirror, tying the collar. "I shoulda washed my hair and got some extra money from Tina. You shoulda told me last night we were going today."

"I told you that you couldn't tell anybody. We'll be back tonight."

"Good, 'cause I don't wanna miss supper."

There was a vague light coming from the end of the hall—moonlight. "I forgot my gloves. I need to get my gloves."

"We don't have time for that. We have to be the first on board."

"But I need to—"

"Go on and brush your hair and wash your face, but be quick about it—and be quiet."

The screen door creaked slightly as they stepped out

onto the porch, the rockers barely visible, the smell of honeysuckle thick in the night air. Dew had settled in on the grass and the gravel path they were following to the old school bus that sat under a tree off to the side of the main house. "There's nobody here. You must have got the wrong day," Tab said, still whispering, although there was no need now.

"No, we're just early." She stuck her fingernails in the worn rubber gaskets, pulling back the folding door and holding it for Tab. "Go on. Get in."

Tab climbed up to the first seat and sat down. "No, go on back. We need to go to the very back."

"Why?"

"Just because—go on back and we can lie down and get some sleep while we wait for the others to come."

"How many others?"

"There won't be many. Mr. Spivey is coming. My father. I think Dora and some of the other Fisk students. Miss Wilma, that old lady from down in south Georgia— mostly students who've been up here at the conference this week."

"I mean, will there be others like me?"

"I'm sure. Now go on to the back. I don't want my father to see us just yet."

"Why? He's gonna see us sooner or later."

She pushed on the small of Tab's back. "Better later than sooner. By then, we'll be too far down the road. Go on back and we'll pretend we're sleeping."

"But I'm wide-awake now."

"Pretend."

Both of them lay pulled up into balls on the bench seat that ran the width of the back of the bus. Dominique was asleep, or pretending sleep to avoid questions. Tab held her white patent-leather purse tightly, fingering it to remember what she had brought along: a lipstick, comb, some Life Savers if she got hungry before they could order their hot dogs, and Aunt Eugenia's cat's-eye sunglasses.

A half hour passed. The sky off to the east began to flush pink. They heard voices gathering outside the bus, eight, maybe ten people. Mr. Spivey was louder than the others, even though he was trying to keep it quiet. Dominique's father was greeting them all as if they were going on a picnic. She could hear laughing and joking.

They all got on the bus and huddled up front around the driver. "Let's get rolling," somebody said. "This is all that's coming—not enough, but this is all. We got to get going if we want to meet the others there just as it opens." The driver, Dominique's father, cranked up. The top of the bus scraped and screeched out from under the branches of a sweet gum. Tab and Dominique were still lying across the back bench seat, their heads together, looking down the aisle at the backs of the others. Most of the windows were pulled open or permanently stuck that way. Cold mountain air rushed in at them. Tab curled up to stay warm.

—•—

"It's been over an hour. We can get up now. We're more than halfway." Dominique sat up in her seat, pulling a comb out of her dress pocket to reshape the hairdo. Tab remained where she was, pretending to sleep. They jostled along, Dominique looking out the window at the passing scenery, humming, waiting for the inevitable. Maybe it was one of the songs they usually sang at night after supper: "This Little Light of Mine," or maybe Dominique's favorite by the Platters, "Smoke Gets in Your Eyes." Tab couldn't tell which, and she wouldn't ask, wouldn't let on that there might be creeping into the back of her mind the thought that Dominique was taking her somewhere she didn't want to go, that she had never had any intention of going, that Dominique had duped her as easily as Tab had sometimes tricked the twins, or Charles Junior, into doing her bidding. She stayed where she was, her head cradled in the elbow of her arm, goose bumps rising on the back of her neck, a knot forming in her stomach. The bus trundled on down the mountain road, the sun rising behind them.

CHAPTER 28

The Sit-in

*E*VENTUALLY, REVEREND CALDER looked in the rearview mirror and saw his daughter. The others had not. He didn't stop suddenly. They were still coming off a steep grade. There were still curves ahead, thin and winding. He didn't say anything to the others. He waited until he found a place to pull over, yank up the hand brake, and turn off the engine.

"I see we have a stowaway." He talked into the mirror. The others looked at him—some still half-asleep, others immediately aware—and then at the mirror and then to the back of the bus. His voice had not been antagonistic. It was proud, almost as if he had stopped the bus to show her off. "Fervor for a cause must be tempered with reason." He still talked to the mirror. "Although I admire your conviction, I am somewhat at odds with your methods. If you had wanted to come, you should have asked me." He was not jeering at her. He was like the parent whose child had hit a home run in Little League: too modest to brag, but aware of what was obvious to all.

The others were shaking their heads, some smiling to boot. One or two were not so sure. "She's too young,"

one of them said. "She could get us in trouble," another
one said, and they all took a moment before that became very funny.

"You wouldn't have let me come if I had talked to
you," she said, her voice loud from that distance.

"No, I wouldn't have." He sat drumming his fingers
on the steering wheel and checking the side mirror for
traffic coming down the mountain. "Well, what's done is
done. I suppose you must have a baptism of fire one of
these days, since we have chosen this rather arduous
path and will continue on it for some time."

"There's more than one." She blurted it out, blunt as
a rusty knife.

Now he twisted in his seat as Dominique poked Tab
with her elbow. She rose slowly. The others turned
around to look. "THE LORD, IT'S LITTLE TAB. YOUR
AUNT KNOW YOU COMING WITH US? IF SHE
DON'T, GONNA BE THE DEVIL TO PAY."

"Of course she knows, Mr. Spivey." Dominique lied in
such an offhanded way, Tab thought for a moment she
might really have asked Aunt Eugenia's permission.

"Most of the time I am admiring of your leadership
abilities, Dominique, but this—this is too much." But
from the tone of Reverend Calder's voice, it was another
accolade for her. She was leading and her sheep were
following. "Come forward, Tab," and when she hesitated, he added, "Come along now." She stood up,
brushing the felt skirt so the poodle would stand
straight. They were all watching her, staring at her as if
she were some strange sight they had never seen before.
In the meetings and at mealtimes, they had given her
passing glances, maybe said hi as they came and went.
Now she thought they were seeing her for the first time.

She slipped her purse over her arm, clasped her hands together, and walked slowly up the aisle. She had been a junior bridesmaid in a cousin's wedding the summer before last. It was the same walk, the same positioning of the hands. Not since that wedding had so many people looked at her with such high expectations.

She wasn't halfway up the aisle before one of the students declared, "I say she stays. Anyone dedicated to the cause has a right to prove it."

"Still too young," another one said.

"She's dressed nice enough," a black girl said. Tab realized that they were all black except for one boy, the white lifeguard, and her thought was that now Tina would know the whole thing. She stopped at the edge of them—they were all bunched up in the front seats. Dominique's father motioned for her to come forward all the way to him.

"I've seen you sitting at the edge of our morning meetings with Dominique. You know what you're getting into by virtue of being at those meetings, don't you?"

She kept her flower-girl pose and nodded her head, but of course she didn't remember a thing about the meetings. Half the time, she had played tic-tac-toe with Dominique. The other half, they had played battleship. And sometimes she hadn't even been there. She and Dominique had been swimming or playing Ping-Pong instead, but Dominique's father had seen them there every time, soaking up every bit of it, every bit of his rhetoric, every bit of the cause. He had seen them as dedicated, as caring. In other words, he had not seen them at all; certainly he had not seen her.

But here on the side of the road in an old school bus that was halfway to Nashville, she couldn't cry or run away or say that she had only the haziest idea of what he was talking about. All her options were gone, and she realized Dominique had known they would be. She turned to look back at Dominique, whose hands were folded, her smile a smirk. Tab turned back to Dominique's father and said the only thing left to say. "Yes, sir. I know what I'm getting into from going to the meetings."

"It's either take her with us or take her back," one of them said.

"We can't go back. We told the others we would meet them before the store opened," another one said.

"WE COULD LEAVE HER IN THE BUS."

"Look at her, all dressed up to come with us. There's not going to be any trouble at this Woolworth's—hasn't been since we started. They close the counter when we sit down, and that's that. We stay an hour and then leave. Let her go with us," said Dora, the student from Fisk.

Reverend Calder told Tab to go back and sit down. He would think about it as they drove on in to Nashville. They were definitely not going back. There were claps and cheers from the rest of the bus. Tab turned on her heel and marched back up the aisle to sit next to Dominique and stare straight ahead. "You got me into this."

"I knew you'd want to come," Dominique said. She smiled out the window, seeing the grocer at the store down the street where she lived in Connecticut. He was piling groceries into her mother's cart, glancing up at Dominique, who must have been all of five years old. "You baby-sitting for the maid?" He put a box of Tide down beside her and rubbed her head. "Cute little pickaninny." And Dominique had pointed. "She's my mother."

"Sure, kid." He had smiled and winked at her mother,

and her mother had said nothing, had pushed the cart
out the door and said nothing.

———•———

The bus pulled up across the street from Woolworth's. It was still early and there was no traffic. It
looked much like the Woolworth's in Bainbridge. Even
the displays in the windows looked familiar: sets of
plastic bowls, Kewpie dolls, school supplies, lunch boxes,
and summer kites. It gave Tab a feeling of comfort. This
was the same store, just a different town. Whereas before
she had been happy at the thought of being left in the
bus, now she was anxious to go with the others. She
could almost taste the hot dog. Reverend Calder had
turned off the engine. He was talking in low tones to the
others, intermittently glancing back at her.

"How old are you, Tab?" one of them called back to
her.

"Sixteen," she replied.

"Sixteen? You aren't any more sixteen."

"I will be—in a few years."

"You know what you're suppose to do when we get in
there, don't you?" Dominique asked.

"I know as much as you do."

"I doubt that. You'll never know as much as I do.
Were you listening at all when they were discussing it,
how to be nonviolent?"

"As much as you were. Besides, why do you care? You
got me in this just so you could have a laugh." They saw
three cars pull up behind them and park.

"I thought so. You're supposed to keep your cool, not
talk back, just sit there quietly. Got that? If they let you
go in, that's what you're supposed to do. No matter what
they do, you're supposed to sit there and take it and take
it and take it and—"

"Oh shut up. I got the picture." But she knew they wouldn't think about bothering her or haranguing her in Woolworth's. She was half-listening to Dominique and at the same time watching the colored people who had just parked get out of their cars, the men in ties and suits, the women in heels and dresses, hats and gloves. Ridiculous to get that dressed up to go to Woolworth's, no matter what they were trying to prove. One of them came on the bus. Again there was talk and glancing back at her.

They saw the manager of Woolworth's arrive and open the double doors on one side of the store. He went inside and locked them behind him, all the while glancing at their bus and shaking his head. This had been going on for two days now.

"Probably gone in to call the cops," Dominique said.

"If he has, I hope you're the first one they get."

Reverend Calder walked back to them. "You're in luck, Tab. Not enough people are here to fill the counter seats, so we need you. You're going in with us. I can't leave you in the bus by yourself and we'll only be in there a short time, until we're relieved by another group that will take our place." He smiled before he turned back down the aisle. "Now, aren't you two glad you made up after that ruckus in the dining room?"

Tab started to say no, she was not glad, that she would be happy to stay in the bus and lie down on the floor so nobody would see her. Instead, she nodded and said nothing. She was remembering that there was a cousin of her mother's who lived in Nashville, wondering if he ever came to shop at this Woolworth's. She opened her purse and got out Aunt Eugenia's cat's-eye sunglasses and peered through them, watching as the manager of

Woolworth's came to the door and opened it for business.

———•———

Muted colors greeted them as they passed through Woolworth's swinging front door. A diffused light filtered in through the front windows. Stale cigarette smoke and the odor of yesterday's grilled cheese sandwiches hung in old air. This Woolworth's was like all the others she had ever been in—wood floors creaking underneath, a hint of Midnight in Paris as they filed past the cosmetics counter, candy piled behind glass cases smudged by wishful fingers. Just like home. Why was she here?

They took seats on the line of stools that ran the length of the lunch counter, settling in to looking at themselves in the mirror that covered the wall in front of them. Dominique was to her left, Mr. Spivey to her right. The mirror was almost covered over with signs advertising what was good about the place: COKES: 5 CENTS. MILK SHAKES: 25 CENTS. CHILI DOGS: 30 CENTS. No one was behind the counter. No one else was in the store. They sat quietly. She took a paper napkin out of its metal container and placed it on the counter in front of her. Habit.

A woman in a light green uniform pushed open the swinging door that led to the kitchen. "Breakfast ain't served. We ain't open 'til later."

"We'll wait," Reverend Calder said.

She disappeared back into the kitchen.

After awhile, they could hear sounds behind them and see in the mirror other customers coming in to shop or to gawk. Some stood off by the candy counter and watched. Others edged closer. Tab sat with her sunglasses on, her hands in her lap, gripping purse straps.

Why in the world was she here, alone with all these people she didn't know?

If she were back at Highlander, she would be getting up and going to breakfast now. She tried to concentrate on things other than the images in the mirror, the ones from out in the store, images that seemed to be coming closer to her, looking intently at her.

On the counter opposite them, silver milk-shake mixers caught the light and mirrored the overhead fans that circled slowly. She knew what was underneath each one of the square metal tops that lined the space next to the mixers: red cherries, nuts, crushed pineapple, strawberry sauce, caramel sauce, and finally chocolate sauce—a bigger lid for that one. The kind of ice cream didn't make that much difference; it was the topping that mattered. "Mr. Spivey," she whispered. She had forgotten they were supposed to remain silent. "Ever had caramel and strawberry mixed together on top of chocolate ice cream?" He looked at her and shook his head because he couldn't hear her, and she realized it was just as well. He had never sat here before anyway, so he didn't even know what was beneath the silvery metal tops constantly wiped clean by the soda jerks and then lifted up with each new order, one scoop at a time, to be poured over the ice cream, something extra you could live without, because the ice cream was good enough, but you got something extra anyway.

She glanced up at the mirror. Dominique was frowning at her.

—•—

Half an hour passed. Half an hour of sitting there, not saying a word. All the while, more and more people were coming into the store. She noticed a blue blur back near the main entrance and looked again, letting her eyes focus on it. Policemen had come in, four of them, and they were standing there watching. The letters on their sleeves, the insignia on their caps—all reflected backward in the mirror.

She wished their time would be up. They obviously were not going to get chili dogs. Another group should relieve them soon, but she didn't see them. She didn't see one black face in the store except for her people.

A loud group of boys—some about her age, she judged from the mirror—had come in and were standing around the toy counter, pretending to test out some of the toys. One of them picked up a baby doll and turned it over and back again, the doll making a whining "Maaamaaa" sound. He wore a leather jacket and had sideburns like Elvis, and he smiled at her when he saw she was watching.

The waitress came out again to get some napkins and was turning to leave.

"We would like service."

"Well, you ain't getting none from me."

A black lady who worked in the back came to the door and stuck her head out.

"You a disgrace to the race." She was a nice-looking colored lady with a crisp white uniform, probably been working at this Woolworth's for years, and she thought they were wrong. She was the kind of colored person Tab knew—kind and caring and Christian. What had they gotten her into, the likes of Dominique and her father? The image in the mirror had on ridiculous-looking sunglasses.

Suddenly, Tab realized the boys at the toy counter had moved up closer, were spread out in a line behind all of them. Some older people were mixed in with them. One of them down the line, near Dominique's father, said, "Did you hear that? Even the coloreds think you ain't worth killing." One of the boys from the toy counter was almost touching her shoulder. She could smell tobacco and see the pack of Camels sticking out of the Elvis boy's jacket pocket.

She looked along the mirror. There were people in back of all of them now, three or four deep, laughing and calling out things to them, asking them where they came from, asking why they had come to this town. Why didn't they stay home in their own town if they wanted to cause trouble? Each remark seemed to give credence to another and then another, getting louder and louder. She noticed a girl standing in the crowd; she had on an angora collar like Tab's. Suddenly, one of the bystanders down the line picked a catsup bottle up off the counter, unscrewed the top, and began pouring catsup on Reverend Calder's head. Sounds of much laughter erupted from the crowd. The Elvis boy bent down and whispered something in Dominique's ear. Her expression never changed. Seeing no response in the mirror, he leaned over to Tab. "What's a white whore doing in amongst the niggers?" His next words, she had never heard before. No one had ever said words like that to her before. Who would? She wasn't even sure what they all meant, but she knew they were insulting, as every word he said was meant to insult. She wheeled around on the counter stool to hit him, was grabbing the top of her purse to whack him as hard as she could. Her arm was in the process of coming around when Dominique caught it and held fast.

The boys were delighted to get such a rise out of her, whooping and hollering to their friends. "This one done forgot she ain't supposed to do nothing."

Dominique was holding her arm suspended, hand

wrestling her in midair. Then she slammed it back in her lap and there was nothing Tab could do but sit there as her heart raced and tears rolled out from under the cat's-eye sunglasses. She might faint or she might start crying hysterically, but no one would help her no matter what she did, the black or the white, and the Elvis boy had grabbed a catsup bottle. She could be finished with breakfast by now, would probably be back in her room changing to go swimming. He was unscrewing the top.

She stared at the huge mirror as she might a Norman Rockwell or a Grandma Moses. *Home for Thanksgiving, The Country Fair,* or maybe this, *A Day at Woolworth's.* Rampant colors spilled onto the canvas. Red catsup, a blue dress, brown suits, a yellow necktie. The clapping white hands of the girls come to cheerlead, their matching sweater sets in pale pinks and blues, their pink lipstick lips, smiling. Bright red Coke signs on either end of the mirror, and in the background the blue blur of uniforms. Dark brown people seated at the counter dressed in their Sunday best, staring back at themselves. A gigantic wood frame held the mirror that reflected the image that captured the moment at the lunch counter of the Nashville Woolworth's in the morning hours of a new day.

She saw the sunlight on the water as they swam out to the floating dock. The catsup poured on her head, trickled onto the angora collar, dribbled down her sweater front. This is your fault, she was thinking. Why couldn't you be happy with us swimming in the lake? Why couldn't you be happy giving me a black eye, telling me I was past ignorant, not knowing what you know, *n'est-ce pas?*

The Elvis boy slammed the empty catsup bottle down on the countertop. The others laughed at the noise, at the catsup, at anything that humiliated. He took the pack of Camels out of his pocket and lit one. "That should do it." She watched the tobacco glow red and turn to a gray-white ash, which he deposited on top of her head. More laughter. She watched the glowing red center, knowing that he might get the idea, and he did—holding the end close to her face. "I think you need a tattoo to remember me by." She squeezed her eyes shut, waiting. She heard the voice of one of the girls doing what girls did, cajoling him out of it. "Now Dwayne honey, she ain't worth it."

He must have been sweet on her. He brought the cigarette back slowly away from her face and took a big drag. "Yeah, you're right." Instead, he put it out on the top of Dominique's hand, jamming it into the dark flesh that gripped the counter. She never moved. She shuddered, but she never moved her hand, never gave any other indication there was pain. Tab had been the only counter person to see. The others were too busy dealing with their own catsup, their own taunts. Tab thought she heard skin sizzle, and took faint pleasure.

"Teach you to go grabbing a white girl's arm," the Elvis boy said.

—•—

Replacements arrived, edging their way into the crowd until they were standing behind them to take their places. The crowd was renewed. Fresh meat.

Mr. Spivey helped Tab lift herself off the counter seat and walk out, most of her weight on his arm. She hoped she didn't look that foolish—catsup and tears. She tried to stand up straight, to look dignified like Dominique, who was walking out in front of them, stiff-backed, arms at her side.

They passed by the blue uniforms leaning up against

the candy counter. "Arrest 'em? Why arrest 'em? They got comeuppance enough." The gun belt scraped against the glass case that held the lemon drops. "What a mess. You wanta have catsup all over the patrol car?"

They were outside and climbing on the bus. Mr. Spivey let her down in a seat near the front. Dominique had gone straight to the back.

Somebody had brought paper towels. They were passing them out. No one was saying anything. Mr. Spivey tried to wipe away some of her catsup and then gave her extra towels and began on his own head and neck. He took off his red-streaked yellow tie and wadded it up, depositing it in his pocket. Silent minutes passed as they busied themselves with cleaning. She didn't look around to see where Dominique was. She didn't care.

They hadn't realized the bus had started. Reverend Calder was having a hard time pulling out. The patrol cars had parked too close in the front and he didn't dare touch a bumper in order to get out. He was slowly moving up and back, gaining inches of space with each try. When the front of the old Blue Bird finally pulled clear, it was their release. A cheer went up. They were free again, and everybody began talking at once. Relieved laughter broke out. Dora, the Fisk student, sitting in front of Tab, turned around and patted her on the knee. "You did good, girl." And then back to the others. "Did you see that white trash with the leather jacket trying to unnerve Tab here?"

"Did you hear them cops?" another one said. "Believe this catsup saved us from the pokey. Wasn't gonna mess up their patrol cars with catsup, much less niggers like us." The laughter was out of control, hilarious. People were holding on to the sides of the bus seats, trying to catch their breath.

"Thought for sure we was all going to jail when I saw them police come in."

"Lucky, we're lucky dogs. Had my toothbrush, ready to stay the night in the Nashville jail."

Tab wiped her hair. She was taking off her catsup-soaked angora collar when she realized the others had thought they would be going to jail, had thought they would most probably be spending the night in jail, and still Dominique hadn't warned her. She was sitting in the back, looking out the window. Catsup dribbling down her neck had settled into her Afro, making her head look flat and distorted. She held napkins in her hands but wasn't moving to use them.

"TAB DON'T SAY NOTHING. SHE JUST SIT THERE." Mr. Spivey was talking and laughing at the same time. They all were. The release of hours of anticipation and then the ordeal, and now everyone was edging toward hysterics.

"Didn't serve us, but they didn't serve nobody else." Bursts of laughter, slapping of shoulders, stomping of feet. "And we used up all the catsup supply." More laughter, loud and high-pitched, and Tab found herself doubled over, tears running down her face. The funniest thing she had ever heard. She looked back at Dominique sitting alone and laughed even harder. She felt euphoric, as if she had run some mighty race.

"I"—she had to catch her breath, "I, I felt like, like a hamburger." She could have said anything and they would have laughed, and they did, some rolling around in their seats with relief.

"At first, when I was sitting there, I coulda killed Dominique for tricking me into coming along."

More laughter. "Get outta here, girl."

"Yeah, I was sitting there thinking, I'm gonna kill you, Dominique."

"Go get her, girl, lying to you."

"Now, now that it's over, I feel great." She jumped up out of her seat and did a shuffle on the aisle floor. "We did it," she shouted, not really knowing what they had done, only feeling that they had been in some deep, dark place and had emerged victorious, vindicated.

The bus had stopped at a light. Reverend Calder put the gearshift in neutral and pulled the brake up before turning around and, in a low voice, "What do you mean she tricked you?"

Tab was standing in the aisle, still ecstatic about being out from under. "Oh nothing," smiling at her group and they back at her.

"No, you just said she tricked you. What did you mean by that?" Reverend Calder got up out of his seat slowly. The light was still red.

Embarrassed at her own ignorance now but feeling too much a part of them to try to hide it or somewhere in the back of her mind remembering how she had hated Dominique when she was sitting at the counter. "I"—she was grinning at them—"I didn't know we might go to jail."

The others were losing their smiles, knitting eyebrows.

"I didn't know I was gonna get catsup on my head."

Again, smiles. "Ain't that the truth."

"Dominique told me we would go in and order a hot dog and maybe get served or maybe not and that would be the end of it." She laughed at herself, shaking her head and inviting the others to do the same. The others were glancing at Reverend Calder and then back at Dominique. Tab was still explaining her naïveté. "It was all supposed to be over in just a little while. Can you imagine I thought that?"

"Is this true?" He had forgotten Tab. He was directing his attention to Dominique now, had stepped a few feet down the aisle, moving closer to her. "Is it true that you let this child come along not knowing what might happen, that she hadn't an idea we might all end up in jail?" He looked down at Tab. He was almost standing over her now. "Weren't you listening in the meetings? Didn't you pay attention?"

She tried to shrug her shoulders. "It's over now anyway. I'm fine now." And in a smaller voice: "Anyway, it's over."

A low, ominous tone from the back of the bus, "Just like you to say that—just like you, Tab." Dominique was braced up against the backseat, half-standing, her shoulders pressed against the window glass, her legs stiffened. "Just like you to say it's over when it's never over, like stepping in and out of the rain just when you please." She made a face in imitation of Tab and spoke with a flat southern twang. "It's ova, Raveren, and Ah kin go hame naya." She went limp, sinking back down into the seat and giggling. "It's ova, Raveren." Sweat had beaded on her forehead. She hugged herself, arms glistening with perspiration.

When she looked at them again, the face was menacing. She was the preacher she had seen him be so many times, shouting from the pulpit. "It's never over." The others were silent, looking at her. "You think it's over? It's never over." And now raging at them: *"It's never overrrr."* She pushed up out of her seat, walking toward them, holding out her fisted hand—the burn mark not that visible on her black skin, but Tab knew.

Her eyes were wild with searching, "You don't know that? You people, you people are so, *so stupid.*"

"*See this? Do you see this?*" She fanned her fingers and held her hand spread out to them. "He had a chance to do it to *her.* But he did it to *me.* He had a chance to do this to her." Her hand whipped back in and hit her chest. They could feel the sound, a dull thud, pushing air out. "But he did it—to me, to *me,* and she, she was sitting right there. Right there . . ." Her voice trailed off. She was up to Tab now and grabbed her shoulders, turning her around to face her father. "See this? See this? They had a chance to do it to this, but they did it to me." She pushed Tab forward into her father. Her voice tried to regain some normalcy, her eyes on the verge of spilling over. "I did like you wanted. Don't say you didn't want it."

"I didn't. You are mistaken, as usual."

She looked down at her hand, brought it to her lips in a long kiss, her chest stuttering in and out as if she were crying, but she wasn't crying.

Car horns were sounding from the rear. The light had gone green and red and green again. One of the students said, "Reverend, you want I should—" Reverend Calder waved him off. "I meant that you were a natural leader, that you had the best of both worlds," trying to explain, not necessarily to her. He looked around at the others. "I meant that she—"

"I know what you meant. You've said it every day since she left."

He tried to take her arm. She began backing away.

"Reverend, the cars behind us." The student eased past him, slipped in the driver's seat, let off the brake, and shifted into first. He inched forward and, to anyone who might know, "How do you get out of here? I'm not from around here." No one heard him.

Reverend Calder stepped forward again, pushing Tab aside. She fell back in Mr. Spivey's lap. Dominique's head was down, looking through furrowed eyebrows—cornered and daring him to come closer. "You didn't even see, did you?" She dangled her hand in front of him, trying to show what she had suffered, what he had missed, kept missing. She backed up and he came closer. "Don't touch me. Don't touch *meee*."

Each time he moved toward her, she stiffened and moved back, giving ground one bus seat at a time. Horns were blaring from outside. The new driver was getting impatient. "Where do I go?" he shouted at anybody. "Where in the hell do I go? We're gonna get arrested for a traffic violation if somebody doesn't help me." One of the other students got up and went forward to help. The older woman, Miss Wilma, stood and put a hand on Reverend Calder's shoulder. "Clarence, why don't you go on back up there and get us outta here. Lemme see what can I do about Dominique."

He jerked around and spit out at her, "Don't you see how she has it confused in her mind?"

"Sure I do, Clarence. Now why don't you go on back up to the front of the bus and help us get outta here. Else we gonna be in more trouble than before. Here"—she gestured to the others—"y'all take Reverend back up to the front." Two of the students came forward. He twisted his shoulders to loosen their hold, but Miss Wilma raised her eyebrows to them and their grip held. "Come on, Reverend. Hear those cars? They gonna have the police on us if we don't get outta here. We need you in the front."

"You see how she has it confused," he said back over his shoulder.

"Yes, sir, we see, sure do."

And Dominique was greatly amused, watching them pull him away, pointing her finger and laughing at him.

"Here baby, let me see to your hand. Didn't nobody know you was hurt. Let me see, baby." Dominique backed away like a child, whimpering and holding her hand cradled at her chest. Miss Wilma followed, but kindly, moving forward slowly. "Dora, bring me that thermos of water. We gonna clean Dominique's hand. Lemme see it, baby."

Now the bus moved forward with a purpose as Reverend Calder gave directions. The others were talking quietly among themselves, looking alternately up at Reverend Calder and back at Dominique, whispering their individual thoughts, the feeling of euphoria faded and gone.

Tab got up out of Mr. Spivey's lap and sat down in the seat across the aisle.

There was the sound of bus gears grinding forward as they picked up speed, and a small whimpering noise that could have been Dominique. She wouldn't turn to see.

CHAPTER 29

The Gift

*L*ORD, *WHAT* IS GOING ON up there in Nashville? Seem like peoples getting crazy and the police don't do nothing." Miss Laura clicked off the radio she and Maudie had been listening to while they washed Sunday dishes. "Nice to be here where everything quiet, everybody friendly. Don't know as I'd wanna get myself messed with, just so I could drink the white water."

Maudie and Miss Laura were the only ones left. Jessie had gone on back to his house. JD was out in the yard, playing. "Let's us sit out on the porch awhile." Miss Laura folded the damp dishcloth and hung it on the peg by the window. "Usually a good afternoon breeze by this time."

She followed Miss Laura outside, taking a seat in the swing at the end of the porch. Miss Laura sat in the metal lawn chair she preferred and picked up a cardboard fan to encourage the breeze. Maudie used her crutch to give herself a push. The scent of petunias, red, white, and pink, cascading out of the coffee cans drifted around them. Off in the distance, the noise of a car as it crested the hill. "You sure Jessie wants us out here in the front where everybody can see me?"

"Aw pshaw, don't pay Jessie no mind. His bark worse than his bite. Besides, that was when you first come and Jessie didn't know you." She waved as the car passed by the front yard. "Now I think he's getting so he's partial to you, going to voting school and all."

They both sat in silence, breathing in the day. A hawk circled up over the pastures that spread out across the road. Another car passed and scattered rust-colored dust up on the black-eyed Susans at the road's edge. They could hear JD out back, playing soldier, swinging from the rope attached to the hayloft pulley.

"You know, I remember talking to your aunt Carrie before she pass. Say you was in that polio place down there in Tuskegee for a long time. Say something 'bout you must be on the right side of the Lord on account of you surviving all that polio business and a big storm to boot. Say they was even some folks killed in that storm." Aunt Laura looked at Maudie and, getting no response, turned her attention to the scenery.

"I was lucky."

"That right?" Aunt Laura searched the pasture again. "Look at them crows after that hawk. Must be after a nest of eggs." She pointed her fan.

Maudie continued sitting there, but suddenly her heart was pounding. She was hearing the howl of the night wind in Tuskegee. People were yelling, glass was flying. Nurse Betty was calling to her; Yolanda was begging. Just as suddenly, she was watching the crows again. She said, in what she hoped was a normal tone, "Yes, there was an acquaintance, a little girl named Yolanda. She didn't survive."

"Oh my, didn't know 'bout that." Aunt Laura had stopped fanning and was looking at her.

"Well, as I said, she was just an acquaintance, not kin. I suppose I need to be leaving now."

Miss Laura looked at her watch and said probably she should.

—•—

Maudie liked walking home this time of the day, when she could take her leisure and watch the goings-on along the way. She waved to a passing car as she started out on the dirt road that sloped down all the way to the church driveway. Boys in the passing car whistled at her. It had happened the last time she had walked on the road. She had started wearing formfitting dresses, had taken them up to reveal more of her figure, and she had started styling her hair so that it fell down loose and soft around her face. For the first time, she had noticed the men in church watching her. Perhaps it had happened before, but she had not noticed it, and so for her, it had not happened. She was beginning to believe she might be pretty.

When she got within seeing distance of the back of the church, she noticed Jessie's car parked in the drive. Just as she turned off the main road onto the church path, she saw him standing there watching her as she found good footing on the gravel drive. He had a hammer in his hand and smiled as she came closer. He seemed more ready to do that now, to smile at her instead of fixing her with a blank stare.

"What is it?"

"Thought Aunt Laura was gonna keep you all afternoon. Told her to keep you, but not all day."

"Keep me for what?"

Just then, she noticed Mr. Calvin and Roy Boy. Mr. Calvin's car was parked over near the trees, out of the way. They stood at the back of the church building, waiting for her. "'Bout time."

"What are y'all doing here?" She came around to the backyard. They parted to let her see the wooden swing sitting at the edge of the clearing, in between the woods and her garden. It hung from chains attached to a two-by-four they had nailed high between two pines.

"Where did that come from?"

They didn't say anything, just smiled at her, until they all began to talk at once and then all stopped at once. Jessie rubbed his hands on the sides of his jeans, looking to her like JD up to mischief. "Mr. Calvin bought the wood. I built it."

"What's you mean, *you* built it? We built it," Calvin said. He cocked his head toward Roy Boy. "Ain't we been sitting here all afternoon handing him nails?"

"Sho have."

"Is it for me?"

"Well, it ain't for Reverend Earl. He don't stay put long enough to sit, much less swing."

"We knowed how you partial to swinging," Mr. Calvin said. "Now you can sit out here looking at what you be calling a garden."

"All day, hoping something gonna grow," Roy Boy said.

They stood there shuffling feet in the dust, looking first at the swing and then back at her. Jessie said, "Well, go on, take a seat." They watched as she slowly moved to the swing, stood in front of it, and pulled on the chains. "Told you it was steady."

"She ain't no fool," Mr. Calvin said. "She knowed who put it together."

Maudie turned around to look at them standing there grinning and she tried to say something, but nothing came, so she sat down and used her crutch to push off. "It's lovely," she finally managed to say.

Mr. Calvin went to the car and brought back a Coke for her and a glass jar in a paper sack. "Now I guess we can get to celebrating. Been meaning to bring this out all afternoon, but old Jessie here afraid Brother Earl gonna show up." He handed the Coke to Maudie and passed the paper sack around.

"Brother Earl liable to be the one drink the most if he do show up," Jessie said, taking a full swallow.

"That's what I'm saying." Mr. Calvin winked at Roy Boy. "Reverend Earl show up and won't be none left for us workers. You ain't saying much, Miss Maudie."

"Did Miss Laura know all along what y'all were doing? Did she suggest it?"

"What's you talking? We done thought of it by ourselves." Mr. Calvin got the bottle again and took a big drink. Roy Boy held out his hand for another. "Naw, you gotta drive. Gotta get me back in time for prayer meeting." He handed the jar to Jessie and then took one more drink himself before he screwed the top back on and got up. "Come on, Roy Boy."

"I was thinking I might stay on," Roy Boy said. "I ain't got to be back for no prayer meeting."

Mr. Calvin was halfway to the car and didn't even turn around. "Get on out here, boy. We late as it is."

Roy Boy moved a step toward Maudie. She looked up, waiting for him to say something, but he just stood there and then turned to follow Calvin to the car. "The name give to me is Roy, just Roy," he called after Mr. Calvin. "And much obliged if you'd remember it now and again."

"Thank you," she called to them, "thanks."

—•—

Maudie sat swinging and watching Jessie gather up his tools. He placed them all in the metal box he had brought down for the job and then began cleaning up the surrounding area. Shadows from the church had stretched almost to the swing. The sun was down to the tops of the trees that lined the road above the church.

"Used to call him Roy," he said. "Worked in the pouring room, like everybody else. One of the best they was, 'til it happened." He picked up stray wood chips left over from making the swing. "I seen it," and pitched a handful of chips into the woods. "Didn't turn in time. One of them casting molds caught him upside the head. Bleeding like a stuck pig, and then some melted iron splash out on his back." Jessie's body jerked in a shudder. "Still remember that yell he let out." He stooped down to pick up more wood chips. "Just one wrong look, one minute looking the wrong way. I seen it coming. I was gonna yell, but it done caught him by that time.

"I picked him up—didn't want to—run out the door with him, me yelling to everybody. When I let loose of him to put him in the car for the hospital, skin from his back come off on my arm. Big pieces of it just stuck to my arm and come off." He took the rest of the wood chips and sailed them out into the woods. Then he came to take a seat beside her. "He always saying someday he's coming back to the pouring room, but we always say, 'Roy Boy, you done done your time.'" He sat down with her as the light disappeared from over the hill and cricket sounds came up around them.

She swung back and forth for several minutes before asking, "Did you ever build Carlie a swing?"

"Carlie? What she want with a swing? Lord girl, you

wanna make me out the fool? Carlie wouldn't never stop dogging me if I did that."

There was silence again, only the creak of the swing.

"Y'all go to the same high school? Is that how you met?"

"Didn't go to no high school. Been working in the fields ten years by high school. Carlie asked me to take her to the movies. Said I was more a man than them high school boys." He turned to her. "You know how that make me feel, going with a high school girl and me not getting past first grade?"

"I guess that was nice." She looked down and watched the dust rise in little clumps as she pushed off with her crutch. "I guess it was."

"Hell yes it was, and when she say she want to get married, wasn't nothing else to do." He was still looking out at the garden. "I wasn't no fool. Worked at the foundry by then. All them men coming round, slapping me on the back, saying how lucky I was, 'cause she so pretty." His elbow rested on the arm of the swing and he rubbed his chin. "I wasn't gonna be no fool," he said again, almost to himself. "I didn't marry Carlie, peoples gonna go to saying I got a little too much sugar in me."

—•—

In the coming dusk, the shadow of the church building stretched out over them. Tree frogs joined the cicadas' whine and lightning bugs left tiny sparks in the air. She felt so relaxed, sitting there with him, almost sleepy, except for the touch of his shoulder against hers. Until now, she had never trusted her thoughts to anyone else.

It was deep dark when she began telling him about the night she killed Yolanda.

CHAPTER 30

Yolanda

*E*VEN AS SHE HAD USED HER CRUTCH to hold open the door of the Tuskegee library, she could feel it coming, had lived too long in north Alabama not to know the signs of a tornado.

That day, she had made the trip to the library, pretending to get a book to read to Yolanda, but really it was to get away from her. The doctor had come again the night before. Each time, it would take longer for him to clear Yolanda's breathing. There were horrible gurgling noises, as if she might be drowning. Maudie could hear her little body heaving in panic. She would sit on her own bed, trying to breathe for her, feeling as if she might be drowning with her.

Each time, after the doctors and nurses had left, she would go to Yolanda. "We still off to California, ain't we?" she'd ask, and Yolanda would try to smile. Her eyes had become dull black marks.

"Tell—me," Yolanda would say, and Maudie would begin to talk, telling her about California, about what they would do when they lived there; about how they would go to the Piggly Wiggly, because Yolanda would be out of the iron lung for an hour or two each day by then.

They would load their cart with milk and Snickers and Life Savers, because Yolanda would have to drink milk to regain her strength, but she could always have a candy bar with it. They would pass John Wayne shopping in the meat department, because men liked to get the best cut of meat, and Susan Hayward's housekeeper would be in front of them in the checkout line, because lady stars didn't go shopping in person, not like the men. And they would go to the beach. There must be a beach out there someplace. She had seen photographs of the stars standing on the sand, holding beach balls. Rock Hudson might throw them a ball, if they happened to be out there at the same time he was, if he didn't have anybody else to throw it to. Maudie had talked on and on, spinning tales until her head ached, and still Yolanda would be looking up at her asking for more. "Tell—me." Only one word at a time now. "We'll—go—together?"

"What's you think, Yolanda? I'm gonna let you get out there 'fore I do? You crazy, girl." And that would elicit a faint smile.

The night before the storm it had been the same thing. But afterward, Yolanda had stared dull-eyed at Maudie and said to her, "No—more." And Maudie had first thought she meant she wanted no more stories about California.

—•—

A delightful breeze, way too perfect to be up to any good, had drifted past her into the library's front hall. That was when she took a long look out over the library grounds and noticed the birds were silent in the trees and no squirrels darted about on the lawn.

She rushed back, her crutch chafing under her arm, and hurried over to take the elevator to the second floor. She saw the nurses laughing if she tried to warn them.

Wind blew in through the elevator door as it closed. When she walked into their room, she could see the dark cloud out the window, off at a distance, around the western edge of the campus. "Think we gonna have some rain maybe."

Doreen had glanced up and then turned a page of the magazine she was reading. "Well, don't say nothing. You get Yolanda and Macy all het up."

Maudie watched the children in the yard below being ushered inside, some in wheelchairs, most on crutches, a slow procession. She could hear the attendants beginning to call to them to hurry before the rain came.

Yolanda looked out from her mirror. "Rain?"

Maudie didn't answer. She could hear it now, a faint, steady sound in the distance, barely discernible, a background to all the other noises around her. If she hadn't heard it before, she wouldn't have known.

Minutes later, it was there in full rage, coming front and center, blocking out everything else. The wind picked up to a tearing force. Small hail began to ping the windows. A massive flash of lightning swept away all the shadows in the room. Seconds later, the matching crash of thunder shook the building and knocked out all the electricity. The iron lungs sputtered to a standstill.

Doreen had put down her magazine and stared at Maudie.

The wind was banging to be let in. The hail had grown huge and was threatening to shatter the window glass. A branch on the pine tree just outside broke off and came crashing through their window, sending glass and splintered wood across the room. Maudie watched the funnel cloud dipping down, then back up into its body, then back down for good, a whirling, churning drill, gouging out a path on the ground, headed straight for them. She didn't remember hearing anything else. Maybe Yolanda was calling her. Maybe Doreen and Macy. She was too taken with what was happening. She couldn't do both at the same time—watch and realize.

She felt her bed roll over toward Yolanda and crash into her iron lung. She saw Doreen's bed slide past hers. A large piece of rusted tin roofing swept through the open window and knocked her back across the room, and then everything went black.

When she regained her senses, the roar was drifting away, but rain still poured in the windows, dumping out what was left. She came to, sitting on the floor. She could hear large pieces of what sounded like board being carried or dragged. Beds were being pushed around. Nurse Betty's voice and other nurses' voices could be heard from downstairs as they shouted to one another.

She looked down at her hand. There was blood and a long gash running the length of her forearm. From where she lay on the floor, metal bed legs and the frames of iron lungs loomed quietly above her. No one else seemed to be in the room. Pillows were scattered on the floor; sheets were hanging off mattresses. She began inching toward the lung she thought was Yolanda's. Still the shouts came from downstairs as she crawled over to lift herself up, holding on to Yolanda's frame. She pulled up near her head. Yolanda was still there, her eyes closed, one blue ribbon left in her hair. "Yolanda?" she whispered. "You hear me, Yolanda?" Her eyes fluttered but didn't open.

"NURSE BETTY, GET ON UP HERE." She worked her way back to the other end of the iron lung, pulling along the sides until she reached the back, and then began to engage the hand pump, trying to imitate what she had seen the nurses do before whenever the electricity had gone off. She hadn't thought of anything then except to save Yolanda.

"NURSE BETTY," she screamed again. "Old Nurse Betty be here soon enough. Don't you worry none, Yolanda." She screamed again and peered to the other end of the lung, trying to see Yolanda's head, looking for any sign. There was only silence and muffled shouts from below. She pumped furiously, trying to imitate the compressions the iron lung would give if there were electricity. A curtain rod on one of the front windows gave way at one end and swung down, creaking as it dangled back and forth on its remaining brace before the whole thing fell to the floor, clanging itself to a standstill. Maudie stopped pumping and edged back up to the other end. "Yolanda? You hear me?" Yolanda opened her eyes. It wasn't a frightened look. She was staring at Maudie as if she was trying to say something. It was then that Maudie thought maybe God was trying to tell her what to do. Maybe He had sent down this great storm as a sign of what she should do. All that was left for Yolanda were nights of suffering, days of hanging on.

She bent down, brushed back the black curls, and kissed Yolanda's forehead. "Yolanda girl, you gonna go on to California without me. You gonna beat me getting there." She patted her head. "But don't go bragging about it, you hear me?" She thought she saw the slightest smile on Yolanda's face. She wasn't sure what she saw, but after that, there was no thought of ever going back to pump.

—•—

Nurse Betty finally did come. She and the maintenance man had found a ladder, braced it against the window frame, and Nurse Betty had crawled up to the second floor through the rain and what was left of the wind and come into the room, stepping over the jagged rain-dripping pieces of glass left in the windowsill, a stetho-scope around her neck.

Maudie remembered now what a fool she must have looked like screaming at Nurse Betty, swearing at her for taking so long, using the scattered beds and chairs to lean on, sometimes crawling, as she made her way over to get the gold braid out from under her mattress, yelling for Nurse Betty to do something and yet knowing there was nothing to do—Maudie had made sure of that—and then coming back to put the braids in Yolanda's hair. And all the while, Nurse Betty not saying a word, just watching as she wrapped the black tubing of her stethoscope around its metal earpieces, stuck it in her pocket, and moved on to the next person.

—•—

She had said all this to him as they sat there in the swing, the dark all around them and so making it easier to see what had happened. She wasn't sorry, she said. Yolanda was breathing easy now. It was the first time she had remembered she had done that with the drapery braids. Did he think she did that because she felt guilty for killing Yolanda or did she do that because she loved Yolanda?

He had been leaning forward, his elbows resting on his knees, looking out at the night and listening to her story. He had felt so much love for her that he had wanted to stand up and pull her to him, but he knew it wasn't about his love. Instead, he leaned back against the swing, letting his shoulder touch hers. "It was 'cause you loved her. You do for the ones you love," he said.

CHAPTER 31

The Cross Thing

*T*HE *BAINBRIDGE DAILY* had endorsed Brad La Forte for governor. Several volunteers who had been working for A.W. dropped by La Forte headquarters and said they were switching sides. James Mitchell, president of the bank, said he was voting for La Forte. It was about time the business community took note of the economic impact of the segregation thing, he said. People weren't aware of it, but there was money in the black community. Recently, he said, he had been made aware of that.

Most noticeably, Sunday dinners were beginning to fray at the edges. There was silence at the table, only the clicking of silverware, the tinkling of ice in tea glasses. Ora Lee cracked the swinging door from the kitchen to peek out and then let it ease back shut without bringing more biscuits.

Mary felt some small obligation to converse before she and Charles had to leave. As soon as they could get away, they were going to head down to the campaign office. There would be a group stuffing envelopes this afternoon, mostly Episcopalians and Presbyterians, a few Methodists. On a Sunday, they had not asked Baptists or Church of Christ members. Time was running short.

Every hour, every minute seemed to count now. At least that's how they were beginning to feel—an urgency that hadn't been there when there hadn't been a chance. A paper over in Huntsville had endorsed La Forte on Friday. Each time something like that happened, it sent Charles into a panic.

"Did I tell you," Mary said, "that we got another letter from Tab and Tina yesterday?" She directed her question to Miss Hattie's end of the table. The other end was in no mood for small talk.

Miss Hattie tried to go along. "Oh really. Is everybody still having a wonderful time, like I knew they would?"

Nobody else said anything. Tom shook the ice in his empty glass and Helen reached around behind her to the huntboard and retrieved the pitcher.

"Yes," Mary said, going on without them, "seems Tab has a friend who speaks French and won't tell her what she's saying." Now she looked to Helen, who was not a traitor and only smiled, going immediately back to her fried chicken.

Tom had had enough, as it never took much for Tom to have enough. The glass of iced tea sat down stridently in its coaster. "You know what you're doing, don't you? Splitting the vote. That's what the hell you're doing," he declared, forgoing apologies to the ladies for cussing in front of them. "You're splitting the damn vote, and that means Wallace is a shoo-in." He looked at Charles and tried to cover an almost evil grin by taking a drink of tea.

Mary had put a hand on Charles's knee, but she couldn't contain him. "That's absolutely hogwash, Tom, and you know it. A. W. Ladd never had a chance—will never have one, not if he runs for the next twenty-seven years in a row."

"'Hogwash'?" Mary said. "Charles, you sound like

you're running for dogcatcher." They stared at each other and both started laughing.

This only gave Tom cause. "You can both sit there and laugh if you want to, but A. W. Ladd was a viable candidate before y'all started all this nonsense with Brad La . . . *La Stupid.*"

Mary burst out laughing again. "Oh, very clever, Tom—as usual." She hadn't meant to say it, and immediately she added, "Sorry, I didn't mean that."

"I hope to goodness you did not mean that." Helen was pointing her drumstick at Mary, as Tom was not allowed to answer an insult from a woman and, in addition, was probably not aware he had been insulted.

Miss Hattie picked up the dinner bell and rang loudly, adding her own voice. "More biscuits, Ora Lee. Hurry on now." Ora Lee eased open the kitchen door, bored with all of them. She came to hold the bread basket in front of Mr. Ben.

"I do think y'all will like this second batch," Miss Hattie said, "sweet-potato biscuits, a new recipe Bessie Turner gave me last week at missionary meeting. And speaking of missionary meeting, Mary, you haven't been for the last three times."

"And . . ." Tom had not finished with them. "And think of how this looks to everybody else in town, you lining up with the rich Jew against your own people."

"Now listen here, Tom." Charles was halfway up out of his chair.

"*Enough!*" Mr. Ben had finally decided to enter the fray. He held his silverware on either side of his plate, his hands clinched into fists. Narrowed dark eyes glared out at them through wire-rimmed glasses. The whole room stopped eating, "I'll not have talk like that at my table. Are you forgetting we wouldn't even have a church to pray in if it hadn't been for the Rosensteins?" Mr. Ben settled back in his chair, easing into a more normal tone. "We don't forget our debts, no matter who, no matter what."

——•——

It was at about this point in the campaign that the cross thing happened. That's how everybody in the family referred to it, "the cross thing."

It was on a Thursday morning that Jimmy Vallen— every bit of fourteen and the neighborhood paperboy/town crier—rushed in the back door to tell about it. Mary was in the midst of making pancakes, a family treat, so everybody had come to breakfast on time. Charles was sitting at the table, glancing at the morning headlines, when Jimmy banged open the back door into the kitchen. Mary was flipping the last of the pancakes onto the platter. Evidently feeling she alone wasn't worthy of his news, he motioned for her to follow him as he walked straight through to the dining room to tell it to the head of the household and everyone else present—Charles Junior and the twins. He began without taking a breath, knowing that the moment they heard, they would be grateful for his coming. "I was the first one seen it, 'cause I'm the first one to be out and about in the morning, you know."

Charles calmly lowered his paper and, as if he had been expecting Jimmy for breakfast, said that, yes, he realized this because he remembered Jimmy had told him on numerous occasions that he had to get up at five o'clock every morning to be on time to pick up his papers and fold them before he could throw them.

Jimmy, because of his years of accumulated experience, was looked upon with great admiration, even awe, by Charles Junior and the twins. So if anything, they were honored to have Jimmy in their presence, even if they were sitting there in their pajamas. Mary had followed him in the room with a steaming plate of pancakes. The stage was set for his news.

"The way it happened was this," addressing Charles, although the others were welcome to listen. "I was riding my bike up Hawthorne, throwing all the while, nearly to the Trousdales', when I spotted it way up the block, still glowing and smoking." He paused, waiting for the question.

"What glowing and smoking?" Charles Junior obliged.

"It is not the biggest one I ever seen. That one is in the yard of First Baptist around Easter time, the one in the middle with the purple cloth draped around it where Jesus was hung, but this one's bigger than the ones on either side, where the thieves was nailed up."

"You saw a cross burning." Mary put down her pancakes.

"Yes, ma'am, right there on the front lawn of the Rosensteins' house, and nobody seen it but me—it being so early and all. I peddled straight away up there to have myself a look-see. Then I, quick as you can imagine, knocked on the Rosensteins' door to tell 'em about it, 'cause I knew they would still be asleep, them not getting up 'til eight o'clock."

Charles's attention to the cross was momentarily diverted by Jimmy's seemingly intimate knowledge of the sleeping habits of the Rosensteins. "How in the world do you know when the Rosensteins get up in the morning?"

Jimmy wasn't even challenged. "The kitchen lights is never on when I pass. The maid don't come walking down the street 'til eight-fifteen, when I'm finishing up my route. So anyway, he comes to the door after I knocked for seems like twenty minutes, hair all messed up and still in his bathrobe, and I say—handing him his paper, of course—was he aware somebody done burned a cross in his front yard?" Jimmy paused, having picked up the smell of the pancakes, and he looked at Mary and then at the empty seats that would have belonged to Tina and Tab had they been there.

"Would you care for some pancakes, Jimmy?"

"Don't mind if I do." And he was in a seat immediately, borrowing a napkin from Charles Junior and tying it around his neck. Mary passed him her plate and silverware and began to pass the pancake platter around the table. She sat down in her chair, glancing at Charles and waiting for the rest. Jimmy continued, while remembering his manners and waiting his turn. "And you know what he said? Looked out at the cross still smoldering away in his own front yard and he says, 'It's about time. I was beginning to feel all of our work was going for naught.'" He turned to Charles Junior, who was hanging on every word and holding the pancake platter. "*Naught* means zero—learned that in school." Then he forked three pancakes, took the platter from Charles Junior, and placed it on the table in front of him. "Would you pass me the syrup, little Charlie?"

"Not as big as the one at the First Baptist Church on Easter, you say?"

"No, sir." His mouth was full of pancake. "But nigh on to as big as the smaller ones."

"Was it burning full out when you saw it?"

"No, sir. Looked like it was just half-burned to begin with."

"And you say you were the first to see it? Nobody else was out there at the time?"

He paused to swallow, making sure that this fact was

clear to everyone present. "Yes, sir, the very first one. Not a soul out there before me." He took another big bite— as paper carrying is hard work. "Course, I did tell plenty others as I was finishing up my throwing."

"And did the rest of the family come out and see it?"

"Girls wasn't home—off at camp in Vermont."

"How did you— Never mind."

"Course, the wife seen it and she commenced to blubbering." By this time, his mouth was stuffed with pancake and he was fast losing interest in the subject. "My pa said I should come by here and tell you, you being such a pal of Mr. Rosenstein, going to high school together and all, working on the campaign together and all. Would you gimme that syrup bottle again, little Charlie?"

"Did you see any other signs in the yard or any markings on the cross?"

Jimmy shook his head, no.

"Why did you ask that?" inquired Mary. "Are there usually signs or markings?"

"If it's the Klan, more than likely there would be. I have a feeling that this is a prank that's emanated from the opposition—which one, I haven't a clue—just part of politics this day and time." Charles took a last sip of coffee and stood. "I better get over there. I'll call and let you know what's going on."

—•—

He called Mary when he got to the farm that afternoon. "By the time I got there, the police had arrived, along with most everybody on the block. They took pictures and asked a lot of questions—mostly perfunctory, I think. There's not much to go on. It was a rather pathetic-looking cross, as cross burnings go. Half-burned. Whoever it was didn't stay around to give it a good light.

"Was Reuben terribly upset?"

"That was the funny thing. I think he was delighted, as if, for the first time, someone was taking into account his liberal bent and the fact that he wasn't his father."

"What's this 'liberal bent' stuff, white man? We're in that same boat."

"Nobody would bother us. We're too much like them."

"Do I resent that? Should I resent that?" She laughed.

Charles laughed in turn. "Sometimes it's not all bad being able to hide in the forest with the rest of the trees.

"Reuben was a hoot. He was laughing and joking around with the neighbors. I've never seen him so chatty. Saying that it was not the quality of cross that one might get if one lived in south Alabama. In the Black Belt, they did themselves proud with their crosses. This, he said, was your typical north Alabama cross, too utilitarian, no imagination.

"Another funny thing. The neighbors came over, ready to offer condolences and he was having the maid serve iced tea on the lawn. I think some of the neighbors left thinking he was a little touched in the head."

"Well, I'll tell you something else strange. Your sister Helen? She called this morning, and of course she had heard about it. Actually had driven by to take a look. Said she thought it was so tacky to do such a thing, she might even vote for Brad, Cousin John Lester or no."

—•—

Two weeks later, they found the culprit. Not because of precision police work. The police had forgotten all about it and had gone on to other things. The culprit confessed. He was a schoolboy. Said he'd been buying a hot dog at the soda fountain at Woolworth's when the man sitting next to him had struck up a conversation and offered him fifty dollars to make a cross and place it on the Rosensteins' lawn, pour gasoline on it, and light it up. He had confessed because his father had found what was left of the fifty dollars and thought the boy had come by it in some illegal way and was about—according to the boy—to beat the tar out of him. But the boy said that there was nothing illegal about it at all. He had just been sitting at the counter, having a hot dog, and the old man sitting next to him had been having a big glass of sweet milk and had started talking to him and hired him to do a job. He didn't know why the man wanted it done, but it was the most money he had ever earned.

Paul Davis, down at the paper, ran the story, never mentioning A. W. Ladd's name, but using the exact words the boy had used. So everybody knew who was responsible, even if the police wouldn't conduct any further investigation and the other candidates wouldn't accuse any one person.

The result was—much to the delight of the La Forte campaign—that Brad La Forte began to pick up quite a few crossover votes from people shamed into leaving the A. W. Ladd camp.

Mr. Ben let it be known at Sunday dinner that the original Klan would never have done such a thing. Now he felt obligated to vote for Mr. La Forte, even though he might not agree with his politics.

CHAPTER 32

The Rising Tide

"*D*ID I MENTION that Brad called a couple of nights ago?" Charles was trying to be casual about it, trying to see if it sounded ridiculous coming out of his mouth. "Said if he was elected, he would seriously want to consider me for Conservation Commissioner, and asked if I was interested." Charles stopped to see if Reuben had any reaction that was discernible. There was none, so he continued. "Of course I said yes, but only if I could name a state park after myself."

Reuben smiled but didn't laugh. "Don't feel insulted by that. He's just trying to show you that he appreciates your support."

"Why should I feel insulted?"

"It's so demeaning, a political appointment, like a payoff. Probably a pittance of a salary, and you would have to travel down to Montgomery every time the legislature meets."

Charles didn't say anything, but since that phone call from the candidate, he had begun to see things in a new light. It had never occurred to him that he might be considered for a post of that caliber. Sure it was a political payoff, but somebody had to fill the position, and

Charles would do an honest job. Probably do it better than most.

After Brad had talked to him, he lay in bed the whole night, wide-awake, thinking of what that could mean to him, to his family, to the farm. He had watched Mary sleeping and had been afraid to mention it to her, to get her hopes up.

He wouldn't tell Reuben, but the yearly salary for that position was almost twice as much hard cash as he had ever cleared on the farm in a year.

People like Reuben looked at all the acreage, at all the workers swarming over the fields in the cotton season and they just naturally assumed. But it was large amounts of money in and large amounts out and not much left in the final reckoning.

Now, for the first time in years, that old feeling began to creep in. It had not been there for so long—since he had first come back to the farm. Now when he drove onto the property each morning, the whole place began to take on a dingy, worn-out look. The fields ill kept— the workers slow and undependable—and fences that he had overlooked before needed mending now. There was farm equipment that he now realized would have to be replaced in two or three more seasons, tractors and combines, which meant thousands upon thousands of dollars outlaid. Something he had not even wanted to think about before, because before there was no way of thinking about it.

As he drove onto the farm this morning, his truck automatically turned down the road to the springhouse. Could he be the one, would he have to be the one to break the line—the first one in over a hundred years to sell off the whole thing? The thought had never even entered his conscious mind. Now it could, because the additional thought had occurred to him that if the politics worked out like he wanted, he might be able to do both—keep the farm and make ends meet. He could look at everything more realistically now—now that there might be avenues of escape.

He would check the springhouse, the rest of the farm, and then leave to drive back into town to Bainbridge's La Forte for Governor campaign headquarters.

—•—

He never really had dreams—except for the Nat King Cole dream. That one, he would have every once in awhile. He never knew what triggered it. He would just wake up the next morning and tell Mary he had had the Nat King Cole dream. She would be brushing her hair or her teeth and would raise an eyebrow. "You Alabama good old boys," she would say.

And he would say, trying to keep the disgust out of it, "Don't put me in that category." She would rinse her mouth out or put down the brush and say, "Sorry." And that would be the end of it—for her, but not for him.

Many times during the day, he would see parts of the dream flash through his mind, negative pictures backlighted in an eerie blue, flashing before his eyes as if posed snapshots from his old Kodak Pony camera. It would begin with a picture of Mary and him, sitting in the audience of the Boutwell Auditorium in Birmingham. He had saved for six months so they could take this little weekend trip to Birmingham, a getaway, a surprise for Mary. She had been working as hard as he had since they'd come back to the farm. It had been hard for him, and he knew something about the farm life. She had known absolutely nothing about country living. She had been raised in the city, had had her own car by the time she was fourteen, had always had cooks to prepare all of her meals. She had been thrown into a situation where she had no indoor plumbing, not even any electricity for the first years, but she had stuck it out. Finally, they had moved to town and had the modern conveniences. It had never been easy, not with five children and so little money.

He had planned for them to stay at the Tutwiler, have breakfast in bed. He would tag along behind her while she shopped. They would eat at Ollie's Barbecue for lunch, and to top off the whole thing he had purchased tickets—and good seats—to the Nat King Cole concert that would be in Birmingham that weekend.

It had all gone according to plan. She had bought a hat at Loveman's. He had told her how cute she looked in it. The saleslady had been amused that a husband had come along shopping with his wife, rare indeed. They had scurried around to find a chair for him while Mary tried on one hat after another, and he had smiled his approval.

That night, they had had prime rib for dinner and key lime pie for dessert at The Club, courtesy of one of his farm friends, who was a member.

They had gotten to the auditorium in plenty of time to take their seats. She loved Nat King Cole, wanted especially to hear "Mona Lisa" and "Stardust." The audience had been full of college-age kids—up from the university in Tuscaloosa for the evening. Some had driven over from the college in Auburn. It had made him and Mary feel like kids again. They were smiling and holding hands.

The lights had dimmed; Nat King Cole had walked onstage to tremendous applause—standing ovations and cheering. They all loved Nat King Cole. He was a na-

tive son. He had launched into his first song. Charles
could never remember what that was. He was about to
sing his second song, "Mona Lisa." Charles remembered
that because the orchestra had been playing the introduction, lulling them into the wonderful mood. And
then suddenly, out of nowhere, three rednecks had
come rushing up onstage. For a split second, no one
knew what was happening. They grabbed Nat King Cole
and started beating him. Charles remembered seeing
one of them throw a punch to his stomach. The whole
audience was momentarily dumbstruck and then
screaming for somebody to do something. Police had
rushed onstage and dragged the white boys off. Nat King
Cole didn't appear to be terribly hurt. He had left the
stage. As they sat there with the rest of the audience, ab-
sorbing what had happened, Mary had become enraged.
Charles's stomach had tied itself in knots, feeling the
blows. The whole evening, the joy of the entire trip—all
was instantly washed away.

She had dropped his hand, had practically thrown it
back at him. "I can't believe you disgusting rednecks."
She had turned on him as if it were all his fault. "How
can you put up with people like that? Aren't you even
civilized down here?" The more she talked, the more
outraged she became. It turned into a tirade against
everything she had had to put up with since she had left
her home and come to live in his. People around them
were staring.

"My Lord, Mary. Do you think I'm responsible for
that? Do you think I would ever condone anything like
that? If it were up to me, nothing like that would ever
happen."

She didn't want to hear him. She kept on and on,

venting frustrations she must have felt for years. This weekend had been meant to soften those frustrations. It had, but by using Charles as the battering ram.

Eventually, Nat King Cole had come back onstage. They had all clapped, standing on chairs and cheering—shouts of "The show must go on." He had stood before them until the noise died down and then had said—not with malice, but in the most unassuming way—that he was an Alabama boy. He had just come to entertain them. Despite himself, tears had welled up in Charles's eyes when Nat King Cole said that—that he was an Alabama boy. Charles, whose whole life was anchored in a strip of land along the river to the north. He had imagined the disgrace of not being welcomed in your own homeland. Then Nat King Cole canceled the concert and walked off the stage. Some few in the audience, Mary included, had immediately clapped at his canceling the show. Others were still speechless at what had gone on.

Although they had planned to stay the night, they canceled their reservation, packed, and drove home. Mary had regained her equilibrium somewhat on the ride back and had apologized to him, had said she knew it wasn't his fault. She knew he had worked so hard to make it a perfect weekend.

Much later, they had even smiled when they remembered her outrage. It was so unlike her. But it had stayed with him, the Nat King Cole night. And lately it had been coming back more frequently: the punch in the stomach, the stringy, thin-faced rednecks thinking, in some grotesque world, that they were being heroes. Flashes of light illuminated the scenes one by one. He would wake breathing hard, sweat-soaked, and trying to sustain the thought that if it had been up to him, nothing like that would ever happen.

He knew the election was the thing that was making him revisit the Nat King Cole trip. Lately, he had been neglecting everything to work on the election.

CHAPTER 33

Izzy and Lou Ann

BY MIDSUMMER, four others had joined Maudie's voting school. Two were men from the foundry. They had heard Jessie say that they could learn how to write a check. They would come, missing a class now and then, more interested in knowledge acquired to help them in everyday living than the once-a-year ritual of voting. Maudie liked them, felt at ease with them. They followed her instructions without question.

The other two—Maudie had been astounded when they appeared—were Izzy and Lou Ann, the girls from the drive-in. One night, halfway through class, the front door had suddenly been flung open and in they swished, the aromas of Evening in Paris and Juicy Fruit swirling about them. Everyone stared, which didn't seem an unusual occurrence to them. They stared back.

"Miss Maudie done invited us to come, when we seen her at the drive-in with Carlie, so here we is." They stood for an instant in the shadows just outside the circle of light, waiting to see if that reasoning would fly, and in the drop-jawed moment Maudie gaped at them, they must have decided it was her acceptance and so proceeded to step closer, spiked heels finding every crack in the sanctuary floor. The men—grinning—looked from woman to women and back again, thinking they might be the ones designated to throw them out. Izzy and Lou Ann recognized the looks. "We a woman, just like she a woman. We got a right." And they settled themselves in front pews, stretching skirts down to decent levels.

Watching them, Maudie realized she needed every warm body she could muster for voting school, even if only lukewarm. She instructed them to take seats at one of the two tables that were now in the sanctuary. They jumped up, grinning, and proceeded to fuss over the chair next to Roy Boy. Izzy, being the stronger, won out. After she had jerked the chair away from Lou Ann, she went demure, crossing long, bony legs, adjusting a bra strap, smiling at Roy Boy. Lou Ann settled for a chair at the end of the table.

Maudie continued with the lesson, but for the remainder of class she had to talk over the constant smacking of Juicy Fruit. When class was finally over, she thought she must establish some ground rules, so she asked the girls to stay for a moment after the others had gone. There was a look of hesitation. "Can't stay if we wanna get a ride. Roy Boy say he—" Roy Boy said he and Mr. Calvin would wait on them in the car.

"Now there's one thing I don't allow in my class," she began, trying to say it with authority, in a way that wouldn't elicit smart remarks—of the drive-in variety. "It's about the Juicy Fruit."

Their eyes immediately turned bright, and Lou Ann said, "Ain't it something? Got it off a fellow we—" Izzy punched her. "Let's us just say it was give to us by a gentleman we done a favor to . . . for." The grins broadened into giggles, each poking the other.

"Never had none before," Lou Ann said. "Smell just

like perfume, don't it?" Suddenly, Izzy slapped her knee, realizing why they had been kept after school. "She be wanting a piece," she said to Lou Ann. "Look there in your purse, Lou Ann, see can we spare one." Lou Ann pulled the strings to open the top of an evening bag that had seen better days, remnants of fake-pearl stitching hanging off its sides.

"Got three left. We give you one."

Maudie stood holding the stick of Juicy Fruit as the girls waved bye and ran to catch their ride, sure now that they had bought their way into voting class—familiar as they were with bartering favors.

—•—

Later, Jessie held up his hands to ward off her suspicions. "Didn't have nothing to do with them girls coming. Told me they heard refreshments was served at the voting school."

"Well, who then? Carlie?"

"Now don't go bad-mouthing Carlie. They just cotton girls. Izzy and Lou Ann don't know nothing but the fields. Born and raised in the cotton fields. That's all they know."

"That's not all they know."

"Why, Miss Maudie, what's you talking, and you a schoolteacher."

"I think Carlie sent them."

"If she did, it'd be to get shed of 'em. Probably stay awhile, get bored and leave."

—•—

But they didn't leave. Izzy and Lou Ann said they believed it was time for them to get some schooling. Their calloused hands with the split, dirt-imbedded nails would grip the pencil each held, both trying mightily to imitate the others and sometimes succeeding. The men were tolerant, smiling at one another when Izzy and Lou Ann walked in late, talking and smelling loud. Sometimes, the class could hear a car pull away after dropping them off. Other times, the girls would stand holding on to the front door of the church, slipping back into their high heels before coming forward. When they couldn't get a ride, they walked to class barefooted. The cotton girls had found a new home.

—•—

Jessie had come early and put two plates of Miss Laura's cookies in the middle of the tables in the sanctuary. The members of the class had come to know one another enough that conversation was not stilted. Sitting in and on the edges of the spread of light from the naked bulbs, they talked and waited for Calvin and Roy Boy. Izzy and Lou Ann sat at the far end of the table, an empty chair between them. They took special care to have a place reserved for Mr. Calvin. They liked looking at Roy Boy, but they had heard tales of Mr. Calvin's bank money.

Roy Boy and Mr. Calvin arrived half an hour late. "We liable to commence without you." Jessie had taken it upon himself to chastise anyone who was late or who might start to doze off during class, no matter how hard their day had been. "Miss Maudie"—he had started calling her that in front of the others—"don't have no time to waste on people being late."

Maudie had been standing there with a copy of the voter-registration papers. She was trying to bring up the subject of registering—for a third time. "I heard on the news the other night that there's a man running for governor this time—against Wallace—a white man wants to treat everybody more equal, and if you registered to vote, then you might—"

There were immediate hoots and shaking of heads. "What rock you been hiding under, Miss Maudie?"

"Only white man I'd vote for done been crucified long time ago," one of the foundry men said.

"And if I recall correct," the other one added, "he wasn't laid low by no colored, neither."

She persisted. "They say he's from down in the middle of the state, near Tuscaloosa. If you had the vote—"

More hoots and laughter, "Oh, now you talking. Tuscaloosa got the biggest Ku Klux in the whole state. He probably the chief Klux."

And Izzy, "Thought this here was real school—didn't know it was no *fairy-tale school.*"

And Lou Ann, "You ain't nothing but right, girl."

Maudie glared at them but decided to let it drop, for now.

Mr. Calvin sat down. "Sorry we late. We was delivering the float paper by the courthouse. Boss give it to us when we was headed out the door, had to drive all the way back in town to drop it off."

One of the other foundry men leaned back in his chair—Ed, from up around Crossroads, who was married and had six children. "What kinda float we having this year? Old lady Peters gonna pretend she Miss America and fall off the thing again?" The other men began to snicker. "That white woman musta been drinking for two days 'fore she got up on that float."

"A parade?" Maudie asked.

"Parade at the end of the summer," Roy Boy said, "suppose to honor the working. Anybody can make up a float, and we all get off work to go watch. Got cotton candy, American flags all stuck up and down the lampposts, hot dogs for sale out on the street. Anybody can buy one and eat it."

"What did you mean, 'Anybody can make up a float'? Who enters?" She was looking down at the voter-registration papers. What if she sat here all summer and came away with one person having a bank account and the others only learning to read the signs at the drive-in?

"Oh Lord," Mr. Calvin said, "she gonna get us in trouble now." He reached over and took a cookie off the plate and pointed it at her. "I see that look in her eye. Done seen it the day we was at the bank and she start gathering up the money off the banking table."

"We could have a float sponsored by the voter-registration school."

"I told you she was gonna get us in trouble."

"He say anybody can make up floats," Jessie said. "Didn't say no *colored* anybody."

The cotton girls could immediately see the possibilities. "I could use me a ride on a float. Everybody get to ride?"

"How do you register to enter a float?"

"Got to go down and take one of them papers off the counter at the courthouse and fill it out and go back and drop it in the box," Roy Boy said. "Me and Mr. Calvin done it the past five, six years. It don't change. You get a parade number when you turn it in and pay five bucks. Then you bring in your float on the day of the parade, hand the number to the man, and he tell you where to line up."

"How'll they know what we're gonna do?" Maudie asked. "We just get a number and the day of the parade we show up—that's all?"

"If you pay the five dollars," Mr. Calvin said. "You get the number and show up—nothing to it."

All eyes turned to Mr. Calvin. He was not unhappy with his new reputation as a rich man, now that all his money was out of harm's way. He patted the knees of the cotton girls. "Well, all right then, long as y'all let me be the Miss America." The girls giggled, wiggled hips and hit on Mr. Calvin's shoulder.

Even as she had said it, Maudie was standing it up next to sit-ins in North Carolina, or Freedom rides in south Alabama—some kind of shabby homemade thing they might build. "We need to enter, since we haven't gotten around to registering anybody, and we don't have long to go before Izzy and Lou Ann have to start back picking. This'll be our voter-registration project." When they didn't say anything, she hurried on. "There's just one thing. We can't tell anybody we're doing this. Everybody will be coming round here minding our business, messing with our float.

"What you 'spect, we ain't gonna tell Reverend Earl, and the float sitting right here in the backyard?" Jessie said. "And peoples coming to church every Sunday?"

They all watched her, standing there staring at the obvious. She sat down in the nearest chair and picked up the registration papers, fingering them. "Okay, we'll tell everybody we're making something else. We're making a place behind the church to show people how to register. That's what the float really is anyway. People coming to register to vote, only we won't tell them it's going to end up being in the parade. We'll tell them it's just a model, a place to come see what it's like to vote."

—•—

The next week, Roy Boy brought the form to class. Mr. Calvin produced, with great flourish, the five-dollar bill needed to complete the entry.

"Wait till they see us riding down River Street. The

colored band marches, but they ain't never seen no colored float. Gonna be white floats all up and down and us in the middle. I'm gonna have a time waving to y'all up there," Roy Boy said.

"What's this 'waving at y'all' stuff? We're all going to be on it," Maudie said.

A silence fell across the room. The cotton girls looked sideways at Mr. Calvin. The reality of actually getting on the float was not as fun as imagining it. Jessie watched the pencil in his hand tapping the table.

Ed, from the foundry, spoke up. "This crazy. Where we gonna get a truck at? Where we gonna keep it while we get it ready?"

"Where we gonna get the money?"

"What money?" Maudie said. "We don't need money. We can use what we got—old barn boards, things like that—maybe spend a little for crepe paper."

They looked other places—out the window, down at the floor.

"Can't write no signs," Lou Ann mumbled.

"Ain't got no big paper," Izzy said.

"We can get poster paper. We can borrow a truck from somebody in the church. I can teach you how to do the signs." She hit the floor with her crutch. It only made them turn away more. She would evoke the one thing they would all have to heed. "I think the Lord gave us this chance," she said. "Here it is right in our laps."

"What if peoples start throwing things at us? Can't take no more hits on the head," Roy Boy said.

"What if peoples laugh at us?" Lou Ann said.

They were all looking at anything other than Maudie. She began to stack papers and pencils on the table. "All right, we'll think about it. Either you want to do it or not." She squared the pieces of paper until they were perfectly stacked, hoping for a response. "What I want to know is, what were you coming here for in the first place? Did you want to know how to read and count money and then be reading about where you can't go—be wishing you had money to count? Don't you wanna go to a bank and not be laughed at?" She slammed all the papers down and took her crutch from the back of the chair, surprised at how adamant she was about this. "Are y'all always going to be sitting behind the split-rail fence listening to—to somebody else's music?"

The foundry men looked at Jessie. "What she talking—a split-rail fence?"

"Don't pay her no mind. She talking crazy."

Maudie pulled up out of her chair, weary with prodding.

"Now just hold on here," Mr. Calvin said. "I think Sister Maudie got something here. The Lord done seen fit to visit this here on us. We be in a lot more trouble if we don't listen to what He say." Slowly, and for effect, he reached for his hat and rose up out of his chair. "Now here's my thinking. We gonna think about it, like Miss Maudie say, but come next week, I'm gonna come on back in here with this five-dollar bill to put down on the float papers." He winked at the cotton girls. "Might even pick y'all up some of that fancy colored paper while I'm at it." He glanced at Jessie before he walked out the door. "Come on, Roy Boy. Done all we gonna do tonight."

——•——

By that next Sunday, Reverend Earl had heard about it, or at least he had heard something about it, not quite all, but enough to take note during announcements.

"Hear tell they gonna be a model set up outside here, showing how to get registered to vote, compliments of our voter-registration school, sponsored by Word of Truth. Gonna show people how to go down to the courthouse and register. Think we should give a big hand to our voter-registration class and Miss Maudie."

There was curious applause.

"Matter a fact, hear they need a truckbed to build it on, and I'm gonna surprise 'em by saying right here and now I'm gonna lend mine to do the job."

More applause.

"Use it for hauling food round in the winter, but I can spare it for a time."

—•—

A guest at Miss Laura's table, Reverend Earl took down his Sunday dinner napkin. "Surprised you 'bout the truck."

"You coulda knocked me over with a feather," Aunt Laura said, and gave him the biggest piece of fried chicken off the platter. "I was wondering what they was gonna do for a place to put it."

"It was supposed to be a big secret." Maudie glared at Jessie.

"I done told him we was gonna build a voting exhibit, that's all."

"*That's all?* What do you mean, 'that's all'? That's a heap," Reverend Earl said. "Think you finally getting your feet wet, Sister Maudie. Just like I knew you would." He helped himself to collards. "Have people see what's it like if they go down to vote. Let 'em test it out. Ain't no use in rushing things. It'll come soon enough."

Jessie gave the corn bread to Maudie and winked. "Butter it while it's hot, girl."

CHAPTER 34

The Float

"THIS OLD HEAP OF JUNK won't even make it halfway to town." Roy Boy had his head stuck down under the hood of the preacher's truck. Brother Earl had brought it over the night before. "What Reverend mean, giving us a heap of junk like this?" Maudie was holding a flashlight for Roy Boy's look at the engine.

"It's because he thinks we ain't got a need to move it." Jessie closed his car door and walked over to them. "He thinks it don't matter if it runs or not—matter of fact, he told me he was taking the battery 'cause he knew we wouldn't need it."

"See, Jessie, we should have told him what we were up to." Maudie clicked off the light. "He would have helped."

"Maybe so, maybe not. Brother Earl funny 'bout things sometimes," Jessie said. "He like to be the one say when to gee and when to haw. When the ladies first say they want somebody like you down here, he flat set against it. Took him a long time to come round."

"And you were for it right off, were you?"

"Don't go messing with me, girl. I'm here, ain't I?"

It was decided that they would fix up the truck as a

surprise for Reverend Earl. "Besides," Roy Boy said. "What's Brother Earl gonna do 'bout it if we tell him the thing don't work? He ain't got the money to fix it up no way."

From the beginning, it became the gathering place for all of them. Maudie would sit in the new swing, imagining what it might look like when they finished. The cotton girls began coming most every day. They didn't have that much to do during the day, till picking time, they said. They began to walk around it, looking at it and thinking of what they might do with the crepe paper Mr. Calvin had bought them, seeming to feel that it was theirs to do with as they pleased. In truth—although the cotton girls wouldn't let on—they had never come in contact with crepe paper before, had never handled such bright stacks of color, and if they had, they would not have thought of using it in such a mundane way as to decorate an old truck.

Miss Laura found some old chicken wire in her barn and had Jessie take it down to the church and nail it to the sides of the truck. When it was in place, the cotton girls began stuffing each hole with strips of meticulously cut crepe paper. The sides of the float began to take on the look of an abstract painting, random colors splashing out in all directions on the wire.

On Sunday after services, church members would stand by admiring it. The cotton girls got wind of the compliments to be had and began showing up for church. Hungover and high-heeled, they would walk in through the back door and sit next to Maudie and Miss Laura in the front pew, dresses so tight, they were hard-pressed to sit in one place for the whole hour. While there were plenty of raised eyebrows, Reverend Earl made it a point to say that everyone was welcome at

Word of Truth. The cotton girls twitched shoulders and gave loud amens.

On occasion, Lou Ann and Izzy even became interested in some of the Bible stories Reverend Earl used for making points in his sermons. One Sunday, at the end of a story about the wisdom of Solomon, Lou Ann—long arms lounging over the back of the pew, chewing gum to cover the previous night's activities—had leaned over to Izzy, "You mean that Solomon king was gonna cut that baby in half right there in front of his mama?"

"That's what he say."

"That son of a bitch." she had said, in grave contemplation of the injustices in this world. Later, Reverend Earl had reminded her there were children present, and Lou Ann had agreed. "I was wondering how come you telling such a no-count scary story in front of them little children."

There were tarps to cover the float each night to keep out the dew and possibly the rain, although it was a very dry summer. One morning, when Maudie went outside to look at it, somehow the tarp had slipped off and half the crepe-paper decoration had been ruined by a heavy dew or maybe rain, but the ground looked bone-dry. When the cotton girls came that afternoon, they were in tears, having never created anything so beautiful, and then to have it ruined. Mr. Calvin, who had taken to dropping by every afternoon or so, came up close to inspect. He said for them to dry their eyes. He would buy more crepe paper. They still had plenty of time to begin again.

Jessie, when he came, said that he had remembered putting the tarp on tight and anchoring it with the cinder blocks. They were all sitting to one side now. The others said for him not to worry, that it wasn't his fault he forgot. He said he hadn't forgotten.

For his part, Jessie was building a registration counter like the one used at the courthouse. They decided to have a policeman dressed in uniform standing to one side, police usually being involved in such things. Miss Laura was making the uniform. And there would be a big American flag.

It didn't get dark until almost eight o'clock, so they had plenty of time to work. The cotton girls spent hours deciding on which colors to restuff into the chicken wire. Now that they were doing it for a second time, they had worked out a grand design, which they were not revealing to the public, the public consisting of everyone except the cotton girls.

Roy Boy could be heard from under the hood, clanking and cussing. Sometimes in the evening, Miss Laura would come to sit in the swing, sewing on the policeman's outfit as she watched the progress.

Every Sunday, church members congregated to comment on its progress and ask when they would get to walk through and try the thing out. Maybe they should have a party, they suggested, and invite the other churches around the Crossroads area, Pleasant Valley CME and Reverend Earl's other church. There had never been a project of such grand scale associated with the Word of Truth Missionary Baptist Church—stuck back in the woods, down in a gully, a building so old that on rainy Sundays, buckets were placed at strategic locations to catch the leavings of a leaky roof.

Some of the mothers had come to Maudie. In the fall, might she consider starting up an afternoon tutoring session here at the church, for their children, the ones who were behind and needed help?

On the Sundays when Reverend Earl was preaching elsewhere, Miss Laura led the congregation in singing, Jessie would make announcements and then various members would get up and speak as the spirit moved them. Lou Ann and Izzy listened with great interest to the confessions of faith, to the stories of Christian conversion that had caused the members of Word of Truth to be born again. Before this time, they had always been just two of twenty or so in the fields, only concerned with scavenging cotton bolls to make their weights and pay at the end of the day. There had never been anything that interesting to do before midnight. Now they began showing up early every Sunday to explain to the children who followed them around just exactly how it was that you went down and registered to vote. As soon as they were finished with this particular crepe-paper beautification project, they themselves were headed down to the courthouse. Maudie had already taught them how to write checks, and wasn't it logical that if you could do that, you could vote? After that, as soon as they got some money, they were going to open up a bank account. The children of the church stared up in awe.

After he had scraped his knuckles trying to get the rusted bolts to loosen, Roy Boy had finally replaced the truck's water pump. Now he was replacing all the old belts and gaskets, remembering as he went along that he knew more about cars than he had realized. Perhaps, if he got too tired of being assistant janitor at the foundry, he might ask Jimmy, down at Jimmy's Battery Shop, if he could use a good mechanic.

The foundry men were building a big wooden frame—one like they had seen used on the foundry float—to fit over the front of the truck cab. It would eventually be covered with crepe paper, leaving a peep-hole for the driver. Ed, the one with the six children, brought them out to see the float one Saturday, let them stand up on top of it, drew a picture in the dirt to show them what it was going to look like when it was finished.

Mr. Calvin took it upon himself to bring out two cans of gasoline. Reverend Earl had left the truck that empty. He placed the cans under the flatbed behind the crepe paper. They would be ready when Roy Boy got the truck in driving shape, or maybe as an incentive for Roy Boy to hurry up and finish so they could try it out.

It became natural for the two of them, Jessie and Maudie, to sit and talk each evening after the others had gone. Maudie thought it reminiscent of talks with her mother or brothers. Jessie was amazed by it. Before, he had always been awkward with words. Now the conversation was effortless. He had never felt so at home with anyone: not with his child, certainly never with his wife. All through the evening as they were working, he would think about being there with her, just sitting in the swing when the work was done.

From the time Jessie was eight years old, he had known nothing but work. It had been like breathing. Up in the morning and out to the fields, men and women and children. He had not been aware that there was any-thing else or anywhere else until he was older—twelve or thirteen—and had traveled with his father along the red clay road, which had become a bigger clay road, and fi-nally the blacktop highway that was Crossroads. He had stood by while his father sat on an old nail keg outside the Crossroads filling station and played checkers with other men. He had watched in amazement as the few cars traveling from Huntsville to Bainbridge had stopped to fill up. He had never seen cars like that—shiny, with chrome fins and white sidewall tires. Trucks and tractors, or older worn-out cars with bald tires and gas tanks always on empty—that's what he had known.

As much as this was a revelation, traveling to Bainbridge when he was fifteen had been like going to the moon. Before the war and electricity, they hadn't even had a mailbox. Not having one had probably saved him. His mother had told him this when he didn't get a draft notice at the war's beginning. Everyone else close to his age in surrounding tenant houses had gotten one. He had not. His mother had kept him on the farm, with few excursions to Crossroads during those first years of the war. Later, when he could get a ride, he ventured back into the city of Bainbridge, drawn by the local movie house, oranges all the way from Florida at the corner fruit stand, and people who actually went into a store to get their hair cut.

On one of these visits to town, wild good fortune had struck. A man had come up to him and handed him a piece of paper. "You look like you might be strong enough." The man had given him the paper and walked away. He stood holding it and watched as the man looked around at the other people standing outside the corner fruit stand, choosing the few other young men he saw standing there and handing them a paper. Jessie had no idea what the paper said, school being ten miles from his house and impossible for him to get to on a regular basis, even if they could have spared him in the fields. He edged over to another man, who had also been given a paper. The man was standing next to a girl, maybe his sister or girlfriend. Jessie heard her ask the man what his paper said. "Say they hiring down at the foundry. Come

Saturday morning at seven, and they hire you if you can do the lifting."

"You going?" the girl had asked.

"Nah, ain't going. Soon as the war's over, they gonna take back all them peoples gone off now."

The girl had taken the paper from him. "Look like good pay. Wonder do they take girls?" The man had laughed so hard, she had thrown the paper in his face and walked off, but the part about good pay had not escaped Jessie. He had taken the paper home. A friend of his father's at Crossroads had told him what it said.

It had been his wildest dream come true to get that job, to get real money, which he alone could spend or dispense as he saw fit, or as he and his mother saw fit. And the work had been child's play compared to what he was used to doing. He had kept waiting for the hard parts, but there were no hard parts, as far as he could tell. He worked pouring castings. If you were careful, there was nothing to it.

By the time the war was over, he had bought the little house they lived in and was paying on the thirty acres that surrounded it. When he went to the filling station up at Crossroads, people asked all manner of questions about his town work.

Aunt Laura had him contribute to the church fund to build a cross for the sanctuary. It was to be in honor of his mother. She had died the year the war ended. His father died soon after that.

The post office had even started delivering mail to his house. He had had to go out and buy a mailbox.

—•—

They had decided to take in one last movie before the end of summer caught up with them. John Wayne was

Aunt Laura's favorite, and he was playing. They got there plenty early. Reverend Earl was taking tickets. "Y'all get yourself some of that good Brunswick stew we got in the food stand tonight."

When they found their parking place, JD got out immediately and began running with his friends. Aunt Laura had brought her lawn chair and had placed it out beside the car, but she was soon drawn to the cars of other friends. The two of them, Maudie and Jessie, were left arguing in the front seat. "You just looking for trouble, nothing to it. Air just naturally goes out of tires after a time. Ain't natural for it to be in there in the first place." She had taken to speaking in her old way when she was talking with him now. He smiled at her but said nothing about it.

"What you talking, woman? Air stay in tires for years. Somebody done let the air out of them tires. I been seeing them tires on that truck nigh on to the first day it come. Somebody come and let the air out of them tires."

"Why would they do that? If they'd wanted to ruin the tires, they would've cut them, wouldn't they? Ain't that logical?"

"Logical? *Logical?* What's you know 'bout logical when it come to tires? Been working on trucks all my life."

She began to run her finger along the open window's edge, looking out to the line that was forming at the food stand. Now she took such pleasure in teasing him. "I been watching them tires. They been getting lower and lower every day."

"What? You been watching them tires?" He burst out laughing. "You didn't even know them tires was there 'til I showed you this afternoon, all four of 'em, flat as a fritter. His hand came around her shoulder and he caught the back of her neck. "You do beat all." He rubbed her neck and kept laughing. "You been watching them tires? Who you funning, girl?"

He reached over, picked up her crutch, and gave it to her. "Get on out of here, woman. I'm gonna get you a big bowl of that stew. Maybe that'll clear your head." He got out of his side of the car and went to her side, opening the door and calling out to one of the foundry men he had seen walking by. "Come on over here, Ed. Maudie gonna learn you all 'bout tires." They strolled over to the concession stand, Jessie holding her free hand, making sure she didn't fall on the loose gravel, and all the while telling Ed about going to the float that afternoon and finding all four tires on the truck flat, and now they were going have to spend hours with a hand pump. They weren't damaged, he didn't think, just out of air.

Maudie walked along, listening to them talk and saying hello to all the people she knew now—and who knew her. Now, at night, she slept with a peace she hadn't known in years. She had remembered again that she had wanted to be a teacher. Maybe now she would think about going back to school and becoming a teacher. When she mentioned it to Jessie, he had laughed. "What you think you are now, girl? You a teacher." She had smiled and said nothing, because Jessie wasn't educated enough to know that to be a teacher took years of training. "What you think the voting school is? It's a school," he had said, "and you our teacher."

They were approaching the food stand. Nat King Cole's voice was floating on warm heavy air: "Many dreams have been brought to your doorstep . . ." She glanced out to the west at the huge orange glow that had been the sun and thought she had never been happier, and that's why, at that very moment, she truly believed the tires had gone flat, all four of them, just naturally gone flat of their own accord.

CHAPTER 35

The Telling

$\mathcal{L}$OU ANN AND IZZY had finished their masterpiece. Inside the red border, blue crepe-paper stars danced on a white background. Red-white-and-blue streamers hung from each corner of the float. In the center of the crepe paper surround, in bold black letters, it read WORD OF TRUTH MB CHURCH, BROTHER EARL WATTS, PASTOR.

That evening as they all gathered around, the cotton girls were the first to speak in favor of telling the church members that it was really intended to be a Labor Day float. It had become like birthing a baby and not being able to tell. Pride was getting the best of them, overshadowing any logical fears they might have had earlier. They had kept their crepe-paper sign, honoring Word of Truth and Reverend Earl, under wraps until the last minute so that no one would suspect anything, but it was too beautiful to hide. They were members of the church now—Reverend Earl had baptized them last week down at Twelve Mile Creek—and they felt they were being downright deceitful not telling everybody the truth.

Ed, one of the foundry men, spoke in favor. "Everybody wanta come on into town and see the parade, if they know Word of Truth having a float." Mr. Calvin agreed. Said he didn't mind if people knew he bought all the crepe paper went on the thing. Roy Boy had wanted to tell from the beginning. Jessie was the only one not talking. He leaned up against the trunk of one of the pine trees, listening, and when he didn't say anything, Maudie asked.

"We said all along we wasn't telling," he said. "Now what if something happen to the float 'fore the parade? All sorts of no-count people out there. You hear them drive-in boys coming by on the road all the time, hooting like they was up to no good."

"Something happen? What could happen? Them drive-in boys been doing that for years. Ain't nothing gonna happen," Izzy said.

"White peoples don't even know it down here, and black peoples, they ain't studying us," Roy Boy said.

Jessie stood away from the tree trunk. "All right, all right if, and I say *if*, somebody stay here with it 'til it's time for the parade."

Immediately, there was grumbling, "What's you 'spect? I'm gonna give up my job at the foundry?"

"Got cotton to tend to. Can't do that," Izzy said.

"Somebody already here," Lou Ann said, "Maudie."

"Maudie? *Maudie?*" He threw down the piece of sassafras he was chewing on. "You gonna leave Maudie to take care of the whole thing, and her cripple? What's Maudie gonna do, beat 'em off with her crutch?"

The others winced and glanced at Maudie. Roy Boy looked away and mumbled, "Ain't no call to say that."

"Well, I didn't mean nothing by it." Jessie turned toward Maudie, who was staring at him, her crutch limp in her hand. It began to fall away from her and she jerked it back.

"What I'm saying is, she can't do no good if some big

man come along. Ain't fair to ask her to do the whole thing, and her . . ." He looked around for some support and heard none. "Well, what if two big men come along? They always riding around in them cars, honking horns and yelling."

"Maudie be taking care of herself," Izzy said, as everyone else was too embarrassed to speak.

"What I'm trying to say is . . . Why, hell . . ."

Mr. Calvin stopped him before he could do more harm. "Well now, if two big men come along, you ain't gonna find me nowhere in the *vicinity*." He winked at the cotton girls. "That's one of Miss Maudie's big words."

"Sure right 'bout that," Izzy said. "Ain't gonna find us nowhere in the *vicinity*, neither." She hit Lou Ann on the shoulder.

"Well now, if one *good-looking* big man come along . . ." Lou Ann grinned. Everyone laughed, relieved to have pulled the conversation out of Jessie's awkward corner. They agreed that they should be at church next Sunday when the announcement was made. Gathering up their tools, they prepared to leave, ignoring Jessie, glancing sideways at Maudie. It had not gone unnoticed that Maudie had barely smiled at their jokes. She sat in the swing, pushing her crutch in the dust, watching the others call good-byes to her as they headed for their cars.

Jessie waved the last car off up the hill, pretending to laugh at some joke the cotton girls shouted out the window as a farewell. Jessie pushed off the tree trunk, picking pieces of stray crepe paper off the ground, flexing his shoulders all the while because Maudie staring at his back was like some sort of hot ray between his shoulder blades. He didn't have to wait long.

She began through clinched teeth. "What do you

mean, 'can't do nothing'?" When he didn't answer she hit the side of the swing with her crutch. "'She's crippled'? 'She's gonna beat 'em off with her crutch'?" Again she smacked the crutch on the side of the swing and didn't stop banging, hitting it again and again with each sentence. "I came here crippled. I'm staying here crippled. All those nights nobody even cared if I was alive or dead. All those nights here by myself, no running water, no plumbing, didn't have no nothing," she yelled. "Back here in this backwater place. Everybody else marching in Mississippi, everybody else doing something worthwhile, and I'm sitting here with the likes of you. Turn around and look at me, Mr. . . . Mr. 'I can't even read and I can't even write, but I know it all' Jessie. Turn around here and look at me." Tears were choking her. "I thought you . . ." She pulled up by the swing's chains and hurled the crutch at his back.

Maybe it would hit him. She hoped it would. It skittered past him along the ground and came to rest on a mound of trash—discarded lumber, bits of crepe paper, bent nails. Slowly, he walked over, picked it up, and walked back to her. She didn't look at him.

"Guess you right, just ignorant. Don't know no better," he said.

"You don't know *any* better," she said. "*Any better,*" she yelled. She grabbed the crutch out of his hand and stood up, trying to walk to the back stoop of the church. He followed along beside and tried to hold her other elbow. She jerked away and threw the crutch up against the porch.

"I'll fix it tomorrow," he said, and held out his hand.

"Don't you know *anything* about *anything*?" she yelled. She took his hand to step up and then tried to push it back at him, but he wouldn't let her go. He pulled her around to him, so close that she caught her breath, so near that she was afraid of what she might say next.

"Guess I don't know nothing 'bout nothing, but I know this." He gripped her arm. "You listening? You listening to me?" his face inches from hers. She nodded. "It ain't the float or the church or the voting school I care 'bout. Remember that night you told me 'bout Yolanda and you ask me, 'Did I do it cause I felt guilty or did I do it cause I loved her?'" She didn't say anything, looking down at the buttons on his shirt, the scent of him making her dizzy. "I said, 'You do for the ones you love.'" She turned her head. Her face brushed against his shirt. "You hear? You do for the ones you love." She nodded.

He pulled away, still holding her hand as he stepped down off the porch. "Before you, I didn't know that." Then he let go and walked out to his car.

—•—

Days later, she had made him take her out on the highway to Joyce Ann's Fashions, the only store out in the county that sold clothes she might be able to afford. The tables were stacked with remnants left over from town stores and bought by the pound.

When she came out, she wouldn't let him see her purchases. There had been a new skirt, long and light blue, and a blouse, fitted, with lace around the collar. The thing she was most proud of was the madras shirt, a pale blue plaid, extra-large, with short sleeves. To show off his muscles, she said when she gave it to him later. She had searched for half an hour in the stacks of men's shirts. It was an irregular, but the imperfection was on the back of the shirttail, where nobody would notice.

And he had brought her a gift, an old double-barrel shotgun, the only thing he had in the way of protection.

It had been his father's. He had, even as she protested, shown her how to use it, then left two cartridges on the table beside her bed. Two would be all she would need if it ever came to that, he said. "You put them two in and pull the trigger, ain't gonna be nothing left of whatever you was pointing at. And if you miss with that thing," he had said, laughing, "ain't no help for you." Immediately, he had raised his hands and backed off. "Course, I ain't saying you need no help."

CHAPTER 36

Dominique

AFTER THE BUS RIDE back from the sit-in, Dominique had disappeared. She was in the infirmary, someone said. It was a rumor. For the next few days, rumors of every ilk spread like confetti over Highlander: She wouldn't talk to her father, to anybody. There was to be another sit-in. Her hand had become infected. The police were coming to take them all to jail.

Tab had not paid attention. She had not cared what happened. She was fed up with all of it, or maybe she just wanted to go home. No, she didn't want to go home. She couldn't face going home now. She couldn't face being here at this place, either. The food had lost its flavor. The lake was too cold to swim in. Nothing was right.

Eugenia had been white-faced on Tab's return, and then when she saw her safe, she had turned proud, having a niece do what she would have done—if she had been invited—if someone had had the decency to invite her along. She was the one who believed so fervently in what they were doing. She was the one who should have been included, should have taken a leading part in the sit-in, and she had told the leader this.

"It was not up to me, Eugenia. It was up to the ones

who organized it, the ones who live in Nashville. Perhaps you might think about getting involved in your home state. I understand they have a candidate to challenge Wallace this time—fellow might not be half-bad, they say." Eugenia nodded vaguely and let it drop. Change—revolutionary, bone-crushing change—was the answer, not some insipid, ordinary, and everlasting political process. She would find another way to help.

In one way, Eugenia felt she had accomplished what she set out to do all along: bring the girls—one anyway—to a new light. Through it all, Tab hadn't cared to tell her that the sit-in was a fluke, that it had all been a big mistake.

Tina hadn't said much to her sister. The lifeguards had told her the story. Tab hadn't told her about the cigarette ember glowing next to her face, about what the Elvis boy had whispered in her ear.

Everyone seemed to forget about Dominique in the telling of the Nashville sit-in. She was a minor moment in their remembering of it. The catsup stories ran rampant. The howling rednecks, the sluggish blue-uniforms in the corner. Radios were on at night after supper, people listening for the news. Newspapers were brought in from off the mountain and grabbed at first light. Something was starting; at least it seemed that way to Tab. Or maybe it had already started. She didn't care either way. She lay in her bunk at night, thinking of what she might say to Dominique if she saw her again, what she might do to her. One night, she had a dream in which she held Dominique's hand and kissed it right on the burned spot. She woke up gagging, sticking her tongue out, wiping it with her sheet.

On the third day after the sit-in, Reverend Calder and Dominique walked into the dining room together, Dominique holding on to her father's arm. Not that many people noticed. Eloise looked up, poked Tab in the ribs, and went on eating. They sat down at the table with Miss Wilma. Dominique looked stiff and tired, but otherwise she seemed unchanged, except for her hand, which was noticeably wrapped in white gauze. Tab could hear Dominique in snatches over the rattle of dishes and conversation, that same clipped Yankee voice giving her apologies to Miss Wilma for the trouble she had caused. Tab could see her father listening, making sure it was sufficient. And Miss Wilma answering, "Honey, wasn't no trouble to me. How's your hand doing, baby?"

After dinner, Dominique and her father walked over to Tab. Dominique had taken her father's arm again, not leaning on him, but holding on. Tab felt her face going hot, all she had imagined saying now stuck in her throat. And Dominique's apology, so full of tricks and turns, not an apology at all, but passing her father's muster as she stood there still holding his arm. "Certainly you realize I never would have asked you to go with us had I been aware that you were not listening to what might happen in the first place, that you were too young in the first place. I had always assumed you were fifteen, my age." And the last part, hardest to get out: "I hope you will accept my apology."

She stood there with her father, waiting. Her father was already preoccupied with someone across the room. Hearing no response, Reverend Calder momentarily turned his attention back to them. "Oh sure, I accept," Tab said, and wished she was the one standing next to her, helping to steady her.

"Fine, fine." He took Dominique's hand off his arm and patted it before releasing it. "Now you children sit down and make up. I need to speak to Jeffrey over there."

And then Dominique said—so blatant that Tab had blushed—"But Daddy, we were going walking."

"We'll walk later, Dominique. I need to catch Jeffrey before he goes back to New York." He left them to hurry across the room.

Dominique pulled out a chair and sat down next to Tab and Eloise, inhaling in stutter steps, staring out past them. Most people had left the dining room by then. Helpers were beginning to clean up. They watched her father talking to one of the men as they walked out of the room. "He needs to talk about going to Mississippi this summer." Tab nodded. They sat watching dishes being scraped. "We need to go down there and help out." She picked up a stray glass of iced tea and took a drink, hiding quivering lips that were about to fall into disorder.

"Hey, you drinking old man Spivey's leftover iced tea," Eloise said.

"No she's not. That's my iced tea. I told her she could have it."

"You lie like a rug, Tab. That there's your iced tea you got in your hand."

—•—

Dominique came back to their room that night, appeared in the doorway—wooden blocks some child might have stacked precariously on top of one another, a tower that might scatter with the slightest touch. Tab was afraid to look at her, would not have dared to speak to her. Tina glanced up and went on with what she was doing. Dominique didn't look at either one of them. She climbed up to her bed, lay down, and opened a book.

"Just so you'll know," Tina said to the lump that was

on Dominique's bunk. "We, the lifeguards, we've taken it on ourselves to go out and patrol the school after dark." She had changed into jeans and a T-shirt, hopped up on her bunk, and began applying makeup. "We haven't told anybody about it. We don't want to alarm the older people. We just feel it's necessary."

Dominique didn't take her eyes off the book she was reading. She nodded her head in agreement. "So you won't mention it to anybody?" Tina said. Dominique nodded again.

Eloise came in carrying a load of laundry. "You going out messing with them boys again tonight?" Tina, concentrating on eyeliner, didn't bother with an answer. Eloise dumped laundry on her bed and began to fold it. "What's gonna happen when you out there kissing and somebody sure enough do come along?" And getting no response, she mimicked. "Come on over here, Mr. Policeman. I give you a kiss, too."

Tina exhaled and put down her eyeliner and mirror. "It's not just the lifeguards. There are several of us. We don't want to upset the older people, so we're doing it in secret." She glared at Eloise's back. "Gravy, I do believe you're worse than Tab."

"I seen you out there the other day making eyes at the colored one."

"You saw no such thing."

—•—

Tina waited for half an hour after lights-out before pulling the sweatshirt from under her pillow and slipping out the door. By that time, Eloise was making intermittent gurgling sounds in her sleep and Tab was listening for Dominique.

She had watched her that evening while she pretended to read a *Seventeen* magazine Tina had left lying on her bunk. Dominique had stayed in her bed, answering in one syllable the questions Eloise fired. "Do your hand hurt? Did you have a conniption fit on that bus like they say? Did your daddy give you a spanking? Mine woulda. You think the police coming to get us 'cause of what y'all did? And that wasn't any of our doing."

She had answered yes and no, yes and no, not hearing the questions, or caring about the answers. After awhile, she put the book on her face and pulled the sheet up to her neck, much like that first day.

When Eloise had turned their lights out sometime past nine o'clock, she didn't realize Dominique hadn't dressed in her pajamas, hadn't brushed her teeth or washed her face. Eloise had curled under her covers and was sleeping minutes later.

The one window in the room was open and tree frogs were setting up a chatter. There was a full moon that moved a square of light slowly across the floor, reflecting up onto the walls, giving long shadows to the bunk beds' frames and the look of small mountains and valleys to the rumpled bedcovers.

She could hear Dominique taking uneven breaths, trying not to cry. She hated the sound. It was too common for Dominique, way beneath her dignity. She wanted to tell her to shut up. She put the pillow over her face and tried not to hear. It didn't block out a thing. She punched the pillow up, put it back under her head, and watched the light from the window inch its way across the room.

The jagged breathing and sniffling wouldn't stop. When she was to the point of wanting to scream, Tab ripped off her sheet, went to the bathroom, pulled toilet paper off the roll, came back to their room, and climbed up the ladder to Dominique's side. "Here." She rustled the toilet paper on the top of the sheet and waited before a hand came out and took it. Dominique sat up in the bed and blew her nose, then flopped back down and pulled the sheet up.

"Scoot over."

For a long moment, the covers didn't move.

"I said, 'scoot over.'"

The sheets rustled and the body underneath moved to one side. Tab pulled back the cover and slipped in beside her. She was stiff, like Tab imagined a corpse might be. She could feel her shorts were still on, and her shoes.

They lay there in the darkness, listening to Eloise's deep breathing, the tree frogs, and a screech owl's intermittent call, feeling the warmth of their bodies next to each other. After awhile, Dominique's breathing seemed to ease. She sat up in the bed and blew her nose again, then lay back down, finding Tab's hand with her bandaged one. Tab pulled Dominique's hand up to her chest and held it there. "What I was thinking was, maybe you could come live with me for the rest of the summer—you know, while he goes down to Mississippi."

What she had said—the absolute absurdity of it—was slow in coming to them. For that moment, the outside noises covered them, until Dominique began shaking—the whole bunk bed creaking. She put her hand over her mouth, trying to suppress it. "You people," she tried to whisper, but she couldn't and burst out laughing. "You people are so, so—"

"Okay, I just thought—"

"Are you a complete idiot?" She held the crumpled toilet tissue over her mouth trying to hush. "Oh God, why does he bring me to these places, introduce me to people like you? Completely useless people like you, and

I must stay in this place and stay in this place . . . and no way out." She took deep breaths, trying to even out her breathing. "I might just go stark raving crazy. That's what I might do, go stark raving crazy."

Tab grinned up at the dark ceiling and fingered the bandaged hand she was still holding. "I could take you to get a hot dog at the Woolworth's in Bainbridge. They got lots of catsup." They both had to sit up now—in hysterics. Tab used the sheet to wipe the tears that were running down her cheeks.

Dominique was trying to blow her nose in between trying to catch her breath. "Have I not taught you one single solitary thing this summer?" She flopped back down on the bed, bending her knees and kicking them up in the air. "I can't believe you said that," she almost screamed. "You are such an *idiot.*"

"I know," Tab said, trying to conjure up the ultimate, "We could go swimming at the Crystal Plunge."

Dominique jammed the pillow down over her face; her whole body rolled from side to side.

"Hey, Dominique, what you doing up there? You waking me up."

She held the pillow up long enough to say, "Go back to sleep, Eloise. I'll be quiet." Then she dropped the pillow back over her face.

After a time, they calmed down. Dominique put the pillow back under her head. The sounds from outside came in around them again. The moonlight had moved up the wall now and was slowly disappearing out the window.

"I meant it, though," she whispered, and Dominique turned on her side and pulled Tab in close.

"I know you did." And now she was crying again, not crying as ordinary people cry—she was long past that.

Tears were there and she was breathing in an erratic way. It was as close as she could come to giving in. She inhaled and wiped tears away before she let out a long breath. "I know you did."

The moonlight was completely gone out of the room now. The darkness encased them as if they were suspended in fathomless water—and then she asked, just this once, "If you want to, you can tell me—what it would be like, what we would do."

And Tab told her, deep into the night, everything she could remember of her old life—of Coke floats at Trowbridge's, of nights on the front porch at her grandmother's house, of listening to the old stories, of sitting in the middle of the family pew at the First Methodist Church of Bainbridge, looking to either side and seeing it lined with parents and siblings, aunts and uncles, cousins and grandparents, and, in the rows in front and back, neighbors and friends.

A life defined by its narrow, unblinking vision, a life bound by an irrational moral code that had gone unquestioned for generations, a life made secure by a love that accepted her—unequivocally, lovingly accepted her—and made rock-hard her sense of place in the world. Any attempt to dissect the whole might bring into question some of its parts, parts she might not be able to live without, and so why bother—save for this girl lying beside her, crying in the night.

CHAPTER 37

The Raid

RETRIBUTION WAS SWIFT IN COMING. It arrived in a cloud of dust, four cars in all, winding down the road and through the entrance to Highlander just as the sun was setting over the mountains. They must have known the leader was off traveling, that there was a woman in charge while he was gone. They must have thought they could intimidate her.

A few people were sitting out on the lawn, some in rockers on the porch. Most of the others were in the dining room, watching a movie, the evening's entertainment. Dominique and Tab were in their bunk room, changing bedsheets.

"As soon as I'm old enough, I'm going to France and live with my mother. I think she's a schoolteacher. That's what she used to be."

"Don't you know? Doesn't she write to you?"

Dominique flipped one side of a sheet over to Tab. "She didn't leave me, if that's what you mean. She left him, and when I'm old enough, I'm going to live with her."

There was yelling in the hall. Someone ran by, stopping just long enough to tell them, "The police are here, stay in your room," and then ran on and, of course, the girls didn't stay in their room. They dropped the sheets and ran up the hall. Doors were slamming. Blinking red lights were reflecting off the porch windows. Brown uniforms were getting out of the cars. One of them from the lead car walked up the front steps, where Eugenia was chatting with several other women. He stood over her. "You in charge here?" The girls were watching through the front screen door. The officer had some papers in his hand and was about to give them to Eugenia. She pointed to the other chair. "Officer, I'm not in charge. This lady is."

"I am." The black woman, Septima Clark, sitting next to Eugenia was rocking and fanning herself with a folded newspaper. "I'm in charge," she said, and never stopped rocking.

"I mighta known." He walked over to her and handed her the papers. "We have a warrant to search the place. Had some complaints y'all might be selling whiskey on the premises."

She put down her fan to accept the papers from the officer. "Whiskey, you say. That's a new one."

"Officer," Eugenia was rising out of her chair. "You can't come here and push your way in—"

"It's a violation of Tennessee law, selling alcohol at a private residence." He looked around at the others watching him. "Probably some other violations going on here, too, if I was to look." He turned back to the rocker. "But that's what that there paper is for, selling whiskey." Three other men joined him on the porch. "You ain't gonna give me no trouble, are you?" he said to the black woman.

"Of course we're going to give you trouble." Eugenia came to stand behind Septima's rocker. "We are citizens

of the United States. We have every right to be here. You
have no right to—"

"No, we're not going to give you any trouble." The
black woman was folding up the papers. "These are in
order. Do your searching, and then leave."

"We'll leave when we're good and ready." He turned
to the others standing by the cars and dispersed them to
different buildings and locations on the grounds. "And
make it out-and-out thorough, like I told you."

One of the policemen started toward the door. Tab
and Dominique backed away as he whipped it open. He
shook his head at their two colors together. "Get to
where you belong." They backed down the hall to their
room and sat on Tab's bunk, listening to chairs being
overturned, glasses rattling in the kitchen, and voices
coming from the projector in the dining room. Those
that were watching the movie had remained riveted to
their places, staring at the screen.

By the time the officer got to their room, he was tired
and Dominique was ready for him, a bad combination.
"I'm sure," she said, halfway standing as he entered,
"that you will find a case of beer underneath this very
bunk." Tab tried to pull her hand to sit her back down,
but she jerked it away and walked across to her bunk.
"This is mine. You won't find anything but vintage Dom
Pérignon, I think—'39, a very good year."

"She's just kidding."

"I mighta known y'all would all be sleeping together."
He pushed Tab aside and pulled the mattress off her
bed, pitching it in the middle of the room. He did the
same with Tina's, tearing apart her small canvas makeup
bag.

"My, doesn't he have strong muscles. Probably his
mother coupled with one of the local bulls."

"Dominique, will you shut up," Tab whispered.

"What's the nigger saying?"

"She didn't say anything."

He turned and pulled Eloise's mattress off and then grabbed Dominique's. She stepped toward him, but not in time. "What's this we got here?" He reached up on the exposed slats and pulled down a small leather-bound book with lock strap and a small keyhole. "Will you lookie here. Somebody's keeping herself a diary."

"Give me that."

"Why don't you give me the key? Oh, you don't have the key? Well, I might have to open it up myself."

She had stepped away now, trying a new tack. "You're supposed to be searching for whiskey."

"I might find a clue in here." He waved it in front of her. "Let's us just see." He took a finger and ripped back the leather strap. A photograph fluttered to the ground. He stepped on it as she reached to retrieve it. "We'll just leave that lay while I look at this here other first." He began to leaf through the pages. "Hell, this is some kind of foreign language. Are you some kind of Communist? The chief is gonna be interested in this." He began turning the pages slowly. " Lookie here, it ain't all foreign."

She grabbed for the book, but he turned aside and her cheek caught his elbow, knocking her back again. "Now let's see here. It's to somebody named Roman. Got a boyfriend, do you?" He began reading. "'We rejoice in our sufferings'—hell, girl, that's a good one for you— 'knowing that suffering produces endurance'—you gotta have lots of that if you wanta stay ahead of the Tennessee police—'and endurance produces character, and character produces hope, and hope does not disappoint us because . . .' His voice trailed off. He snapped the diary shut and pitched it across the room. "Not much there. No wonder you writing in a foreign tongue." She made no attempt to retrieve it. Her attention was intermittently on his foot and his eyes.

There was a loud crashing sound from the kitchen area. Someone had let pots and pans slip, or be thrown, to the floor. Shouts came from the dining room, where the movie was being shown. The noise from the projector had stopped and now there was a deadly quiet. The officer watched them as he reached down to retrieve what was under his shoe.

Dominique was standing rigid by her bunk, hands gripping its frame, the same look on her face that Tab had seen that afternoon on the bus coming from Nashville.

Until that very moment, it had not dawned on Tab what might be in the picture. In her world, a world defined by absolutes, the thought of options, the possibility of options, had never entered her mind. She had no idea that something could be menacing and precious at the same time. "It's *my* picture." She stepped forward. "Give it to me."

"This your picture, is it?" He was studying the photograph, closely taking in every image on it. He looked up at Tab. "Oh yeah, what's in here, then?"

"It's . . . it's a picture of a white woman, my mother." She held her hand out.

"What else?"

"Other things."

"What other things?"

"Just other things, background things."

He held the snapshot out in front of her, dangling it from side to side. She could see a black man in uniform; the Eiffel Tower was in the background. The black man had his arm around a white woman and there were crowds milling about, a band parading down the street, everyone smiling and happy. "After she took up with a colored man, she left out for Texas. They all go to Texas when they get in trouble, you know." Tab tried to smile at him.

"This ain't no more yours than fly me to the moon."

"It's got the Eiffel Tower in the background, see? I'm gonna go see it someday. That's how come I keep it."

"No more you don't." He began to rip it in two.

"Don't." Dominique rushed at him, trying to grab the picture out of his hand, but he pushed her away.

"Thought you didn't claim it, nigger girl."

"It's not hers. It's mine." Tab grabbed at his arm. He pushed her down on the mattresses piled on the floor and went back to the picture, putting the two pieces together and tearing again. She was up and took a flying leap, trying to grab him around the waist, hitting her nose on his gun belt.

Dominique rushed for the hand that had the picture pieces. "It's my only one, you redneck jerk." He grabbed her bandaged hand and slung her into the bottom bunk and smiled as he proceeded to tear the picture into bits.

"I knew it was yours all along, half-breed. I could take one look at you and see that. Klan ever find out your daddy been humping a white woman, that'll be all she wrote."

Tab got up off the floor, yelling at him. "You're disgusting, *you people.* You're disgusting!" She charged him again, even as she heard herself saying it. She lowered her head and butted into his stomach, bouncing off hard muscle. He grabbed her arm and twisted it, pushing her into the bunk on top of Dominique.

"That's the problem with you lily-white do-gooders. Hell, you don't know what the real world is."

By this time, Tab was raging at everything she had been made to learn in this place, against everything she had been forced to betray—against love that doesn't have a history. The nearest thing to grab was an orange crate filled with clothes. It might have been Tina's or Eloise's. Tab wheeled around and picked up the crate, clothes and all, and flung it toward him. His back was turned. He was looking toward the closet. When the orange crate hit him, it was an automatic reflex to grab for the gun and swirl.

They stood facing each other—her nose trickling blood, his eyes riveted on her, the barrel of the revolver catching the light from the overhead bulb. She had heard the hammer cock back as he turned. She looked straight into the black hole of the barrel and waited for the bullet to come out and tear into her.

"Joey?" a voice called from down the hall. "Joey, where you at?" It came closer. Joey stood frozen, gun in hand. "We ain't got all day. Where are you, son?" Joey pulled up from his crouched position and let the hammer ease back into place. "I'm in here." He holstered and snapped the leather safety strap as easily as he had removed it.

A face appeared in the door frame, a face like Joey's, young, perhaps not twenty years in this world. "Come on, we found what we was looking for—beer, a can or two in a bucket. They been selling beer. It's against the law. Since the head man ain't here, we gonna arrest the colored woman." He looked around. "What's going on?"

Joey glanced around and turned to go, pitching what was left of the picture up into the air, "Nothing," he said.

Tiny pieces of the Eiffel Tower, of the black serviceman and the white Frenchwoman floated down though space, landing gently on the floor. The rap of nightsticks and leather holsters against thighs could be heard down the hall.

Dominique was off the bed and on her knees shepherding in stray picture pieces. She corralled the lot into a heap beside the mattresses and began picking up each piece and positioning it in the palm of her good hand, trying to fit back together what had been so long gone. "It was the only picture I had—the only one." She brushed tears away so as not to let any moisture come in contact with the black-and-white shine of bits and pieces. "How will I remember her?"

Tab sank down on the box springs, her body involuntarily shaking. "Joey—it's such a baby name." She looked down at her trembling hands. "Dominique . . . he was gonna shoot, and he had such a baby name."

CHAPTER 38

The Leaving

*I*T HAD BEEN A PLACE of slamming screen doors, of the scent of simmering meals floating through the morning air, of laughing and shouting, down by the lake, up in the dining room. The conversation had spilled from the house onto the front porch, out into the yard. Great hopeful talks of what was now, of what might be tomorrow.

Just as suddenly, it was a place of memories. The lake glassed over, and the buildings stilled, a shell echoing the night singings, the rowdy square dancing. The sheriff came again, this time to close down Highlander Folk School forever.

—•—

"It's absurd anyway, to think you can close down an idea. I don't care about the buildings; the time has come for the idea." Eugenia was paraphrasing what the leader had said as he stood by and watched the sheriff padlock the main house. She had said it, too, but she couldn't bring herself to believe it, not the way the leader did. He had actually smiled at the sheriff as he put on the padlock.

Not so for Tab. She came of stock that held dear the

solid physical foundations of land and family and place. It made no sense to her that the idea would not be imbedded in the thing—the thing in the idea.

Now Eugenia was repeating her thoughts to those she stopped to talk with on the way to her car, lugging suitcases and clothes on hangers abruptly gathered up in the rush. The others weren't thinking so much about the idea as they were about where they were going to sleep that night. They had been given only enough time to pack their clothes and get out.

Eugenia had the trunk of the Buick open and was arranging suitcases. Tina had gone off to be with the lifeguards and say good-bye.

Dominique was sitting on her suitcase out by the Ping-Pong table, waiting for her father to finish talking to some of the others. Her elbows rested on her knees, chin in palms. She was looking out at the floating dock when Tab walked over. "Remember that day out there, when you said your parents were divorced and I acted like such a ninny?"

Dominique's eyebrows rose slightly.

"Maybe we could write each other sometime."

Dominique didn't look up. "I doubt it."

"Why? Are you gonna put it all in French?"

"I don't even write to my mother. Why should I write to you?"

"'Cause I like you better than your mother likes you?"

She still didn't look up. "Take that back, you shithead."

"Sorry."

They both watched the sun playing on the water out near the dock. Tab saw it reflecting off glistening shoulders as Dominique flashed by, beating her in that first race.

"I don't blame her. She couldn't take it. That's what he said—she couldn't take it, but I can. That's what he said. I can take it and I'll be the stronger for it."

"He would," Tab said, and grimaced, expecting to be cursed or at least have some French something thrown back at her, but it didn't happen. Only the quiet of the morning closed in around them. A breeze caught early-turning red sourwood leaves and settled them down on the water's surface, tiny boats sailing away from the shore.

"Well, I got to go. Aunt Eugenia's packing the car. We're going home."

Dominique didn't say anything, just shook her head.

Tab got up and walked off toward the Buick, was halfway there, almost out of range, when she heard Dominique. "Wait a minute." She had gotten up and was walking toward Tab, reaching down into her jacket pocket. "I want to show you something." She stood there holding her hand in her pocket until they were close enough to touch shoulders. Only then did she pull it out. "I never showed it to anybody else."

"I know what it is. Let me see it. I never got a good look."

Dominique pulled it out of her jacket. She had pasted it back together on a piece of cardboard. "Be careful."

"I will." Tab took it with both hands and stared down at it. So many jagged lines crisscrossed the surface, it was hard to tell that it was a picture at all, impossible to see any details—as Dominique must have seen them in all those years of opening her diary each night and studying the picture, as she must still see them now.

"I want you to tell me."

"What?"

"Do you see me resembling her much?"

There was such a catch in Tab's throat, she was afraid she wouldn't be able to speak at all, so she pretended great concentration on the picture pieces even as she blinked back tears.

"Well?" Dominique said. "Yeah, yeah, I know—they look happy, and they were, back then, but what do you think? I think maybe our noses and our eyes and our profiles. What do you think?" She turned sideways so Tab could see her profile. "I haven't seen her since I was five, but I've always thought we did."

Tab glanced at the profile and back to the picture. "Oh yeah, sure. I see it. I thought I saw it when the policeman was holding it up in front of me the other night."

"Yeah?"

"Sure, and your body type. You're gonna be tall like she is."

Dominique had her hands in the back pockets of her jeans and was still in profile so Tab could get a good look. "I think the older I get, the more I'm going to resemble her. Most people miss it because of the skin color, but"—she turned to look at Tab—"I knew you wouldn't."

Tab handed the picture back, and as soon as Dominique had it safely in her pocket, Tab grabbed her around the neck and hugged. "You look just like her."

"Yeah, I always thought so, too." Dominique held her for a moment and then backed off. "Don't get carried away." She patted Tab on the shoulder and then turned to go.

Tab watched as she walked back toward her suitcase. About halfway there, she turned. "Maybe one of these days, I'll write to you, *mon amie.*"

—•—

Tab was still wiping eyes on her sleeve when she got back to the car. Eugenia was trying to get too many things into the trunk. Material things had also been added to their load. The hanging macramé flowerpot holder Tab had made in crafts class one day when Aunt Eugenia had been in charge of the children's activities. A new thing out of California, she had said. Also reams of notes Eugenia had taken and a coffee mug Tab had commandeered from the dining room—no one would be using it now anyway, and she needed it to remember by.

Eugenia looked up and saw her. "I know how you feel. I had a good cry myself last night. Several of us did. The idea that in America, a thing like this could happen. It makes you want to bite nails." She crammed the last suitcase in and slammed the trunk shut, using both hands.

Tab leaned against the fender and watched Tina walk toward them, lugging her suitcase. "There's nothing we can do about it now. I just want to go home. I feel a great need for a Coke float at Trowbridge's."

"Do about what?" Tina let her suitcase drop to the ground.

Eugenia bit her lower lip and opened the trunk again. "About this whole thing—closing us down. Those troopers coming in, ransacking the place just to find some excuse." She heaved the suitcase up and began trying to squeeze it in, hammering it with her fist when it wouldn't fit. "The balance of power in this country has gone haywire."

And then both Aunt Eugenia and Tab stood gawking as Tina gushed forth—a tirade completely unexpected. "I don't care about a balance of power. I don't care anything about this place. Why did we come here anyway, just to get to know people we'll never see again and . . ."

She took a tissue out of her pocket, "I"—she swiped at the tears, furious they were there—"I think we should have left it like it was. Why should I get to know somebody when I can't ever see him—them—again, and if I did, it wouldn't be allowed anyway." She stopped to get out a fresh tissue to blow her nose. "This whole thing is *stupid*," she screamed, hitting her hand against the car fender, then kicking the tires. They watched her jerk open the back car door and fall inside. "Let's go," before she slammed the door.

Tab looked at Aunt Eugenia, who was staring at Tina's head through the back window. "Mama says she's just a teenager and she has outbursts like that, and she's glad I haven't started it yet."

"I should say." Eugenia began pushing the trunk lid down again. "I know this whole thing has been . . . well, not quite what I expected, but you have learned, have experienced . . . haven't you, Tab?"

"Sure, Aunt Eugenia." Tab added her weight to the trunk lid and heard the lock click. "Let's go before I get teary again."

As they pulled away she was still sitting out by the lake, waiting.

CHAPTER 39

The Campaign

CHARLES WONDERED if he had bullied Reuben into going. Had he done that all of his life, bullied Reuben into doing things, or was it Reuben who pushed him?

Mary was waiting supper and Charles was in a hurry to eat—the meat loaf would get cold—and so he tried to end the conversation quickly, twisting the phone cord in his hand as he talked. "I know you don't want to go, but you have to." He held the kitchen phone and listened. Mary passed by him, carrying the meat loaf and its aroma. "Because we're having a meeting before the rally, and the treasurer has to be there." He waited a moment to let Reuben try to talk his way out of it with some lame excuse. "Don't be ridiculous. Fort Payne is just as peaceful as any town around. That lynching thing happened years ago, way back in the thirties. Lynchings happened back then." He listened for a moment more, then burst out laughing. "Nobody does that kind of thing anymore, Reuben, only the far-out elements. We're not the far-out element, for gosh sake. Rednecks aren't interested in candidates like Brad." He listened a moment longer. Mary was taking hot biscuits out of the oven. "You're just looking for excuses, Reuben. I'll pick you up at three-thirty tomorrow afternoon. Remember, I'm taking time off from work, too." He hung up while the meat loaf was still hot.

—•—

The next day, he was out front at 3:25, waiting. Reuben dragged himself out the front door at 3:40. He was holding his head back as he walked, spraying something in his nose, an oversized briefcase in the other hand, a coat slung over his arm. He stuck his head in the open window on the passenger side. "I really shouldn't go. I'm not feeling well."

"Get in, Reuben. We're late." Reuben got in. Charles circled the drive, glimpsing the patch of black left in the grass. "This should be fun, riding in the campaign plane. I know you may have done this kind of thing before, but not me."

Reuben didn't say anything. He sprayed more nose drops.

"Well, have you—been in a private plane before?"

"No, I can't abide small airplanes."

"It's the only way to get into Fort Payne and keep Brad's schedule, what with things heating up like they are. Did you see the poll in the *Birmingham News* today?" He picked the paper up off the front seat and waved it in Reuben's face. "We're running a close third. If we can beat out Comer, we'll be neck and neck with Big George. The paper said it was only a matter of time." Charles almost ran a stop sign. "God, Reuben, can you imagine what a difference this could make if he wins—in education, in the integration thing, in everything? It'll be a new day for Alabama, for the South." Charles glanced at Reuben. "Why are you so dead set against going? After all, you're a veteran now. You've had a cross burning in your yard. That's more than I can say."

"It's safe where people know you." Reuben replaced the cap on the nasal spray and slipped it in his coat pocket. "I never liked that town. I had an unpleasant experience once on a train stopover."

"What kind of experience?"

Reuben looked out the window as they passed over the river bridge. "It was a minor uncivilized incident."

Charles changed the subject, as he always changed the subject when Reuben began to think dark thoughts. At least that's how Charles saw it, that Reuben had a propensity to a darker side and the best way to assuage him was to change the subject.

"Yessir, tonight should be great fun. We have none of the responsibility for the goings-on. We'll have our meeting, go to the rally, and then hop back in the plane and be home before you know it. We should be back by midnight. Brad has to fly back down to Tuscaloosa after he lets us off."

They drove on in silence. Reuben was not one to embrace new experiences, and Charles knew it. He would come around. The campaign seemed to be helping that along—inches at a time.

"I had an interesting theater occurrence today," Reuben finally said.

"Don't tell me. You integrated another movie."

"Hardly." Reuben didn't bother to see Charles's grin. Charles slowed for a stop sign and waved to another car. "Well, do you want to talk about something to take our minds off this wretched flying business or not?"

"Oh, I do, I do." Charles had stopped at a red light and honked at a friend crossing the street. "Now Ed," he yelled out the window, "don't forget who you're voting for." He shifted into first as the light changed. "Ed Mal-

lard from over in Courtland." He looked at Reuben.
"You know Ed, good family."

"I know Ed." Reuben drummed his fingers on the
window frame. "Are you interested or not?"

"Oh yeah, sure, go ahead."

Reuben brought his hands together in his lap.
"Today . . ." He paused to make sure he had Charles's
full attention. "Today, I had a visit from a black preacher,
a Reverend Watts. He told me he had been trying to see
me for some time now and that my secretary would not
let him in." He thought a moment and said, almost to
himself, "Another subject entirely. I'll deal with it later."
He cleared his throat and began again. "He was really
quite a charismatic fellow. You should have seen him. He
had on his best suit—at least I assumed it was his best,
because he seemed to consider our meeting important."

"Of course he would, Reuben. You're a very important fellow." Charles waved to someone else he knew.
"Did he want to get all his congregation in the movies
for half price?" Charles grinned and waved to another
friend, then, and hearing no disgruntled retort, said,
"Sorry. I couldn't resist. Go ahead. Tell me what he said,
this reverend."

"Absent any further vulgar interruptions from you."

"I won't say another vulgar word."

Reuben began again. "It seems he runs the Negro
part of our Crossroads Drive-in. That's up near your
farm, isn't it?"

"Yes, Crossroads Drive-in. Been there for years. Never
heard of a Reverend Watts, though. A Negro man?"

"Yes. He seemed somewhat ill at ease, so I offered him
a Coke and we sat and talked."

"Just a minute." Charles pulled into a parking place
along River Street. "I want to pick up an extra copy of

our paper to take to the meeting. Everybody's seen the *Birmingham News*, but not the *Bainbridge Daily*. Did you see that editorial today?"

"Yes." Reuben took a deep breath and again tapped fingers. "Yes, I saw it."

"Just hold your horses there, Reuben. I'll be back in a second." Charles left the door open and ran into Anderson's Newsstand. He dashed back out and pitched the paper through the window into Reuben's lap, then got in and started backing out. "Told you it wouldn't take long."

"We're late as it is."

"Who was fifteen minutes late in the first place?"

"Be that as it may." Reuben brought his knees together, shoes lined up parallel. "May I continue with my story now?"

"Sure. He was ill at ease, so you offered him a Coke. I was listening."

"Yes, he didn't want to sit down at first, but I insisted. We had a lovely chat. He said he had been ministering to that part of the county for years. Said he had been running the black concession at the drive-in for years." Reuben turned in the seat to face Charles, seeming to forget about how miserable he felt. "Now here's the interesting part. He said my manager out there was trying to cheat him out of his share of the business. They had said originally that he could have fifty percent of the ticket take in the Negro part, and *all* of the money from the black concession stand, but now they were only letting him have twenty-five percent of the tickets and they wanted fifty percent of the money he made on the concession stand. He uses the money to help his church members."

"Is that what he told you?"

Reuben looked straight ahead—thin-lipped. "I can tell you don't believe it, but I did."

"Did I say I didn't believe him?"

"You know what I told him? I said I would do better than that. I would integrate the entire thing."

"The entire what thing?"

"Are you listening? I told him I would write our manager out there and say that it was time for us to integrate the entire drive-in, that Reverend Watts had come to me and I agreed with him that we must move forward with integration—and do you know what? And this is the strange part. It seemed to upset him no end. He got out of his chair and immediately began backing toward the door. 'No,' he said, all he wanted was his fair share, kept repeating it, his fair share. He said he had to have it to support his congregations."

"And what did you say—'you'll assuage my conscience and take integration or nothing, Reverend?'"

"You think you're so humorous. No, I reluctantly agreed that if that's what he wanted, I would go along with his wishes and make sure he got his fair share, but that it seemed to me he would want equality for his people, never mind the revenue." Reuben paused to think about it. "I hope I didn't insult him, but that's what it seemed to me."

"What's the name of the church he's supposed to be supporting with all this largesse he's passing around?"

"The Word of Truth Missionary Baptist Church."

"The what?" Charles burst out laughing. "Now I've heard it all. The Word of Truth Missionary Baptist Church?" Charles was pulling into the airport parking lot. "I know the Pleasant Valley AME and Harvest Moon CME. They're presided over by Brother Earl, but I never heard of that one." Charles turned off the key, grabbed the paper out of Reuben's lap, and opened the door. "Sounds to me like you've been had, Reuben. The Word of Truth Missionary Baptist Church? That's one for the books."

Reuben opened his door and slammed it, following along behind to the airplane. "I most certainly have not. It's located up near your farm. He said so. I most certainly have not. I wrote a letter today to my manager out there and told him in no uncertain terms that from now on he was not to take advantage of Reverend Watts."

Charles was still laughing when he got to the plane. "Reuben, if there is a Reverend Watts, you have succeeded in putting him in harm's way with all the good old boys at Crossroads Drive-in." Charles stepped on the plane and shook hands with the candidate, who was sitting up with the pilot. Reuben did the same and took a seat beside Charles, searching for his seat belt. "I most certainly have not put anyone in harm's way. I merely gave my manager a directive."

Charles looked out the window, shaking his head at Reuben's complete ineptitude when it came to handling people. "Do you think your manager will take kindly to getting a letter from you in which you say you believe a Negro over a white man?"

"Well, you would, wouldn't you?"

"You're not dealing with me. You're dealing with a bunch of men mighty set in their ways—and that's putting a good face on it."

CHAPTER 40

The Reckoning

THE TRIP HAD GONE WELL—at first. The campaign-planning meeting was more like a pep rally. Everyone on the election committee had read the morning paper and the poll tallies. Various chairmen gave reports. Reuben, who seemed to be feeling better now that they were back on solid ground, reported that the coffers were in good shape and more contributions were coming in. It was the first time most of the other men had met Reuben. He reported on every contribution of any size. He handed out pages and pages of calculations, estimating their budget requirements from the present time until the election. There was a round of sedate applause when Reuben finally sat down. Charles watched several of the men glancing at each other, unable to keep from smiling. Brad La Forte ended the meeting by saying that he wanted volunteers to stand with him on the platform so he could acknowledge their fine work. Several raised their hands. Brad pointed to almost everyone there, having his secretary record the names for a press release. Reuben was the only one who did not get recognized. Of course, Reuben had not raised his hand in the first place. He told Charles that the thought of actually standing on a platform and having other people gawk at him was abhorrent.

After the meeting and before the rally, the men went to the local barbecue house for supper. Four carloads of them pulled off the highway and into the dirt lot that was the parking area for Bama Barbecue. Reuben, in his usual unwieldy way, had opened his door too quickly and banged it into the side of the pickup parked next to them. The two men in the pickup had glared at him and Reuben had apologized profusely—only making it worse.

Inside was a different matter. There was a festive air, the place full of friendly locals, some getting ready to go to the rally. It was warm and smoky. The smell of barbecue had long ago soaked into the walls and heavy wooden tables. A waitress took her towel and slapped crumbs out of the dark red vinyl booth before Charles and Reuben and two others of their party could sit down. Men with ice in their glasses periodically disappeared outside for refills stored in their pickups. Snatches of Eddie Arnold floated from the Wurlitzer in the corner.

There were four of them in the booth. Charles, Horace Ramps, and Jessie Camp, from over in Bullock County, ordered the sliced barbecue plate, iced tea, and pecan pie. Reuben ordered fries and an RC, meticulously dipping each fry in the mound of catsup he poured in the center of his plate.

Horace and Jessie directed most of their conversation to Charles. Reuben had been oblivious, hunched over his fries—intermittently smiling at Charles, injecting precise figures and campaign calculations into the conversation whenever they were fumbled over by the other three. His voice, without an accent, but with a high nasal tone, cut through the smoke and smell of barbecue.

They had all finished eating and were getting ready to leave when Charles went looking for Reuben, who had excused himself to go to the men's room, but that had been some time ago. Charles searched every part of the restaurant and was about to tell the others he would catch up to them later, but just then Reuben came hurrying back in the front door. "Where have you been hiding? I've looked everywhere."

"I went out to get in our car, and those men parked next to us were being insolent."

"Reuben, you're imagining things. We're in a hurry here." Charles had turned a deaf ear, embarrassed for Reuben, or maybe for himself.

They got to the rally site about the same time clouds rolled in over the hills lying off to the west. Fort Payne was in the center of a valley, bound by what passed for mountains in this part of Alabama. Charles felt the wind picking up. Stadium lights, set on telephone poles, cored paths down through the gathering darkness. Bunting rippled in the wind. Cars and trucks lined the grass parking area. Whole families had come for the speech making. In a rural county, a political rally was half social. Several local churches had set up food tables to earn extra income for their mission work. All manner of other candidates vying for county offices were wandering in among the crowd, using the gathering to pass out their campaign cards before Brad La Forte made his grand entrance. It was an acceptable practice for the sucking fish to feed off the whale.

Charles moved about in the press of people, passing out cards with "Brad La Forte for Governor" on one side and the Alabama and Auburn fall football schedules on the other. Reuben followed close behind, carrying extra cards, he said, in case anyone might run out. Charles tried to ignore him. At eight o'clock, as a few drops of rain could be felt, all the men in the candidate's party walked to the stage—all except for Reuben. Charles could see him standing down by the ten-yard line, leaning against the steps that led up to the bleachers. The only set of bleachers was on the north side of the field, so the speaker's platform faced it.

Charles was seated on the dais, trying to calculate the size of the crowd, half-listening to the speeches, when he saw the two men from the restaurant parking lot come up behind Reuben. They were younger than he remembered, probably in their mid-thirties, dressed as if they might work at a gas station: brown pants, heavy brown shirts. Reuben was standing with his coat over his arm and a small box of candidate cards in his hand when they appeared on either side of him, the tops of their shoulders even with the top of his head. He had begun fumbling in his coat for something and then dropped the nasal spray when he finally managed to get it out of his pocket. He reached down to pick it up. The men appeared to reach down to help him and then all three disappeared as Brad La Forte made a point to the crowd and it erupted in cheers. When the banners and balloons were back down in place, Charles couldn't locate Reuben or the two men. Charles sat on the platform for another few minutes, scanning the crowd, trying to keep from being overcome by a rising sense of panic. When the next cheer went up and everyone on the platform stood to applaud, Charles stepped to the back and hopped off the stage. He circled around the crowds of people and, finding no sign of Reuben, went out to scan the parking area. He caught sight of something moving in a dark corner several yards away from the line of cars that would take the candidate and his entourage back out to the airstrip. As he was running toward them, one of the men was hitting Reuben hard in the gut. They both had their backs to Charles and were facing the large oak tree against which they had pinned him. When Charles yelled, the two men didn't flinch, but just turned slowly and began to walk away.

"Hey." His yelling hadn't seemed to affect them. They were walking casually toward him. "What in the hell's going on here?" They walked as if they had heard nothing of Charles yelling, as if he had known what they were doing all along. They brushed past him out into the parking lot.

Reuben's legs gave way and he slid slowly down the tree trunk to a sitting position.

"Reuben, you okay?"

"Apparently . . ." He tried to smile. It turned to a grimace. "Some sort of welcoming committee." He followed this with an attempt to laugh, but the effort was so painful, he stopped immediately and used his arms to brace his ribs.

"My God, Reuben, what happened?" Charles dropped to his knees beside him and at the same time called to the two Highway Patrolmen stationed by the candidate's car, serving as escorts for the evening. "Those men. Get those . . ." By the time he pointed in their direction, the two were gone. Charles yelled as he stared at Reuben. "Can't you see somebody's hurt over here? Get the hell over here." The officers began to jog toward Charles, holding in place thick leather belts laden with law and order.

"I'm fine, fine—just don't touch me for a minute. Let me just rest here." Charles helped him ease back down to a sitting position. "This is supposed to be your job, isn't it? Where were you, damn it?"

The officers looked at him, nonplussed. "We was right here all along, guarding the candidate's car," one of them said. "Like we're supposed to," the other one added. "We didn't see nothing."

"Sir, you wanna swear out a warrant? We can do that if you're willing to . . ."

"We should swear out a warrant, Reuben. Really, it's what we should do."

"Just get me out of here, back home."

He yelled out in pain when Charles tried to help him. Just then, a roar went up from the stadium as the candidate made a point that particularly pleased the crowd. Charles glanced over his shoulder. The huge stadium lights were gathering swarms of night creatures flitting in and out of the beams. Cigarette smoke drifted up through the lights.

"Don't. Don't. Let me do it. I think they must have cracked some ribs." Charles stood up and watched as Reuben made several futile attempts, but in the end Charles had to pick him up and carry him over to one of the patrol cars. He had the mass and weight of a child. "Is there a hospital close by?"

Reuben's fingers gripped Charles's shirt. "I don't need a hospital."

"Big one over at Turvey City," the officer said. "Wanna go over there? Takes 'bout a hour."

"An hour? Don't you have something else closer, a local doctor that can take a look at him?"

"Doc Tram. He's off fishing for the week. That's alls I know of."

"I'm feeling better now, honestly." Reuben wet his lips and tried to speak distinctly to reassure Charles. "Have him take us to the plane. We can wait on the others at the plane."

"All right, take us to the airfield, then." He eased Reuben down in the backseat of the patrol car, then ran around and got in beside him. It had begun to sprinkle. The patrolman pulled out on the road and turned on the radio to look for the weather. The dial hummed past country and western, past good-time preachers and more static. The rain set up a tinny noise on the roof.

"What happened?" Charles whispered.

Reuben let his head rest against the backseat, eyes closed. "You know what happened."

"No, damn it. I don't know, Reuben. People just don't hit for no reason."

"That's something you couldn't imagine, could you, hitting for no reason? I heard what they said when they passed you. You heard it."

"'Jew boy'? Ignorant rednecks."

"'Faggot Jew boy' was the exact phrasing." Reuben's eyes were still closed, his breathing labored; yet there was a half smile. "It's easier not to see—isn't it?"

"No, it isn't," in a tone so abrupt it might have implied all this was Reuben's fault.

The patrol car pulled onto the paved strip of asphalt that was the airport. It was raining harder now. The windows had fogged over. The officer got out and ran to the porch of the cinder-block building that served as the waiting room and Unicom station. He switched the porch light on, came back out, and opened the door on Reuben's side—rain dripping in. The wind blew the patrolman's raincoat, slapping it up against Reuben's pants leg. "Nobody's here to unlock the place. They'll be along soon as the rally's over." He leaned down to look through to Charles. "Want me to carry him?"

"No. That's all right. I can manage." Charles stepped out in the rain and went around to Reuben's side. The patrolman took off his plastic raincoat and held it over them as Charles managed to get hands behind Reuben's back and under his legs and carry him, like some offering, up to the porch of the old building.

There was a sagging wooden swing at one end and a couple of worn cane-back chairs. "There," Reuben said, gesturing. The chains clinked as Charles eased him down.

The patrolman shook out his raincoat. "Always too much drinking at these things. That's why I don't like 'em. Roads is gonna be full of crazy people tonight."

Charles walked the patrolman back to the front of the porch. Thunder rumbled across the sky out over the landing strip. "When do you think you'll be back with the others? We need to get going soon as we can."

"Shouldn't be no longer than half hour or so. Gully-washer like this'll break up things at the high school for sure." He handed his raincoat to Charles. "Maybe the little fellow can use this."

He stepped off the porch. Charles watched his lights disappear down the rain-glazed road, then walked back to Reuben. "You doing okay?"

Reuben began to wheeze, trying to cough. He couldn't inhale enough air. He tried to reach into his pocket for a handkerchief. Charles leaned over, got it, and handed it to him. Reuben coughed into the hand-kerchief and then gripped it in his fist.

"This whole thing is my fault. I practically forced you to come."

There was that look on Reuben's face—tired disdain—the same one Charles had seen each time they had, on rare occasions, seemed to come to a dead end in their talks and had actually played a game of chess through to the end, Reuben making precise killing moves—as close as he could come to anger—bringing the game to an abrupt end, with Charles at checkmate.

"You don't have to worry, Charles. Long ago, I chose propriety over peace of mind." He looked up at Charles, trying to find some good in the path he had chosen. "But being there in the restaurant tonight . . . I felt . . . I felt I contributed enormously. Didn't you?"

And Charles nodded, only nodded. Of all the times in his life when he could have said more, he had only nodded. That would haunt him for the rest of his days.

—•—

Off in the distance, car lights bobbed up and down, coming through the rain and hitting every pothole as they came. Suddenly, four carloads of men were on the porch, stomping wet feet and congratulating each other on the event. The airport operator was unlocking the door to the building and flipping on lights; the door to the men's room was slamming open and shut. The patrol car's blue lights still flashed around in circles, hitting the building and then shooting out onto the airstrip to reflect against the plane, which was being pelted by rain. The sounds of the weather were completely drowned out by the triumph of a winning evening.

"Charles, we were saved by the bell." Brad La Forte walked over to Charles and Reuben. "You should've seen it, fellows. The minute I finished my last sentence, the heavens opened up."

"It was like word directly from above," one of the other men said. "'Verily I say unto you, vote for this man or there shall come forty days and forty night of storms.'" There were rounds of laughter and handshakes and congratulations as most of the others prepared to get back in the cars and leave.

The candidate took Charles aside. "One of the deputies said our treasurer had a little too much to drink. Is he okay?"

"He's fine. He'll be fine when we get him home."

Brad raised a hand in Reuben's direction and then drifted off to talk to his other supporters as they were leaving. The pilot went inside to get the latest weather report now that the Unicom operator was there. He came back out a few minutes later. "If we can get above this cloud cover, it's smooth sailing." He was saying this to Brad. Charles and Reuben would be the only other passengers in the Aero Commander.

"What do you think?" Brad asked the pilot. "I know everybody wants to get back tonight if at all possible. My boy has a baseball game tomorrow and I promised I would be there. Course, I'm not pushing you. The final decision is up to you."

The pilot scanned the dark skies. "Tell you what. I'll do my preflight and we'll see what it looks like then." He stepped out into the drizzle and walked over to the plane. Brad went inside to the men's room. Charles walked over to Reuben and asked if he thought he could stand.

He didn't open his eyes. "When the time comes."

It had almost stopped raining when the pilot signaled to them to come on.

Brad stayed on the porch, talking to the Unicom operator, waiting for Charles and Reuben to load first. The Unicom man spat tobacco juice out off the porch. "Tell your man to be mindful of them winds around the mountains up there—comes in fits and starts. Course I know he knows that."

Reuben was able to stand on his own, but he couldn't walk. Charles grasped his belt and was as gentle as he could be, given the steps and the rain-slick asphalt.

The pilot was in his seat, dialing in his radios, by the time they got out to the plane. At one point, Reuben cried out when Charles pushed too hard, trying to heave Reuben up the narrow passageway. Reuben dropped his handkerchief and grabbed Charles's arm. Finally settled, Charles fastened Reuben's seat belt and then did the same for himself. The last thing he remembered saying to Reuben was, "We make a pair, don't we?" Reuben hadn't answered.

Brad climbed in the front seat. The pilot started his engines and turned on his taxi lights. Charles looked out through the rain-draped window to the tarmac and saw, in the flashing plane lights, the handkerchief Reuben had dropped. It was soaked in red. As they rolled past, blood was seeping out onto the asphalt in little rivulets.

Charles could feel the plane airborne and then suddenly, still moving forward, the tail began to shift from side to side, as if the pilot was stomping the rudder pedals. The engines were at full throttle, but they weren't gaining altitude. Charles thought, This is what Reuben hates about flying, this turbulence. I'll never hear the end of this. He looked over to Reuben, expecting to see "I told you so" in his eyes, but Reuben's expression had not changed. He was sitting slumped over, his eyes closed, his mouth slightly ajar.

They were well off the ground and straightening out when the plane began to drop, sucked down, the propellers almost useless as they tried to cut through airflow that wasn't there. He remembered being thrown about, not being able to control his arms or legs, even though he had his seat belt well fastened.

He was never able to tell if the last sound he heard was the right engine misfiring, or maybe that last sound had been the tops of pine trees scraping against the belly of the plane.

—•—

When Charles came to, he could feel raindrops splashing on his head, and he thought, since it was pitch-dark, that the wetness he felt on his face was rainwater. The cabin in front of them, what he could see of it, appeared twisted out of line with the rest of the plane. As his eyes adjusted to the dark, short circuits in the wiring spit out sparks, which gave off just enough light to see that the pilot no longer had a head. A large metal object, perhaps in the shape of a propeller, rested to the side of the pilot's shoulder. He couldn't see the candidate's side of the cabin.

He remembered thinking how quiet it was, that they must be on one of the mountains that circled the air-field. He could hear sizzling noises—rain on hot metal—and cracking, popping sounds—wiring systems trying to reconnect with their home boards. Then the whooshing sound that comes when flame finds fuel. The wing out to his right caught on fire. He knew it held one of the gas tanks, and the surge of adrenaline, the sudden panic on top of panic, caused him to begin jerking at his seat belt. "Reuben, we gotta get out of here." He could hear himself mumbling this and then repeating it louder—"We gotta get the hell out of here, out of here, come on"—because somewhere in the back of his mind he realized Reuben hadn't called to him, hadn't moved. He tried undoing the seat belt with his right hand, but it didn't work. The hand didn't hurt, it just didn't respond to what he was trying to get it to do. He used his left hand, and the belt finally came free.

"Reuben, get up. We got to get out." He reached over to shake Reuben and then felt for the seat belt he had fastened not five minutes before. He jerked it free with his left hand. "Get up, get up!" He kept shouting at the dark lump that was Reuben. He was struggling—on his knees now—to pull Reuben out of his seat. He couldn't stand. There were obstructions all around and above him. He remembered pulling Reuben's body over on his back and holding one of his arms with his hand, then crawling forward toward the place where he felt the rain pouring in.

He had crawled out on the side opposite the flames, glancing back and seeing them licking the underside of the wing and growing stronger as he scooted backward away from it, pulling Reuben along between his legs, holding the collar of his coat with one hand and pulling with the other arm over a mulch of soggy, rotting pine needles.

The burning wing was behind the cockpit, probably sheared off by trees as they had skidded to a landing. An explosion was inevitable. He pulled back several more yards in among the trees, dragging Reuben with him, not wanting to look. And when he did, when he finally did, Reuben's face—reflected in the light of the burning wing—held the same expression it had before takeoff.

"Reuben," over and over, "damn it, Reuben," repeated and repeated, as he reached down, patting Reuben's chest and straightening Reuben's coat collar and realizing then that the whole evening—watching him give his report, having supper with him, and berating him for not being on time—he hadn't noticed: Reuben was wearing his wretched party tie.

—•—

It was an explosion so dazzling, it seemed to coat them, so strong that it created its own wind, blowing their hair, flinging pine needles and leaves past them. For a moment, there was light that obliterated the shadows. And then, as if asking forgiveness, it retreated back into a warm glow, remnants of their hopes lingering in midair—shimmering small pieces of debris, silently drifting back down through the trees, in among the raindrops—luminous, sparkling stars falling on Alabama, consecrating this place that had put an end to their dreams.

CHAPTER 41

The Road Home

THE BUICK HADN'T BEEN DRIVEN in weeks. Dust swirled off the hood as they pulled away from Highlander, Eugenia and Tab in the front seat. Tina, in the back, was still not speaking. Turning down off the mountain, road signs popped up at them: LUCKY STRIKE MEANS FINE TOBACCO. YOU'LL WONDER WHERE THE YELLOW WENT WHEN YOU BRUSH YOUR TEETH WITH PEPSODENT. Sliding back into the familiar old roads, the old signs—maybe even the old life. In just that long, Tab felt a million miles removed from the mountaintop.

When they came to a split in the highway, Eugenia stayed west on 64 instead of turning to go south to Alabama. Tab was so weary, she didn't want to ask. She closed her eyes and let her head rest against the window. The side vent blew air in her face. Tina was furiously flipping through a *Seventeen*, the same one she had left in the backseat the day they first came into Highlander. "Gravy, I can't afford these clothes. What do they expect me to wear this fall?"

Maybe Aunt Eugenia was afraid to go home. Maybe she couldn't think of a way to ease them back into the old life unannounced. Maybe that was the problem.

Tab's head was still up against the window and her eyes were still closed. "What we can do is tell them that we told Miss Bebe to call them and say we were coming home early, only Miss Bebe forgot to call."

Aunt Eugenia didn't say anything.

"What do you think about that? They'll never know, and we won't tell, honest."

Eugenia kept driving.

Tab sighed, "Okay, Aunt Eugenia, where are we going?" She reached up to tap the cloth stitching just above her head. Dust from Highlander sprinkled down over them.

"We need to go to Pulaski. There's one last little thing I need to do before I can go back to California in peace." She pressed down on the accelerator.

The pages of *Seventeen* stopped flipping in the back-seat. "What one last little thing?"

"We'll just take some small nonviolent action to show our displeasure. Then we'll move on, that's all." She twitched her shoulders, still gripping the wheel. "Not being invited to sit-in in Nashville, at least I can make some statement on my own."

"*Our* displeasure?" Tina pitched the *Seventeen* and tried to get Aunt Eugenia's attention in the rearview mirror. "See me? You are looking at a person who does not have any displeasure. I am happy—aren't we, Tab?"

"Oh yeah, happy, happy. And no, not one bit of displeasure do I have. I am done with making people mad," and to add emphasis, "Aunt Eugenia, did Granddaddy ever tell you about the lynching he went to up here in Tennessee when he was a boy? They don't take kindly to outsiders up here, Aunt Eugenia."

Eugenia said nothing.

"And you're about as outsider as they come."

Tab tried again. "Aunt Eugenia, people don't care about the plaque. All they want is to eat at Woolworth's, to go swimming in the heat, things like that. I never heard anybody say they were mad about the plaque, not Dominique, not Eloise." She began to think of Dominique. She would love this. She would love doing whatever it was they were getting ready to do. Tab couldn't suppress a grin.

Tina flopped back against the backseat, hands hugging her waist, "Jeez, I've had such a hard day. I don't need this. You know I'm not like the others. I didn't go on the bus trip," She sneered Tab's way. "Even though I was asked."

"You weren't. Who asked you? And what do you mean, saying, 'Jeez'?"

"Who do you think asked me? But I have more sense than some people."

They drove on down off the mountain, passing perfectly normal-looking farmhouses and pastures and farmers driving tractors in the fields. It seemed to be a perfectly normal day—for those people.

The ends of Eugenia's scarf caught the breeze and fluttered out the window. "There is a dark side to our family history we mustn't forget," she said.

"Oh no, Aunt Eugenia. You got that wrong." They both began shaking their heads too much in unison, hoping this would discourage her, since they seldom agreed with each other. "Our family," Tab said, "it's got a perfectly good history. We go to church. We're nice people. Uncle Arla, he died in the war, fighting the Nazis. Mama, she's president of the Red Cross auxiliary, for heaven sakes. Pop, he's president of the Rotary."

"The plaque, it's just some old piece of metal," Tina said, "put up there because the men were saving southern womanhood." Eugenia turned to look at Tina, reaching up to lower her glasses and get a clearer picture. Tab put a hand on the steering wheel, swerving to avoid a possum. "I know all about it," Tina said. "Don't look at me like I don't know all about it. Grandmother told us the whole story."

"We're not supposed to talk about that," Tab said. "Grandmother told us never to talk about that."

"Oh really." Aunt Eugenia was momentarily diverted. "I'm sure I've already heard it, but what did she tell you, just to refresh my memory?"

"She told us the story of Cousin Annie Sue Harden, her mama's first cousin. You remember her talking about Cousin Annie Sue?"

"I remember seeing her. She was an old lady when I was a child, but she died when I was little, so I don't remember much. What about her?"

"You better not tell that story," Tab said. "Grandmother cried when she told us that story. You're gonna get in trouble."

"You can tell me, Tina."

"It was about that time she was out in the cotton fields, after the war, trying to make a garden because there was nothing to eat and they needed food 'cause her husband had been killed in the war and she had two little children to feed, and along came a gang of freed slaves, and they took cousin Annie Sue down to the creek and . . . and they made her take off all her clothes and . . . and she was horrified. That's what Grandmother said. Cousin Annie Sue Harden was horrified to tell, but she went into town and told the Yankee general that was in charge, and after she told him, he just laughed and said it served her right. And then she had to go to Texas for a whole year to have the baby." Tina stopped to take a breath and Tab took it up, because the cat was out of the bag by then, and besides, she did feel for Cousin Annie Sue Harden, she really did.

"And so Cousin John Lester and the rest had to do something about it, 'cause if they hadn't, it woulda happened all over the place."

Aunt Eugenia drove on. It was a two-laner and she decided to pass a tractor that was pulling a hay baler, with a truck coming in the opposite direction. Tab slid down in the seat and closed her eyes. After a minute or two, when they weren't dead, she sat up and looked out.

"She never told me that story, her own daughter."

"Well, it's true," Tina said.

"It's just an old wives' tale," Aunt Eugenia said. "The family is full of old wives' tales."

"How do you know that?" Tina had her arms over the front seat, watching Aunt Eugenia's face in the rearview mirror.

"I saw a picture of Cousin Annie Sue Harden. Grandmother showed it to me," Tab said. "She said she had to leave her baby in Texas with some Mexican family 'cause it was so dark." Her mind wandered for a moment, thinking about that baby and what had ever happened to it and if Cousin Annie Sue was like Dominique's mother. Did she ever wonder about Dominique? She had never before considered Cousin Annie Sue's baby and what had happened to it, only Cousin Annie Sue.

"Your grandmother would not tell you a tale like that. I know it."

"We were sitting right there on the porch. I remember it because it was when Great-Uncle Colton was visiting from Georgia and brought her the peach wine he'd made. We were sitting there, just the three of us, and she was sipping and rocking. Every time I smell peaches, I think of that night," Tina said.

"It couldn't be true," Eugenia said again.

"How do you know?" Tab asked.

—•—

Aunt Eugenia ordered tea and butter beans. "I'll have butter beans, cream corn, string beans, sweet potatoes, fried chicken, corn bread, sweet tea, and pecan pie for dessert." Tab handed the menu to Tina.

They had passed the sign advertising Aunt Joleen's Kountry Kitchen just outside of Pulaski. That's when Tab remembered she could say she was hungry, since it was already past dinnertime. Aunt Eugenia would have to stop, even though she was anxious to get on with it. It would slow things up a bit. Tab needed time to think about this. Maybe her father wouldn't like it. She knew for sure Dominique would. Granddaddy would not. Grandmother would not. Why was she taking a vote? The twins and Charles Junior wouldn't care. Uncle Tom would hate them doing this—whatever it was they were going to do.

Tab dawdled over her green beans and the pecan pie. She struck up a conversation with the waitress. "Miss Cora"—her name was right there above the purple lace handkerchief blooming out of her breast pocket—"mighty good pecan pie. This y'all's specialty?"

"That and the peach cobbler," Miss Cora looked at the rest of the table. "Anybody wanta try the peach cobbler?"

"I do."

"Aw honey, you can't do that," said Miss Cora. "You've already 'bout busted a gut with what you done et so far." She stood there, with pencil and pad, adding up the bill. "Y'all on your way to Memphis?"

"Directly, but first we gotta look round a little more." Tab was bad to go along with the local talk. Aunt Eugenia only wished she could, it having been completely washed out of her, probably someplace in India.

They watched Miss Cora still adding up the bill. Miss Cora was not a fast adder. "Lordy, I was wonderin'," Aunt Eugenia said, trying to affect a country air and it not coming off at all. "Do y'all got any idea of something of historical interest round these here parts that we might lay eyes on?"

Cora looked sideways at Aunt Eugenia, like she had just run her fingernails across a blackboard. Then she rolled her eyes at Tab.

"What she means is," Tab said, "how do you get to the Ku Klux Klan plaque from here?"

Tina folded her arms around her waist and looked down at the floor.

"Oh that. You take Second Street for a couple of blocks and then turn left on Jefferson. Go past the courthouse and it's down there on your left. You can't miss it. Lawyer offices now. George is away for the week fishing, but you don't need to get in. Right there on the outside of the building."

Aunt Eugenia was opening her purse to get out money and her cat's-eye sunglasses. "That's very kind of you. We're truly much obliged." She snapped her purse shut. "And by the way, where is the nearest hardware store?" Tina put her elbows on the table, rested her head in her hands, and groaned. Miss Cora gave them a funny look, but told them.

When they left, Miss Cora was standing at the next table. She was taking the orders of the three men sitting there. Once, she pointed her pencil in Aunt Eugenia's direction.

After she picked up the paint and a brush at the hardware store—Aunt Eugenia said she had chosen white for purity—they headed to the plaque.

Tab caught Tina glaring at her from the backseat, as if she was some kind of traitor just because she was sitting up front and somehow couldn't keep the grin off her face. She was thinking of Dominique: I'll have something to write to you about soon, *mon amie.*

"I am not taking part in anything unlawful," from the backseat.

"That's what I used to say."

"I am not breaking the law."

"This is nothing compared to the other. I'm getting used to this." Tab did notice, out of the rearview mirror, as they left the hardware store, that there was a blue Dodge following them, about a '56, like the one that had been parked next to them at the Kountry Kitchen. It had disappeared by the time they pulled up to park in front of the plaque.

"You may come or not," Eugenia said. "It's up to your individual conscience." Tab opened her door.

"What are you doing? Egad, do you know what you're doing, Tab? You could get arrested. What would Mother say?"

"I am going, Tina, to *look* at the plaque. That's all I got in mind—to *look* at the plaque." Tab closed the door and talked through the window. "I am *not* the one carrying the gallon of paint. I am *not* the one with the paintbrush. You can see that plain as day, can't you? Besides, there's nobody around. They've all gone home to dinner."

When Aunt Eugenia said she couldn't get the top off the paint can, Tab did go back to the car and get a screwdriver out of the glove compartment.

"I'm telling. I don't care what you say." Tina flopped down in the backseat, covering her face with the *Seventeen*.

A few minutes later, they opened the back doors of the car, dropped some things on the floorboard, slammed the doors, hopped in the front, and drove away.

Tina lifted the *Seventeen*. "Just wait 'til we get home."

"I"—Tab was leaning over the backseat, smiling—"I did not have a hand in opening the paint. That was all Aunt Eugenia, and you can't tell on her. She's an adult."

Aunt Eugenia was in a state of euphoric shock, white knuckles gripping the wheel, a silly grin on her face, mumbling, "I can't believe . . . after all these years," followed by giddy laughter.

"And when she wrote the word *shame* in big letters across the building and put an arrow pointing to the plaque," Tab said, "I did *nothing* but stand back and say that I thought an exclamation point would be in order."

"Oh gravy."

"The next part, where she accidentally brushed up against the plaque and realized that it was loose in its bolts, so then she took the screwdriver out of her pocket and began to pry the plaque off the wall . . ." Tina sat up slowly, staring at her. Tab shrugged her shoulders. "I had nothing to do with that. I don't know why I was grinning when she did it. I just was. I was just caught up in the moment or something."

Tina didn't move, but her eyes shifted to the floorboard.

"I did pick up the paint can and the brush—no fingerprints left behind. Looks like you could be happy about that." Tina moved to the corner opposite the plaque, huddling up, like it might strike out at her.

They were not even out of the city limits when Tab noticed the blue Dodge several cars behind them. She decided to break the news slowly. Tina was not used to the protest life. "You know how you feel, Tina, just before you get to the top of the first hill on a roller coaster? You know, like you should take a deep breath 'cause pretty soon you won't be able to take a breath at all?"

"What are you mumbling about, and at a time like this? We could all go to jail."

"Oh nothing." She thought better of it and turned to Aunt Eugenia. "Aunt Eugenia?" Both of her aunt's hands were gripping the wheel. There wasn't much paint at all on her fingers. "Aunt Eugenia?" She had a glazed look on her face and it was blushing red. "Aunt Eugenia, did you notice that car back there? I think it was the same one as at the Kountry Kitchen. If I was a betting person, I'd say Miss Cora tattled."

"I knew it," said Tina, not daring to turn around and look. "I knew it. I knew it."

"Can't you say something useful," Tab said, "like 'Where is the nearest police station?'" Then after a moment's consideration, "Never mind, we couldn't go there."

Tina turned slowly and looked out the rear window, catching glimpses of the blue Dodge several cars back. "How much gas have we got?" It was time to face up to things. "How much?" she said.

"Just a minute and I'll tell you." Tab moved one of Aunt Eugenia's hands down on the wheel to get a look at the gauges. "Less than a quarter of a tank."

"Not enough, but it'll have to do. Gimme that map

outta the glove compartment. We gotta get out of this state." She looked back at the blue Dodge and then up at Tab. "Course it's just a coincidence. I'm sure it's just a coincidence. Soon as we clear town, it'll go its way and we'll go ours."

"That's what I think also," Tab said, to make her happy, just as Tina was trying to make Tab happy. Aunt Eugenia was beyond happy. The whole of Sherman's army could have been behind them now and she would not have cared. "We made a clear, nonviolent statement for all the world to see."

"And so what's the world gonna see?" Tina was feeling vindictive. "There is now a hole in the wall and the word *shame* painted on the side of the building, with an arrow pointing to the hole, like you were saying, It's a shame the plaque is gone."

It was a particularly bad habit of Tab's that she would start laughing in the worst types of situations. That was why Grandmother never took her to funerals anymore, but she could picture it: all the people of Pulaski walking along and nodding their heads and saying, "Why, yes, it sure is a shame the glorious plaque has gone missing."

Tina drummed her fingers on the map and waited until Tab had stopped laughing. "You are gonna *think* funny if that car back there keeps following us. Turn left here at this next corner, Aunt Eugenia. That's county road Thirty-three.

"Left here?" Eugenia was slowly coming out of her trance. "Why would we want to turn left? That takes us southeast; we want to go straight south. See that sign that says 'Lawrenceburg, nineteen miles'? That's where we want to go." She sailed past the left turn and headed toward Lawrenceburg, jiggling the wheel, swerving across the middle line in the road to punctuate her point. "I must call Val tonight."

"That was the last turn south 'til we get to Lawrenceburg." Tab was hanging back over the front seat, looking at the map with Tina. "We can turn south in Lawrenceburg. It's not far from there to Highway 72 and then home to Bainbridge," Tina said. She looked down to consult the map again. Tab watched the blue Dodge. There were two cars and a truck between them. "Besides, this is the main road out of Pulaski. If some native persons are out in their cars and headed this way, they just naturally have to be on this road."

"So," Tina said, trying to be casual about it, not wanting to send Aunt Eugenia off in the wrong direction, "what do you plan to do with the plaque? You're not gonna"—she pretended to laugh—"gonna take it back to Granddaddy, are you?"

Aunt Eugenia laughed. "Don't be silly."

The girls looked at each other, "Don't be silly," in unison.

"Of course she wouldn't do that," Tab said.

"So," Tina said, "what might we think about doing with it?"

"The obvious, my dears." She tapped the horn of Grandmother's Buick to make her point.

"Aah, the obvious." Tina was nodding.

"We will hurl it into the muddy depths of the Tennessee River, upon whose banks our ancestors perpetrated untold anguish and heartache."

"My ancestors did not—" Tina put a hand over Tab's mouth.

"That's a great idea, Aunt Eugenia."

"I don't know if I want to do that to the plaque," Tab whispered.

"What do you want to do, take it home to Grand-daddy?"

The Blue Dodge edged closer as other cars on the highway left the main road for the sanctuary of home.

CHAPTER 42

The Blue Dodge

NOW SHADOWS WERE LONG off the passing trees. Traffic had thinned to an occasional tractor lumbering along on its way home. The blue Dodge was still four or five car lengths behind, but there was no one in between now. The girls could no longer imagine that this might all be happenstance. Eugenia was still off in her own world, contemplating the vast implications of a bucket of white paint on a brick wall. They would hear about this in Berkeley.

"Aunt Eugenia, remember that car I mentioned before? Have you noticed that it's still behind us? It's been following us since Pulaski."

"Must be going on down to Birmingham."

"No, ma'am, I don't think so. I think it's following us on purpose. I think they know about the paint in Pulaski, about the plaque."

"Don't be ridiculous. How could they know that? Not a soul was around when we did it."

"I'm sure they're just country boys out for a good time," Tab said, "but if they get to drinking too much, we're in big trouble out here, out of our state and nobody to call on." The thought gave rise to an acid taste in her throat. How was it that now, suddenly, they had no one to call on, when before, always before, they had lived in the center of founding authority?

They were coming into Lawrenceburg. "This is absurd. I'm going to stop now and get some gas. You watch. That car will go right on by." And it did go on by, but it stopped down at the corner as they gassed up the Buick.

Tab kept an eye on them while Aunt Eugenia went to the ladies' room. "Probably calling home to say they're gonna be late on account of they have to run some outsiders off the road into the river and to keep the chitterlings warm."

Tina bit a nail and watched one of the three of them get out and make a phone call in the booth on the sidewalk. An empty beer can was pitched out the driver's side.

—•—

What happened next turned into a blur of asphalt and trees and sky. As soon as they were on the outskirts of Lawrenceburg and on a lonely two-lane road, the blue Dodge pulled up behind them and began tapping their bumper. When a sheriff's car passed at the next intersection, the Dodge backed off, but it came at them again when the patrol car was out of sight. What began as worry over scratches to Grandmother's car quickly turned to panic that something far worse might happen.

The whole car would shake each time there was contact with the back bumper. If Aunt Eugenia slowed down, the bumps were harder and more frequent. If she went faster, contact was more erratic and caused both cars to sway wildly over the road. "This is asinine. I'm going to stop and talk to them, whoever they are."

"Are you crazy, Aunt Eugenia? Out here in the middle

of nowhere and it getting dark? And we got the plaque here in the car with us?" They were too afraid to think of crying. With each contact, the girls were holding on to anything available or bracing against the ceiling. The blue Dodge began to honk right before it would hit. Dust was rushing through the open windows. There was not another car in sight.

The next stretch of road was curving and the Dodge couldn't get at them as easily as it had on the straight-away. Eugenia floored the gas pedal. "We're coming to the Alabama line; they'll pull back now."

Tab reached over and turned on the car lights. They could see the Welcome to Alabama sign in the high beams. All that was left of the sun was an orange glow through the trees off to their right. The blue Dodge had turned into two headlights, cutting through the dust as it flew past the welcome sign.

"They're not turning back, but we're coming up on Crossroads. We're not that far from home." Suddenly, Eugenia made a hard left turn onto a dirt road and the Dodge boys overshot the turn. The big Buick swerved and careened from side to side as the road got smaller and rougher. At one point, they may have even cut across a pasture. Fence posts zipped by in the dark. "If we can find a house, they won't dare come into the yard," Eugenia said. That's what she thought.

The Buick took the next left and began bumping down steep, hard-packed clay toward a large clapboard house. They were bound to hit it if Tab hadn't started yelling at Eugenia, who was looking to her rear. The car skidded to a stop right past the house, coming to rest in what seemed to be its backyard.

They were momentarily lost in a cloud of dust as the Buick shook itself to a stop, high beams coursing through dancing red clay particles. They sat perfectly still, all of them, not wanting to move, for fear it would bring on the Dodge boys.

The settling dust gave way to a strange sight: an old flatbed truck covered with crepe-paper streamers, eerie in the Buick's high beams. Long crepe-paper arms were swaying in the night breeze. A table and several chairs sat on the top. A fake window painted on a piece of plywood leaned up against the back of the cab—maybe an empty stage, or perhaps a plaything for children. "What in the world?" Eugenia began brushing the dust off of her shoulders, staring at the thing, half-expecting the Dodge boys to skid in behind them any minute.

Tina was in the backseat, burying the plaque under her sweater, and then her periscope eyes rose slowly to take a look around, coming only to the top of the front seat. "What is that thing?"

"Who cares, long as we lost 'em." Tab was trying to figure how to turn off the ignition and the lights so as to look casual, as if all along they had meant to end up down here in this gully behind this broken-down old building—just in case anybody was here in the first place, in case anybody was watching.

They sat in the car for a moment, getting used to the dark, listening to the quiet. There was the click of the door handle as Eugenia opened it and got out. The girls followed, walking around to meet in front of the car. The moon was in and out of the clouds. A whip-poorwill called in the distance. It was such a contrast to what had gone before; the silence was ringing in their ears. "Must be a child's plaything." They moved closer to it. Tab reached out and pulled at one of the streamers.

"Don't go messing with the float," a low voice said from out of the dark. They all jumped and backed up into one another, searching for the source. There was a creaking sound and they could make out the outline of a man sitting in a swing under some pine trees. The figure slowly rose and began walking in their direction. Eugenia, her voice unsure, began talking to this shadow figure. "What a lovely night we have here," she said, trying to straighten her scarf, brushing dust off her dress. "I hope you'll forgive this interruption." The black man—now they could tell he was an older black man— said nothing, just kept walking toward them. "I see you're building a lovely, lovely . . . thing there." Eugenia took a few steps back, as did the girls.

Their eyes were adjusting and they were beginning to see by the full moon that was coming up over the fields. Tab could hear the call of a screech owl out in the woods, much like the one she remembered from their Highlander nights.

"You ladies lost?" The black man clicked his flashlight on their little cluster.

"Lost?" They looked at one another, delighted with that explanation. "Lost? Lost! Yes, that's what we are, lost," Aunt Eugenia said, and Tina and Tab nodded their heads in violent agreement. "Lost—yes, we've been circling around here forever and a day."

"Where 'bouts you headed?"

"Headed?" Eugenia said. "Well, we were trying to get to—"

"Home," Tina almost shouted. She cleared her throat and said it again, trying for more dignity. "We would like to go home . . . to Bainbridge."

He swung his flashlight up into the darkness, pointing it toward the road. "Wouldn't be having a disagreement with that coming yonder, would you?" Heads jerked around. Being behind the building, they couldn't see the car, only a glow up on the road, moving along slowly, streams of reflected light shining up through the trees as it came toward them.

They stepped closer to the black man. Aunt Eugenia began to gush. "What happened was that we were minding our own business and that . . . those . . . that car full of—"

He stopped her. "Why don't you ladies come on inside 'til whoever that is up there finds whatever it is they looking for."

"That's an excellent idea, excellent," Aunt Eugenia said, and all three followed along behind him, centipede-fashion. He opened the door to a back room that was so dark, they couldn't see anything. He said for them to follow close behind him, which they did. They went into the next room, which was bigger. He pointed his flashlight and told them to have a seat on one of the pews. That was when they realized that they must be in a church of some sort.

"Everybody gone to the drive-in picture show right now. Ain't nobody here but me. Sit on down. Let me go look can I see up on the road."

"I don't think I would have any dealings with those gentlemen if I were you," Aunt Eugenia said. "And this," she called to the man she had decided must be the minister of the church, "this is a lovely sanctuary, Reverend."

"How does she know that? I can't see a thing. It's black as pitch in here." Tab was whispering into Tina's ear, holding on to her shoulder. The black man walked slowly to the front of the church.

Looking through the window, they could see a glow of light from up on the road. He opened the door a crack and looked out as the light passed. Then he closed it and came back to where they had taken seats on one of the front pews.

"Look to me like they gonna be back. Driving slow, like they looking for something." He stood for a moment, flipping the flashlight on and off, watching the small circle it made on the floor. "Now they can't see the car you come in less they be round back." He turned the flashlight off and put it in his pocket. "We don't want 'em coming round back, and Jessie be bringing them others from the drive-in anytime now. They see all the lights on, bound to know something wrong." He nodded his head as if he had decided. "Y'all get up under them pews. I'm gonna turn on all the light I can find. Wouldn't want them to see you."

"Oh, now sir, I don't think that's a good idea. You don't know these men. They're—"

"Been knowing them kinda men all my life. Them kind put off by a lot of light, and it'll warn the others that's coming."

"But—"

The preacher held up his hand. "Now miss, I know what I'm doing here, and we ain't got much time. They driving slow, like they looking for something, and they ain't gonna leave less they come down and see to this place, it being the only turnoff between here and Hollow Road. Strange car, ain't never seen it round here, probably from out of the county. More'n likely, they gonna be turning round right now."

"I'll do it," Tab said. "I'll get up under this one." She dropped to her knees.

"Scoot over." Tina scrunched in beside her. Tab ended up in the floor space between the first and second pews. As she scooted forward, her hand touched a piece of paper on the floor and it made a slight cracking noise.

"Shhhh." Tina was lying full out on her stomach, her head hugging the floor.

"Now listen here." The preacher's voice had dropped to a whisper. "These boys mean business—think I seen a coon tail on the antenna." A faint glow of light stopped him. It was still some distance off, but coming slowly back down the road. "Quiet now." He turned and walked up the aisle, the echo of his footsteps bouncing off the corners of the church walls. Tab touched the paper again without meaning to. It made a rustling sound.

"Will you shut up?" Tina had raised up long enough to whisper it, then pressed her cheek back down on the pine flooring, eyes squeezed tight.

Eugenia sat down on the floor with them, her arm resting on the seat as if to protect them. "This is just ridiculous. How did this ever happen?"

"How do you think it happened?" Tina said in a loud whisper, the anger welling up past the fear. "You go making a lot of trouble and somebody's gonna notice. Didn't you think about that? Don't you ever think about that?"

And Eugenia, "They wouldn't hurt a man of God."

Tab could see the reflected glow through the front windows of the church, very faint but coming forward, not stopping, not going away. They were stuck, trapped down here in this gully, in this church that didn't even look like a church. If something happened to them, nobody would even think to look down here. And it came to her, for a moment, just one moment—Dominique's constant way of being.

Tab heard faint clinks and closed her eyes to what seemed a bright light. The preacher had pulled the strings on two of the lightbulbs closest to the entrance. Tab kept her eyes closed to let them adjust to what was a dim, faded light when she opened them again. She inched forward enough to look down the aisle and see the silhouette of the preacher standing under the light, opening the front door.

Eugenia said, "I don't know how we got into this. I honestly don't, but if—if it was my fault—"

"Shhh, Aunt Eugenia, please, just please, be quiet." Tina buried her face again.

The Dodge's lights bounced up into the trees and down on the red clay as it turned off the main road and came down the drive toward the front of the church. For an instant, the lights shot through the front door and hit against the opposite wall, illuminating a cross that was nailed there, momentarily casting its shadow on them.

Eugenia scrunched down a little bit lower to the floor. Tina whispered into her hands, "Oh Lord, oh Lord," and it raced through Tab's mind also—thoughts of contrition and absolution, hoping that the Lord knew that it had not been her idea to steal the plaque, but of course He could see that in the first place and He could also see that none of this was her doing, and if He would just get them out of this, she would go straight home to Bainbridge and stay there for the rest of her natural life and never again be tempted by some rabble-rousing outsider California aunt.

Not only had the preacher turned on all the lights but he had proceeded, as casual as you please, to stoop down and wedge the front door open with a stick just as two of the Dodge boys—they heard them but couldn't see—

slammed their doors and came walking up to the front door of the church.

"Evening," the black man said, as if it were Sunday and he was greeting his congregation. "When I seen them lights, thought you was the first of the all-night prayer meeting people coming."

Voices came out of the dark. "Prayer meeting? Ain't it a little late for a prayer meeting, uncle?" They sounded friendly enough. Tab thought they sounded that way.

The black man never stopped fussing with the door, making sure that it was pushed back up against the wall. "Well now, yes, sir, may be, but at Word of Truth Missionary Baptist we always have us a night of prayer before commencing with revival." He managed to position the door as he liked it. "Yes, sir, revival once a year. Early for a revival, I know, but I like to get a jump start on the Devil." This was followed by a hardy laugh.

The others didn't say anything.

"You'll excuse me, I'm gonna need to sweep this here stoop. Like to have things neat when they gets here."

Still silence.

He stepped back and opened the coat closet just inside the door, took out a broom, and began to sweep. "Rest of the congregation coming long any minute now. Something I can do for you gentlemen?" He finished with the doorway and stepped out onto the stoop, still sweeping. "Yes, sir, be long any minute now."

Tab strained to see just beyond him into the dark.

Suddenly, a hand reached out from the shadows and grabbed the reverend's broom, jerking it away from him, knocking him off balance. There was a low cracking sound, like a bone breaking. Two pieces of the broom were thrown back up on the stoop; they rattled across the pine floor, landing at the preacher's feet.

Tina reached over and touched Tab. Her whole body jumped. "Shhhh."

The voice out of the dark again: "We ain't interested in no prayer meeting, Reverend. Looking for a woman and kids been by here in a Buick."

"That there is my sister and her kids," another voice. "You seen 'em?"

The preacher needed only to point down the aisle in their direction. That was all he needed to do, but he was conditioned, as they were not, to a world of higher stakes, of greater consequences, a world that was ordinarily out of balance. He was standing very still, not lifting his head, not taking his eyes off the pieces of broom that lay on the stoop. "No, sir, can't say as I have."

"You sure?"

His eyes were still fixed on the broom and his story. "Yes, sir. Just getting ready for the all-night prayer meeting is all."

A light came on in the blue Dodge as the third man got out of the car. "We ain't got all night. What's he say? Where they at?"

"Says he ain't seen 'em."

"Hell, he's bound to. This the road they come by."

The first man stepped up on the porch and grabbed the reverend's coat and pushed him back against the door frame. "Don't you go lying to me, nigger. This the road they come by." The preacher's head jerked back as the man slapped him across the face.

"What is it? What are they doing?" Eugenia eased forward to look up the aisle. "We just must stop this right now."

Tina grabbed her skirt. "No. You might get him killed." She caught her ankle and held tight. "And us."

"Naw, sir, ain't seen nobody." The reverend had taken a handkerchief out of his pocket and was wiping his face but sticking to his story. "Just been getting ready for the prayer meeting. Everybody be long any minute now." And just as he said it, as if he might have prayed them up, car lights appeared on the road. They turned off and came down the church drive, slowing when they saw the Dodge and pulling right up behind it.

"Maybe there really is a prayer meeting tonight," whispered Eugenia, ever the believer.

Tab could hear the sounds of car doors slamming, of other people talking in accents and with a cadence that was familiar to her. She heard the reverend greeting the newcomers, saying in a pointed way how glad he was that they were here for the prayer meeting and maybe they might have seen a car full of white women.

"Go on. Go on and tell the gentlemen if you seen somebody," the preacher said, his voice drenched in sincerity. "I'll go on back in the sanctuary and turn on them outside lights to see better by." He slowly walked away from them, leaving the Dodge boys to question the newcomers.

—•—

He was standing beside them now but not looking at them. "You ladies," he whispered, "crawl on out the way you come in. Go on and get in your car. When I give you the signal with my flashlight, you turn on your engine, but don't turn them lights on. Then get on out of here."

Aunt Eugenia started to get up off the floor, whispering to the preacher. "I'm terribly sorry about placing you in danger, Reverend. We never meant to—" He put his hand on her shoulder and pushed her down hard. "Go on and get, like I told you, while the getting's good."

"But I feel so responsible for—"

"This ain't nothing. We handle this. They talking right now, asking the others if they seen y'all. The others done seen the situation. They hold 'em long as they can, but pretty soon they gonna wanna come in and search the sanctuary. Now when they do and I blink my flashlight, you drive on out of here, and remember, don't turn them lights on."

Tina and Aunt Eugenia had crawled out before Tab. She backed up under the pew, her hand touching the paper again, her fingers gripping it as she backed and turned to crawl after them. They had made it to the smaller room and were standing when somebody called to the reverend to ask if he had found the outside light switch. He said he was trying it, that it must be burned out.

The voice of what sounded like an older black lady was saying that she believed she would come on in and practice her hymns while the gentlemen were looking around, and for everybody else to come join in singing with her.

As they were easing out the back door and making their way to the car, the Dodge Boys were coming in the front. The piano struck up "I'll Fly Away." The singing was loud and fervent. Tina slipped in the front seat with Aunt Eugenia. Tab tripped over the plaque and closed the back door. They began to creep away as soon as they saw the flash of the reverend's light. Aunt Eugenia backed out very slowly and then shifted into forward and started up the drive in the dim moonlight. They got a glimpse, only a passing glimpse, through the two side windows. There looked to be a young woman holding a crutch or a cane and a boy and an older man all standing by the piano and singing along. A few notes of a new song drifted out to them as they passed.

They went up the drive, turned left, and drove for a mile or so before they found Highway 72, not a word among them. The night air blew at their faces. For the first time, Tab felt the paper in her hand. She had made sure she held on to it, hoping to find out where she had been. She unfolded it, thinking it might be an old church bulletin. She would know where they had been, who it was that had saved them. She reached up and turned on the overhead light.

"Are you crazy? Turn that off. Do you want them to see us?"

"Just a minute." She unfolded the paper. It wasn't a church bulletin at all, just cheap writing paper, like a child might use to practice penmanship—faded, awkward letters written out in obedience to the lines on the paper: "50 cents per person." Vacation Bible School in the church was what she figured.

"Will you turn off that light?"

"Okay, okay." She turned it off, wadded up the paper, and threw it out the window, not knowing where they had been or who had saved them from a fate that might have been worse than Cousin Annie Sue Harden's.

They were coming to Twelve Mile Creek, not the Tennessee River, but it crossed under the highway bridge just before it spilled out into the big river, so that counted. Tina didn't turn around, just reached her hand back over her shoulder and pointed. "We're coming up on the bridge. You should get rid of that thing before we get too close to home."

"Me?"

"Yes, you. So get ready."

Aunt Eugenia slowed the car to a crawl. "Let's get rid of this business once and for all." Tab looked down at the sweater that covered it, brushing her shoe over the top. "I don't hear you moving, Tab. Get ready."

Tab bent down, pretending to busy herself with the plaque. They were on the bridge now. The moon had come out from behind intermittent clouds. She could see moonlight reflected on the water ripples below. She lifted it up to her lap. She could hear the bugles sounding. She pushed the sweater aside to stare in the face of it. She could see his blond hair reflected in it as the moon caught the metal surface, his hat sitting at a jaunty angle, a boy's smile forever on his face as he marched forward into the swirling mist, to the sound of the drums, to the shouts of the—

"Will you throw the thing?"

It was too heavy. It wouldn't lift off her lap, like a child gone completely limp, not wanting to do her bidding. They were coming to the end of the bridge. Aunt Eugenia was slowing to a stop. No car lights were visible in either direction. "Throw it, Tab, or give it to me. I'll throw it," said Tina, trying to reach over the backseat.

"No, I'll do it." Tab couldn't even see the plaque now. It was a hazy dark lump. "If we're gonna do it, I'll do it." The car had come to a complete stop. She opened the door and got out, holding the plaque in both arms, bent over from its weight. A strange wind was blowing through the bridge girders, the sound of Yankee reinforcements coming off the steamboats at Pittsburgh Landing, thousands of them, headed for Shiloh Chapel. She lifted it up and let it rest on the bridge railing. The moon eased its way from behind the clouds again. She looked down into its murky burial ground.

Aunt Eugenia had gotten out of the car and come up beside her. "We've got to get going," she said. "Either you do it or I'll do it."

"I'm not doing it," Tab said. "You can do it. I'll watch you do it, but I'm not doing it."

Aunt Eugenia tipped it forward with a flick of her finger. It lost its balance and fell headfirst. The moonlight caught it in flashes as it sank beneath the water.

—•—

It was almost ten o'clock when they hit the front drive of Grandmother's house and then walked up the steps to the others, who were enjoying ice cream and watching the lightning bugs.

"I'll bet," Tab said, out of breath from running to them, "I'll bet y'all are not surprised to see us." In fact, they were all sitting there looking dumbfounded.

Aunt Eugenia was right behind. "Didn't Bebe tell you we were coming? I told her to call you."

"She didn't call you?" Tina tried to look incredulous.

"We told her two hundred times before we left to call you and tell you we were on the road." They looked at one another, shrugging shoulders, "Musta slipped her mind."

Tab plopped down in the wicker swing after kissing her mother, grandmother, grandfather, and her aunt and uncle, then waving to the cousins, who were still up, and out in the yard playing hide-and-seek. For the moment, she and Tina hadn't noticed their father was missing, thinking he must have stepped in the house and would be along presently. Grandmother took the top off the freezer, spooned out some ice cream, handed it to Tab. "Why on earth are you wearing those ridiculous cat's-eye sunglasses and it's pitch-black dark?'

Tab looked at sweet old Grandmother and all the others sitting there like they hadn't moved since she had left them.

"It's in keeping," she said, swallowing a spoonful of strawberry, "with my new self." She pointed her spoon at Grandmother. "I'm not saying right this very minute that it is gonna be my new self, but—"

"Oh Lord," said Grandmother.

CHAPTER 43

The Last Night

*J*ESSIE STAYED LATE, tying up the Kentucky Wonders and weeding the corn. Maudie made tuna fish sandwiches, using lettuce and tomatoes fresh from her little garden. They had eaten sitting in the swing, looking at the float. Recently, there had been trouble with some white crackers from up in Tennessee coming by the church and messing with Reverend Earl. It had made Jessie even more watchful. He had been with her constantly, had made sure the old shotgun was close by her bed, in easy reach. He finished two sandwiches and an RC before he got up to go. "Be back in awhile. Gotta go get some medicine for JD. Had a bad ear for two days now. Doc at the pharmacy say he's ordered medicine from over in Huntsville, gonna bring it home so I can pick it up at his house—save me a trip to town. Coming back once I get the medicine."

"Go on to JD, no need to come back."

"We see."

She remembered thinking how big his shoulders were as he walked away from her to the car, wearing the new shirt she had given him.

—•—

It was late when she heard the noise out back. She had turned off the light some time ago, and usually by this time, she would have been asleep. She had half-expected Jessie to come back by, but she herself had told him not to come, to go on and take the medicine to JD. Now she lay there wondering why, if that was Jessie, she had not heard his car. She sat up in bed and heard the noise again, a rustling sound, nothing ominous. Curiosity got her out of the bed, not fear. Maybe a possum was on the float, eating the crepe paper.

She was strapping on her brace when a light flickered outside for a moment. Still she thought maybe it was heat lightning. She picked up her crutch and eased over to the window. Someone was standing by the float. Again the light flared. The match went out and it was dark.

At first, safe inside the church, she thought she would let him do it, whoever he was. Burn down all their hard work in the same way he had pulled the tarp off the float and let the dew ruin the crepe paper, and later let the air out of the tires. She watched, more fascinated than afraid, more amazed than mad. Whoever this person was, he wasn't someone to be afraid of. The other acts, if he had committed them, had been so benign, so half-hearted.

Even as she walked over to it, it passed through her mind what she had heard about nonviolence up at Highlander, but this wasn't the civil rights movement. This was just a backwater church in the middle of nowhere, with a homemade parade float sitting outside. Even as she laid the gun on the bed and felt around for the cartridges, even as she slipped them in the chambers, she had no idea of using it. She kept the gun on the bed as she snapped the old barrels back in place. The feel was clumsy and heavy, a throwback to the time when she'd had to use two crutches.

It was chagrin that was driving her as she walked back to the door and turned the knob. What would they all say when they came tomorrow and found a shell of what they had worked on all summer, their pride and joy, the thing she had made them believe in—the cotton girls, Jessie, Mr. Calvin, all the others.

Would she say she had seen the whole thing and done nothing? Would she say she had stood at the window and watched him burn it down without so much as shouting at him? She could hear them as she pulled a crack in the door. "Wasn't like you didn't have nothing. You had a gun. Couldn't you a done something to scare him away?" This pathetic white boy, drunk, maybe her age, maybe even younger? She had probably seen him on the other side of the split-rail fence. And now here he was ready to make a show so he could go home and brag to his friends: "Burned down the nigger's plaything."

She jerked the door open, letting it swing back against the wall with repeated bangings, and walked out on the back stoop, holding, almost dragging, the gun in one hand, her crutch in the other. And only then, as he heard the steady tapping of her crutch, did Reverend Earl raise his head.

He looked as if he had been expecting her. With the next match, the newspaper torch caught fire. "Them crackers over to the drive-in, always asking me . . ." He waved the torch through the air to get a good flame, all the while mumbling to himself. She could understand snatches. "He say, 'You hear 'bout a voting school going on round here?' And I say, 'No, sir, ain't heard nothing 'bout no voting school, Mr. Bowie. . . . Shit!" The torch had died again. He searched his pockets for another match.

She watched, still denying it. "You be careful there now, Reverend. You might start a fire with all this wood and paper around here."

"He say, 'You wanna keep your business going, I better not hear nothing 'bout no voting school.'" Reverend Earl looked at her now, talking directly to her for the first time. "Him standing out there, watching this here pass by, and my name on it." He stared at the match in his one hand, trying to line it up with the paper in his other. "I got peoples depending on me. See this? See this?" He waggled the match in front of her. "Gotta put a stop to all this foolishness. Here you go, putting my name all over for everybody to see. Too many peoples depending on me. Can't have none of this foolishness."

This time, the flame caught on the ragged edges of the half-burned pieces of newspaper and flared into a steady flame, revealing eyes yellowed and worn-out from too many years of accommodating a system grossly one-sided in its weights and measures, and yet one he had adjusted to. Using the rules he had been given, Reverend Earl had fashioned a world for himself and his people and was too old now—too long old to start over. "Them ladies always talking 'bout 'Brother Earl, we gotta have us a voting school, for the children, to show the children.'" He brought the torch down to the crepe paper and held it fast. The sight of the flames writhing and gnarling the paper strands seemed to calm him. "Church ain't my business, church my calling. This here gonna keep my business going.

"Sitting round here playing school, like you was doing something." He watched the flames creeping along the chicken wire, curling up: REVEREND EARL WATTS, PASTOR.

"Where you think the money come from to keep the church going, from them no-count collection plates? Ain't enough in there to feed the chickens." He lifted the torch out of the flaming paper and touched it to another section. "Where you think I get the money to patch the church roof, food for Miss Luella's babies, work boots for Edward so he can get a job to support his mama? Keep three churches going with the drive-in money."

Maudie moved closer to him. "Maybe we can get some water and put the fire out if you give me that." She held out her hand. He swiped the torch through the air, backing her off.

"And me thinking going to the man own the place gonna make it right. No-count white man, sitting up there in the cool, saying, 'Now Mister Watts,' calling me Mister. Ain't no white ever call me that. . . . Saying, 'We gonna integrate the whole thing.' Now he's telling me. *Now* he's telling me." He poked the torch at her, as if he was jabbing at a fire in the grate, furious he had been brought so low. "What's he saying to me? I come this far. I made do. . . . Now he saying he wanna change, wanna change everything we go by."

His weary eyes caught the light of the torch. "Why you think I put you in my no-count church? Why you think I got the crippled girl, couldn't get round? And here you go, making peoples think they care 'bout you." He leaned forward, the torch coming within inches of her face. "You think you matter? No, child. I'm doing the Lord's work. Can't nobody stop the one doing the Lord's work."

She heard Jessie's car pull off the main road and come careening down the hill, and she relaxed, knowing he would take care of Reverend Earl now. There would be time to repair the float. "It's Jessie," she said half to herself, half to him.

"Ain't never gonna get it out now. Lord see to that." He threw what remained of the torch up on the top of the float. The hand-painted sign on the counter—REGISTER TO VOTE—began to catch. "Had to be done," he said. "Had to be done."

She could hear Jessie's car door slam and his footsteps running toward them. Flames were shooting straight up in the air, casting the whole thing in black and white. The shadows beyond the church were impenetrable, but the light right where they stood was white-hot, so that all their faces were not colors, but flat, one-dimensional surfaces. "What happened?" she heard him shout as she rested the gun on the back stoop and started searching around for something to put out the flames.

"It was her," she heard the preacher say. She almost laughed, knowing Jessie would find that ridiculous. She found an old piece of cloth and began slapping at the burning crepe paper.

"*Her?* What the hell you talking 'bout, her?"

"I done found her out here. Tried to use this here gun to scare me off, but I done took it away from her."

Suddenly, there was no movement, only the crackling of the flames creeping through paper, their shadows dancing up and down the wall of the church, the reverend's shadow cast stock-still in among them. Very slowly, she lowered the cloth and turned her head to see Jessie standing between them, Reverend Earl holding the gun. Jessie stood motionless. "Had a little to drink, has you, Brother Earl?"

"You Brother Earlin' me now, are you?" Reverend Earl chuckled as he cradled the gun in his arms. "Wasn't

Brother Earlin' me when I was asking for more money to fix the roof, was you?" He seemed to close one eye, as if he was starting one of his sermons. "Wasn't Brother Earlin' me when I say we gonna have to help sister Luella 'cause she down in the back, or when I say where we gonna get the money for the Willard twins 'cause they orphans now. Everybody saying, 'Can't help out Old Brother Earl. Got to do for me and mine.' Done forgot the Bible say, 'Love thy neighbor.'" He held the gun in his arms, running one hand along the barrel. "White folks up there in the mountains gonna send you down here to get peoples registered, and I ain't even got enough food to feed my own."

Jessie glanced at her. He didn't say the word, but she knew what he meant, and she shook her head that, yes, it was loaded.

"Now Brother Earl, you don't wanna go messing round with that old double-barrel. My daddy had it. Safety done broke long time ago."

"Ain't messing with nothing," he said. "Just standing here watching a fire, watching the Lord's fire."

Flames began to creep up on to the voting counter and into the fake window they had made, and she was standing there doing nothing. She felt she couldn't catch her breath. She felt she might faint. Jessie shouted for her to get back in the church.

"Leave her be. She the one made me do it. She the one cause it. Tried being polite about it, leaving that broke-down engine, letting the air out of them tires. Trouble with y'all is you ain't got sense enough to know what somebody trying to tell you."

"Got sense enough to see you ain't nothing but a drunk old man." Jessie began walking toward him.

"Stay on back. Go on and stay back."

"You ain't gonna use that on me. Give it here."

Even as drunk as he was, Reverend Earl had no intention of using the gun. He had known Jessie since he was a young man, had baptized him down at Twelve Mile Creek. Jessie was part of the flock he had somehow guided through all the storms that had rained down on them over the years. He had made do, one way or the other, balancing everything—the white and the black, the good times and more bad times. He had tried to give them all what they wanted, but now he was old and tired and the way had become too treacherous and the new rules too confusing. And so, on this night, in the light of the moon that rose out of the north Alabama pines, the Reverend Earl Watts, never meaning to, held them all— for one moment—suspended between the tail end of an era and what was the inevitable rush to a new day. And then he turned the double-barrel to one side, but forgot to take his finger off the triggers. Both barrels exploded, spraying out beyond Jessie into the heart of the burning Labor Day float and into the center of the fumes left in the gasoline can Roy Boy had thrown back under the truck a few nights before. The fumes, the full gas can next to it, and the half-empty tank of the old truck blew almost simultaneously.

A ball of fire rose seeming to circle up and up right above them, until it disappeared into a black column of smoke. The explosion had thrown Jessie up against the church wall and Reverend Earl to the ground. Pieces of wood splintered and shot out in all directions. The frame of the old flatbed cracked and fell in on itself. Swirling black smoke rose off the burning tires. A large piece of make-believe voting counter landed on the roof of the church and the surrounding shingles began catching.

Jessie couldn't hear anything at first. The sound of the explosion had been so loud, it had knocked out his hearing for the few moments he lay there. He rolled over to his knees, all the while calling to her.

Reverend Earl was lying on the ground, moaning and rolling back and forth, trying to put out the flames on his coat and pants.

—•—

She had thought she was going to save the float in the seconds before the explosion. She had imagined that if she could get the lower part out, then she could crawl up on the flatbed and somehow save the rest of it. She was just moments, just seconds away from doing that—so close to saving it. It brought to mind the time when she was a child fishing on the river and she had come too near one of the big river barges and it had almost run her down. She and the white girl, Tab, had come within inches of getting hit and being drowned by the barge, but they had made it. They had made it with just seconds to spare.

She lay on the ground now, unaware of how she had gotten there and why she was thinking about that, about how whole lives might go one way or the other in fickle moments. She seemed to be rising up, looking back at herself. Her clothes were smoldering—the pieces that hadn't been blown off in the explosion. She watched as she tried to lift her arm, but it was limp beside her, and she thought how strange it was that she wasn't in any pain. It was likely that her leg brace was red-hot and burning her leg, but she couldn't feel it. She saw Jessie running toward her. She couldn't hear him, but she could see him. It was like watching a silent movie. In the firelight, she saw the look on his face when he rushed up to her and she saw the tears running down out of those beautiful brown eyes, and she thought she asked him, hoped she asked him—because she had been wondering about it ever since Reverend Earl said it: Did he think the voting school mattered? Did he, Jessie, think the voting school had much mattered to them, to him? She could see that her eyes were closed now, but she thought she saw his lips moving and saying, as he gathered her up in his arms, that, yes, yes it mattered; more than anything in the world, it had mattered to him.

—•—

Now all that was left were the crackling flames consuming every part of the Word of Truth—charred pieces of planking dangling, then falling on smoldering pews; a discordant note as rafters fell in on Miss Laura's piano; the glass from the side windows cracking and shattering—and, somewhere back in the woods, a screech owl.

Smoke rose, disappearing in the darkness, and out near the swing, he held her, the random and inevitable fallout of cataclysmic change.

—•—

He was still holding her when Miss Laura came rushing to them, called from her house by the explosion. He watched through flickering firelight as other members of the congregation arrived. He backed them all off with his stare. He held her as a pickup came down the hill and men carried Reverend Earl, unconscious now, to the truck for the trip to the hospital. It was only after Mr. Calvin came that he let them take her. Only after repeated assurances from Calvin did he carry her to the hearse that had come out from town. He watched as it climbed the drive. Then he took a seat in her swing.

By first light, most of the congregation was there, milling around, walking up the three steps that had been the back entrance to the church, staring at what was now a dark piece of smoldering ground, pointing out the remnants of a pew, a charred piece of the pine cross. Then they would turn and walk back down the steps, slowly circling the ruins and standing on what had been the front steps. Some came over to the swing, patting him on the shoulder, murmuring things he didn't hear. Others helped Miss Laura cut away what remained of his shirt, cleaning his cuts and burns and wrapping his swollen wrist. One of the men brought him a glass of whiskey that he held warming in his cupped hands. Lou Ann and Izzy were there, had taken up a vigil on either side of the swing. They stood holding the whiskey bottle and a white handkerchief, the one and the other, at the ready.

—•—

Eventually, he found himself sitting there again, on the swing, at the funeral. They were burying her in the cemetery beside the church—where the church used to be. They had tried to call her mother and brothers but couldn't wait on them to come up, and Jessie was afraid if they did come, they might want to take her back with them, and so he insisted they go on with the funeral. Her old family would arrive later. They were her family now.

Aunt Laura sat beside him in the swing—JD in between them. The others, all the congregation, formed an arc on either side of the swing, making sure his view of the grave was clear.

Mr. Calvin did the preaching. Preaching, he said, was not much in his line, but he wanted to do it for her, wanted to say something she had read to them, something a black man wrote, because, he said, he would never have known a black man wrote something so beautiful if it hadn't been for her, and then he repeated what he had memorized from the famous poem by a famous black man. "'Weep not, weep not,'" he said, "'She is not dead; she's resting in the bosom of Jesus.'"

It was hot and still out under the pines. Flies were brushed aside by paper fans; grasshoppers danced in the weeds that had grown up beside the graves. An occasional car passed by on the road above. A white car stopped to stare, but mostly, mostly, everybody black from around Crossroads had come to pay their respects. "Steal Away" was the closing hymn, sung a cappella, the voices, without the constraints of ceiling and walls, drifting out into the air, up past the tallest pines, perhaps even farther.

—•—

Everyone had brought food for afterward. They set it out on card tables and car hoods. Jessie remembered looking around and noticing that it was a beautiful day.

The cotton girls had tried to tempt him with barbecue and ham. Later, they had brought a dessert plate mounded with pie and cakes. It all sat on the ground beside the swing, gathering ants.

Hours passed. There was quiet laughter out under the shade trees. Children chased around through the cars and people. The sun was almost to the tops of the pines when Roy Boy came to sit down beside him, the swing creaking under his weight. Jessie winced at the movement. For the first time since the fire, the pain was beginning to break through to him. His body was aching all over, the soreness from being thrown across the yard, the cuts and bruises from flying debris. "My fault for leaving her. Shoulda stayed right here the whole time. Knowed it from the beginning."

Roy Boy took a waiting glass of tea from Izzy and

started to give it to Jessie, but then, lost in contemplating what Jessie had just said, he took a drink himself. "If you wanna look at it that way, I 'spect you could. You done caused it." He downed the rest of the tea. "Now the way I see it—wasn't you," and he pointed a finger skyward. They sat quietly, letting precious minutes distance them from it, each passing moment building a barrier, paper-thin now, but the beginnings of a march toward perspective.

—•—

Dusk was settling in out across the fields and most of the people had gone when Roy Boy said it. "You know what they waiting on, don't you?" And Jessie turned to look at him, not sure what he was talking about. "You know, don't you?" he said again, and Jessie shook his head.

"Waiting for you to tell 'em what do to. Waiting for you to tell what we gonna do, now she's gone."

He looked up at the cotton girls on either side of the swing. They were staring straight ahead, pretending they hadn't heard. Mr. Calvin was leaning up against a car fender, talking to some of the foundry men but intermittently glancing at him—waiting. Miss Laura had packed up all her empty food containers and had taken a seat on one of the folding chairs somebody had brought. Seated on either side were Viola and Dottie Sue, along with some other ladies of the congregation—all talking quietly, glancing over to Jessie now and again. Small groups of men were hunkered down on their haunches, smoking and watching the ground.

"It's over, Roy Boy. Nothing to do now. It's over."

Roy Boy was staring at what was left of the burned-out truck—wheel rims and a frame. "Ain't got but one gear. Wasn't born with no ability to put it in reverse," he said.

"I'm one knows 'bout that." He got up and wandered over to inspect one of the blackened wheel rims.

It was almost dark when Jessie lifted himself up off the swing to face them. It didn't matter, he said, that they only had a few days left. It didn't matter that they would have to start from scratch. They would rebuild it in time for the parade.

CHAPTER 44

Home

It never came—the sense of relief Tab hoped she would feel with their homecoming. In the back of her mind she had thought there would be some great reckoning, a scene in which she would break down and confess the whole thing. They had not gone to Chattanooga. They had almost been killed on the way home. Told in this setting, back home where she belonged, where she felt safe, she could make full sense of it. She had, in a way, looked forward to it. It never came to pass.

What she and Tina had forgotten—probably not Aunt Eugenia—was that while they had been gone, their parents and the rest of the family had been getting on with their lives. Their world had not stopped just because Tab and Tina had gotten off it for a while.

That night on the porch, after they were welcomed home a few days earlier than expected, the conversation had quickly turned back to what they were talking about before being interrupted. Their mother cleared her throat to break the news as the others on the porch turned to her. There had been an accident, she said. Their father was fine, but he had been hurt and Mr. Rosenstein had been killed. It was an airplane crash.

The man running for governor, the one their father had written them about, had been killed, as well. "But your father is fine. Your father is fine." She kept repeating it until she saw the worry easing in their faces. He was out of the hospital and at home. She had just dropped by to give everybody a report. She would take them home soon and they could see for themselves. He was sleeping.

In all of the tumult, no one bothered to ask anymore about their trip. What Tab and Tina had done was so far out of the realm of anything the porch people could imagine that they had done just that—not imagined it, not thought anything but that the girls had had a wonderful time playing in Chattanooga while they themselves were still here in the real world, coping with tragedy.

There were a few polite inquiries as the girls were eating their ice cream. "And I'll bet you had a grand time with Miss Bebe," Tab's grandmother said.

"I'll bet she fed you some wonderful meals," Aunt Helen said.

Soon they had turned back to the important news of the day—the crash—hardly interested at all in the sweet pleasures of children.

After finishing their ice cream, Tab and Tina sat down in the shadows on the top steps of the porch, listening to the news. They must have looked the same to everyone, sitting there in their same places on that same porch. After Tab realized her father was safe, the whole thing—what had happened to them at Highlander, the trip home—gave itself over to a sense of melancholy, and there was no one to share it with but her sister.

—•—

The fact that the candidate had died in the crash was all the papers talked about. The additional fact that the pilot had been a married man and had four children and that Reuben had died in the crash was always mentioned, but only way after the candidate and what the political implications of his death held for the rest of the field. It was an incidental fact that Charles survived, having suffered a gash on his head, a sprained wrist, and a broken leg—something even he had not realized until he was found by the rescue team and asked if he could walk, and then ended up being carried down the mountain on a stretcher.

It was never pointed out in the newspapers, but the air-safety investigators had wondered out loud to Charles why Reuben had ended up with massive internal injuries and he, Charles, had come out of it relatively unscathed, especially considering that the main impact had been to the front of the plane. The back cabin had hardly been touched. The vagaries of airplane crashes, the air-safety investigators had concluded.

The family was so glad to have Charles alive, everyone acting as if he were a hero, when all he'd done was survive by some odd fluke—some pine tree growing two yards to the right of where the wind might have blown its seed. God's plan? he wondered. What an ego to think he might discern it.

He would get through the funeral and feel better—rid of the nausea and fatigue, the breathing spells that would come on suddenly. He had awakened at night trying to catch his breath. Mary had heard him and thought it was the trauma of the crash. He had let her think that.

Big Abe had come by to see him, ringing the front doorbell, an ominous shadow through the curtained glass. He apologized for disturbing them as Mary led him into the bedroom. He looked as if he hadn't slept in days, and if he had, it had been in the suit he was wearing now. He looked like Charles felt, forcing himself to keep believing what had happened. Big Abe slumped down in the chair Mary brought to the side of the bed, took off his hat, and patted strands of hair over his balding pate, the old face ruddy and used, his fingers kneading the brim of his hat, circling it round and round. "We have a history of this, you know." And Charles didn't know whether he meant being Jewish and persecuted or that his other son, Stanley, had died as a young man also. It didn't matter.

"I'm sorry" was all he could think to say, and Abe nodded his head.

"Knew he would want me over here. He always thought the world of you, always thought I wanted him to be more like . . ." He paused there.

"His last moments, in his last moments he was thinking of you." Charles hadn't planned to say it; it just came out—years of placating, of keeping everyone balanced in the boat. He was going to tell Big Abe—just make it up as he went along—all about how Reuben had talked of Big Abe in his last moments, how Reuben had loved and respected his father, but Abe couldn't hear it.

"We'll talk later," he said, breaking down right there in front of Charles, tears rolling down old gray cheeks. For the first time, Charles wondered about the nickname, Big Abe. He wasn't big—broad shoulders and a big head, but not tall, rather squat, in fact. Charles watched him pull a damp handkerchief from his pocket.

"He would have wanted you to be a pallbearer." He blew his nose and wiped it, stuffing the handkerchief back in his pocket. "You aren't in any condition . . . I'm listing you, you'll sit with the family."

Reuben's funeral was huge. Mr. Ben and all Charles's

family were there. Much of the Methodist church of
Bainbridge came, remembering their debt. Jews from all
over north Alabama and Mississippi, from as far away as
the Delta, had attended. Charles had never known there
were so many in this part of the country.

He had taken great solace in seeing all his friends and
family. It was what community and family were for, comfort in a time of trouble, stability in a time when there
was no stability. He wondered what might have happened had he gotten up right there in the middle of the
funeral and told them about that night—that Reuben
was most likely dead before they were even airborne,
that he had had the stuffing beat out of him by some
bigot rednecks. How fearful Reuben must have been
that night in the parking lot, while Charles could only
berate him. "What a coward."

"What? What did you say?" Mary whispered, and took
his arm. She was sitting beside him. They were still at the
funeral. Several people sitting around them turned to
look at him.

"Are you all right? You're perspiring."

"Fine, fine." He took out his handkerchief and wiped
his face. "Nothing."

What if he got up right here at the funeral, confessed
to everyone that he had practically thrown Reuben to
the wolves?

He reasoned it would probably have been like his
Sunday school teachings. He had taught adult Sunday
school at Bainbridge First Methodist for years, too kind-
hearted to believe, as some did, in the hellfire and
damnation part of God's love. He always tried to em-
phasize the history. He talked about other monotheistic
cultures that had developed during the time of Jesus.
People were not offended. They thought he was com-

paring to underscore superiority. People believed what they wanted to believe—as he had.

—•—

Aunt Eugenia had left two days after they got back from Highlander, telling the others she was driving to Memphis to pick up Uncle Val at the airport. They would drive back across country together, taking a different route.

She told Tab and Tina that actually she was meeting some civil rights workers in Mississippi and donating the white jeep to them for their work. The workers, down from New York for the summer, would be driving her to the airport in Memphis. She would be back in California the next day. Feeling she had accomplished for them what she had wanted for herself in her early years, she was packing up to leave—satisfied for the moment. "But I'll be back next summer. You can count on it."

The girls sat on her bed in the upstairs room of their grandmother's house.

"I remember sitting on that very bed, looking out this very window, like you're doing right now, longing for something else, knowing I wanted something else." She dropped the shirt she was folding into her suitcase and came over to sit on the bed with them. "Listen." She took one of their hands in each of hers. "I know it didn't turn out exactly as I planned. I'm sorry about that little unpleasantness with the plaque, but you do understand the greater significance, don't you?"

They nodded their heads, not sure at all what they were supposed to understand, only sure that she had lifted them out of their place in the puzzle, that she had reshaped them just enough so that now they might never fit back in place.

—•—

When they first got back, Tab had rushed, almost in desperation, to find Mary Leigh and Harriett and go downtown shopping. Mary Leigh was trying out for cheerleader. So was Harriett. They said they had to have exactly the right clothes, the perfect lipstick. They wanted to talk about it incessantly. Tab tried to stir interest, but none was there. Mary Leigh had wanted to start out shopping for nail polish at Woolworth's. It had gone downhill from there. After trips to all the dress shops on River Street, Tab had herded them to Trowbridge's, sitting in the back, spending upward of fifty cents playing the old songs, trying to conjure the old self—but nothing.

Tina said she was tired of going steady with Jack. She had told him so, had given back his letter jacket. She had taken to her room, spending long hours reading library books.

They found themselves, of all things, ill at ease with anyone other than each other. They acknowledged this not by saying so but merely by being together all the time, having some vague idea of keeping alive what they had been through. They couldn't seem to talk of anything else. They had even borrowed their mother's car one day, saying they needed to go shopping at a place they had heard about near Huntsville. Tina driving, they had searched for hours, trying to find the little church in the gully. They had said it was because they wanted to thank the black man who had saved them that night. "We're bound to see it, what with that weird old truck out front with all the crepe paper on it."

"I don't think it was out front. I think it was in the back and I think the minister said it was a church float, some kind of a float."

"Way out here? Fat chance."

"Let me just get out and ask at this house up here with the blue shutters. It won't take but a minute," Tab said.

Tina had pulled into the drive and was looking at her watch. "Hurry up. I got to get home and wash my hair. I have a date tonight."

Tab had run up the steps to the bright blue door and knocked. As she stood there waiting and looking around at the neat coffee-can planters all in a row on the front porch, a breeze ruffled her hair and set the porch swing moving. She thought she heard music—a hymn, maybe, coming from somewhere far off. She knocked again, but the house was closed tight. Tina honked. Tab stepped off the porch and trotted back to the car. "I just feel like we're so close."

"We've been thinking that for three hours." Tina backed out of the drive and headed for home.

CHAPTER 45

Trowbridge's

THE AFTERNOON of the Labor Day parade, Tab and Tina had wandered downtown to eat at Trowbridge's. It was packed. Half the school had stopped by to eat and drink before the parade began. Band members were roaming around in their uniforms, athletes in letter jackets. Cheerleaders, although not cheering, felt it a valid excuse to dress out.

The jukebox blinked in the corner. Tommy Edwards was singing. "And he'll kiss your lips and caress your waiting fingertips and . . ." Steam rose off the hot dog cooker behind the counter. Lucille, the headwaitress, because she had been there the longest, was jerking up topping ladles, building five sundaes at a time, loading a tray to be held shoulder-high and distributed to tables and booths. The girls grabbed the first empty place. Lucille brought them a chicken salad sandwich, a chocolate malt, and a strawberry sundae. They sat talking quietly—at least they thought they were.

"You liked him, didn't you—the black one?"

Tina was sucking on the last of the chocolate malt. "Gad, of course not. If you were to say that out loud in here, I'd never get another date."

Leaning closer in, Tab said, "But you liked him, didn't you?"

"Maybe."

"A lot?"

"I guess." She churned the straw. "He was almost white, you know. He looked almost white."

"But he wasn't."

"We would walk around to the other side of the lake at night."

"And make out?"

"And *talk*—he was very interesting, you know. All the places he had been, was going. Okay, once, toward the end. I had been arguing with myself the whole time whether to or not. I knew he wanted to." She fingered her straw, watching Tab. "If you ever tell that, I'll be considered the town whore, making out with a black person. You know that, don't you?"

"At first, I thought I hated Dominique, but guess what? I asked her if she wanted to spend the rest of the summer with me, here in Bainbridge."

"You're crazy."

"No more than you, kissing a black person. It's all the same."

Tina looked over her straw and said nothing, sucking in the last of the malted milk. "Smoke Gets in Your Eyes," her favorite, was starting.

They had been talking for over an hour before they looked up and realized people were staring at them. There was still music on the jukebox, but the hum of voices had quieted. "We weren't talking that loud— were we?" Tab whispered. "They couldn't hear, could they?"

"I don't think so." Tina pasted a smile and flashed it.

Still, people were intermittently glancing their way. They had been watching and listening the whole time.

"And who cares if they did hear us?" Tab made a face out into the room and then began singing along with The Platters: "'When a lovely flame dies, smoke gets in your eyes . . .' You're not telling me to stop. 'Theeey, asked me how I knew—' What's got into you?"

Tina sighed. "I guess I'm getting used to it. Besides, you'd have to go a long way to top that ridiculous brawl up at Highlander."

Jack Carter, Tina's former, left his booth and came over. He stood there, not sitting down, even as they invited him to.

"We wanna know . . ." he began. They looked past him to the others. "Smoke Gets in Your Eyes" was winding down. "Everybody wants to know how you have the gall, especially you, Tina."

"What?"

"Even my dad said everybody abided by the rules when he was young. You know better."

"Whose rules?" Tab said. "Your rules? She can see who she wants."

"Not in here she can't."

"Oh yes she can."

"You keep out of it, little jerk."

Tab glanced at Tina and grinned before she said, "Are you gonna make me? Just answer me that, Big Jack. You think you can make me?" She could hear Dominique in her voice. She had said it too loudly, but once she had let fly, it was easier to do it a second time. After a few times, she realized it almost came naturally. She wasn't at all surprised at what she was about to do. "She can do what she wants to," Tab said loudly, so the others would hear. "It's none of your business and if you're gonna call her a . . . a lady of the evening for doing it, then—" There wasn't much left in the glass, mainly slivers of ice, but she did sling the slivers his way. She could hear Tina trying to stifle a laugh.

"Are you crazy?" Jack said. She had heard that before, but before, she had been the one saying it.

"Crazy? *Crazy?*" she said, crossing her eyes at him, making a face. "Maybe so." She jumped out of her seat, stepped on it, and then up on their tabletop, towering above then—a different view now. The whole place was watching. Lucille had stopped in mid-soda jerk. Chubby Checker was beginning "The Twist." "Now this," she called to all of them, "is crazy." She had hands on hips and began tap dancing, shuffle-ball-change, shuffle-ball-change, as in first-year tap, faster and faster. She added a spinning motion, twirling around on top of the table.

Tina grabbed her empty sundae glass from under frenzied feet and leaned back out of the way. She smiled at Jack. "A little something she learned over the summer."

Tab's glass and sandwich plate vibrated to the floor. Now Chubby was in full swing. "Come on baby. Let's do the Twist . . ." She twisted along, finally ending it in a great flurry of hands and legs swirling through the air, penny loafers tapping madly on the table, everybody staring.

Lucille, jaded to everything Trowbridge's had offered up over the years, put down her half-composed tray of sundaes, sighed, and walked over as Chubby was ending and Tab was taking a bow to a gawking audience. "Get on down off that table, honey. You're gonna scratch the Formica."

Breathless, Tab called out to them, "Now that's crazy. Other things are not crazy. *That* is crazy!"

So then Jack said to Tina—because the rules said he should not converse with the younger crazy one—"I don't know who she thinks she is, Doris Day or somebody, but even if she is your sister, junior highs do not come in here and sit in the same booth as senior highs. It's the rule."

Tina, openmouthed, put down her soda glass. "Oh, *those* rules. She looked up through sweaty legs to the limp ponytail towering above her and they both burst out laughing. "He meant *those* rules."

And Lucille, hands on hips, "I told you—off the table, honey. You've acted the fool enough for one day."

Tina slid out of the booth and held out her hand. "Come on, Doris, you've danced your way into everybody's heart. Time to go."

—•—

They walked the four blocks down River Street, jostling in and out of crowds, laughing as, intermittently, Tab did short versions of her tabletop dance. They were headed toward the river to meet the family, because always, from earliest memory, the family had watched the Labor Day parade, sitting on blankets and chairs spread out in front of the VFW, Tab perched on the barrel of the World War I cannon that stood in the middle of the lawn.

They could see all the family settled in chairs and on blankets, the children chasing around, their mother waving to them as they walked toward her, passing under American flags hanging on the lampposts that lined River Street, the dazzling sun in a cloudless sky giving a clear-eyed view of it all.

Their mother was holding out something as they approached. Down at the opposite end of the street, the Bainbridge High School Band was forming up to the cadence of the bass drummer, and the fire chief's siren was beginning its whine up the scales. Her mother shouted above the din as she handed her the postcard. "Who in the world do you know in Paris, France?"

The Parade

$\mathcal{A}$LL THINGS BEING EQUAL, most people would have been down at the river on a day so hot as this one, but nobody was because of the Labor Day parade. Somehow over the years, this parade had become a big event in Bainbridge, bigger than the Christmas parade, much bigger than the one on the Fourth of July. Tab's father had said it was because, for a long time, nobody much around here celebrated the Fourth of July, that kind of being a Yankee holiday. Now all that was changing. Now they had a Fourth of July parade, too, and it was getting bigger every year. Not as big as this one, but a nice size.

It was to start up at the far end of River Street and come straight through town, ending up down by the river. After that, everybody would go home to sit under fans or stay down at the river to swim.

Most of the family had gotten there early, taking up seats on blankets and chairs in front of the VFW hall that faced River Street. Soon, most of the neighborhood was there. Mary had walked down with the twins and Charles Junior. A little later, Charles drove up. The cast was off his leg now and the bandage on his forehead had been reduced to a square of gauze under a strip of adhesive tape. He still walked with a noticeable limp, using an old cane that he had found in the umbrella stand, probably his grandfather's.

Uncle Tom and Aunt Helen had brought lawn chairs and spread them out around the grassy rise that was the front yard of the VFW. Several neighbors came over to Tab's father and talked about Brad La Forte, saying what a shame it was, the plane going down and all. Her father had said they would never have a chance like that again. Tom had said, thank God they would never have a chance like that again, and tried to laugh when no one else would.

The police chief's siren was heard, the high-pitched whine careening up and down the street, bouncing off buildings, then the thump of the bass drum. From her perch on the old World War I cannon, Tab put the post-card she had been studying—all in French—back in her pocket and waited for things to commence. She could look up the length of River Street and see parade marchers and floats gathered, waiting to be given a place in line as the parade fed out behind the ROTC honor guard carrying the American flag and the flag of Alabama.

After the honor guard, the police chief's car, then the World War II veterans—men about her father's age, sitting in the backseats of Ford convertibles and waving to all their friends. Uncle Tom and her father waved back, Tom shouting time-honored insults about their age or their shrinking uniforms. It got the thing off to a good start, especially since the school band came next. Music—patriotic music—always gave integrity to things. After that, the floats began, every kind imaginable, decked out in days of handmade effort. The themes were not so much tributes to laboring America as they were symbols of community. The Girl Scouts had one, advertising the cookie sale. The bank sponsored one full of kindergarten kids throwing out play money. The First Methodist Church had a scene from the Bible—children dressed like Romans and gladiators, the theme being: Be sure to come to MYF on Sunday nights. Interspersed with the floats were marching ROTC units from the high school, politicians running for election, fire trucks from the main station.

Uncle Tom had settled in his lawn chair next to Helen and Mary, critiquing each float as it lumbered by. It was a tradition for the onlookers to clap for those floats that were considered particularly well made-up, and to amuse the ladies, Tom would give a loud cat whistle to those he thought were tacky. Fingers in each corner of his mouth were almost as loud as the siren.

Far up the line, Tab saw Hills Grocery Store's float and swung down off her place on the cannon. It always came toward the end and threw out hard candy for all the children. She wanted to be near the street and ready, but in a nonchalant way, as if she just happened to be there as the candy was thrown. She was too old now to pretend real interest in candy. Besides, the band from the black high school was coming, and seeing the majorettes up close was not to be missed. Whereas the white majorettes marched in a sedate line, twirling batons in unison, the black majorettes seemed to each have their own agenda, twirling, prancing, or dancing, depending upon their talent or mood—free of standard.

Tab was walking away, opening a piece of peppermint, when she heard her uncle say, "What the hell is that supposed to be?" It was third from the last. After it came a float from Jimmy's Battery Shop, then a patrol car bringing up the rear. It had been made on top of a beat-up old Ford with a flatbed loose on its frame. The motor kept dying. One of the black men in the cab would jump out and lift the hood, jiggling something to make it start again. It was lagging behind the rest of the parade, opening a gap in the line. Most people didn't really pay much attention, gathering up lawn chairs and calling in children, preparing to leave.

Charles was folding a quilt when he glanced up. "By that cross on the front, it's a church float of some kind."

"No church around here." Tom squinted to see. "They wouldn't put out something looking that crummy. Thing looks like it's on its last leg." The motor died again. One of the men in the cab got out and raised the hood.

Her father bent over to see if he could look in the cab. "That's old Calvin from down at the foundry sitting in shotgun."

"Word of Truth Missionary Baptist Church—that's what it says on the sign," Tab said.

Her father stopped what he was doing, putting the quilt on one of the lawn chairs. "What? Where does it say that?" He took up his cane and began walking out toward the street, Tom following. "Well, I'll be damned . . . Reuben. There really is . . . a Word of Truth . . ." Her father never cussed in front of the ladies or the children, so they all turned and watched the float from the Word of Truth Missionary Baptist Church as it got started again and came toward them—those few who were left, those few who hadn't already packed up their chairs and blankets and headed home or on down to the river.

And Uncle Tom, taking her father's words all wrong, was just in the process of letting out one of his whistles when her father said to him, very quietly, as if he was having a hard time getting the words out, "Don't do that, Tom."

"The hell you say." Tom turned to smile at the ladies, put two fingers in his mouth, and took a deep breath.

It was the first time Tab had ever seen anything like this from her father. Suddenly, his cane was raised in the air, and if Tom hadn't stepped back, he might have been hit. "I said, You make one more sound and I'll—" Her father stopped, and brought the cane to the ground. Tom shrank back, raising his eyebrows at Helen.

Tab watched her father's face turn ashen. "Family or no, I'm so tired . . . tired of that, Tom." He was leaning more heavily on his cane, although still managing to turn and move toward the street.

"What's got you so teed off? Look at that thing. Why the hell can't I whistle? That float's a disgrace. Doesn't have a damn thing to do with Labor Day, and look"—he pointed—"everybody behind is having to wait."

Charles was breathing hard now. "I might know that float . . . those people." He caught the side of the VFW cannon barrel with his free hand.

"Pop, you all right?" Tab turned around, searching for her mother. "Mama," she called over to her mother, who was talking to a neighbor. Mary walked over toward them, bringing a lawn chair as she came.

"Charles, I told you you've been doing too much lately, not giving yourself enough time." She unfolded the chair into the back of his legs, "Sit down, sweetheart." And then she got a good look at his graying face. "Charles? Are you all right?"

He slumped down in the chair, feeling the desperate breathing coming on in front of all these people and powerless to do anything about it. The wind from the explosion of the starboard wing blew by him. Rain dripped off his face and onto Reuben's coat. "I'm fine," he said, but he could feel a new sensation, had felt it the minute he recognized the sign on the side of the float—pain in his chest and shoulder.

"Look at that thing." Tom was still jeering. "Not a flag on it. Typical coloreds, always the ones to think up the queerest thing around."

"For heaven's sake, Tom. Never mind that. Come here." Helen had followed Mary over to Charles. They were looking down at him. He brushed the rain out of his eyes, trying to get a clear picture of them.

"Go get the car, Tom," Helen ordered. "Mary's right. You've just overdone it, Charles."

"Pop, are you okay? Pop?" Tab was searching back and forth between his face and her mother's.

"I'm fine, just fine. Go tell me what you see on that float." Tab was gripping his arm. He put his hand on her shoulder. "Do that for me. Tell me what you see."

Mary was trying to stay calm. "Your father's right. Go look at the float and tell us what it's like. We'll be here when you get back. Go on. It's all right." The float was almost on them now. It had managed to start again and was tottering forward.

"And clap," he said. "You might clap when it passes by."

Her mother nodded her head. "Go."

Tab backed away from him, taking comfort in pleasing him. She turned and ran to the edge of the street.

The women, Mary and Helen, stood there waiting for Tom to come with the car, hoping to divert Charles by trying to guess what it was supposed to be.

It was, after all, a strange-looking thing. The wooden frame set up against the back cab of the truck might be a drive-in movie screen. The long crepe-paper streamers attached to the sides were waving in the breeze. Somebody had written "Three minutes till the movie starts" up on boards that had been nailed together in a square and whitewashed. Next to that was a tall black man, standing behind what could be a ticket taker's booth. There were what looked like toy cars made out of cardboard boxes probably taken from some Dumpster back of Crossroads General Store and painted bright colors, still drying in the afternoon sun. Black people were sitting in all the cars, facing the screen. Three older women sat in the first cars next to the screen, one of them with a big bag of popcorn she was passing to the other two. Behind them were two young women seated in their toy cars, bright and tight dresses almost, but not quite, obscured by long crepe-paper streamers tied to their wrists, continually swirling about in the air as they blew kisses to the crowd. There was a boy, sitting somberly, drinking a Coca-Cola. From time to time, he would spring out of his car to walk forward and grab a handful of popcorn.

There were others, grown men, barely able to squeeze into the little spaces that were the car seats. Beside each car was a wooden post with a shoe box on top, painted black to resemble a speaker. The cars and speakers filled the back of the flatbed. Nailed down the sides of the truck were Burma Shave–type signs: 50 CENTS PER PERSON, and TURN OFF LIGHTS AFTER ENTERING, and NO

ALCOHOL ALLOWED. On the tail end of the flatbed, as if discarded to make way for new things, were pieces of old split-rail fencing.

There was something about it Tab thought she recognized, the disheveled old truck, the long ribbons of crepe paper floating up in the breeze. She took the postcard out of her pocket and waved it to get Tina's attention away from the boys who were talking to her. "Hey." Tina looked up and Tab pointed to the float. "Was that what we saw?" Tina started toward her, all the while studying the float. "Was that the thing in the churchyard that night? Didn't it look like that?"

Tina was standing next to her now, watching it, hand raised to shield her eyes.

"You think?"

"Maybe," Tina said. "Kinda scruffy-looking, and I don't see the preacher anywhere on it."

"I think we should clap," Tab said, and she stuck the postcard from Dominique back in her pocket and they stood there clapping. Perhaps one of the older women on the float seemed to acknowledge this, dipping her head slightly as it passed.

"Come on, Tina," Tab said. "We need to see about Pop." Before she turned to go, Tab stepped off the curb to get one last look.

The float from the Word of Truth Missionary Baptist Church lumbered its way forward, down the road toward the river—all on board knowing for certain they had created a thing of unparalleled beauty. Not to be vain about it, but it would be impossible for anyone watching to miss the majesty of it, all decked out in bright, swirling colors, glistening in the afternoon sun, the culmination of days and nights of continuous toiling, the first of its kind, really. The voting school—indeed, all of the members of Word of Truth—would not rest until they got it just like they thought she would have wanted. Was she watching them now? Could she see the white girl standing there in the road, enthralled by the beauty of it?

Tab ran to catch up with Tina. "I think that's it, the thing we saw in the backyard of the church, that night we got saved."

EPILOGUE

It was almost dark when they finished cleaning out the house. Tina's husband had taken one more load to the dump. Tab's sons, Charlie and Ben, had gone with him to help unload. Tab's minivan was stuffed with boxes of letters and the old portrait of Lee on Traveler. They had divided the books out of Mr. Ben's library. All else had been hauled off by a mover—and none too soon. Tab had been in charge of the closing, which was yesterday, and the new owner was coming by to pick up the key.

Traffic out front had slowed to an occasional passing car. Shadows off the old oaks danced on the cracks in the front walk. "If it gets any darker, I'm going to start seeing the twins on their Radio Flyer, careening down into the boxwood," Tab said.

Tina watched the shadows conjure up long ago summer evenings they had spent on this porch. She could see the breeze from the floor fan ruffling her mother's skirt, hear the pop of the newspaper as her grandmother turned back its pages. She watched herself—a lifetime back—sitting on the steps, young and impatient, waiting for some great revelation. "Why don't we have our fathers speak to us more before they go?

Was it what happened that summer or was it that first heart attack that changed him?"

Tab sighed and stretched aching legs, worn out from carrying boxes all day. "We'll never know everything about him—about his whole generation."

A car pulled up in the drive behind Tab's van. The driver waved and opened the door. "You didn't tell me the new owner was black."

"An engineer, with the new Ford plant that's going in across the river. Says he graduated from Tuskegee. Has a wife and a little girl about five."

A tall dark man, broad shoulders and receding hairline, perhaps a few years younger than Tab, strolled up the walk toward them.

"Thanks for waiting. It was my turn to pick up Maudie from the sitter." The little girl had clicked open her seatbelt and was following behind.

"Here's the key. I don't think you'll find a speck of dirt in the house because it's all on me." Tab laughed and handed it to him. "You new around here?" she asked. "My sister and I don't know anybody much anymore, since we moved away back in the seventies."

"Been working up north," he said, "but I was born and raised about fifteen miles east of here, out Highway Seventy-two. Not much left out there now."

"Really." There was a long silence. "Wouldn't happen to remember a church out there called Words of Truth—something like that?" Tina said. "We think it used to be somewhere in that vicinity, years ago."

"Sure I remember it," he said, "Word of Truth Missionary Baptist Church." The little girl tugged on his pants leg and he leaned down to pick her up.

AUTHOR'S NOTE

For the purposes of the story, I have compressed civil rights–era events that took place in a larger time frame. Actually:

- The Highlander Folk School was raided, padlocked, and later auctioned off by the state of Tennessee in the early 1960s.
- The race for governor of Alabama between George Wallace and a man much like the character Brad La Forte took place in the mid-1960s. Many believed Ryan deGraffenried would be the first New South governor for Alabama. He died in a plane crash while campaigning.

The KKK plaque remains in Pulaski, Tennessee—its face turned to the wall to discourage photographs and vandals.

READING GROUP GUIDE

AUTHOR'S COMMENTS

The question I am asked most often is this: What does the book's title mean?

You—as reader—may have other ideas, but here's my take on it.

The era of the summers in which we got saved was a time when the black church rose up and said, in so many words and deeds: *You, white man, brought us to this country and you indoctrinated us into the ways of your Christian religion. Now that we have learned to truly believe in its concepts of brotherly love and compassion for our fellow man, we are going to throw those beliefs back in your face, and you can either put up or shut up. And if you don't, you will be living in the very sin that you have taught us would bring about eternal damnation.* And that is why white people had no choice. And in having no choice, they were saved by the black man, lifted up by him to a higher moral ground, saved by their own teachings—come home to roost.

—•—

You know by now that this story is about ordinary people trying to cope with monumental social and political change. The epic change in this country, in my lifetime, was the civil rights movement—hence the setting. Some other writers might have chosen the Vietnam War or the war on terror. In any event, the perfect vehicle for me was the 1960s.

In the prologue I tell you that there is a road and, in traveling it, you will meet two radically different philosophies, implying to you—I hope—that the story will take place between these two viewpoints.

I am sometimes perturbed by the way history overlooks the valiant effort most folks make in living their own lives and, at the same time, trying to do the right thing as they see it. During the civil rights movement, they (we) were kicked back and forth, rebuked by both the elements of change and the traditionalists. In fact, ordinary people—and most of us fall into that category—were the ones who held the fabric of society together, kept everyday life stable and moving ahead while the two ends of the spectrum had a go at each other. If we hadn't been there as the ballasts, the pendulum might have swung wildly from one extreme to the other. In the end, they (we) were the ones who took the small definitive steps that moved us onward and upward.

History books record the likes of Martin Luther King Jr. and George Wallace but, in the end, the Everyman among us is the final arbiter of any rock-solid change that will take place.

And so, in light of that background, a brief look at the characters.

The aunt—Aunt Eugenia was much like my own Berkeley-based aunt, who would come south to visit in the summer and immediately begin to tell us what we were doing wrong. It was not a vindictive telling, but one born out of genuine concern. In the story, she is so single-minded in her pursuit of justice that, at one point, she endangers the lives of Tina and Tab. (Think of reformers throughout our history: John Brown, Susan B. Anthony, the feminist of the 1970s, etc. Remember the monks in Vietnam who would set themselves afire, so determined were they to make a point?) My aunt was a natural to lock horns with the rest of my family who had stayed south, steeped in their own traditions, especially my grandfather.

Mr. Ben—The grandfather was inordinately proud of the fact that he was kin to one of the founders of the Klan, content with living in the past and glorifying it. This made for some interesting dinner table conversation. As a child I didn't contribute much, but I certainly absorbed a lot. And that is the genesis of this story.

Charles—Patterned after my own father, Charles is, along with the Reverend Earl, one of the two real heroes of the story. Both were torn between trying to make a living and needing to do something about the segregationist society in which they lived.

Charles, like so many men of his generation, was expected—by his family, by the community and by the church—to play multiple roles. As firstborn son, he was responsible for taking care of his parents and carrying on the run-down family business. He was head of his own family and the only breadwinner, expected to be a loving father and husband and, as a responsible member of the community, expected to give over some of his time to public concerns. When I look back to that period, I think it should have been the men who fomented the feminist movement. They were that overwhelmed.

Maudie—Like many African Americans caught up in the changes that were taking place and, perhaps at first, not realizing their significance, Maudie gradually realized that she was making a huge difference. During the civil rights movement, one of the most effective grass-roots methods used to bring about change was the voting school for blacks. These schools proliferated throughout the South in the sixties, conducted by African Americans. In my mind, Maudie represents the essence of what the civil rights movement was about, the African American who stood up and made the ground-level changes that were necessary to its success. And like many blacks of that time, she had to pay the ultimate price. Her death, though not premeditated, was part of the random fallout that comes with great cultural up-heaval—consider the children in the Birmingham church bombing.

The Reverend Earl—He is especially dear to my heart. How many black people, like the reverend, had carved out a place for themselves—for generations—on an uneven playing field, only to be threatened by the very movement that would eventually give them equality? Sometimes, even those who would benefit most are the very ones dead set against change. (Think of the black funeral homes, the black-owned insurance companies, the black restaurants and eating establishments that would be upended by the coming transformations.)

Rubin—One of a small minority of Jewish merchants, sprinkled in towns throughout the South. A brilliant man, monetarily well off and out of touch with the day-to-day reality of segregation, but having great empathy for black people because he identifies with their plight. He works behind the scenes, through his more socially accepted friends, to bring about change.

Tina and Tab—Somewhat like my sister and me in our youth—they were happy with the life they had been given and very reluctant to look at its flaws for fear it would upset the balance of things. I think Tab and Tina represent so many whites in our country at that time. They were slowly leaving behind the age of innocence that had served them—but not their black brothers and sisters—well.

—•—

DISCUSSION QUESTIONS

1. Consider the characters and discuss how each one of them reacts to change. (If I were a guest at your reading group, this is how I would tell you that I see them. You may view them differently.)

    a. The reformer aunt
    b. The traditionalist, old-school grandfather
    c. The naive teenagers
    d. Charles and Reverend Earl—the real heroes
    e. Rubin—the awkward outsider
    f. Maudie—change at the ground level

2. Which character are you most like when dealing with some kind of traumatic change? If you have a book group, each member might take a piece of paper and write down—but not *sign*—which personality most closely resembles him or her. Hand it in and have the leader tally.

3. What kinds of radical, national change are we experiencing now that can compare with the changes people were going through back then?

4. What role would you play if you lived back in that time? What role are you playing now?

ACKNOWLEDGMENTS

Many thanks for the interviews granted to me by Dr. John F. Hume, MD, retired director of the Tuskegee Polio Unit and Edith Campbell, MPA, a childhood survivor of polio who still resides and teaches at Tuskegee University and who, along with Dr. Hume, wrote the very helpful monograph on the Tuskegee Polio Unit. A special thanks to Dr. Scott Bates, longtime member of the Highlander Center board of directors and professor emeritus at the University of The South. He took the time to show me where the old Highlander Folk School was located and to relate myriad facts about the school and its founder, Myles Horton.

And to the staff of the Giles County Library; they were kind enough to direct me to points of interest in Pulaski.

I am indebted to my aunt Beth Kennedy, longtime supporter of Highlander Folk School. In her ninety-fourth year, she and her husband, Van, still reside in Berkeley, California. And thanks, as always, to my sisters Joanne, Sally, and Helen, who are always kind enough to take the time to read and comment on early drafts.

Thanks to all the folks at Warner Books, especially my wonderful editor Maureen Egen. I so appreciate Harvey-Jane Kowal guiding me through the maze of editing and Carol Edwards and Michele Bidelspach. To my agent, Molly Friedrich and to Frances Jalet-Miller and all the folks at Aaron Priest—thanks to all.

Selected Bibliography

Adams, Frank and Horton, Myles, *Unearthing Seeds of Fire: The Idea of Highlander.* Winston-Salem, NC: John F. Blair, 1975.

Barnard, William D., *Dixiecrats and Democrats: Alabama Politics, 1942-1950.* Tuscaloosa, AL: The University of Alabama Press, 1974.

Barnard, F. Hollinger, ed., *Outside the Magic Circle: The Autobiography of Virginia Foster Durr.* Tuscaloosa, AL: The University of Alabama Press, 1985.

Branch, Taylor, *Parting the Waters: America in the King Years, 1954-63.* New York: Simon & Schuster, 1988.

Brown, Harry Bates and Ware, Jacob Osborn, *Cotton.* New York: McGraw-Hill, 1958.

Buck, Irving A., *Cleburne and His Command.* New York: The Neal Publishing Company, 1902.

Chappell, Edith P. and Hume, John F., *The Black Oasis: Tuskegee Institute's Fight Against Infantile Paralysis, 1941-1975.* March of Dimes Birth Defects Foundation, monograph aided by Basic Research Grant No. 1-1046, 1987.

Clark, Septima, *Ready from Within: Septima Clark and the Civil Rights Movement.* Trenton, NJ: Africa World Press, 1990.

Fosl, Catherine, *Subversive Southerner: Ann Braden and the Struggle for Racial Justice in the Cold War South.* New York, Palgrave Macmillan, 2002.

Glen, John, *Highlander: No Ordinary School.* Knoxville, TN: The University of Tennessee Press, 1996.

Horton, Myles et al., *The Long Haul: An Autobiography.* New York: Teachers College Press, 1998.

Johnson, James Weldon, *God's Trombones: Seven Negro Sermons in Verse.* New York: Penguin Books, 1927.

Kehret, Peg, *Small Steps: The Year I Got Polio.* Morton Grove, IL: Albert Whitman & Company, 1996.

Lester, J. C. and Wilson, D. L., *Ku Klux Klan: Its Origin, Growth and Disbandment.* New York, The Neale Publishing Company, 1905.

Lollar, Mary Alexander, "My Colbert County Families: Lanes, Prides, Goodloes, Rutlands and Bartons." Unpublished, 1972.

Sanders, Don and Susan, *The American Drive-in Movie Theatre.* Osceola, WI, Motorbooks International, 1997.

Seavey, Nina Gilden et al., *A Paralyzing Fear: The Triumph over Polio in America.* New York: TV Books, 1998.

The Adventures of a Radical Hillbilly, videocassette, directed by Sidney Smith. New York: Public Broadcasting System, WNET/Thirteen, 1981.

Westmacott, Richard, *African-American Gardens and Yards in the Rural South.* Knoxville: The University of Tennessee Press, 1992.

William, Warren Rogers, et al., *Alabama: The History of a Deep South State.* Tuscaloosa, The University of Alabama Press, 1994.

Wright, Richard, *Native Son.* New York, Harper & Brothers, 1940.